THE
WIDOW KILLER

THE
WIDOW KILLER

A NOVEL
Pavel Kohout

St. Martin's Press ❦ New York

Translation copyright © 1998 by Neil Bermel

Book design by James Sinclair

Endpaper art: Karl's Bridge, Prague, circa 1944 (Corbis-Bettmann)

Library of Congress Cataloging-in-Publication Data

Kohout, Pavel.
  [Hvězdná hodina vrahů. English]
  The widow killer: a novel / by Pavel Kohout. —1st U.S. ed.
      p.   cm.
  ISBN 0-312-19363-7
  I. Title.
  PG5038.K64H8813   1998
  891.8'6354—dc21   98–21112

First published in the Czech Republic under the title *Hvězdná hodina vrahů* by Mladá Fronta, Prague, 1995
First published in Germany under the title *Sternstunde der Mörder* by Knaus Verlag, Munich, 1995

FIRST U.S. EDITION: NOVEMBER 1998

10   9   8   7   6   5   4   3

for Jelena

ACKNOWLEDGMENTS

Remembering with gratitude my long-term late friend and agent, Joan Daves, New York

P.K.

FEBRUARY

When the doorbell rang just after the siren, Elisabeth, baroness of Pomerania, was sure the caretaker had come to escort her down to the shelter; she donned the black fur coat she had just hung up, picked up her small emergency suitcase, unhooked the door chain, and realized that she had just let her murderer in.

Earlier, at the Vyšehrad cemetery, she had noticed a man with a bulging bag over his shoulder; it was common these days to see Czechs decorating the graves of their patron saints. His appearance reminded her of a repairman, and she could barely see him because his face was obscured by the sun. Now she saw eyes of glass: no color or expression. He calmly wedged a scuffed shoe into the crack; a lanky body bundled in a cotton jacket followed it through the door. And there, finally, she saw the long and strangely slim blade. A poultry knife! she thought.

The baroness knew she was going to die, but she did nothing to prevent it. She was the only occupant left on the top floor, and the roar of airplane motors would have drowned out her screams. Besides, she had no desire to live.

For a Catholic, suicide was unthinkable; divine punishment was the best she could hope for. This unjust war would only end when those who began it were destroyed. A Russian partisan had shot her husband; a Maquis had killed her son in Brittany. It seemed logical that now a man from the Czech Resistance had come for her.

The patrician house began to shake as the eerie ringing grew more and more insistent. With each approaching explosion the windowpanes, the chandelier crystals, and the goblets in the sideboard shuddered wildly.

Merciful God, Elisabeth of Pomerania prayed to herself, retreating into the salon as if he were her guest; a bomb, a knife—who cares, as long as it's quick!

Her killer's foot slammed the door shut behind him, while his free hand opened a satchel of straps.

Thunder, mused Chief Inspector Buback, in *February*? It was over before he knew it. A large aerial bomb, he realized, and it had fallen uncomfortably close by.

The building of the Prague Gestapo, where Buback worked as liaison officer for the Reich's criminal police office, swayed wildly for what seemed like an eternity, but did not collapse. The proverbial quiet followed the storm; time stopped. Eventually sirens began to wail, and the officers and secretaries trooped down to the shelter.

He stared, motionless, at the two faces on his desk.

Buback disliked the shelter, in the basement of the old Petschke Bank. Some of its safes had been converted into cells; he'd heard a good interrogation there helped political prisoners remember all sorts of forgotten details. So he stayed upstairs, thunderstruck: the blast and the shaking had brought Hilde and Heidi back to life.

Their framed picture had traveled with him throughout the war. The offices changed, as did the cities and countries, but everywhere they had smiled radiantly at him, older and younger versions of a quiet, soothing loveliness. He conducted meetings and interrogations as they gazed at him from that final peacetime summer on the Isle of Sylt; for the most part he barely noticed them. But not an hour went by without Buback remembering in a flash of joy that they were alive.

They had been on his desk last year in Antwerp as men in other departments prepared for the retreat by burning documents in the courtyard. He had sneezed as the pungent smoke tickled his nose, and for a moment he did not understand the voice on the telephone telling him that both of them were dead. The smiles in the picture still glowed inside him; they flatly contradicted what he heard. Then the official from Berlin headquarters read him the police report.

Two years earlier he had sighed with relief when Hilde and Heidi were sent away from threatened Dresden. Wine was the only significant industry in the medieval Franconian village where Hilde went to teach war orphans. Therefore, it could not possibly be on the Allied target list. A stray bomb killed Hilde and Heidi—and them alone—when it fell unexpectedly in broad daylight on their apartment.

When the news finally hit him, the picture's glowing expressions froze into lifeless grimaces. He still kept the little frame on his desk, but when he looked at it he felt nothing, not even regret. Until just now, when another bomb fell close by.

Yes! Suddenly he was sure: they had been sitting opposite each other, with an empty chair and place setting for him at the end of the table, as always. Which meant that, in a sense, he had been with them even at the moment the blast and heat transformed them instantly into smoke and ash.

With the unexpected bomb, a feeling of liberation exploded inside him: it was an angel of merciful death that had first carried off his loves and now returned them to him. The motionless features softened; their old warmth returned. Entranced, he noticed only dimly that Kroloff had come in with a stack of papers.

Buback's adjutant—and, he suspected, his secret overseer—had been assigned to him by the Gestapo; Kroloff shaved his high, narrow brow every other day so that his thinning hair would look fuller come peacetime. He announced that a direct attack had taken out the corner house on the block. Just opposite the National Museum, he said regretfully; a few yards further and the Czechs would have had a taste of what happened in Dresden!

A few yards further, Buback thought, and I would have been with *them,* smoke and ash. . . . Only half listening, he had to ask Kroloff to repeat the second piece of news. He had thought he was beyond surprise, but Kroloff's announcement quickly proved him wrong. Colonel Meckerle should hear about this directly from him, he decided.

M orava barely recognized Prague. It was as if seven years later the city had finally recovered from the shock of the German occupation. As they left the police station on Národní Avenue, his driver had to wait for long lines of fire engines and ambulances to roar past, belching acrid fumes from wartime gasoline substitute. People hurried along the sidewalks toward the river Vltava. All day the illegal foreign broadcasters in Kroměříž had been reporting last night's deadly Allied bombing of Dresden. The recent air raid, despite its brevity, had panicked the Czechs: would Prague meet the same fate?

Assistant Detective Morava didn't think it would. In the first place, he was a born optimist, and in the second, he didn't believe that at this stage of the war the Allies would flatten the capital of an occupied nation. What was more, Air-Raid Control had already determined that only a couple of bombs from a few planes had hit Prague. The prevailing opinion at police headquarters was that a navigator had confused the two cities and made a tragic mistake.

Even so, emergency plans were automatically set in motion. Workers from all departments spread out to the affected areas to supervise the excavation work and report on the damages and losses. Moments earlier, Morava had been heading out as well, but Superintendent Beran sent him back up to his desk.

"Catastrophes bring out the criminals as well as the Samaritans; you'll hold down the fort here, Morava."

Morava's boss had become the legend and the terror of the Prague underworld in the interwar years, but because Beran had always steered clear of politics, the Germans left him in his post. Of course, now he only had jurisdiction over Czech wrongdoers; Germans were tried (and sometimes even punished) by the occupiers.

Morava knew he should fill his time with useful work on his assigned cases. The front moving west toward Prague swept in criminals along with war victims, but at the moment he wasn't in the mood to deal with them. He put on the radio to find out more about the raid. They were broadcasting solemn music, apparently while the censors tinkered with the official statement.

He thought of Jitka and longed to see her. Why not use her sensational chicory coffee as an excuse? Summoning his courage, he crossed the hall to Beran's office. She raised her large brown eyes, disconcerting him as usual. This house of horrors was no place for a shy lamb like Jitka! But otherwise he never would have met her. . . . Before he could speak, the phone rang.

"I'm sorry," she answered like a well-mannered schoolgirl, "the superintendent is out in the field. . . . No, I don't know . . . everyone is out on call after the air raid, but I can let you speak with the assistant detective. . . . Yes, one moment please, I'll put him on."

She handed him the receiver, but he was so enchanted by her serious smile that he did not realize who was barking at him.

"What's your name?" the voice snapped.

"Yours first," he retorted.

"Rajner, as in the police commissioner. Now, if you please . . . ?"

"Morava . . . Jan Morava. . . . I'm sorry, sir."

"So, Morava." To Morava's surprise, the much hated and feared commissioner softened a bit. "Listen closely. Take a driver, or a taxi, for all I care, and get over to Vltava Embankment, number five, top floor, but fast! Someone's put away a wealthy German lady; apparently it's a pretty messy job."

Morava wasn't following. He decided to object.

"But, sir, the Gestapo takes care of German cases. . . ."

"They're the ones who asked for Beran. Until I can get hold of him, I'm sending you. But watch out, kid, do you understand?"

The long arm of the Nazis hung up. Morava stood immobile, his face burning, with the receiver clamped against his ear. Jitka was shaken.

"Gosh, I . . . I forgot to tell you who . . ."

He hung up and flashed a smile at her.

"It's fine, believe me. Is there a bicycle around?"

"I'm sure I can get you a car. Wait downstairs a minute."

He hurried after her, mesmerized by her supple gait. He felt vaguely jealous when the garage manager, Tetera—the pretty boy of Four Bartolomějská Street—who also fell under her spell, agreed to drive Morava there personally in a freshly washed car.

They had barely turned left just past the National Theater when Morava smelled the fire and spotted a column of smoke. The corner house down by Jirásek Bridge (renamed Diensthoffer by the Nazis) was aflame and half in ruins. They drove onward into a black snow-storm; particles of soot and flecks of half-burned paper drifted down from a blue sky. The car wound past a line of stopped trams and came to a halt at a blockade of fire engines. Morava and the driver gazed upward, openmouthed. After a while, the detective had grown accus-tomed to murder victims; they were nothing more to him than strange-looking store mannequins. He had never seen the prolapsed innards of an apartment house.

The top four floors had collapsed down onto the second, leaving a motley chessboard of paint, wallpaper, and tiles on the outside wall of the neighboring building. Paintings, tapestries, mirrors, wall lamps, bookshelves, racks with towels, hooks with bathrobes, even sinks and toilets hung forlornly in space. Morava thought about the people who had used them and shivered. In his line of work he had learned to think of violent death as a temporary suspension of societal norms. Often there was a motive—sometimes a poor one, but it could always be traced. Scores of people in this building would have welcomed the fliers as angels of salvation; wiping them off the face of the earth made no sense at all.

An anxious policeman ordered them to move along. Morava sent Tetera back, praying that he wouldn't go to Jitka for payback on the favor. Showing his papers, the detective dodged past the rescue workers and their machines to Number 5, two buildings down. A pair of dis-figured corpses on the pavement did not faze him; they were no worse than the cases he saw every day. As he walked, he took care not to get his imitation leather boots wet in the puddles near the fire hydrants.

He rang the single bell, which must have led to the caretaker's apart-ment. There was no answer. Tentatively he tested the handle of the heavy double doors and found them unlocked. The entrance hall, its marble mosaic dominated by the inscription SALVE, led to an elevator of dark wood as spacious as a small bedroom. It bore him silently upward, with a regal slowness. Even as he stepped out of the elevator at the top, he could have sworn he was at the wrong address.

Immediately the apartment door flew open. On the threshold was a man in a leather coat who had to be from the Gestapo.

"Der Hauptkommissar? Well, finally."

"The superintendent's on his way," Morava replied. "I'm his assistant; Commissioner Rajner sent me."

His decent German had the desired effect. The man gestured—a bit more politely—for Morava to follow him. In the bedroom, a number of men were standing around. And on the table was an object unlike anything he had ever seen before. When he realized what it was, he felt his stomach heave.

H e had a fabulous view from his bench on the far side of the Vltava. It's like being in a box at the theater, he thought happily; no! it's like being in the choir loft! Even past noon, the weak February sun struggled to break through the mantle of cold air, but he was still dripping hot. He unbuttoned his jacket, placed his satchel between his legs, and rested his arms on the back of the bench. Relaxed and at ease, he drank in the spectacle before him and slowly regained his composure.

He was delighted that no one was around to disturb him. The embankment was deserted; the city had crawled into its shell at the first sign of danger. To the left across the river, fire engines and ambulances swarmed around the destroyed corner building. However, he was most interested in the building he had just left—how long ago? He stared at his left wrist; he could see the hands of his watch, but could not read them.

It felt like ages. He had passed the burning wreckage and traipsed across a bridge covered with shards and chips of brick. A while later, a siren had sounded on the other side and the first fire engine appeared. Two private vehicles had pulled up at HIS house much sooner than he'd expected. That man, he remembered, that oaf I met on the stairs! He deserved it TOO. . . .

No! He couldn't kill an innocent person, especially not a man. He was not a criminal; he was an INSTRUMENT. He was chosen to CLEANSE. That was why the METHOD had been strictly defined for him. He'd blown it that time in Brno, true; he'd been a terrible disappointment. They'd said in the papers that the person who'd done it was a DEVIANT. But he was not a deviant; he had just been clumsy. It was his fault they hadn't recognized the MESSAGE. He was lucky he hadn't been punished for his failure. Or was it luck?

CLEARLY MY SERVICES WERE STILL REQUIRED!

He laughed aloud with joy: today he had pulled it off perfectly. What must they be thinking? What do they make of it? This time they must have understood! The newspapers won't dismiss it so easily this time. Maybe they'll use photographs too; yes, definitely—after all, words can't do it justice. The only thing he lacked now was proof of the deed, and the papers would take care of that. An indisputably faithful picture of his work, just like the picture SHE had once given him as a guide.

Only now did he fully remember what happened in that apartment. While he was doing it, he'd been curiously detached, as if an outside force were directing him. He had neither felt nor perceived anything he had said, seen, or done. But it had all been recorded, and now it began to play itself back, like a film rewound to the beginning.

The past became present; the sun and the river vanished: now, in the twilight of the room, he relived each of his movements, noticed each of her reactions. And he marveled at his calm and efficiency as he quickly and precisely performed a horribly complex task. No, he was no longer a third-rate hack from Brno; in those lean, empty years he had matured into a master, just like that unknown painter.

She must have sensed it as well. The whore in Brno had squirmed and squealed like a crazy woman, even fouled herself—ugh! that was what had repulsed him most afterward—while this woman had immediately recognized his AUTHORITY. Maybe she wouldn't have screamed without the gag, but he couldn't have risked it. He couldn't tell when her life ended, because even in death her doglike stare followed him. Now he had finished the task, and when he stepped back, he saw that IT WAS GOOD.

The film ended, the lights came up, and the river was back again. He was even more tired after this rest than he had been before it. Sternly he ordered his muscles to pull him upright and grab his satchel. Now he had to find a place in this unfamiliar city where he could inform the ONE who gave him the task that it was complete.

Through a blast-shattered window the chill day entered the room. Its pungent air stilled his stomach. Meanwhile, Assistant Detective Morava mustered his strength, as he had often done before, so he would not look inexperienced in front of the Germans. There were six of them, all but one clad in the long leather coats that had become the secret police's civilian uniform in the Protectorate. Their apparent leader was a giant whose chest threatened to split his coat open.

Morava introduced himself. They merely nodded expectantly, which he took as permission to go about his business. Briskly he pulled out a folded tablet and opened it to a clean page, so he could take notes for a later briefing, as Beran had taught him: the pathologists may laugh at it, Morava, but this is how we get the human picture before it disappears under a mountain of professional jargon.

The Germans left him alone, conferring among themselves sotto voce, as if they didn't want to disturb him. He watched them in his peripheral vision as he worked, trying to guess what they might want from him. At least it prevented him from devoting his full attention to the gruesome spectacle on the table.

Only the civilian in the beige overcoat acted like a detective; he silently watched Morava wade through the mosaic of fine shards around the table with the woman's torso on it, filling the pages of his notebook with tiny handwriting. However, when Morava finished, it was the hefty one who addressed him. The man's high Gestapo rank was almost palpable; he stood, feet apart, and planted his hands on his hips in imitation of his Führer.

"Your opinion?"

Morava answered as concisely as possible, the way he'd been taught.

"A sadistic murder."

"We figured that out already," the German snarled at him. "Any other bright ideas?"

Morava had always found it difficult to talk to people who raised their voices. His windbag of a father had labeled him a scaredy-cat, and this reputation followed him to Prague. Only Superintendent Beran had realized that it was an inborn aversion to the sort of violence that hides intellectual weakness.

Morava had to clear his throat again, but then he answered firmly. "At the moment, I can only tell you what I see. I'd have to investigate, but given the nature of the case—"

The man he took to be a detective broke in.

"The colonel wanted to know if you recognize an MO."

Morava looked over at the corpse again. This time his training prevailed; he examined it dispassionately, as an object of professional interest. The bizarre and horrible tableau did not remind him of anything he'd read or learned in his few years as an apprentice. He shook his head. The man probed further.

"Do you know of any religious sect that might have done this?"

He should have thought of that himself. Yes, there could be a ritual behind it, but what? There was nothing like this in Czech history, at least.

"No, not offhand."

"Where the hell is your boss?" the large one exploded.

When afflicted, Morava used to imagine his tormentors without their clothes. It still worked; the overfed pig in front of him wasn't the least bit frightening.

"With the rest of my colleagues, at the air-raid sites," he explained. "The city was just bombed for the first time."

"No! You're joking!" The Gestapo officer turned caustic again. "How could we have missed it? You want to know what bombing is, kid? Go have a look at Dresden!"

Suddenly he sounded almost insulted. Morava imagined the sinks and toilets hanging from the walls of the corner house, things their owners had been using just a short while ago. Those people certainly hadn't missed it.

"The police commissioner is having the superintendent tracked down," Morava assured him. "I'm sure he'll be here as soon as he can."

The practical one spoke up again. Slender and gray-haired, he looked like the most reasonable of the lot and differed noticeably from the rest in his behavior and tone.

"Will you wait for him or start the investigation yourself? How quickly can you put a team together?"

A fellow detective, that's why. He tried to explain it to him again.

"Our department is only authorized to investigate criminal acts committed by Czechs. . . ."

"This one will be transferred to you."

"But the victim is German," Morava objected.

"Unfortunately so. Except the murderer is Czech. The building's caretaker met him."

Morava was dumbfounded. Privately he had been betting on a refugee or a deserter hoping to extort money and jewelry from a fellow German. But that was no motive for butchery like this.

"Well, hel-lo," he whispered in Czech.

I n addition to years of experience in the field, Chief Inspector Buback brought an extra qualification to his new post in Prague. He was a Praguer by birth and had an excellent command of Czech.

The young detective's involuntary gasp amused him.

Buback imagined all the things he would overhear in the near future. Hanging this case around the neck of the Czech Protectorate's police was one of the masterly moves Colonel Meckerle was known for.

The tactic had nothing to do with the nationality of the criminal or the victim. The von Pommeren clan had a problematic reputation: in addition to the government's general distrust of the German aristocracy, there were doubts about this particular family's loyalty to the Führer.

In the eyes of the Czechs, however, the baroness represented the German elite; her murder could prompt another bloody reprisal. Of course, at the moment that wasn't a possibility. It would be unwise to inflame the natives when this land would soon be the site of Germany's decisive battle with its enemies.

Meckerle knew that until they could deploy the nearly completed ultimate weapon, they would need perfect order in the Protectorate. And for this he needed absolute control of the police. Now that the small and unreliable Protectorate Army had been disbanded, the gendarmes were the only Czechs with an arsenal—even a small and militarily insignificant one—and, more importantly, a good communications system.

The murder investigation would be transferred to the Czech police: a matter of the utmost importance, they'd be told. They'd be hostages! Finding this sort of criminal was like looking for a needle in a haystack, Meckerle had assured Buback. We'll run them ragged! We'll dig in the spurs and pull the reins at the same time! And then, using you, he explained to Buback, we'll get our hands around their throat!

"Elisabeth von Pommeren," the superintendent now told the Czech, "was a member of the oldest noble family in Germany; her husband was a general of the Reich's armed forces and was posthumously awarded the Knight's Cross. For this reason, we are invoking the Security Decree of the Protectorate of Bohemia and Moravia, signed on first September 1939, section two, paragraph twelve, according to which—and I quote—'the police departments of the Protectorate are required to act on the instructions of the Reich's criminal police,' end quote. What's more, the imperial protector will no doubt offer a reward for the capture of this criminal. The murderer must be found. Lack of diligence will be treated as sabotage."

Buback watched the youth scribbling in his notebook, concentrating so hard his tongue nearly hung out. The kid wasn't their intended audience, but he would convey the message accurately to his superiors. Thirty-three months ago, thousands of Czech hostages had paid with their lives for the assassination of the Nazis' acting imperial protector, Reinhard Heydrich. The boy could certainly imagine the carnage to come if Germany decided that this murder had a political motive.

"Do you want your people to keep the evidence?" the youth asked with surprising practicality.

"I'll tell you what we want," Meckerle thundered. "I want that monster's head. How you get it is your business! Detective Buback will be watching your every move. Unless he finds incredibly good reasons for your mistakes and delays, I will personally bring them to the attention of the Prague Castle and Berlin."

The colonel's explosions always rattled his own men; therefore, it irritated Buback when the kid merely cleared his throat again.

"I understand. May I use the telephone?"

Meckerle gestured with a glove.

"Tell your supervisor that his absence today is quite exceptionally excused. Tomorrow at eight hundred hours I expect to see his personal status report on my desk at Bredovská Street. Even"—and here he raised his voice again—"if it's thundering and bombs are falling!"

More bombs were falling on his beloved Dresden as they spoke, Buback remembered. Was his old home still standing? Anyway, what was the difference . . . ? Once the others had trooped off, Buback took his anger out on the Czech.

"Is there a problem? The telephone is in the entrance hall; hop to it and look smart. We haven't touched anything here, it's your neck on the line now."

The kid rushed off and was heard asking a Jitka to get him an autopsy team quickly. Buback was alone in the apartment for the first time. He looked at the unbelievable object, which someone had created not long ago from a human being, and shivered.

H e described in a whisper how he had done the deed and, as expected, heard praise. He left the church a new man; the unbearable tension of the previous days was behind him. He had done it! He'd erased the shame of Brno. He had proved he was worthy of TRUST, and now he, and no one else, would carry out the rest of the assignment. This morning he had still doubted himself; would it be humanly possible? But incredibly SHE had calmed his fears and confirmed him as HER judge on earth.

For the first time in years, his spirits were high. However, he had a new problem. He had less and less control over his body. Even after a long rest, he felt as if he'd been marching all day. But even when doing IT he'd just stood there; there had been no resistance. Why this stupor; why did even a light bag weigh him down?

The answer he received was so simple he had to laugh. A woman rolled her bicycle out of a nearby courtyard; as she walked she bit into the heel of a loaf of bread, and his stomach immediately cramped up. Of course, he realized; with all the excitement, he'd had nothing to eat or drink since yesterday.

He placed his satchel on the sidewalk and pulled his wallet from the inside pocket of his raincoat. Sure, he had tons of ration coupons left, even halfway through the month; he'd neglected himself completely the last few days. This would have to stop. If he was to succeed and fulfill the HIGHEST OBLIGATION, he needed strength.

He looked around the unfamiliar street and wasn't the least bit surprised to find a restaurant directly opposite. "Angel's." How appropriate. His spirits revived immediately and he could feel his saliva start to flow.

S uperintendent Beran had an excellent alibi. At the ruins of a building in Pankrác that had housed German bureaucrats' families, he had met the entourage of State Secretary Karl Hermann Frank. Frank was the Protectorate's eternal second fiddle, but he had outlived all the first fiddles; he ordered Beran to accompany him as he toured the path of the raid. When the messenger from Police Commissioner Rajner delivered Colonel Meckerle's command, Frank had merely shaken his head briefly.

However, the report, which reached them less than an hour later, roused the impassive Nazi to anger.

"How repulsive—disgusting!" he screamed at the superintendent, as if he had suddenly discovered the Czech to be responsible for the murder. "I expect you to find the murderer immediately. And I hope, for your people's sake, that it's some deviant and not a bloody Resistance fighter trying to frighten the Germans in Prague. Otherwise you Czechs will pay for it from now till doomsday."

Beran proceeded immediately to the scene of the crime but found only a locked building. The single policeman out front was on his way home. The on-site investigation had just ended, he told Beran, and they'd taken the remaining pieces back to the pathology lab. What pieces? The officer hadn't seen them himself and his secondhand description sounded like the product of a sick imagination. The superintendent returned to the Bartolomějská Street office, wondering whom he could put on the case. The Germans had shot his best homicide detective in the Heydrich affair—for "condoning" the assassination—and his senior detectives, both aces, were ill with the flu. He was glad it was the ever-diligent Morava who'd stepped in in a pinch, but his country-born assistant could be as stubborn as a mule; he hoped the kid hadn't made waves.

The assistant detective was now sitting on the other side of his desk. The photos had not yet arrived, so Morava was reading his notes from the scene to Beran. They were far beyond anything even Beran had ever witnessed.

"Point A: The victim, forty-five, a well-bred woman in good physical condition, evidently offered no resistance. Apart from the mutilations listed below, there are no scratches on her skin, and her nails show no traces of a struggle;

"Point B: Using several strips of wide tape (the sort used at post offices and to protect windows against bomb blasts), he taped over her mouth and genitals; the doctor's preliminary investigation suggests that she was not raped;

"Point C: The perpetrator tied the victim to the dining-room table with straps—judging by the cuts on the skin—on her back, so that her head fell back over the edge; he tied her arms at the elbow to her legs underneath the tabletop;

"Point D: The perpetrator cut off both breasts just above the chest and placed them next to the victim on an oval serving dish, which he apparently took from the sideboard;

"Point E: The perpetrator sliced open the victim's belly from chest to below the waist, pulled out her small intestine, twisted it skillfully into a ball, and placed it in a soup tureen;

"Point F: The perpetrator cut the victim's throat almost through to the spinal cord; however, he did not cut the cord itself, so the head remained hanging beneath the body and the blood ran into a brass container, which he had taken from under a potted ficus tree;

"and finally, Point G: Not even the doctor could determine in his first examination when the victim died. But the panic in her eyes," Morava added, closing his notebook, "leads us to conclude that unfortunately she did not die immediately."

His boss reacted much as Morava had at the scene of the crime.

"Good job, Morava. Is it the dream of a mad butcher?"

"Or a surgeon . . ."

"And the Germans think it's the Resistance?"

"The perpetrator was Czech; that's all they needed."

The superintendent studied the closely written notes he had made during the presentation.

"Was anything missing?"

"The victim had precious stones on her hands and neck. More valuables and a considerable sum of cash were found in her handbag and in a small air-raid suitcase by the apartment door."

"How did the murderer get into the apartment?"

"She must have opened the door for him herself. The keys were in the lock, inside. When he left, he just pulled the door shut."

Morava watched tensely as Beran worked his way down the feared list of question marks. For years now it had been his goal to answer all of them correctly. So far he had never made it; today he sensed he was the closest yet. An idea popped into his head: if he did it today, he'd go talk to Jitka too, before someone else beat him to it.

"Was the front door of the building unlocked?"

"No, but every occupant has a key."

"Who could have let the perpetrator into the building?"

"Apparently the victim herself did it."

"Arguments for."

"From his apartment, the caretaker saw her come in and heard the elevator going up. Soon after that the sirens sounded; he wanted to make his usual rounds to see that everyone was in the shelter. But the bombs were already falling, and he ran out onto the embankment in a panic—as he realized later, not just in his slippers, but without his keys. If the door had been locked, he wouldn't have gotten out. So she was the one who forgot to lock up, and the murderer took advantage of it."

"Unless he was waiting in the apartment."

Morava gulped.

"How could he . . . ?"

"Can we rule out the possibility that he got into the building before she did? Say, as a repairman? Or that he got the keys from her?"

Morava saw both his goals recede into the distance.

"No . . ."

"So we can't determine how long the slaughter took him."

Slaughter! His boss had found the precise word for it. And at the same time was testing him.

"That we can. After all, he couldn't have started without her."

Beran grinned in agreement and Morava's confidence grew; at least he hadn't fallen for a trick question. His instructor plowed on through his thicket of notes.

"The caretaker says he began his rounds a quarter hour after the raid."

"I'd say half an hour after."

"Why?"

"I went back along the route with him. He waited under the bridge in case there were more bombs. He was already in a state of shock."

"Even half an hour isn't much for such a complicated vivisection. We can draw some conclusions from that."

"One thing's clear as day." Morava excitedly put forward his theory. "He was prepared in advance; he knew exactly what he wanted to do and how to do it. He had everything with him, like a master craftsman. I doubt we'll even find his fingerprints. And he must be incredibly skillful; the caretaker didn't notice anything odd about him, even after that butchery."

"What did he think when he met him?"

"Outside all hell had broken loose; men from the gas and electric companies were going building to building to assess the damage. . . ."

"And have you simply ruled out," Beran asked, with obvious incredulity in his voice, "that it might be a false lead?"

Morava was shocked.

"You mean that the caretaker did it himself? Mr. Beran, you'd have to meet the man! When he found the apartment open and saw the butchery, he knew he'd met the murderer. He was sure the guy would be back soon to kill him too, and he lost control of his bowels right there."

"Morava, don't exaggerate."

So Morava described the incredible picture of the witness pulling down his long underwear during the interview.

"He can't remember anything. He was still walking around in his slippers when I got there. Even our doctor couldn't get anything out of him. He insisted that the raid took down the building right next door, and he'd even begun to persuade himself that the bomb did it to her. He remembers that he met a man on the steps, but that's all."

"Is it really?"

Morava was on guard because Beran's expression announced he had missed something crucial.

"Except that it was a man. . . ."

"So how did he know the man was Czech?"

Uh-oh, Morava thought, his heart sinking. I should have been a postman instead. . . .

"I don't know . . . ," he admitted humbly.

"Which of the Germans said so? The head?"

"No, their detective. Of course, he could have been bluffing."

"Where's the caretaker?"

"At home, I guess. . . ."

"Have Jitka get us a car."

Thank God for the "us," Morava consoled himself as he left the office; he could have just sent me packing on a burglary case. The girl smiled warmly at him as always and his heart began to thump. Does she feel sorry for me, he wondered; has Beran told her what a loser I am? It was depressingly clear he would never impress either of them.

As he wiped the plate with the last bit of dumpling he felt so wonderful that he remembered HER again. Something yummy for your tummy, SHE used to say. Their Moravian cabbage really hit the spot; how had they learned to make it in Prague? He wasn't a beer man, but even this fairly weak stuff had a kick to it—astonishing in wartime—that spoke of kegs stored deep underground and well-maintained pipes. The pub was nearly empty; a pair of regulars huddled by the tap. Their loud argument triggered his memory. The raid! There had been an air raid. . . .

He racked his brain, trying to recall what had happened. Yes, he could see himself doing IT, wading through glass shards which appeared out of nowhere to cover the carpet. There he was, passing a house recently leveled by aerial bombardment; how could he not have heard anything? Strange. No matter how hard he tried, everything that happened just before and after IT was gone; the only thing remaining was IT itself.

The cemetery—yes, that he still remembered. His ACT had even drowned out the bombs. No coincidence that they began falling here today.

Of all conceivable feelings, only relief and pride made sense. So why was he suddenly uneasy? And why was his stomach still growling so unpleasantly? Why was the tension he'd released at noon building up inside him again? What was his brain trying to tell him? After all, he'd done the deed, gotten the approval. Suddenly he knew. THE MAN!

The one who'd appeared out of nowhere on the staircase. He'd been so surprised he'd just let him pass—even said hello to him! This was the one person who could RUIN everything. How could he have let him go? To fulfill the MISSION he had to remain anonymous. He'd have to get rid of his comfortable army coat and his favorite bag before he went a step further. And what if this man had a good memory for faces?

What could he have been thinking? The man must have been going to see her; where else could he have been headed? She had no husband;

they had been seeing each other. Yes, of course he'd have wanted to drop by after that scare. Like a pig in rut. And people like that deserve PUNISHMENT!

But who was it? Where would he find him? Now that he knew the source of his discomfort, the fog lifted and he could think clearly. The fellow had been in slippers and a shirt, no jacket, in February. Probably from the same building, then. But those apartments were for the wealthier classes; the man certainly didn't belong there. And why trudge up the stairs instead of taking the elevator?

Of course. THE CARETAKER.

He rose to pay and perform the deed.

The building's service apartment consisted of a tiny kitchen and a small living room. Small details revealed the caretaker to be a widower who tried to maintain order and cleanliness. They could see him from the sidewalk, repairing the shattered windowpanes with tape—the same kind the murderer used, Morava remembered. The old man opened the door for them with the light off, and then shuffled away to pull down the shades. Morava was intrigued by the way Beran was sniffing. Could he smell the underwear?

The caretaker was still unable or unwilling to remember what the man on the staircase had looked like. To distract him, the superintendent asked a few questions about the baroness. He gleaned only a couple of superficial observations; no one in the von Pommeren family knew Czech, and the caretaker's German consisted of barely two dozen indispensible expressions. The general had been transferred here from Berlin just after the occupation of Czechoslovakia. Both he and his son had fallen on the front, and the baroness had had both urns buried at the Vyšehrad cemetery nearby, where she visited them every day.

Morava followed studiously as Beran reeled in his line, bringing the conversation back around to the morning's events.

"You greeted the man first, right?"

"Yep," said the caretaker without hesitation.

"How?"

"Well . . . 'dobrej den,' I guess. Just 'hello.' "

"And he said?"

"The same. He said, 'Dobrej den.' Yep, I'm sure of it."

"So that's exactly what you remember?"

"Well, he said it sort of strange like. . . ."

"Strange in what way?"

"I dunno. . . ."

"Did he stutter? Hesitate? Mumble? Mutter? Did he have a lazy *r*? A hoarse voice? Or a high one?"

Morava was amazed at the stream of possibilities his boss poured forth, but the caretaker kept shaking his head.

"What was so strange about it?"

"Dunno . . . something just wasn't right."

Morava dared to enter the game.

"Something about his clothes?"

"Maybe. . . ."

Beran lunged into the gap.

"So how was he dressed?"

"If I knew, I'd tell ya. . . . Look, I had enough for today; did this young feller tell ya what happened to me? Crapped in my pants."

He sounded almost proud of it. The superintendent decided to call it a day and stood up. Morava had a flash of inspiration.

"So you definitely said to him . . . how was it?"

"I said, 'Dobrej den.' . . ."

"And he said . . ."

"The same thing."

"And could he have said it slightly differently, maybe 'dobrý den'? So, 'dobrý' instead of 'dobrej'?"

"Yeah. That's what he said. Just like you said it. Like how they teach us in school, in books, you know?"

Beran's gaze suddenly turned respectful. Morava warmed to his task.

"And something about his appearance didn't fit with how he spoke?"

"I suppose . . ."

"What would have fit?"

"Um . . . what you're wearing: a hat, a winter coat . . ."

"And what wouldn't have?"

Morava was encouraged by Beran's continued silence.

The caretaker looked briefly down at his thermals.

"What I'm wearing. . . ."

"So was he dressed in something similar?"

Morava had noticed long ago that when people of low intelligence were forced to think hard, the exertion made them suffer almost physically. When the man finally spoke, there was a pained expression on his face.

"Look, lemme sleep on it, I'm worn out today."

The superintendent had the caretaker let them into the baroness's apartment. A bitter cold welcomed them. They pulled the brocaded drapes closed over the blown-out windows and turned on the lights in the now darkened apartment. Beran walked around the table, the glass crunching under his feet as he sniffed, doglike.

"Did someone change the carpet here?" he mused.

"We didn't touch a thing," Morava protested.

"From the way you described it I expected pools of blood."

"I told you, he knew what he was doing. He got all her blood to run out into that ficus container. I sent everything to Pathology."

"The breasts too, and the . . . intestines?"

For the first time ever, Morava saw his boss shiver.

"Yes. The guys there were horrified by it; they said they'd put in a rush order."

" 'Scuse me," the caretaker called from the entrance hall. "I think I'm gonna be sick again; could you lock up after yourselves?"

"We'll go with you," Beran decided.

Back downstairs the man had regained some color but was still distressed.

"How'm I gonna sleep tonight?"

"Surely you're not the only one here."

"But I am! The dentist who lived upstairs left for the country; his office was on my floor."

"And on the other floors?"

"Used to be Jews living in those apartments. Now the Germans have some offices there or something."

Morava opened his mouth and closed it again when he caught Beran's warning glance. The caretaker opened the main door. Outside, the darkness reeked of ashes. The firemen had left; only a few curious onlookers were hanging around near the ruins.

"Good night," said the superintendent. "My assistant, Mr. Morava, will come by tomorrow morning to see if you've remembered anything overnight. Litera, step on it."

The caretaker nodded and glanced longingly into the car at them. Beran wrinkled his brow as they drove off.

"I think we can forget about him. Even if we put the perp right under his nose, he's too frightened to recognize him."

"Which our murderer doesn't know," Morava realized.

"What do you mean by that?"

"I'm surprised he let him go. Almost an eyewitness. Must have been an oversight that he let him slip away."

"Good point, Morava. So logically . . . ?"

"The murderer will certainly be back."

Beran nodded.

"Make arrangements right away. Then come to my office."

At Bartolomějská Street, Morava stopped to transmit Beran's order. Back in the anteroom of Beran's office, he was surprised to see Jitka at this late hour and could only manage a loopy smile.

"Hi . . . what are you still . . ."

"I thought maybe you'd need something . . ."

Well, yes: he needed to touch her, to confess that for months he'd been thinking only of her; she was the only reason he hadn't fled when he realized that he'd be saddled with mutilated corpses from now until retirement. But despite his recent success with Beran, he still couldn't find the courage, so he blurted out an inept question instead.

"Like what?"

"I brought a bit of soup from home; I'm heating it up for the superintendent, if you'd like some too . . ."

Suddenly the stench of blood and smoke was gone, replaced by one of his favorite childhood smells.

"Sausage soup!"

"My family"—she dropped to a whisper as she admitted to a grave crime against wartime economic measures—"slaughtered a pig. . . ."

"I'd love some," he said softly. "I . . . thanks. Thanks, yes."

He couldn't tear his eyes from her and so walked backward into his boss's office. Beran was just hanging up the phone.

"I spoke with Pathology. The autopsy confirms your report. He dismembered her alive, almost to the end. But he took something as a souvenir."

"What?"

"Her heart."

"My God!"

"And also, of course, . . . ?"

"What else?"

"The straps he used to tie her up. Which means . . . ?"

Morava the student knew.

"That he'll do it again."

"Exactly. I'm declaring an emergency."

E rwin Buback put the dead woman out of his mind. It wasn't his case. He probed for the contentment he had felt at noon and to his joy found it was still there. Not even the disgust he'd felt in the apartment—the worst ever in his career—could destroy this feeling. In his pragmatic way, he had broken the deed down into a series of colorless facts, just as the young Czech must have done.

He had been sitting alone for over an hour at the end of the bar in the German pub Am Graben; his evident lack of interest in human contact kept the other patrons at a distance. As he sipped a mediocre brandy of suspect origin—oh, where was sweet France?—he considered, for the first time since he lost Hilde and Heidi, what he would do after. . . .

That unknown After. Would it bring sorrow or new hope? When would it finally come? What form would it take? And how should he prepare for it?

Was he exaggerating his skepticism? Or was he dangerously deformed by a profession that made him disbelieve everything he heard?

Why not give it a try? Admit, for a start, that the Führer could be preparing a gigantic trap, part of which was a false retreat on all fronts?

If victory destroyed Europe's existing social order and made way for a new era in history, what would it bring for Chief Inspector Erwin Buback?

If that fateful After came soon (it would have to, he thought, since they were running out of places to retreat to), it would find him just past forty, with a high-placed police job, an excellent salary—and alone.

On the day an unfamiliar voice, callused by years of these messages, had informed him briskly that the two reasons for his existence had perished, a large part of him died as well. The women who tried to comfort him hit a wall of ice. It was his awkward attempt to strike a bargain with Fate, as if his faithfulness would allow Hilde and Heidi to rise miraculously from the ashes.

Today's noonday bomb had made him whole again. When the building shook, his long sleep ended, and he realized that over the past few months Hilde and Heidi had quietly become part of his living self. Interrupted contacts met again, like severed nerves. He began to feel once more.

If the Reich actually won the war—and if he himself did not die in it—he could not spend the rest of his life mourning them. The dead had to be replaced. Germany was paying a terrible price for victory (the lot of all great nations, he supposed) and would need new blood. If Hilde and Heidi had survived him, they would definitely have felt the same way. But which way was that?

The bar was filling up quickly, the noise grew louder. To stay meant risking the company of one of Meckerle's thugs. They had the disturbing habit of drowning out their own fear with proclamations about the Final Victory; it would instantly make him doubt the very thing he was trying so hard to believe in. And starting tomorrow, he would be taking concrete steps to help bring it about.

H e gave a wide berth to the deserted, reeking remains of the corner building and walked as slowly as he dared past HIS house, guided by the balustrade that ran along the sheer drop down to the towpath. In the black of night no one would recognize him, but still he only glanced quickly up at the top floor. The memory of his achievement filled him with contentment. Now he would eliminate the remaining threat to his continued success.

They were still working feverishly on the nearby bridge. Apparently a bomb had fallen there and tipped over a few statues. A crane lifted one of them off the tram tracks; it looked like a giant corpse. He halted and looked around. He was alone on the embankment.

He set his bag down on the sidewalk, opened it, and rummaged deep inside for IT. The wax-paper package was still soft; carefully he placed IT back in the corner of the bag, where IT would be better protected. Then he groped with his fingers for the handle of the knife sheathed beneath his shirt. As he placed it under his jacket he took care not to cut himself. That was how his failure in Brno had begun.

Across the street, a thin streak of light lined the bottom of the windowshade in the ground-floor window. He had it all thought out. He would ring the bell and say—if necessary—*Luftschutzkontrole!* Air-raid control! Better take off his hat and modify his voice, since he'd been stupid enough to speak to the man earlier. What else would he need? His foot, as a wedge; his elbow, as a crowbar; and, to be on the safe side, two quick blows. He had just stepped into the street when the sirens went off.

The freshly wounded city reacted quickly. Shadows hurried from the bridge down to the shelters. The last echo had barely faded into the distance when the sirens wailed yet again, their strange rising and falling glissandos prophesying an air raid.

THOSE FUCKING POLICEMEN!

A few yards farther and wide green steps led down to the towpath; he had planned to use it as his escape route afterward. Instead, he headed directly down toward the dark water. Nothing to be done; he'd come back later, once he'd changed his appearance. How much time left till the train? He had to put his watch up to his eyes to read the hands. Then he saw night become day.

The whine of planes high overhead and the distant bark of anti-aircraft fire explained the light immediately. He knew the shining signal rockets on parachutes would dazzle the air defense systems, but instead of fleeing he stood mesmerized, watching the whirl of countless foil strips designed to distract the German gunners.

The fireworks had to be a thank-you message from HER!

T
he unearthly light show found Morava in Jitka's company.
"Take a motorcycle, drop Jitka off, and go home; I want you here bright and early tomorrow," Beran had decided. The tram lines to Pankrác and Podolí were out of service and the superintendent had felt guilty keeping them late into the night under these conditions.

Morava turned cartwheels inside at this unexpected assignment; it turned a bloody day into a private celebration. Despite his good fortune, he would have seen her to the door of her suburban house (hidden in a romantic blind alleyway on a craggy wooded slope) and said good night with a courteous handshake—if not for the bombardiers. At that very moment, instead of dropping their bombs, they decided to rain a slowly descending radiance onto the city. Evidently they were trying to avoid another tragic error, but Jitka saw it as a warning of impending doom.

"Hurry," she ordered with a firmness he had never seen in her before, "into the shelter!"

Of course, he did not protest, trembling as he obeyed the command. So they waited with last year's potatoes, alone in a quite ordinary cellar. Half of it had been quickly cleared and redecorated with garden furniture; the landlords—a waiter and a cook—were working for a German military hospital in a former north Moravian health spa. When the all clear finally sounded, she invited him up to her attic room for tea with rum, since the kitchen downstairs was unheated.

Finally, he was warm enough to reclaim his courage.

"Please excuse me. . . ." He had to clear his throat again before continuing. "Please excuse my rudeness in asking, but I'm not in the habit . . . do you think . . . that I could . . . that you could . . . that we might get to know each other better . . . ?"

Meckerle was on the rag again; the entrance guards spread the word as usual after he had chewed them out. Immediately there were rumors as to why. Yesterday's firestorm at Dresden had swallowed the villa the colonel "Aryanized" some years ago; it had been a symbol for him of his station. Of all the officers, only Buback was not quaking in fear.

Buback knew the rest of them were incompetent amateurs who owed their posts to their connections; he was the only one who understood his craft. He was sure Meckerle realized this. The giant SS agent was capable of anything, it was true, but Buback found him particularly capable of pulling the right strings in the occupation government's crucial central office—even in times when there had been no recent victories.

Buback agreed with him that the baroness's murder offered a unique chance to illuminate the inner workings of the Czech police, which had so far proved surprisingly resistant to the Gestapo. German informants found themselves isolated from all interesting information with amazing speed, a fact that pointed to the existence of hidden structures. Just yesterday Buback had turned his brigade, based in the former Czech college dormitory in Dejvice, over to his deputy Rattinger, an experienced detective he'd brought with him from Belgium. Buback recognized both Rattinger's yearning for promotion and the primary impediment to his career. Rattinger drank too much and Buback covered his blunders, which obliged Rattinger to him and secured his loyalty. The fanatical Kroloff watched their every misstep like a hawk, apparently convinced that they were the sort of people who were causing Germany to lose the war.

With Meckerle's backing, Buback would inflate the importance of the case by investigating the widow's murder personally. This would force the Czech police superintendent to make the same gesture. Except Buback would move into their camp and engage his secret weapon: his knowledge of Czech. After years of experience in similar organizations, he felt sure he would be able to ferret out any Czech police conspiracies against the Third Reich.

When the colonel had cut his senior minions down to size and then thrown them out, Buback was left alone with him in the room. As he had anticipated, Meckerle instantly calmed down and offered him a shot of surprisingly good cognac. He was uncharacteristically open with Buback.

"Those swine." The giant threatened the distant pilots with a fist. "Soon we'll be the ones flattening their cities. Headquarters reports the Allies are on the brink of collapse. V-1 and V-2 are toys compared to our new weapons. And I wish the Allies would keep bombing so the Czechs would lose interest in stabbing us in the back."

At exactly 8:00 his aide came to announce that the Czechs had been sitting in his waiting room for some time. Meckerle let them cool their heels a while longer as he had two more cognacs. Melancholically he showed Buback photos of his luxurious villa, and when asked politely if at least the inhabitants had survived, he informed Buback gloomily that by sheer coincidence his wife had been in Prague. (Buback, like everyone in the building, had heard of the chief's passionate liaison with a member of the temporarily closed German Theater.) For a short while longer the two men reminisced about their beloved Dresden, until finally Meckerle, purple with fury and regret, stood up sharply and swept the empty glasses off the desk.

"So, let's give it to them."

The trio entered. At first sight these representatives of the Czech Protectorate's executive forces were less than impressive: the police commissioner, small and round, reminiscent of Pickwick; Superintendent Beran, tall and thin, a Don Quixote; and the kid from yesterday, broad-shouldered with small, pink cheeks. Just like Silly Honza, the hero of Czech fairy tales, whom Buback had loved as a child and therefore now especially disliked. He knew, though, that a Czech's appearance is a sadly deceptive thing. Those innocent and harmless-looking Honzas were the worst sort of traitors, and their cunning multiplied their strength.

The colonel had his own opinion about the Czechs. He did not acknowledge them or their lackadaisically raised right hands, and bellowed at them as if they were new conscripts.

Once he had repeated what they had heard individually from him and State Secretary Frank, he concluded: "The Third Reich believes the brutal murder of Baroness Elisabeth von Pommeren is a signal from agents of the traitorous London government-in-exile. With this act, they are unleashing a wave of terror against all Germans in the Protectorate. The guilty party must be detained, and an appropriate punishment meted out. Otherwise the Reich's retaliation will be even more severe and extensive than after the Heydrich assassination. The empire of Greater Germany stands on the brink of a decisive reversal in its all-out war against the plutocrats and Jewish Bolsheviks; we will annihilate them on their own territory! The empire will destroy anyone who even contemplates knifing it in the back!"

Or perhaps slicing its stomach open, Buback thought.

"We will drench the soil of Prague in rivers of Czech blood if doing so will save a single drop from German veins. It is in your hands, gentlemen." (It was evident how little he meant by that word, Buback thought.) "Will you protect your countrymen from a calamity planned by a handful of cynical expatriate mercenaries? I authorize you to form your own investigative team; you will bear full responsibility for the results. The liaison officer of the local Reich Security Office, Chief Inspector Buback, will be my representative. He will be providing me with detailed information about the state of the investigation and can secure the cooperation of our offices for you, should you need it. That is all. Now, which of you will answer personally for the team's activity?"

Police Commissioner Rajner bowed as respectfully as his paunch would allow, and his gaze—till now fixed upon the colonel—slid over to his scrawny neighbor.

"Superintendent Beran. . . ."

Buback had expected it. It would be interesting to work with a man whose name had been a household word for years. He recalled the way the papers had praised Beran during one particular case. A jealous man had killed his wife and her lover, and Beran had stepped forward from the barricade of officers around the house, shouting, If you don't shoot me, I promise you I'll take you for a beer once you get out of prison! And he had undoubtedly done so. Even years later, Beran seemed like a man who kept his word and got things done no matter what. It dismayed Buback that he would have to spy on such an opponent and neutralize him.

Beran nodded agreeably and replied, in accented but passable German, as casually as if he were talking about the weather.

"Given the current personnel situation, I'll still be supervising all of Prague's criminal police operations. As time goes on, we'll be more and more hard pressed by the influx of refugees from the East. Therefore, my deputized representative, detailed exclusively to this case, will be Assistant Detective Morava."

Buback was stunned when Meckerle just nodded; how can he let them foist that kid on us? Careful: the colonel's a dangerous fox. Silly Honza straightened up woodenly, blushing all over. Buback remembered the schoolboy's notebook. You, at any rate, will be mine, kiddo! He tried to answer Beran in the same casual vein.

"That's your business. My job is to see that you get your job done as quickly as possible."

"That's what we ordinarily do," the superintendent replied politely and looked him straight in the eye.

Figures we'd be enemies, Buback thought ruefully; we'd make a great team. At the same time he noticed that Meckerle's attention was slowly but surely beginning to drift. To avoid a general dismissal that would have included him as well, he snapped to attention. At least it would remind the Czechs that this wasn't a social call.

"Standartenführer, permit me to escort the gentlemen to my office to receive their status report."

Meckerle now stiffened up as well and gave them a parting shot for good measure.

"I want that man, here and soon," he bellowed, pointing imperiously at the floor between them. "I want to be the first to ask him personally why he did it. I might even save us the expense of an execution."

Then, finally, he stuck out his arm in the German salute.

As usual, Morava shook off his jitters quickly; the knowledge that he was doing his best calmed him. Feeling Beran's confidence buoyed him as well.

The tumultuous events of the evening before had further sharpened his wits. He had woken, as he'd planned, at five o'clock, even after his first night of love. For a while he had gazed in adoring disbelief at the girl beside him. Once he had made sure that he wasn't dreaming, he went downstairs quietly in the dark, found the chicory in the unfamiliar kitchen, and made himself a quite drinkable coffee. As he sipped it, he wrote down neatly what had already happened, what was happening now, and what must happen in the near future.

He could cross off the site investigation and the autopsy. He had dictated a detailed report (including, among other things, the fact that the murderer had worn gloves and left no traces) to Jitka yesterday in the office—a century ago, he smiled to himself, before that magnificent radiance had descended on them. . . . The superintendent had managed to have the report translated into German overnight, and left it for Meckerle.

In Buback's office, a bulletin was being sent by telegraph or courier to all the police stations in the Protectorate. It ended with a directive to review all the old police blotters; any cases with even a distant resemblance should be brought to Prague's attention. At this point Morava fell silent and looked inquiringly at his boss.

The superintendent turned to the German. "I request your permission to examine the blotters from the former Czechoslovak Republic; we will be looking for any leads in this case."

The German answered without hesitation.

"I will permit it—as long as an agent from the appropriate German security detachment is present at all times; afterward the logs will be resealed immediately."

He's got a good head on his shoulders, and the authority to back it up, Morava evaluated. He finished by asking if the chief inspector had any additional suggestions.

"For now, the press is not to report on this item."

"The censor's office has already been alerted, but it only reviews the Czech press," Morava said, pleased that he had anticipated this demand.

"I'll deal with the German office myself," the man behind the desk snapped.

The upholstered doors opened noiselessly. A young man with a shaven skull handed Buback a sheaf of paper and disappeared. The German looked over the report and turned to Beran again; my first goal, Morava thought, will be to get this man to stop ignoring me.

"Why are your people at the house on the embankment?"

"I ordered them to watch the caretaker," Beran said, taking responsibility. "He's a potential witness for the prosecution; the perpetrator might try to eliminate him."

"Call them off. There are German organizations housed in the building; we'll take care of it ourselves."

Beran nodded again genially. Morava could sense what he was thinking: We'll save on overtime, and now we have a good idea where their counterespionage is.

Buback abruptly stood up. Social graces were clearly not his strong point.

"I expect your reports daily at eight hundred, fourteen hundred, and twenty hundred hours. At an appropriate point I'll join the investigation. Prepare an office for me in your building with two telephone lines."

He did not wish them well, but neither did he say Heil Hitler. From his position at the side of the desk, Morava spotted the faces of two women in a picture frame. Unbelievable, he thought. Despite the events of the last twenty-four hours, Jitka was still on his mind. But could Germans still feel love, after everything they had done?

As they walked down past three checkpoints to the ground floor of the Gestapo fortress, a wave of antagonism rolled over him. These run-of-the-mill sergeants with the skull and crossbones on their caps behaved with incredible arrogance toward the highest officer and best detective of the Protectorate police. They were infinitely worse, he thought, than any Czech guard in Bartolomějská would dare be even to a prisoner. It filled him with a chilling sense of his own insignificance. Only a couple of steps separated them from the infamous basement that had swallowed several of his colleagues, among them Beran's right-hand man. The only way out of there was via the concentration camps or the military firing range in Kobylisy.

Morava believed that Meckerle, who was in charge of all this, was dead serious. If they did not bring him the murderer's head, he'd take one of theirs, and Morava had no doubt which of the three of them would be least missed and would thus suit them best as a general warning.

At times his people's humiliation and degradation had infuriated Morava so much that he would gladly have given his life for their freedom. Thus far no one had ever offered him the chance. But last night for the first time, love had lit up his world more dazzlingly than the pilots' magnesium flares, and now he wanted desperately to live.

That morning, when Jitka had opened her eyes, he had felt fear instead of happiness at her presence: how easily he could lose her or be lost to her in this strange time!

He asked himself: Is happiness a cage for souls to cower in, robbed of their courage?

No! He remembered the passages his grandmother used to read to him from the Bible: It is a shield that would protect him, Jitka, and their children from harm.

My love, I swear to you: in the name of our happiness, I will catch that butcher!

MARCH

An insistent thought woke him: TODAY! He kept his eyes closed so as not to frighten off the long-awaited images.

He saw himself there again as she lay down on the dining-room table transformed into a sacrificial altar. A couple of times in the past few days he'd heard HER reproach him sternly for losing his nerve. He countered that he had a cold, that he must have caught a draft as the pressure wave (he'd remembered it only later) blew out the window-panes. He knew, though, that it was a feeble excuse. Something in him balked; he had gone soft again, and it took all his strength just to keep his workmates from noticing.

Brno still haunted him, though it hadn't been a complete catastrophe. Even if he had screwed it up, at least he'd saved his skin for the next attempt. And after all, the newspapers had hashed and rehashed the story; even in the words they used to humiliate him—labeling him mentally ill—he heard a poorly concealed sense of admiration and horror. In the end, though, a depressing sense of his own failure won out. Add to it the memory of how the girl screamed and fouled herself, and the whole affair had tied his hands for years.

Now that he had finally dared to ACCEPT THE MISSION again, he was eager to see what the newspapers would say. On the second and third days he was patient when the news brought only pictures of disfigured victims from the first Prague air raid—although it annoyed him that his IMMACULATE WORK would not be contrasted with the random results of bomb explosions.

On the fourth day he was constantly tempted to break the strict rules he had set for himself and sneak into the director's office—where the daily papers resided—during the man's short daytime absences. In the end he held out and was all the more disappointed. The focus of attention was the Prague air-raid victims' state funeral; there was not a word of his DEED.

He was alone in the enormous building; he had locked up and made his rounds, and could therefore head home. There, however, he would have to REPORT. Instead, he sat down on the wide marble staircase, turned out the light, and tried in the dark to make sense of it. The silence began to hum unbearably, and the sound, which had no discernible source, made him wonder if he was crazy. Or in shock? After all, a large bomb had fallen close by. He knew from the army what a concussion was; a Hungarian grenade had practically fallen on his head in 1920, instantly ending a promising military career. What if this new shock had turned his wishful thinking into a hallucination?

Finally, a thought saved him. The narrow beam of his flashlight led him down to the cellar; years of practice let him choose the keys from the large ring by touch. He spat angrily at the stone-cold furnace; they'd shivered all through February in winter coats, since the Krauts had requisitioned all the coal. By the back wall, blocks of ice gleamed.

In December, when they stacked the cellar with thick slices cut from the frozen river, he had prudently scouted out a corner where there were already more than three dozen pieces; IT would be safe here through May. Although he could now turn the lights on, he stuck with his flashlight. He leaned against the wall, stretching his free hand behind the ice slabs as far as it would go. His fingers grasped and dislodged a small package.

He put the light on the ground to have both hands free, and unwrapped the wax paper very nervously, because the item inside was unnaturally hard. But it was THE ONE! It was frozen, that's all; how

could he have doubted? He congratulated himself for having anticipated this crisis. It was here, his DEED, imprisoning the wretched soul
which could not fly away.

He arrived home at peace. His mind, free now of distractions, was
calm: those fucking policemen had kept his triumph secret! It seemed
even more unfair to him when he remembered the way they had
harped on his first failure. Will and ambition made him bold again.
Finally he had something to tell HER.

So be it: I will strike again, and SOONER than I planned to! And then
AGAIN AND AGAIN! We'll see whose nerves are stronger. Three will be
enough to start it going; censorship is powerless in this country against
rumors.

Still, he lacked the strength he had last felt in the house on the
embankment. It had melted away as he wearily half sat, half lay on the
park bench. Lunch at Angel's had seemed to set him right, but later
on the train he had fallen into a torpor he could not shake off.

The next day he managed to leave work while it was still light. He
chose a longer route through the city park to air the unheated building's mildewy stench out of his clothes and noticed the celebrations.
A couple of pathetic booths were bravely pretending, in this sixth wartime winter, to be a Lenten fair. He passed a shooting range, where a
youth in a long coat hit five paper roses and the owner grudgingly gave
him a prize. He stopped and stared. It was the thing he'd longed for
since childhood: a Habešan. Of course, the large puppet was only a
shadow of the prewar ones in their shiny colored satins, but here it
shone brightly among the other trophies, the highest attainable goal.

He found himself enviously eyeing the happy winner as a handful
of the youth's peers applauded. The boy gave the black turbaned doll
to a girl, making another nearby plead for one as well. The sharp-
shooter looked embarrassed and balked. He dismissed his friends' insistence and the overlooked girl's reproaches. "I'd never be able to do
it twice," he said.

The stand owner must have thought so too and sensed a chance to
recoup part of his losses. Finally the young man could not resist the
pressure and bought five more shots.

He looked on, paralyzed, recognizing his own dilemma: he too was holding back, out of fear that his single success could not be repeated, that next time he would make a laughingstock of himself again. He knew from his stint in the army that even with a well-maintained weapon, there was almost no likelihood of a second round as good as the first. He faced his own failure as the youth carefully lined up his five lead shots, breaking open and reloading the gun. His fate is my fate, he told himself despondently.

His head cleared when he heard the clamor. The angry stall owner was giving the second girl a Habešan as well.

The image of the puppet lulled him to sleep that night. And when he woke up, he knew he was READY again. Time to find himself an alibi, the instruments, and some new clothes.

Quiet wonder was the only description that fit Jan and Jitka's state "afterward." Throughout their lovemaking she remained silent, although her rushed breath would slowly grow calmer and her eyes, even now, would look at him with the same surprised expression as on the night of February fourteenth, when a new furrow of bombs had threatened to rip across Prague. At that moment he firmly believed that not only would he survive the death throes of the war, but he would live eternally in a suspended moment of grace named Jitka.

Even in that first darkness, which stripped them of their inborn shame with unexpected ease, he felt that this was a moment of truth for both of them. Both came from honorable Moravian stock, where, from time immemorial, couples had first known each other on their wedding night. They confessed the next day how shocked they were at their own boldness, but soon their consciences were appeased by the tacit understanding that they would marry as soon as possible.

Without even asking, he accompanied her home the next day as well, and she did not seem at all surprised. She made him her grandmother's potato soup with dried mushrooms, and then they talked about their families—as it turned out, from villages quite near each other. The conversation was so ordinary that he felt ashamed again. Everything he had ignored the day before, when immediate, irrepressible desire had made it so simple and natural, suddenly became a puzzle. What would happen from here? Where to start? What to say? How to touch her? He bitterly regretted the awkward ignorance and powerlessness that made him feel so uncertain, and finally he decided to slink home to his den. But Jitka just smiled at him and stretched out her hand to the lamp. How simple, he thought gratefully amid the rustling of sheets and clothes; his cheeks were still burning, but after that there was nothing but bliss.

This ritual repeated itself every evening, and Morava soon realized that the same steps led a different way each time. It seemed he was constantly charting a new path across an unknown landscape, but at the same time Jitka was uncovering more layers in him as well.

Morning celebrations soon joined their evening ones. They grew accustomed to falling asleep and waking up in each other's arms: his chin in her hair, her mouth clinging to his breast. They would greet each other with sleepy smiles and a kiss scented with childhood, and close their eyes again until the shrill ring of the alarm clock drove them out of bed.

This silent morning motionlessness opened a new dimension of love in him, and when he would meet Jitka at work later or even just think about her, this was what he remembered. Those Moravian traditions were so ingrained in his character that he never imagined his loved one as she gave herself to him; instead he pictured her in that miraculous state of repose, where instead of touching her body he seemed to approach her soul.

The horrors of their work were implicitly left behind on Bartolomějská Street when the day ended, and they did not waste words on them at home. However, they consciously let the atrocities of war intrude on them more and more each evening. Jan Morava would plug a well-hidden spool (commonly called a churchill) into the radio and cast through the signal jammers' waves for Czech voices bringing hope and fear. Day by day it grew clearer that the world's struggle against the Third Reich would be decided in the battle for the Protectorate of Böhmen und Mähren.

Morava had never frightened easily, despite his peaceful nature. He was from a line of blacksmiths and was never afraid of the older kids;

they quickly learned that little Jan would do his level best to return every blow he received. Although at work he saw on a daily basis the horrors people inflict on one another, it had never occurred to him that he himself might become a victim. Strange, but true: love awakened this instinctual, animal fear in him overnight.

He remembered how as a small child he would wake up in the middle of the night, sure that something awful had happened to his mother. In a flannel nightshirt soaked with warm sweat, he would pad to the door of the sitting room where his parents' solid bed stood, noiselessly open it, and strain his ears to catch his mother's soft breathing beneath his father's loud snores. If he was unsure, he would glide up to the frame, confirming with a careful touch that her hand and cheek were still warm. Although his father was a tall, sturdy man, Jan could not imagine him surviving without her.

More than twenty years later, a similar fear consumed him that an evil force would rip Jitka from his life. While they were making love, death was absurd; together they formed a magnetic field that repelled all harm. However, once he released her from his embrace, she seemed all the more vulnerable, and so he continued to hold her long after the alarm clock rang.

That March morning the heady scent of live soil wafted into their attic from Vyšehrad, Císařská Louka, and the fields of Pankrác and Braník. Ever since he had come to Prague he had lived near the center, and despite the spartan police dormitory room he inhabited, he never tired of the city. My grass is now asphalt and my trees chimneys, he had once written home, scandalizing his mother. From the first he had fit into the city like a native, and he realized belatedly what a wise move it had been not to take over the family smithy. The only thing he occasionally missed were the smells of the land, which at home had told him as he woke what nature and the weather had in store.

That pungent reek, he knew, marked the point when winter suddenly relaxes its grip and sprouting begins. Years earlier, his grandfather had led him onto the dike of the pond and pointed his callused finger at the frozen surface, just minutes before a great expanse of it suddenly cracked in half with a dark thunder, the liberated water gushing forth from the rift.

Morava was sure that scene would repeat itself this morning, but he did not feel the country boy's customary joy at winter's end; instead, fear coursed through him, sharpening as his feelings for Jitka grew stronger.

Tears sprang to his eyes; never had he felt anything like this, not even when his father died. He did not realize that she could see his face.

"Are you crying?" He heard the surprise in her voice.

Unable to speak, he nodded.

"But why?"

"I'm afraid for you."

"But why . . . ?" she repeated, puzzled.

It was the first time he had voiced his fear that they were both trapped in the lions' den. If the war reached Prague, neither Germans nor patriots would be gentle with the Protectorate's functionaries; the dirtier their own hands were, the fiercer they would be.

"When it looks like the end is near, Jitka, you have to get out of Bartolomějská at any cost."

"Where should I go?"

"Definitely not home, the front will come that way and they might tar you with the mess your father's in. You can stay here a couple of days, at worst in the cellar. I'll tell Beran not to look for you, he'll certainly understand. Just promise me, if by some chance I'm not here, that at the first sign of danger you'll do what I said."

"And you . . . ?" she said, without understanding.

"I have to stay with Beran, but don't worry about me; I can take care of myself."

He could see her eyes begin to draw back, and didn't understand at first what was happening. She pulled away from him, rolled onto her back, and threw off the thin quilt. Light had begun to filter into the room, and for the first time he both felt and saw her naked. Her white body, with its full breasts and the shadow of her sex, seemed even more defenseless than before.

"Jan, I'll do as you say, but I also have a request."

"Yes?"

She spoke self-assuredly, in a voice that rang with a mother's severity.

"On the off chance that you can't take care of yourself, I at least want to have your child."

At eight hundred hours Chief Inspector Buback was meeting with Colonel Meckerle. So far, he informed him, he had no reason to criticize the Prague criminal police in their investigation. The Czechs had swiftly collected data on all the sadistic murders from the beginning of the century onward; their records stretched back to the Austro-Hungarian Empire.

It was three weeks since Buback had settled into the office they hastily cleared for him on Bartolomějská Street. After appearing there at random on an almost daily basis, he was reporting on what he had observed.

"I haven't found the slightest sign of activity outside the purview of the criminal police. Superintendent Beran has apparently stayed true to his prewar principle that police work should remain apolitical. As far as the Gestapo is aware, only one of Beran's subordinates violated that commandment—the one who was subsequently executed in July 1942 for sympathizing with Reinhard Heydrich's assassination. His guilt, however, is questionable, since his accuser was an informer he had jailed several times for fraud."

Meckerle, tightly wedged into a chair that would have comfortably fit two normal men, smirked knowingly.

"Now comes the 'but.' "

Buback nodded. His supervisor did not have many likable traits, but at least he was direct; long speeches bored Meckerle and brought out his aggressive side.

"Despite this I do not believe Commissioner Rajner's assertion that the professional departments of the police will remain loyal to us; Rajner is completely in the dark. Although none of the Czech detectives sense or even imagine that I understand them, there is a heightened vigilance in my presence. My frequent visits have blunted this somewhat, and not all of the Czechs manage to hide all their feelings. What's especially interesting is the mood early in the morning, when people trade fresh news and rumors. Even if they aren't listening to enemy radio themselves, the Protectorate's newspapers unfortunately give them more than enough information; the names of eastern cities in the old Czechoslovak Republic appear more and more frequently in announcements from the Reich armed forces high command. During their morning break for rye coffee or herb tea—which they brew up by the hundred-liter—there is a palpable air of excitement throughout the building. Now and then one of them will even drop the pretense of decorum in my presence."

"Do we have an agent in the building?"

"Two, in fact: one is a technician, the primary one is the garage manager. Their reports are muddled, and all I can read from them is that they no longer believe Germany will eventually prevail, and that they are afraid for their own skins. To judge by what happened in the Netherlands, they will be the first to stab us in the back, if it gives them an alibi. Things will certainly be even worse in the operations units of the Czech police, since they are part of the repressive apparatus of a collaborationist government. As the front moves closer to Prague, the danger will grow that they'll turn against us at the eleventh hour to rehabilitate themselves."

"How can we avoid it? Should we lock a couple of them up? Or shoot them?"

What a waste of time, Buback thought; if he can't even come up with a more intelligent idea. . . .

"I'm afraid it would radicalize the Czech police; in Prague alone there are up to two thousand of them—badly armed, it's true, but well trained."

"So then what?"

Meckerle was evidently starting to feel bored.

"Give me a bit of time, Standartenführer. I'll try to gain the confidence of one of the office workers, Beran's secretary."

The giant's eyes once again showed interest.

"Aha. A little 'give-and-take'? At last. You're too young and handsome to play the lifelong widower. Enjoy it while it lasts."

"That's exactly what I have in mind. . . ."

My God, he stopped short; what am I thinking?

He recalled his first sight of the young woman: in the Czech police superintendent's anteroom, the eyes of his Hilde had looked shyly and touchingly out at him, just like when he had seen her for the first time. . . .

"What's new with the deviant?" Meckerle remembered as Chief Inspector Erwin Buback stood up to take his leave.

"The most promising trail leads to Brno. I'm going there with Beran's assistant this afternoon. Brno's close to the front; it will be easier to assess our overall situation from there as well."

At the very same moment as Buback was filling Meckerle in, Morava was reporting his preliminary results to Beran.

The superintendent did not interrupt with his usual treacherous questions; he followed Morava's conclusions without taking notes, and with every page of his notebook Morava's self-confidence grew.

"It can be asserted with almost complete confidence that the perpetrator is the very person who in 1938 committed the sadistic and still unexplained murder of a widowed seamstress, Maruška Kubílková, in Brno. Regardless of differences in the implements used"—Morava raised his voice to drown out his nervousness, for this was the point where he felt his theory was most vulnerable—"it seems probable that the same perpetrator has attempted again what he failed at seven years ago, whether because of inexperience or because the first victim defended herself ferociously."

Even now the superintendent made no objections and took no notes. Morava was already regretting that he had closed the connecting door for fear of exposing himself to ridicule. Jitka could have witnessed his first genuine success; she could have heard his superior appreciatively pronounce that magic phrase, "Good work, Morava!"

"I conclude," he therefore continued at an undiminished volume, "that it would be appropriate to reopen the Kubílková case. Its investigation was interrupted in March 1939 when the two officers assigned to it on the Brno criminal police fled to England after the establishment of the Bohemian and Moravian Protectorate. The file ends with the statement that all significant suspects produced alibis and no crime remotely like it has occurred since then in this country, from which they deduced that the murderer managed to escape abroad as well. Our recent investigation, however, forces me to raise the possibility that he was here the whole time and should be sought first among the ranks of the original suspects."

He finished and, in a new wave of doubt, expected his suspiciously inactive boss to shoot him down with a glance or an observation that would reduce his careful argument to nonsense. Instead, Beran stood up, surprising him with an odd question.

"Would you like to go for a walk? The papers have been claiming for a week already that spring's here."

As he followed Beran out through the anteroom, Morava tried to signal Jitka with a shrug of his shoulders that he had no idea what was happening. The superintendent walked so fast that in spite of his height Morava could barely keep up. He let himself be led as far as Střelecký Island, in the middle of the Vltava River, without daring to break the silence. As the stone steps led them down from the bridge to the park path, he decided that his superior had merely wanted a breath of fresh air, and that there was no harm in asking a question.

"Chief Inspector Buback is waiting to hear what time we're to leave for Brno."

"I know," Beran reassured him. "That's why we've gone for a little stroll."

Morava must have had a somewhat silly expression on his face. The superintendent smiled in amusement.

"You thought I wanted to show you the pussy willows blooming? Jitka can take care of that, I think."

The assistant detective felt his burning cheeks betray him again. But Beran—uncharacteristically—clapped him on the shoulder.

"You can't seriously think I only have eyes for corpses. My congratulations; I'm very happy for both of you. Now all you have to do is survive the war."

"Exactly. She's terribly afraid for her father. He's been locked up for that illegal pig slaughter."

"I haven't forgotten. I'll get to it."

The circular path led them to the tip of the island pointing toward the Charles Bridge. In the clear air the Prague castle rose up before them, from this angle unmarred by the occupiers' flag—not the sarcophagus of an inferior people destined for extermination, but the undying symbol of a metropolis whose glory, according to the old Czech legend, would reach the stars. Even in this distant and deserted place, Beran looked cautiously around.

"What's your opinion of Buback?"

"He's a capable detective . . . to judge by his position, at least."

"Exactly. Kind of a big gun for a little case, don't you think?"

Morava felt hurt, as if his own importance had just been downgraded.

"I had the impression that you were giving this matter the highest priority, sir."

"Of course, of course," Beran said, as if trying to soothe him. "That's why I took the case myself. But in reality, you're the one working on it while I continue directing daily operations. Consider that Buback runs the whole Prague office of the German criminal police; isn't he spending a bit too much time and attention on this?"

"Not given the victim's significance," Morava objected. "After all, she was—"

"That's precisely the point: she wasn't! I put out some feelers and discovered something interesting. The Nazis were deeply suspicious of the von Pommeren family. The general's posthumous decoration was supposed to signal that even the old German nobility supported Hitler, but there's a rumor circulating in Prague's German community that the Russian partisans got him just before the Gestapo did. Von Pommeren had long been suspected of supporting the ideas that led to last year's assassination attempt on the Führer."

"Aha." Morava tried quickly to pick up the thread. "So they're just feigning an interest so they can terrorize us?"

"Berlin—and State Secretary Frank here in Prague—can hardly risk inflaming the populace for no reason, given how close the front is and the way the war is going. No, Morava, the Germans' plan is to keep the lid on us."

"Why should they be so interested in our criminal police?"

"Because in every time and place, it's the heart of the whole force. There's only a handful of us, but we outlast regimes; I'm a living example. And under certain circumstances, our knowledge of the system would let us run the whole force, and not only the force."

Morava was still in the dark.

"Under what circumstances . . . ?"

"Didn't it ever occur to you, Morava, that, railway workers and firemen aside, only the Prague police could defend this castle—and all of Prague with it—from destruction? And who can block the Germans' retreat to the west once the great flight from the Russians begins? Won't it be crucial for the Germans, then, to sound us out up close and neutralize us in time? Buback isn't just a detective, Morava; he's Gestapo."

B arbora Pospíchalová actually enjoyed going to the cemetery. Death had taken a cruelly long time to claim her husband, playing with him like a well-fed cat with a mouse. Its final strike meant freedom for both him and his wife.

After taking years to choose the right man, she had married Jaroslav at thirty for love; the rapid onset of his chronic illness thereafter only strengthened her feelings for him. Therefore she was more surprised than anyone at how quickly she resigned herself to his death. She would have sworn it would be months, perhaps years, before she could lead a normal existence. And it was absurd to think—yes, she had found the very idea distasteful—that she might ever again have a lover, let alone a husband. A month after the funeral, however, she heard a new confession of love and a marriage proposal.

Her suitor was Jaroslav's brother, who had cared for him unflaggingly by her side until he breathed his last. During that whole time Jindřich had never revealed his feelings and even now agreed to her request. This only endeared him to her more.

She had decided to mourn for half a year, and that period was just over. Tomorrow her brother-in-law was coming for dinner, and Barbora was sure he would stay the night. She suddenly realized that even here—where only a layer of clay divided her from the body she had touched so tenderly—she was looking forward to their lovemaking. "Forgive me, Jaroslav, my Jaroušek, my love," she begged in a whisper. For a moment her desires seemed hideously carnal and she weighed writing Jindřich not to come.

Then, as if swimming up from the chilly depths, she heard the voices of the first birds as they returned after winter to the treetops and transformed the cemetery into a park. In the breeze she felt a hint of spring scents and her misgivings seemed senselessly cold. Jaroslav was dead; he was changing slowly into earth, which would soon nourish the fresh greenery. Why shouldn't new feelings grow here too from the love two people bore him, feelings that would join all three of them together?

Barbora had brought water for the bouquet of cowslips and a rag she used to wash the marble stone with its gilded name and two dates. Then, as always, she cleaned out the small blue lantern she had brought for better days: after the February bombing, Praguers had bought up all the unreliable ersatz candles for their cellars, and anyway cemeteries were subject to strict blackout laws. When she had finally finished her prayers, crossed herself, and stepped back from the grave, she bumped into a man.

It frightened her, because she was usually alone here among the dead at noon. The man hastily apologized. His Czech had an unusual accent, but what caught her attention was his odd appearance. The smart black suit, a prewar cut, clashed with a battered brown suitcase. Had he come straight from the train station to a funeral? But there were none scheduled today. Maybe he'd got the time or place wrong?

Of course she had no intention of asking; she simply assured him she was fine and didn't analyze what else in him disturbed her. She had set off toward the exit when he asked her where he could find the grave of Bedřich Smetana. She led him to it; those with loved ones here followed an unwritten code, helping visitors to find the graves of the national heroes who a hundred years before had revived the Czech nation from a similar deadly slumber.

On the way, she could not help asking where he was from, and was shaken by his story. He had lost his wife and home in the recent bombing of Zlín in east Moravia and had set off for Prague, to his divorced sister's. Before she got home from work, he told Barbora, he wanted to lift his spirits by visiting some historic sights he'd longed to see since his school days.

As she bade him farewell at Slavín, a piercing wind blew up and he remarked that winter was far from over. She realized what had disturbed her about him, and asked why he didn't have a coat. It had been in his house, he explained simply, and she reddened with shame that it hadn't occurred to her. Her wardrobe was still full of Jaroslav's outerwear, which would have made slim Jindřich look like a scarecrow, and anyway, she'd feel better without them. . . .

"I don't live far," she said in a wave of sympathy, "and I still have lots of my husband's things. You can take something for yourself."

"God bless you, thank you kindly," he said in his old-fashioned Moravian way—now she could place the accent! He picked up the bulging suitcase and strode after her.

Assistant Detective Morava had met with Chief Inspector Buback several times already, but never for so long and in such close quarters. First he offered Buback the front seat, then tried at least to leave him alone in the back, but the German more or less ordered Morava to sit next to him; otherwise they'd have to shout at each other, he said. With Beran's instructions fresh in his mind, he expected the Gestapo agent to press him for information about the police, and was surprised: Buback merely wanted to hear the facts about the four suspects who had been investigated and cleared of the murder in Brno. With the help of Morava's notebook this task was easily and quickly behind them.

Josef Jurajda, born 5 March 1905 in Olomouc, Moravia (the Brno office had promised to track down his address) was by trade a room painter with the firm Valnoha and Son, which had branches all over the region. Prosecuted several times for sexual deviance, he climaxed without having sexual relations with women. He had tied two prostitutes up with a clothesline, silenced them with a gag, and masturbated in front of them while jabbing them in the chest with pins. His alibi for the fateful moment seemed airtight: he had been working for his firm in Košice, two hundred miles to the east, and the train connections between times when his coworkers had seen him would have allowed him a scant twenty minutes for a complex crime in Brno. Given the low volume of traffic on Slovakian roads, the investigators decided he would not have had time to hitchhike to Brno and back.

Alfons Hunyady was born 16 December 1915 in what was then the north bank of the Hungarian city Komárom. An illiterate Gypsy, he lived off earnings as a day laborer and more often as a petty thief. Among other crimes, he was convicted of rape in 1931 as a juvenile and in 1935 sent to prison for the same offense. In both cases he had tied his victims with wire and cut their breasts to lessen their resistance. Only a miracle stopped the second woman from bleeding to death. Hunyady's alibi for the October night when someone tortured Maruška Kubílková to death was curious. He spent it in jail in the town of Ivančice near Brno; a notorious and therefore oft-imprisoned local criminal would lend out the master key for a small payment. Although other witnesses corroborated the fact, the director of the police station denied the charge vehemently, calling it slander, and for public interest reasons neither the judge nor the prosecutor wanted to risk a perjury trial involving a government official. Alfons Hunyady was tracked until 1941 as the political situation allowed; then the file ended with an ominous note of his disappearance from the personnel register.

The third suspect was therefore of exceptional interest.

Jakub Malatínský, born 6 April 1905 in Mikulov in south Moravia, was the son of a vintner who worked his way up to cellar master in the fabled Valtice vintners' school. His career ended overnight in 1926 when he stabbed his young wife, whom he suspected—probably correctly—of infidelity. What was more, he cut off both the dead woman's breasts, which in court he explained as insane jealousy that another man had been allowed to touch them. The prosecutor asked for life, but after an evidently outstanding defense counsel's fiery closing argument, the court was persuaded that the defendant had acted in a moment of passion and capped the sentence at fifteen years. In spring 1937 he was released for good behavior and sincere repentance and was hired as a custodian for the court building. He was the only one resident in Brno on the day of the murder, albeit as an appendectomy patient. At the time of the crime he was already ambulatory and sharing a room with a demented patient, but even so it was highly improbable that he could have obtained clothing, latched onto the young widow— where there was no evidence that he even knew her—brutally murdered her, and returned to his hospital bed by midnight, when the duty nurse spoke with him. The year before last, he had decided to return to his home county, where his good commendations helped him regain the post of cellar master.

Bruno Thaler rounded out the foursome of potential perpetrators. Born 12 August 1913 in Jihlava of German descent, this trained butcher was sent for psychological treatment when, after repeated vivisections of animals (for instance, disemboweling pigs before slaughtering them), he threatened a female coworker with the same fate if she reported him. His statement that on the day of the murder he had been in Austria as an agent of Henlein's storm troopers was supported by the regional leader's stamp. After the country's annexation, no one dared reopen the investigation.

". . . And because of his German background, Thaler was removed from the Czech office's files," Morava said, wrapping up his briefing.

"We'll look into it," Buback commented laconically.

Then he leaned stiffly into his corner and sat out the remaining four long hours, eyes open, until they rolled into Brno amid the military and civilian trucks. Morava fought sleep strenuously; he did not want to display the slightest weakness, especially in front of this man. He almost regretted that Buback was not trying to squeeze information out of him. . . .

"H ere," she said to the luckless Moravian, "choose yourself some-thing warm."

Barbora Pospíchalová was standing in front of the open wardrobe and had to fight the temptation to close it under some pretext or other. Once again she felt she was treacherously writing Jaroslav off, although as she poured out her whole story, Jindřich included, to this poor man on the way home, her heart told her everything was as it should be. Now her guest stood motionless beside her with his suitcase in hand; he looked uncomfortable, as if he were reading her thoughts. Gallantly she encouraged him, to have it over with quickly.

"Don't be shy; I'd give them away in any event."

The refugee set his case down, opened it, and scrabbled through it. A swath of green material folded several times fell out onto the carpet. As it unfolded, Barbora recognized it as a well-preserved hunting coat.

"But look, you've got . . . ," she blurted, confused, then lost her voice as she saw the straps in the man's hand.

Instantly he struck her between the eyes with the base of his free hand. In the midday light, the familiar room burst into a colored ka-leidoscope. She fell into the wardrobe, slowly sinking into the dense mass of hanging clothes, and the reek of moth powder gave way to Jaroslav's scent.

E rwin Buback was not particularly worried about the Czech detec-tive. The impression the school notebook had made at their first meeting had deepened over time. The kid was capable and hard-working; it was no surprise that Beran trusted him so. At the same time he was a perfect example of a "lotus flower," as Hilde called those too-open and guileless souls. (She'd soon proved herself worthy of the title in his eyes.) In the Prague criminal police's head office, where he had least expected it, he had found two of these characters: in addition to Beran's adjutant, there was his secretary, a near likeness of young Hilde.

As he sat motionless in the car (his standard wartime tactic around citizens of occupied nations, since he felt that a Prussian military bearing induced respect), the faces of the two women merged into a single image in his mind; he could not determine which of them his inner eye was seeing. It was the first time this had happened since Antwerp, and it confused him. Was the Czech girl strengthening his memory of his beloved wife, or had the indelible image of Hilde awakened a connection he'd first sensed that evening in the bar of German House? This striking similarity of features and characters had to be a signal from fate—didn't it?

It was days before he learned anything about the girl, and therefore, in an impossibly short time, he imposed on her many of the feelings he had lost with the passing of his first and only true love. He caught sight of her only in the moments when she walked past behind the eternally open door of Beran's anteroom or when he passed through it himself on the way to see her superior.

A further sign from fate was that he had first seen Hilde in exactly this way. Though she was the daughter of the owner of Dresden's Schlosskonditerei, her responsibilities as a newly trained confectioner kept her behind the scenes of the business, while her parents and brother moved about the stage of the city's favorite café. Buback took a parade of girlfriends there until one day this shy creature appeared behind the café's new technological wonder—a refrigerated counter from Electrolux—to check which delicacies needed replenishment.

This brief eventless event turned his life upside down. He began to spend all his free time in the café, but even so was rarely rewarded with her long-awaited appearance. He prepared his best admiring gaze for her, which, he smugly knew, was infallible—but it never hit its mark: not once did the girl raise her eyes from the sweets.

Later she confessed to a small deception. From the very beginning she had seen him through the grating in the kitchen, so she knew of his numerous companions. He had captivated her from the first with his masculine good looks and suave manner, and for precisely this reason she resolved not even to look his way lest she fall victim to his charm. She was afraid of ending up like the rest of his transitory acquaintances. Hilde had been born and raised for one great relationship;

she intended to offer her love only once and forever. If she were mistaken, she told him soon after the wedding, she would crack. How? he said, not understanding. The way bells crack, she answered; they keep their form, but lose their sound and with it their purpose.

He had no choice but to bring the mountain to Muhammad and, for the first time in his life, take sole responsibility for meeting a girl, instead of letting her do the work. The only polite way of doing so at the time entailed more serious obligations.

"Dear Miss Schäfer," he wrote her,

I beg your forgiveness for troubling you; as an excuse I can offer that I know you by sight, as a regular customer of your establishment. If I may be permitted to make a request of you and your parents, I would like to invite you this Sunday for tea at five o'clock at the Waldruhe Restaurant. Should this request meet with your favor, I will call for you at the private entrance of the Schlosskonditerei at half past four. With deepest respect, I remain

Police Clerk Erwin Buback.

Eventually he received Ludwig Schäfer's letter of cautious agreement (which, he later learned, Hilde's parents had argued over for two days and nights). On the day, he arrived with a bouquet for her mother and had the carriage wait outside so he could converse politely with Hilde's parents, all of which made a suitable impression. Hilde was released with the admonition to be home no later than half past seven.

As it turned out, he only needed the first ten minutes. Before they brought out the service, he had the opportunity to look through her tender eyes into the depths of her soul, and as they stirred the tea, he addressed her.

"Dear Miss Schäfer, I don't know how it happened, and I know this flies in the face of convention, but I am simply in love with you. I've never actually loved anyone before in my life, and I thought I lacked the capacity for true feeling. Then I saw you, and from that moment I've known what love is. I beg you, put aside your shyness and the suspicion you feel toward me, a man you barely know. Please hear me out; I've felt love for the first time and now I know I cannot live without you. What do you say?"

Even now, in the car heading down the shattered road toward Brno, he could see the scene in his mind's eye as if it were yesterday, and suddenly he realized that he could honestly and forthrightly say virtually the same words to the young Czech woman, whom he had known roughly as long as he had Hilde when he proposed to her.

In his comic fashion, Morava coughed timidly before addressing him.

"We're already in the suburbs of Brno, Herr Oberkriminalrat. . . ."

"So?"

"Would you like to go to the hotel first?"

His body ached from sitting turned toward the right; he would gladly have lain down for an hour, but knew that he'd do better to break this train of thought.

"No. Let's get straight to work."

H e sat in the rocking chair and slowly swung his weight there and back. Forward. Backward. Forward. Backward. The regular motion calmed him; it was all he could manage at the moment. His arms and legs had become burdens again; whatever it was that made them part of his living body had evaporated. They had no feeling, no substance to them; they merely WEIGHED.

His mind was fully occupied by the two commands rocking the chair. Backward. Forward. Backward. Forward. Yes, that made him feel good, now he was comfortable! The most effective way to rest and renew his strength would be to lie down on the double bed; he could see it through the adjoining doors at each rock of the chair, but it was too far. So instead he just kept on. Forward. Backward. Forward. Backward.

He had the impression that white smoke was rolling over his brain, as in the Turkish baths he liked so much. It was usually so refreshing;

so why did resting exhaust him instead of reviving his muscles? If it became necessary, he was sure he could . . . aha, he realized, but there's no reason to hurry, and nowhere to go. She had said HERSELF that she lived by HERSELF! The repeated word with its different meanings amused him; he rocked again with renewed interest.

Backward. Forward. Backward. Forward.

He felt safe and blissfully aware that he had done it AGAIN. And FLAWLESSLY. And not only that: out of thousands of widows he had found this one. He had been right to deceive her; she had DESERVED it! After all, she had shamelessly confessed that she was a WHORE! Her new john would be shocked tomorrow when he saw her laid out for her wedding night.

With this thought his strength returned so unexpectedly that it threw him out of the chair. Almost broke my neck, he thought, his heart pounding from fear; they would have found me here uncon- scious. . . . He shook off his fright and stood up. His legs held steady. On the table beneath him he could see his achievement and felt a sudden pride.

NO WHITE DOVE!

Today SHE would be happy to hear his news.

The entire Brno contingent was waiting for them. Matulka, the head of the city's criminal police, owed his job to his faithful collabora- tion; he was a member of the Fascist organization Flag, the pro- German National Union Party in the Protectorate government, and the Anti-Bolshevism League—and was probably an informer to boot. That morning on the island, Beran had described him to Morava as the big- gest stain on what remained of the Czech criminal police's honor. Matulka was even permitted the luxury of not speaking German; it was whispered that through the whole war he had only made it as far as les- son three. Morava therefore translated for Buback and his local Ge- stapo equivalent.

Matulka first fawningly dismissed Bruno Thaler from suspicion, thanks to his Germanic origins and, as he called it, his demonstrated patriotic activity outside the Protectorate at the time the seamstress Kubílková was murdered. Buback commented that the crime took place before the Protectorate existed, and that he would personally look into Thaler's alibi, thus completely derailing Matulka from his script. Morava was struck by the Germans' open condescension toward their local ally. Does treason stink even to those who profit from it?

It clearly affected the man; he began to sweat and stammer until finally he relinquished the floor to his deputy Váca, who seemed equally unprofessional. Reading from a paper he was evidently seeing for the first time, he stumbled through a report on two of the suspects from 1938.

Josef Jurajda had been an invalid ever since he fell down a long flight of stairs while painting the Brno town hall. Currently he was employed as a night watchman in the registry office. Only his wife could supply him with an alibi for the fourteenth of February. According to her, he had slept all day while she had washed dishes at the Grand Hotel. There were no direct witnesses as to when he began his rounds of the building, although the cleaning ladies met him there at five the next morning. The gentlemen from Prague could interrogate him here whenever they wished.

Jakub Malatínský had taken a holiday that day and refused to give details, but stated that in a pinch he could produce an airtight alibi. Brno had directed him, via a local police order, not to leave his workplace. If the gentlemen so desired, he could be escorted here immediately.

Morava was delighted when Buback announced he intended to drop in at Castle Celtice tomorrow for Malatínský. My God, he thought, maybe I'll see my mother on the way. . . .

As far as Alfons Hunyady was concerned, Váca concluded, wiping the back of his neck with a handkerchief, the Gypsy had been transferred to the authority of the Reich's Commission on the Racial Question; further investigation lay outside the purview of the Protectorate police, who could offer the gentlemen no further help. . . .

When he had finished translating, Morava asked Buback whether he would check on Hunyady's case as well as Thaler's. For the first time, his request met with uncomprehending eyes. Then the German told him he could safely forget about the Gypsy. With this the agenda for the meeting was exhausted.

Matulka apparently considered the meeting a mere pretext, since he invited all present to a festive evening which he had organized at the Grand Hotel. Buback declined fairly rudely, set Jurajda's interrogation for 8:00 A.M., and left with the Brno Gestapo agent. So much for Beran's theory that this investigation was a red herring designed to distract the whole Czech police force, Morava thought.

The young Czech could not refuse the invitation and, what was more, did not want to; he was not satisfied with the way the session had gone and hoped to extract more information from Matulka and Váca. Not long into dinner he realized that Buback had their number. The two policemen had failed to invite the rest of their office in the hope of hogging all the credit for the research, and they themselves apparently knew only what their subordinates had put on their desks. The pair even fawned over him, a run-of-the-mill assistant detective, and he quickly sensed that they were in the grip of a practically demented fear.

What plans did the central office have once the front got here, Brno's defender of the law asked when he'd briskly gobbled down the Moravian roast (obtained without ration coupons, which was in and of itself a punishable crime). Everyone in Brno was sure—he assured Morava emphatically, so the message would make it to Prague—that the great German Reich would be victorious, but how should they carry on in the short term if for strategic reasons the Führer found it expedient to withdraw the front temporarily past Brno? Were they perhaps counting on the Brno team's experience to reinforce the Prague police? After all, criminal elements in Prague would be sure to exploit the political confusion.

Morava lost patience with them. They were officers just like their colleagues in Prague, he told them sternly, and he didn't know anyone there who was as obsessed with what would happen after the war. As long as they maintained public order—which was, after all, their only obligation—and had not engaged in extracurricular political activities of their own accord, they'd have nothing to fear. After all, every regime needs criminal police. Now, if they'd kindly excuse him, he'd had a tough day and tomorrow wouldn't be any easier; he had to finish up the investigations their subordinates hadn't completed, so he wanted to get some sleep.

He left them there with their half-empty glasses and looming fears and walked swiftly back to the hotel down dark, deserted streets that he had almost forgotten in his years in Prague. Before he rang for the doorman, he stopped and listened. No, he was not imagining it; a weak but perceptible rumbling rippled through the cold, still air, first weakening, now strengthening and overflowing like the April thunderstorms he remembered over south Moravia.

The front, he realized. They're that close!

Then his thoughts turned to Jitka, because it was the first time in their three weeks together that he would sleep alone.

The man from the Brno Gestapo assured Buback that he could forget about two of the suspects immediately. If Bruno Thaler's alibi for 1938 was problematic, he had one for this February fourteenth that was unimpeachable: he was working as a prison guard at the Buchenwald concentration camp and had not taken any days off this year. Alfons Hunyady had left for another unidentified camp three years ago in a transport of Moravian Gypsies, wearing the label *Parasite*.

Buback had refused Matulka's dinner invitation primarily because the Czech and his deputy were useless to him. Every word they spoke dripped with proof that they were Nazier than the most fanatical Nazis. In a police uprising, worthless toadies like them would be the first to lose their heads.

He had two surprisingly good whiskeys with his colleague and compatriot in the local German casino and managed an hour of small talk. How funny, he thought, that since . . . when was it, Stalingrad, or maybe the Allied landing at Normandy, conversations like this had lost all substance. Under certain conditions even a sarcastic remark about the weather could prove dangerous; after all, it could be a gibe at the constant excuses emanating from the armed forces high command. The situation on the fronts was completely taboo.

They exhausted the murder of Baroness von Pommeren, chatted a bit about Moravian wine, which Buback had not drunk since his youth, and called it a night when they caught each other simultaneously yawning. The chief inspector politely refused an escort home, and when he reached the hotel decided to prolong his walk. Against the dark sky the even darker silhouette of a steep knoll rose close by. He decided he could do with a bit of exercise and set off at a brisk clip up the slope.

Soon the metropolis lay at his feet, darkened, unfriendly, and unknown, the second largest city in the land where he was born. Where does a bilingual German from nonexistent Czechoslovakia belong anyway? Especially one from Prague?

The product of a mixed marriage in which his mother prevailed, Erwin Buback had therefore gone to a Czech grammar school in his native Prague. When his mother died, his father, an insurance agent, married a wealthy German woman from Karlsbad. Erwin attended the German gymnasium there and was sent to Dresden to study law. His parents, who had no further children, wanted to strengthen Erwin's identification with the nationality they shared.

Buback had met Hilde in that wonderful city on the Elbe and stayed until the war broke out. He soon earned his stripes in a field which had never interested him, but which proved reasonably secure in a time of economic and political upheaval. The criminal police, of course, came under Nazi supervision in time, but at least the Nazis understood that to have a dependable judicial and corrective system they had to let some professionals remain at their posts.

That did not mean that the detectives resisted the Nazis, far from it. Buback felt admiration for the verve with which they quickly returned order to a shattered Germany. He too welcomed the Führer as the renewer of German honor, which the Versailles dictates had trampled. His loyalty, though, was a far cry from the fanaticism in other branches of the Reich's government. He was a German, and that was that.

Buback, his young wife, her parents, and their acquaintances applauded enthusiastically when the Führer resolved to return misappropriated territories to a resurrected Germany. They wholeheartedly welcomed the annexation of Austria in 1938. Erwin was greatly pleased when Bohemia returned to Greater Germany's embrace. He experienced a heady Night of Torches in liberated Karlsbad, and tears sprang to his eyes when the banner of new Germany waved over his native Prague as well. He and his colleagues celebrated the lightning victories in Poland and the west.

While at first the newly formed security detachments repelled him with their ostentatious brutality, he came to see his office's connection to them as a necessary evil, an unavoidable consolidation of forces in a nation at war. Sent to France, Holland, and Belgium to ensure the peaceful coexistence of his kinsmen in occupied territories, he devoted his energies, as before, to that task and no other. Some things he saw shocked him others he observed with disapproval; but he felt a direct personal responsibility for all of it.

It was a Sunday in June of 1941, the day Germany attacked the Soviet Union, when he first began to feel uneasy. When he asked Hilde why she wasn't joining the domestic festivities, she brought Heidi's geography textbook and opened it to the map of Europe and Asia. The speck that was Germany butted up against the gigantic expanse of Russia. He controlled his irritation and chided her mildly: she should have stuck to pastries instead of teaching if she couldn't recognize cartographic distortions and, more important, if she couldn't understand that territory was not the only factor involved.

After that the war only permitted him the occasional visit home, when he would drink in as much of Hilde and Heidi's presence as he could. Understandably they kept to personal topics, but he noticed that his wife avoided everything political to the point of awkwardness. Once, however, she slipped, and it led to the one bitter argument of their life together.

On a walk through the Franconian vineyards just one year ago, he had been trying to explain an idea he had just had to Hilde. In retrospect, he had probably been attempting to convince himself more than her. By retreating on all fronts, he had claimed, the Führer was coiling his people into a spring that would then fling the Allies into the Atlantic, the Arctic, and the Mediterranean Sea and across the Urals. Then Hilde unexpectedly asked him if the Führer hadn't lost touch with "his people" long ago.

The low curtains of grapevines stretched out far and wide around them, with not a person in sight, and so he shouted at her. How could she, how dare she lend her voice to such filthy suspicions—now of all times, when only the iron will of a united Germany could overcome their ideologically confused and disorganized enemies?

Endless times since then he had imagined this scene, seen the colors, smelled the scents, heard Hilde and himself, and his regret at spoiling their last day together grew stronger with the suspicion that maybe she had been right after all.

If Germany won, the defeated Allies would rebuild its shattered cities and would cede their poorly managed and sparsely populated eastern territories as reparations—but was there any hope for the basic human values that years of mutual slaughter had ruined? And could anyone anywhere even begin to take the place of his Hilde and Heidi?

Tonight, high above a city that would soon be celebrating its freedom from the Occupation, a devastating analogy occurred to him for the first time: could the German Führer derive the same perverted satisfaction from the worldwide butchery he'd unleashed as the unknown murderer did from his bloody slaughter of women?

He was freezing. Chills crept across his body; he must have goosebumps! Then he realized why.

The reckless comparison he had just drawn instantly made him the worst sort of criminal, the kind most of his colleagues at Bredovská Street would send to the basement and then (after a short trial) to the camps or the old military shooting range in the northern suburbs. He imagined how Meckerle would react if he said it aloud. If it happened face-to-face, Meckerle would relieve him of duty and lock him in the asylum; if it happened during a staff meeting, he would probably kill Buback on the spot.

But it was not fear that made Buback shiver; fear was one thing he had never been prone to, and he knew he was too experienced—or too cunning?—to be hoisted by his own petard. However, he was alarmed at what was happening to him. What was anything worth if out of the blue, after years of faith, he gave in to suspicions that went far beyond Hilde's small question on that final afternoon? Was he a common traitor? A coward, afraid of defeat? A victim of enemy propaganda? Or . . . or had he simply been slow to discover a historic blunder that he helped perpetrate, and now stood horrified at the chilling fate awaiting him and his country?

This last explanation was the most morally justifiable one—but then what difference was there between him and countless other Germans, who, he had heard, paid for far milder speculations in penal gangs, colonies, camps, and at the gallows?

A strange rhythmic sound drowned out the distant gunfire and distracted him from his thoughts. Just ahead, the path ended at a locked gate in a massive wall. The local Gestapo man had mentioned earlier a Brno castle that had been a notorious political prison in Austro-Hungarian days. The good life, compared to today's prisons, his local colleague had said, grinning; Vienna treated them with kid gloves and look what happened!

Now Buback could make out the rustling of last year's leaves, the sound of panting, and two Czech voices whispering.

"Love me! Yes! Love me! Yes yes yes!"

Incredible! A chill night, a steep slope, the gloomy cells a stone's throw away, mass slaughter within earshot, and with all this, two fragile human beings fall in love. And that means hope: an eternal new beginning that repairs the worst brutalities of history.

Suddenly he wanted to live to see it. And the face he pictured belonged to the Czech girl with the brown eyes.

H e found a dozen small jars of lard in the pantry—apparently she'd made individual monthly portions—and a pot of lentil soup with a surprisingly large chunk of sausage, which he heated up on the cylinder stove; all he had to do was shove some wood in. He even discovered a bottle of elderberry wine and tucked into a feast prepared for another man. There was a store of logs by the stove; soon it was almost hot in the apartment kitchen. He packed his booty in wax paper next to the rolled-up straps in the suitcase and placed it out in the chilly entrance hall.

The pale body on the dining table grew warm. He touched the skin on the shoulder. It was rough and dry. He realized with a shock: dead people don't sweat! His own shirt was quite damp after the meal, and the wine had flushed his cheeks. But he did not go into the bedroom, although it might have been more pleasant. This was his first opportunity to get a good, uninterrupted look at what he'd done.

MY DEED!

He was pleased he had finally worked out his opening lines. He'd behaved like an idiot and taken a terrible risk by almost frightening the first two to death. The one in Brno had become an animal fighting for her life; he barely overpowered her. In the second case she had fortunately RECOGNIZED HIM and given herself up; anyone with an ounce of self-preservation would have put up a fight. He had finally hit on it after puzzling the matter over and over at home, and he had decided to start next time by gaining their TRUST.

Today's events had proved him right. He had stunned her so perfectly that he was able to make all the NECESSARY PREPARATIONS without hurrying. She had come to on the table, naked, bound, and trussed, in time to see what was happening to her. He retained the same procedures and was satisfied at how effortless it was compared to the woman on the embankment. This time, all he heard was some weak moaning. The body's jerking did not prevent him from making all the cuts just as he was supposed to. She held out surprisingly long; almost, it seemed, until he cut IT out.

He took his gloves off again and touched first her, then himself, to see if a dead body felt different from a live one. It did not seem to. Her hair was thus all the more surprising. He had held her by it—it was long—when she fell into the wardrobe; the strands had flowed through his palms as he tied her to the tabletop, and were still hairs. As he examined them now, they did not separate; they reminded him of the hemp fiber he had used to clean his freshly oiled implements. So this was a new discovery:

THE HAIR DIES FIRST.

He studied her fingers close up to confirm what he knew from the Hungarian campaign:

NAILS AND MUSTACHES LIVE THE LONGEST.

He remembered helping to bury a lad who had barely grown his first whiskers before they closed the tulle-covered lid on his coffin. Now he raised the severed head and nodded, satisfied: a small mustache was clearly growing on the black-haired woman's upper lip.

Enough for today; it was time to head back. He pulled the gloves back on, changed his clothes, checked carefully that he had left no telltale traces, put on his hunting coat, and on sudden impulse stuffed the brightly glowing stove with wood until it would not close. Let the ROTTENNESS here truly ROT for when her paramour arrives!

He listened at the door. The staircase was silent. The short street was empty as well when he peered cautiously out. He walked down it without meeting a soul. Still he was burdened by the nagging thought that he had forgotten something. At the main train station, he remembered: the caretaker! He had wanted to finish him off before leaving today. But it was still light and night trains were infrequent these days. Anyway, the man couldn't recognize him unless they were brought face-to-face. The main thing, then, was the alibi; he could not afford even a shadow of suspicion to fall on him.

The station loudspeaker in the waiting room boomed a warning over and over about how to behave during the low-flying "tinker" machine-gun attacks from Allied pilots, which strafed locomotives on the tracks of the Protectorate. He knew the announcement by heart; although he firmly believed that SHE would protect him, he always sat in the last car anyway.

In the darkened compartment he read newspaper articles about sunken registered tons of British goods, American planes shot down, and destroyed Soviet tanks, but he barely noticed the figures. He was imagining what they would write in two days' time about HIM.

The sometime room painter Josef Jurajda, now a night watchman, was dragged from under his quilt early the next morning by Váca; he had had a night off. Yes, sir, his wife had gone to Olomouc, he muttered, to bring their daughter and grandchildren back; it looked like there would be fighting in the city, and they had a one-story house there with a shallow cellar. No, sir, he hadn't gone; got to catch up on sleep when you can, never enough of it with this job. Yes, sir, February fourteenth was just an ordinary day for him: he got home at six in the morning, slept through till evening, and at eight was back at work. No, sir, he couldn't swear to it; the years went round like a spinning wheel, one night was pretty much like the rest and he knew even less about the days, but his wife remembered they'd bombed Prague that afternoon, and he'd heard about it from her in the evening. Yes, sir, he remembered her saying it as she woke him up to go to work; he was always the last to know, once the train had left the station, so to speak. No, sir, who would he have run into at work? He gets there long after everyone's gone, and the cleaning girls don't come till morning.

Morava ran out of questions and glanced at Buback. The German shook his head. He too seemed surprised that ten years ago this chubby guy—with the eyes of a rabbit and the cheeks of a hamster—had been jabbing tied-up prostitutes with pins and masturbating at them.

In any event, he made a note that this half-educated retired sadist spoke a quite literary Czech. Like most Moravians, he thought proudly—and immediately remembered what the caretaker from Vltava Embankment had said about the man who carved up the Pomeranian baroness. Of course! A fellow Moravian. That didn't excuse him, but it did narrow the field of possible perpetrators from seven million to three. . . .

He realized that Buback would be missing the telltale linguistic signs, but kept it to himself until he could consult with Beran. He snapped face-on and profile shots of the watchman for the Prague caretaker and recommended to Váca that he let the man go back to bed for the meanwhile. Then they set off southward.

He got in next to the German and asked if he had a particular route in mind. No, he learned, and risked a suggestion: would Herr Oberkriminalrat like to stop for lunch along the way? When Buback nodded, Morava even felt brave enough to propose a location: there was a decent pub on the main road; they would reach it around noon and—if this was acceptable—Morava could meanwhile stop briefly to visit his mother.

For the first time the German showed something like human interest. Morava briefly explained to him that he came, as his surname suggested, from Moravia—more precisely from what was once the Moravian-Austrian border region where they were headed. That was why he'd spoken passable German since childhood. His father, he continued, died a long time ago, and his mother lived alone next to the old family smithy, now rented out, since he, her only son, had fled to Prague to study law and his sister had married a vicar. Later, the Germans closed the Czech colleges and universities, halting Morava's studies, and he'd landed, degreeless, in the police force.

Was an hour enough, Buback asked in telegraphic style, and the assistant detective made a mental note of the debt, one to pay back even if the creditor was a Nazi.

They fell silent (their driver, Litera, Beran's favorite, was more taciturn today than usual) as the car wound along narrow country roads not built for the double load of spring farming and war traffic. When possible they passed the trucks carrying fertilizer and the army kitchen, and were themselves passed by official cars and couriers on powerful motorcycles.

Some soldiers with the insignia of the feared German field troopers (which reminded Morava of a tin spitoon) surfaced unexpectedly just past Rakvice. The policemen's Protectorate identification papers got a good laugh out of them, but as the troopers were turning the car back, Morava's companion showed his usefulness.

My God, Morava realized as he watched the three bandits change instantly into sheep, Buback really is a much bigger cheese than Beran.

The war had by this point squeezed spring off the carriageway; every once in a while deep ruts in the fields leading to the nearby woods hinted at huge quantities of hidden military machinery.

They found the pub on the village square closed. A toothless old man who did not recognize Morava whistled that the landlord had left with his family for Brno. Before the assistant detective's spirits could sink, the German remarked dryly that he was not hungry anyway and would rather have a half-hour walk in the fresh air. Morava was decidedly grateful. They let Buback out, and Litera veered as directed down the muddy lanes toward the smithy. The tenant smith was finishing one horseshoe while Morava's mother tended to the horse.

"Jan! My baby!" she shouted joyfully, and carefully put the hoof down onto the hard-packed soil. "It can't be! It can't! Oh!"

While the driver swallowed slabs of bread and bacon in the kitchen, washing it down with huge gulps of rose-hip tea, Morava's mother repeated those words over and over again in the neatly kept sitting room. Her son, meanwhile, hastily told her that he had fallen in love with the sweetest girl under the sun and wanted to make her his wife, and that he intended to bring his mother back to Prague as soon as possible, so that he and Jitka could give her grandchildren while they were still working.

T he farther they traveled, the more the land resembled a giant army encampment, and Erwin Buback became more and more ashamed of his nighttime funk.

The faces of officers and soldiers on the truck beds and the seats of the official jeeps were not shining with enthusiasm, but that is how members of any army look when they have been practicing the dreary art of war for years on end. On the other hand, there was no faint-heartedness in their faces or even fatigue; they looked rested, radiating a calm resolve and certainty that they would succeed and survive.

He had noticed this phenomenon before. Despite the retreats on all European theaters, a single successful strike was enough to change the soldiers' mood overnight. A step forward, Buback knew, was a cure, even if only for a couple of days; it gave the German soldiers a reserve of moral and physical strength for another month on the defensive.

This broken terrain, its southern slopes covered with vineyards, would be suitable for a new main line of defense. However, treadmarks in the wet soil indicated that a large number of tanks had recently passed by. That suggested this might be the very place where the long-awaited counteroffensive would begin.

Colonel Meckerle, who had excellent connections in the Führer's main council, had recently made it known that the retreat was part of the most magnificent trap in military history. This was no fairy tale, no rumor, gentlemen! Not just one but two Bolshevik army divisions—one and a half million troops—would be flung into a gigantic cauldron and boiled into borscht. Meckerle had the Gestapo officers' cafeteria serve the dish, and its dark red color had a very vivid and encouraging effect.

During his short walk around the village green, a massive artillery column rolled by that they had not seen on the way there; it had evidently joined the main road from a side track. The heavy cabs with their long trailers were a dead giveaway: they had to be transporting howitzers beneath their camouflaged canvasses. And it was the howitzer's percussive fire that launched every major offensive. Buback reproached himself again for his weakness the day before.

Maybe it wasn't wrong for him and Hilde to be so suspicious of Germany's highest leader, however awful it sounded. What difference did it make, in the end? This bloody war would decide the fate of the German people for generations to come—and perhaps even their right to exist. Even if Buback had been right to think that Hitler had failed his country, shouldn't Germans keep trying to avert a total defeat and at least achieve an honorable peace?

Only a year ago he and everyone else had condemned the assassination attempt on the Führer as a monstrous act, carried out by traitors in the pay of the enemy. But maybe the conspirators were simply patriots who had given in to their doubts, just as he and Hilde had. If so, they were not alone. And if Buback was right, there would be more brave men to come who would risk the punishment Meckerle had supposedly described to his closest advisers: being hanged from a butcher hook on a thin string, to die a slow, shameful death.

Buback did not believe there were any altruists of that sort in the Gestapo. There weren't even any real detectives among his own men. They all came straight from SS schools with a political mission, loosely interpreted as knocking out the teeth of true or imagined Resistance workers. After all, they had stopped investigating their fellow Germans' minor offenses a long time ago. But one scenario was probable enough to be vexing. There were many who would be interested in Buback's inner thoughts, because that was their job: to neutralize anyone harboring harmful opinions.

There was only one solution: to support anyone who could promise Germany would not be trampled underfoot, and then wait until they could finally carry out what they'd failed at the year before. And that meant supporting the very army he was now watching and admiring, as it trudged unbroken toward its decisive battle.

His new resolve had an impact on his behavior toward the two Czechs. He knew that for them, Hitler probably embodied all Germans. Suddenly he no longer wanted to contribute to this false impression. And so, to his own surprise, he accepted the gift they brought him: bread with bacon in a fresh white napkin. He continued to keep his distance, so as not to arouse suspicion. However, he felt sure that Beran's assistant was indebted to him, and so, like it or not, would come out of his shell. The kid even explained that he had wanted to let his mother know he had gotten engaged.

Buback kept up the flow of conversation without asking suspicious questions. A competent young man in a demanding job, like Morava, had to be aware that a police liaison officer to the Gestapo might be interested in other things besides a brutal murderer. And that in itself said a lot about the Czech mentality, which had changed drastically during the Occupation.

Then, later on, Morava began to repeat a certain woman's name. Belatedly Buback realized it belonged to the very girl he had been thinking about—these days, more often than about Hilde. . . .

The conversation with his mother comforted Morava. For years he had felt guilty for ruining her dream of keeping the smithy in the family. He visited her regularly, but the weight never lifted.

Until today, that is, when a miracle occurred. As he raced to tell her about Jitka, the tears in her eyes frightened him at first. Would she be jealous now, as well? But suddenly she hugged him and said he had made her unbelievably happy.

He suggested to her that she move to Prague, at least for a while. She could stay in his room, since he would be living at Jitka's anyway. That way, she'd get to know Jitka and they wouldn't have to fear for her safety here, where the war loomed larger every day. Then, with his head turned, his conscience clear for the first time in a long while, he watched the place where his life began to shrink away, until all that remained was a bright spot soon swallowed by the horizon of grapevines.

To add to Morava's unusually good mood, the German's priggishness was noticeably on the wane. Of course, Morava turned even the most innocent of questions inside out before answering, swiftly figuring how Beran would read it. But Buback seemed more interested in the area they were passing through, so Morava told stories about his childhood, confident that he was on safe ground. In some places here the road formed an unguarded border between the Protectorate and the Sudeten territories of the former Czechoslovak Republic, which the Munich agreement had effectively given to the Reich, a goodwill gesture that foreshadowed the annexation. How would things look after the war, he suddenly wondered, would he meet his classmates—if they hadn't fallen in battle, that is—who had saluted Hitler and roared "Heim ins Reich"? Could they still live here, side by side?

To Buback, however, Morava simply described how ten years ago they had thought nothing of switching back and forth between Czech and German; no one would ever have claimed that one was better than the other. Emboldened by a further innocent question, he recalled how they had sung in both languages during wine tastings in the cellars and invited anyone they wanted to the zabijačka, regardless of nationality. What was a zabijačka? the German queried, and Beran's instructions flashed through Morava's head.

He described carefully and yet vividly the Moravian custom of the pig slaughter, in which the most basic human need for nourishment merges with a time-honored ritual of civilization and culture. By offering another person food from your own plate, you prevent the elemental greed at the root of all wars. Without using exactly those words, he emphasized that even in times like these, when food became a rare commodity traded on the black market, in south Moravia the old laws still held. If you had given your neighbor a share of the pig slaughter in times past, then you did it now as well. Which these days could be dangerous for someone who gives generously, he said. Suddenly Morava found himself describing—somewhat more boldly than Beran had advised—the story of Jitka's father, who had slaughtered a pig, not to sell it on the black market, but to divide it among his relatives and friends.

He instantly regretted his move when his neighbor stiffened again, but before he could reproach himself for his simplemindedness, he heard the relatively affable reply that the Reich's offices respect the law but know it needs to be interpreted at times. He, Buback, personally did not believe that the father of this . . . what was her name again? Jitka Modrá . . . yes, of this Miss Modrá—surely she was unmarried, at her age?—would be punished for black marketeering if the facts were as Detective Morava reported them. When they got back to Prague, Morava should tell the young lady that she could call on Buback for help in this matter; the German would certainly look into the case—all he needed was the personnel file.

Ahead, the tower of the castle was rising out of the vineyards; the suspect Jakub Malatínský was supposed to be waiting for them. His absence, however, was not to be the last surprise that day.

The conversation about Jitka Modrá excited Buback. She was undoubtedly a delicate chip off the old paternal block; the girl's father had probably been acting in the spirit of the old traditions, and if so, then he could help her.

Buback's new task assumed a scenario which, if expressed aloud a short while ago, would have been grounds for a charge of high treason: that the proud Reich which had covered most of the continent would shrink back to its core. It was no longer possible to evacuate or liquidate the millions of Czechs living here who had never submitted to their loss of independence; at best Germany might persuade them not to revolt through deft use of the carrot and the stick.

Buback was sure that in the given instance, Meckerle would not object. He could extend a helping hand to Beran and his men that cost nothing and might prove fruitful. The Prague Gestapo supervisor had seen the need for a change of priorities last fall, and now reined in his subordinates as zealously as he had earlier applied the spurs. The girl's father was just a pawn in the game, and Buback, while respecting its rules, could spare the reincarnation of his Hilde any further fear and misfortune.

Then his musings were cut short. As it turned out, the suspect Jakub Malatínský, despite the order from Brno, was not there, and no one had any idea where he might be. Before Buback was forced to dress down the officers, Morava translated for him that the summons could not have reached him; Malatínský had taken two days' leave earlier.

"So what are you waiting for?" Buback snarled at the local policeman, who turned white as a sheet. "Send for him, have him tracked down, whatever, but don't just stand there like God's gift to mankind. I want to be in Prague tonight."

Morava cautiously intervened.

"Could it wait half an hour?"

"Why?" he barked in irritation.

"He should come of his own accord. His shift starts at two."

Is he trying to show me up in public? Buback wondered, but when he looked into those eyes again, even his professionally suspicious glare could find no hint of intrigue. He assented, but as punishment haughtily declined their offer to visit the renowned castle wine cellar. While his guide diligently filled lined pages with facts about the suspect, he continued his pretense of not understanding Czech and stubbornly fixed his sight on a flock of circling crows outside who were choosing a suitable tree to land in.

Malatínský was hauled in by a sweat-drenched police officer at two minutes after two. A giant in linen clothes and felt boots, the suspect barely fit under the door frame. Buback inadvertently thought of Meckerle but immediately dismissed the comparison. Malatínský was a sheaf of sinew and muscle, not a sack of meat. He had a nice, well-proportioned, and sturdy face beneath a black mane without a single gray hair. As he walked he thrust his knees and hips forward, almost like a ballerina, but one with a wild animal's strength.

Buback caught the deferential glance of the assistant detective and signaled him to start. The Czech asked the cellar workers to leave and ordered the suspect to sit down. This too Malatínský did in a surprisingly refined manner, crossing his legs at the knee and clasping his hands in his lap. A native of this mixed border region, he offered to speak German with them. His accent was strong, but his vocabulary was adequate to the task.

After the usual preliminaries, where Morava verified his identity and instructed him, the giant got the same question they had put to Jurajda that morning in Brno. Where had he been on February fourteenth and who could confirm it?

"I don't like to write down where I go." The questioned man grinned.

"Then you'll just have to remember."

"Why is it so important?"

The kid went right to the point, and Buback knew he would have done the same in Morava's place.

"In 1929 you were convicted of a brutal murder. After your release, you were investigated in the fall of 1938 in connection with another one; the investigation was never completed. We are looking for the person who murdered a woman in Prague on February fourteenth of this year in a very similar fashion."

Yes, Buback approved; keep going, if he's the murderer, he knows exactly why we're here and will give himself away. Instead, the vintner laughed as if he had just heard a good joke.

"And why look for him here?"

"The best way to start an investigation is to look in places you know," Buback's famulus said just as casually. "Sometimes it's the best way to finish one as well. Was it you?"

"No," the vintner responded, still with a hint of amusement in his voice. "I'm done with crazy stunts like that. If I'd given her a few good slaps and tossed her rags out on the street behind her, I could have saved myself ten years of life and not missed out on a hundred better women. Except I was twenty, and a complete fool."

"There was nothing crazy about the way you did it," the kid continued in a conversational tone. "The jury called it a repulsive display of extreme sadism. The prosecutor asked for life."

"But the court gave me fifteen years; fortunately they got the point. It was my first woman, you see; I was terribly jealous. I got over it in prison once and for all."

"Where were you on February fourteenth?"

"What day was it?"

"Wednesday."

"At work, I guess."

"No you weren't," Morava shot back. "We already know you took two days' vacation. Why?"

"I was probably exhausted. We'd spent a week cleaning the big barrels."

"So you often take vacations."

"I take them when I want to and when I can. Don't you?"

"And how do you spend them? Today, for instance. You can't have forgotten that already?"

Malatínský laughed until his pearly white teeth flashed.

"No, that I remember."

Not a single filling, Buback noticed enviously. It made the vintner even more irritating. If one of Meckerle's boxers got his hands on you . . . , he thought, and was immediately ashamed: I'm becoming just like them!

"Mr. Malatínský," his companion continued in a suddenly solemn tone, "I should warn you: the victim was a citizen of the Third Reich. This is why Chief Inspector Buback from the Prague Gestapo is overseeing this investigation. If you don't give me proof of your innocence, the Germans will be the next to ask. It's your choice."

He's reading my mind, Buback thought with amazement, and shot Malatínský an icy glare he had perfected. The man opposite them stopped laughing.

"It really wasn't me. I have the same alibi for February as for yesterday. But it'll cost me my job. . . ."

A widening crack appeared in the suspect's self-confidence. The interrogator turned to the local keeper of the peace.

"Could you wait outside for a minute?"

The policeman, who had been following the interrogation with evident interest, misunderstood what Morava meant. Grabbing Malatínský by the elbow, he began to lead him out. When he heard the request a second time, he blushed like a scolded schoolboy and made a quick exit. Only then did the youngster continue, now in an almost affable manner.

"We don't want to make trouble for innocent people. If your alibi holds up, we'll keep it to ourselves."

"I was in Brno."

"What were you doing there?"

"Fucking," the man said in his native language. "I don't know how to say it in German."

Buback enjoyed watching the Czech's discomfort as he translated. The German had been the first in his class to know that word.

"You understand,"—Morava turned to Malatínský again—"that we'll have to confirm it."

"Yes. That's the problem."

"Is the lady married?"

"Which one?"

"What do you mean, which one?"

"Do you mean the one in February or the one now?"

"We're talking about February now!"

"Yes, okay . . . but could you ask her when the other one isn't around?"

"Why should she be . . . ?"

"They're mother and daughter."

The assistant detective suddenly looked like an openmouthed teenager, and Buback had the impression that their suspect was looking for some masculine understanding. It was time to jump in.

"Which one was it in February?"

"The mother."

"And where can we find her?"

"Well, here."

"You mentioned Brno."

"We were at a hotel in the city. I was just there with the daughter too."

"And who is the mother?"

"My boss's wife. He's the administrator. They live here at the castle. But you won't tell her about her daughter?"

"No," Buback said.

"And could you interview her . . . inconspicuously, somehow?"

"Yes," Buback said.

What is it with me? he wondered. First I wish he would get beaten to a pulp and now I'm ready to throw up a triple smoke screen for him? Am I really going to cover for him to his boss and two mistresses?

Except . . . what was the point in turning him in? His detective's sixth sense told Buback that although this man had committed an atrocity, it was not a sign of any inborn deviance, but an eruption of anger at his humiliated masculinity. He felt sure the alibi would hold up. The man radiated charisma; he would not need to substitute torture and murder for pleasure—not with women young and old beating a path to his door. No, today's trip would serve only one purpose: Buback could try to get closer to his guide, and in doing so, fulfill his true mission.

But given his midday musings, what was his true mission any-way . . . ?

M orava was more and more surprised. Throughout their unequal cooperation (with Morava doing all the work while the other merely watched over his shoulder), he had found the German to be a patronizing prig, possibly not as arrogant as others from the Gestapo, but certainly not a colleague one could trust. However, in the last couple of hours Buback had changed beyond belief.

Letting Morava visit his mother, offering to intervene on behalf of Jitka's father, and finally jumping in so unconventionally during the vintner's interrogation could all be classic tricks—if Beran was right—but it was certainly easier to breathe in this new atmosphere. A thaw in relations would bring advantages to both sides; you just had to prick up your ears and watch your mouth a bit more closely.

They turned Malatínský over to the policeman and casually asked the administrator's wife for some rye coffee while her husband was down in the cellars. When she brought it to them, Morava abruptly translated Buback's question for her: where had she been on February fourteenth and whom had she been with? The handsome woman's jaw fell open and her lips trembled; suddenly she sagged into a heap of misery. Before she could burst into tears or faint, Buback had Morava tell her that everything she said would remain confidential; her husband would not find out.

She collected herself with surprising speed, grabbed their promise like a life preserver, and made such an ardent confession that Morava felt hot under the collar. Yes, they had been together those two days and nights in February as usual, but this month they hadn't gone, because he thought they shouldn't always leave at the same time, so instead he went to visit his mother; yes, they always registered legally in the hotel, with his friend the reception clerk putting them in separate rooms, but she'd been with him in one of them and swore he hadn't gone farther than the toilet the whole time; yes, she would even put it in writing, but for God's sake, she was relying on their word that none of the local men would see it, because otherwise it'd be her husband doing the murdering.

With Buback's permission, Morava wrote out a rather short declaration; her hands shook, but she managed to sign it. The two of them finished their drink and returned to the office. Malatínský was chatting affably with the officer. He was still laughing as they walked in, but stood up respectfully. And it was Buback who with an almost genial nod indicated to him that his account had been confirmed. In return, Malatínský docilely let Morava photograph him head-on and in both profiles to show to the Prague caretaker (can't be too careful!). With that they were finished and could go home.

Just before they left, Morava had a memorable experience. As he relieved himself at the employees' ramshackle urinal while Buback went to take in some fresh air, the door banged open and the local policeman appeared at his side.

"Sir, what should we do?" the policeman asked.

"Nothing. Unless we send for him, you can leave him alone," Morava replied.

"That's not what I mean. What should we do in general? If things heat up? Say, if the Germans try to mobilize us. Who do we answer to?"

"How long have you been in the police?"

"Um . . . since 1920."

Morava searched the man's eyes. This was not the panicky fear of a collaborator, but the understandable anguish of a man who for twenty-five years had served the law under various changing powers. The young Czech thanked fate that his work, dismal as it could be, was basically independent of the political weather.

"Or if the Russians come, the way things are looking," the man continued nervously. "Who should we listen to?"

Morava was too much Beran's pupil to trust his feelings completely. A cop who had survived every regime could be a perfectly corrupt bastard and a provocateur, maybe even in the Germans' pay and under Buback's thumb. He decided to play the wise man.

"Did you serve in the army?"

"Yes, the Czechoslovak one."

"So you took an oath?"

"Yes. But under the Germans I also. . . ."

"Willingly?"

"No . . ."

"So what's your question?"

They both buttoned their flies.

"Thank you," the uniformed man said. "We'll keep our fingers crossed until it blows over."

Before he climbed into the car, Morava spotted the administrator's wife on the second floor of the castle. Her corpulent husband in his vest, plus fours, and rubber galoshes did not seem like a passionate soul prone to murderous rages. Despite this, the woman in the window above him briefly clasped her hands and put a finger to her lips. A woman beloved by her husband loved her lover, who made love to her beloved and apparently loving daughter. Jan Morava could not understand their behavior; he felt a deep repugnance toward them.

Why not give this shady vintner a draft of the truth? he wondered. Idiot, he rebuked himself instantly; you work in a cemetery, where every day new graves fill with victims of the chain of abandoned passion and instinctual reaction. Maybe the only reason those feelings don't affect you is that heaven sent you an angel in the form of Jitka. So don't play the righteous man, to yourself or to her!

T he face of the land they had crossed not long ago had changed beyond recognition. In the twilight, only teams with ploughs, harrows, and seed drills passed by; the earth appeared to have simply swallowed up the gigantic army, if it had not in fact been a mere hallucination. Buback, who was used to the appearances and disappearances of military forces, could easily spot the traces of their presence everywhere and was impressed by their unbroken discipline.

From the snatches of conversation he had overheard in the office and Prague's German House bar, he pieced the picture together with what he dimly remembered from school geography lessons. This hilly landscape stretching north across the Moravian-Slovak borderland to Silesia and linking up with the Czech-Moravian highlands farther west took the shape of a mighty natural bulwark. The battle that would decide the fate of the war and the future shape of the world would definitely be fought here.

How must the boy feel, with his mother here, he thought, and immediately asked him. He learned that his companion had convinced her to move to Prague until the wedding. In return, he got an equally intimate question: did the chief inspector also have a family?

"No!" he nearly snapped, and bristled again, but right away he realized that there was no reason to; after all, it was he who had started the personal questions, and he did not want to behave like a member of a master race. So he added, "My wife and daughter were killed last year in an air raid."

Darkness had long since enveloped the car, but when he heard nothing and turned his head to his companion, he saw sympathy in the boy's eyes. The reaction surprised and nonplussed him, and they sat staring at each other this way for a few long seconds before the Czech spoke again.

"I'm truly sorry, Mr. Buback."

He did not remember when anyone last confused him as much as this young man, and the only thing he could think to say was "Thank you."

In Brno they stopped at the vintner's hotel, and the horrified clerk, stammering, corroborated the facts. The onetime sadistic murderer, now tender paramour to two generations of women, was in the clear, and they were back where they had started.

The two of them spent the remainder of the trip in the back seat, half asleep, half awake. Litera could only drive as fast as the narrow beams of the car's blue-painted headlamps permitted. Buback was silent. From time to time he fell into phantasmagoric, contentless dreams, only to wake staring over the unmoving shoulders of the driver into an inky darkness, unbroken by the blacked-out towns that seemed more like stage sets.

Long past midnight he heard the driver's voice informing the rear of the car that they were in Prague; where should he drop them off? Buback nearly answered in Czech and froze: to his surprise, he was less frightened of losing his secret advantage than he was of looking foolish in front of his traveling companion. The Czech deferred to him, and in his fatigue Buback made a further slip when, quite irregularly, he gave his home address. He tried to make up for it by getting out at the very foot of the road. With a brisk good-bye, he headed up the steep slope on foot.

The Czechs now called this neighborhood Little Berlin. What had mostly been Jewish homes were now apartments for functionaries sent here from the Reich. Buback had arrived late, and the only place left for him was an attic studio in a turn-of-the-century house occupied by the chairman of the Prague Volksgericht—"People's Court"—and his large family. They had been overjoyed when he asked for the key to the servants' staircase in the back; it meant he barely ever saw them. Several times, however, the judge had given him a lift to work in his official car, which passed the Gestapo building on its way to the Pankrác prison.

During these rides the corpulent judge, sweating despite the winter cold, would haltingly ask Buback's opinion on the state of the war. As a matter of principle, Buback hewed to the editorial line of the *Völkischer Beobachter* in his answers: the situation on the battlefield was not a reliable indicator, since the brilliant and therefore unpredictable hand of the Führer would make the decisive move, as it had many times before. The judge would enthusiastically echo him, and later, on the evening radio program, Buback would hear news of his neighbor's fresh successes at work, as reflected in the number of new executions.

Now, as he reached the top of the street, he noticed hushed sounds and movements in front of his darkened house. He halted;

for the first time the thought occurred to him that these days, with the advancing front so close, he should be carrying a pistol. The voices were German, however, so he decided to approach them. A large, bulky shadow resolved into a moving van; four strapping fellows were hoisting a long piano into it. Before Christmas Eve dinner last year, his neighbor's wife had played carols on it and boasted that it was a famed Steinway, left behind by the original owners. Even the men's blacked-out flashlights showed Buback that the capacious interior of the van was almost full.

Another hulk loomed out of the darkness and barked at him, "What are you doing here?"

"What are *you* doing here?" he coldly retorted. "This is where I live."

The man, doubtless an officer in civilian clothes, took him for an ordinary Aryan he could push around a bit.

"Your documents!"

"It's all right, officer," a muffled voice called breathlessly; the judge was rushing over to them. "That's Herr Buback, the chief criminal detective; he's our neighbor. Good evening, Herr Buback."

"Evening . . . ," Buback said, and continued to observe the scene until the import of it hit him.

"My mother-in-law"—the words tumbled out of the judge—"has taken seriously ill, and my father-in-law is alone in the Black Forest, so my wife is going to look after her parents. . . ."

Buback could understand why this man, who had ample reason to fear for his own skin, would send his family to safety while there was still time. However, the sight of the Reich's local judiciary chief looting the house with the aid of his wardens took Buback's breath away. For the second time that night he was at a loss for words, and silently watched the grand piano vanish into the van.

"The children are just learning to play," the judge hastened to explain, desperate for an excuse. "We don't want them to be out of practice by the time they come back here. . . ."

You rat, you dirty rat, Buback thought angrily; bloodthirsty rats like you provoked all of Europe until it united against us and now you're the first to leave the ship with your plunder. He lunged toward the back entrance so suddenly that the cowed overseer barely managed to step out of his way. The judge who had sent hundreds to the firing squad and under the knife called after him almost beseechingly.

"Herr Buback! I have permission from the office of the Reich's protector, and of course I personally will remain at my post—"

Buback put all his venom into slamming the door; the blow shook the house, but he knew that no one was asleep there anyway. The judge's spouse and children were doubtless safe in a government car, racing westward through the darkness.

The army advanced toward its historic engagement while this cowardly capitulator snuck away. The thought upset him so greatly that he could not even think about sleep. He ferreted out an unfinished bottle of brandy from the cramped kitchenette and poured it straight down his throat. The pressure in his skull immediately lessened; agitation gave way to a woolly exhaustion. Then he noticed an envelope lying on the parquet flooring near the door.

He ripped it open and read Kroloff's news.

Morava was shocked to find Jitka up so late.
"What's wrong?"

"With me? Nothing. Just waiting for you."

"But I had no idea when we'd be back. We could have been stuck there for days."

"Didn't you get Beran's message?"

"No, was there one?"

"I telexed it to the police station there after lunch."

"Aha," he realized. "The local cop was with us the whole time. And what did it say?"

"He did it again. The butcher."

"No! When?"

"Yesterday. Actually the day before, but they only found her yesterday."

"Who? Where?"

She summarized the latest gruesome tale for him as if they were still at the office. The fire in the ground-floor apartment on Podskalská Street (building 131 in the district register) went unnoticed until relatively late, because the remodeled kitchen had no window. Although the blaze remained localized, the affected apartment was almost completely burned out. The partially charred body was apparently that of the tenant, Barbora Pospíchalová. But yesterday at noon, at the court medical department, a finding turned the investigation on its head: before the fire broke out, the woman—identified by her jewelry and teeth—had been brutally murdered and mutilated in exactly the same manner as the German baroness. The firemen had unfortunately destroyed all the evidence with a stream of water, and then, when they carted the smoking remains off to the dump with the rest of the wreckage, the sliced-off breasts disappeared as well. The missing heart confirmed the link between this brutal murder and the preceding one; the killer had evidently taken the organ with him.

Interviews with the building's inhabitants revealed nothing of any use. The victim's only regular visitor was her brother-in-law, who at the first incomplete account fainted and had to be hospitalized. She had never been seen with any other men. The single, barely credible lead was the testimony of a small girl, who had been watching for her mother from the mezzanine before the fire and insisted that a water sprite had left the building with a big suitcase. From this they deduced that a green coat was involved.

"Want some tea?" Jitka asked when she had finished.

"With plum brandy," he said automatically, trying to digest the realization that the trail he had been following for almost a month had been a dead end from the start. The man who had probably tortured the Brno seamstress before killing Elisabeth von Pommeren and Barbora Pospíchalová was not one of the original suspects. In all likelihood he had a clean criminal record. Because he had taken six and a half years to commit his second murder and less than a month for his third, it was reasonable to surmise he had finally settled on a form of murder that was to his taste.

Morava felt the sharp scent of wartime tea concentrate, softened with home-brewed brandy, rising into his nostrils as Jitka lightly but securely wound her arms around his neck.

"You'll catch him, I'm sure of it!" she said, and he was sure he would not disappoint her.

"My mother," he answered, "is well and is looking forward to meeting you. She sent you her favorite kerchief. And Buback promised he would help your father."

"So what else do we need, Jan?" she asked him. "Just the baby, then, I guess. Are you too tired?"

"Jitka . . . ," he whispered and looked into her eyes, hoping that all those awful images would dissolve in her warm brownness. "My love, where have you been all these years? I waited for you my whole life past, and our whole next life you'll never be rid of me."

C uriosity was stronger than caution. Just to be sure, he pretended to be fixing the lock on the canteen door until the director and his secretary had sat down to lunch (some sort of gray porridge with red beets, ugh!). Then, for the sake of prying eyes, he casually sauntered up to their office with his equipment in hand. He knocked and waited before entering. In the back room he put down his hammer and pliers on the desk and swiftly yet carefully paged through the daily press. NOTHING!

As he stared unbelieving at the back page of the last paper, he noticed that the police blotter reported a fire in Podskalská Street. The sign on the corner the day before yesterday had engraved itself on his memory, because first he had read the German name, *Podskalaergasse*, which made no sense to him. He had to read the article out loud before he realized what it meant. Fortunately, he managed to fold the newspapers up, remember his equipment, and leave before he lost control completely.

Locking himself in the toilet, he sat down fully dressed on the bowl, his hands and legs shaking uncontrollably. Who was foiling his plans! How could sheer coincidence have ruined the next of his masterpieces! He had thought that this time they would have to take notice of him, to start piecing together his motive. Instead, once again there was NOTHING, NOTHING, NOTHING!!

In the meanwhile he had become convinced that his actions should have a regular rhythm, so they could COUNT ON THEM. Discounting the poor start in Brno that had paralyzed him for several years, he had been sure that things would go more or less like last time: he needed two weeks to EXPERIENCE IT, and two weeks to PREPARE FOR IT. Like the moon in the heavens, he realized; he would wane, then wax again.

Twelve a year; the number seemed appropriate and at the same time significant. It too had a SYMBOL in it. But to warn them properly, first he had to let them know he existed; everyone had to understand the rhythm and anticipate the coming PUNISHMENT. That was the only way it could possibly work, the only way the ones who deserved it would fear and repent, become better people, follow the example that would gradually cease to be exceptional, until the world was CLEANSED.

Without the fire, which only SATAN himself could have set, his intention would have been clear by the middle of next month; he would have set a fateful pendulum in motion, destroying another sinner's heart at each swing. And instead? "The flames spared the rest of the building," the item had read, "but raged so wildly in the apartment that the tenant could only be identified by her rings and teeth."

Someone entered the lavatory, pressed down on the doorhandle of his stall, and then began to jiggle it impatiently. Had they found him? How? In a panic he considered opening the ventilation window behind him and crawling out into the light shaft. At the thought of the drop he felt a terrible cramp in his testicles. Vertigo always sapped his strength; he was sure to fall and kill himself at the bottom of the shaft. No! He would turn the lock and open the door so sharply that he'd knock the guy behind it off balance for a few seconds; out in the hall and on the staircase he'd never catch up . . . unless there were more of them!

He broke into a sweat as he realized that he might be uncovered so quickly and simply. A thorough search and it'd all be over: they'd get the straps from his apartment, and here in the basement they'd find his SOULS! He'd never convince them that he was GOOD. They would sentence him just as easily as they condemned hundreds of ordinary people every day. And none of them had come anywhere as close to humbling

EVIL as he had. An image sprang to mind—they were dragging him, bound, to the bloody chopping block—and he felt sick.

The unknown man outside swore, promptly exited, and slammed the door behind him. Meanwhile, he barely managed to turn around and lean over the worn bowl before forcefully throwing up his breakfast. He felt better but remained on his knees, his palms splayed on the filthy tiling and his chin against the cold porcelain, eyes blinded by a gush of tears. Finally his nose felt a piercing sourness. He flushed, scooping the running water into his palms to rinse his mouth out. Checking that he had not soiled his shirt or sweater, he carefully wiped the stall clean with shredded newsprint, and when he flushed again he noticed that his hands had stopped shaking. He could go.

Out in the hallway, fresh air coursed over him. He could see his long-dead friend, one of the first army pilots, who had once saved himself by jumping from a biplane in a parachute. The first thing his friend had requested afterward was to get right into another cockpit again. "Otherwise I would have been afraid the rest of my life," he confided later.

He realized that he too must overcome his bad luck IMMEDIATELY!

M orava got barely two hours of sleep that night. He gave Jitka a detailed description of his visit with his mother and the trip with Buback. She hung anxiously on his every word, and he realized how worried she was about her father. The first flowering of love in the shadow of death, he thought. There was nothing else he could say, so he took her in his arms and stroked her hair and cheeks until the two of them began to fade with exhaustion and simultaneously fell asleep. He came to in her embrace when the alarm clock had just started to rattle, and she dozed on his shoulder as they rode in on the tram.

When Beran arrived, Morava gave him a brief summary of his trip with Buback and asked, heart in his mouth, what he should be working on.

"This case isn't enough for you?" Beran queried.

"You're leaving me on it?"

"Have you lost your courage?"

"I just don't want to cause you any difficulties. . . ."

"So don't, then."

His superior looked meaningfully into his eyes. Morava had to clear his throat again nervously.

"You're aware that it's not just our prestige at stake here," Beran continued. "I tried to explain that to you the other day."

"Yes. . . ."

"If your head is starting to spin again, we can go for another walk."

"Yes. . . ."

"Besides, I heard your cooperation with our colleague was going well."

"Yes, he doesn't seem to have any reservations about our work."

"If the Germans see the second murder the same way we do, they might drop the theory that this is the work of the Czech Resistance."

"But then there'd be no reason . . . ," Morava objected, but fell silent when the superintendent put his index finger to his lips.

"I assume," Beran said, "that out of simple collegiality they won't recall the chief detective just yet. The killer has shown that he doesn't play favorites; German women are still in danger, just as Czech ones are. Mr. Buback can still assist you with security measures for potential victims on both sides. What ideas do you have?"

Morava put forth the conclusion he had reached that morning on the tram. In none of the three cases to date—including Brno, if it belonged among them—was there any sign that the perpetrator had used violence to gain entrance to the apartment; on the contrary, all indications were that he had been admitted willingly, although both Prague women had been mistrustful loners. How did he do it? Where did he first speak to them? How did he win their trust?

"This leads me to question our rationale for placing the case under strict censorship. Panic and fear can't overshadow the positive effect of publicity: women would be warier of unfamiliar men who try to win their favor."

"There's still a risk that the killer might gain confidence from the publicity and increase his activity, like an egotistical artist," Beran countered. "You and Mr. Buback should weigh your options together; both sides need to agree on a single approach."

"It only makes sense to do so," Morava continued, spinning his thread further, "if we have the courage to describe his method in detail. This butchery has a ritual element to it that must have a source. Given how repulsive it is, it has to be some sort of dark art."

Beran frowned. "I'd be afraid of that. At a certain extreme these things exert a repulsive fascination. I've met any number of copycats in my day; I'd rather not inspire some other deviant to try and top the one we've got now. No, Morava, you'll think I'm old-fashioned, but I won't sign off on hocus-pocus like that. Don't be disappointed; a compromise can always be found."

"What sort, in the given case?" Morava asked skeptically.

"Send out a brief official announcement about a deviant murderer who preys on gullible women. And at the same time—I've got it now—send out detailed factual information to all our offices. They'll distribute the description confidentially to individuals whose work brings them into contact with large numbers of people; they might uncover some connection between one of them and what you're calling a ritual. I'm thinking of doctors, teachers, postmen too; you'll certainly come up with others. If you're right, there must be something that inspired him. Assuming Mr. Buback agrees, you can start today; my nose tells me we don't have much time."

Morava also mentioned his conversation with Buback about Jitka's father, and was assured that the superintendent would intervene as well at the first opportunity.

"But, Morava, don't give her any illusions," Beran finished after checking that Jitka was not in the anteroom. "We are all more mortal than we've ever been. Even as we speak, this war is gathering its own momentum, independent of the warlords. Soon laws, institutions, and governments will have no force, and even logic itself—not to speak of morality—will go by the wayside. You can fight an elemental force up to a certain critical point; after that it may be all you can do just to survive it."

With this, his boss dismissed him.

As Morava was dictating a brief message for confidential distribution to doctors, teachers, postal carriers, and other public-sector workers, Jitka asked, "What about clergymen?"

L ike Morava, Buback had kept his report short and sweet. And the chief inspector also concluded that the latest crime made any political motivation for the murders seem doubtful. He agreed that they would nonetheless continue to play up the baroness's case as a threat to German women in Prague, so that the Gestapo's continuing interest would seem plausible. Sharing his observations about the Brno police, he mentioned what he had noticed on their trip to southern Moravia. At this even the powerful Meckerle lowered his voice.

"My dear Buback," he addressed him more confidentially than he'd ever done before, "you are the only detective here with the slightest bit of sense; the rest are worthless shit-for-brains who got in on their connections. That's why I've given you this assignment; it's more important than you probably realize. My sources tell me the secret weapon—the one that will wrap up the war in a matter of days—will be ready for launch in mid-May. I don't have to make borscht for you, and I can spare myself Goebbels's nonsense about luring the Anglo-Americans and the Bolsheviks into the greatest trap in military history. We are retreating because right now the enemy has a severalfold advantage in manpower and materials, and there's no reason to be ashamed of it. Until the new weapon can turn the tide, we simply have to hold on and to prepare ourselves for every eventuality; do you understand what I'm saying?"

He saw that Buback was confused, so he leaned his trunk forward over the desk to make the point more forcefully.

"The Führer has just issued an order, and personally transmitted it to the highest party functionaries in the army, security forces, and state and public offices. According to him, policies we previously applied only in occupied countries will now come into effect in the territory of the Reich as we retreat. I'm talking about the total annihilation of all transportation, communication, industrial, and distribution networks. Total, Buback. Do you understand what this means?"

He did, and felt himself flush. I'm afraid, he realized, my God, I'm afraid! It was an unfamiliar feeling for him; at critical moments he tended to be coolly inquisitive, never frightened. This, however, was truly horrifying news. He nodded in assent.

"I'll tell you more, just so someone intelligent will know what to do and how to do it, in case I don't make it. According to witnesses, Imperial Minister Speer objected. 'My Führer,' he said, 'if we follow through on your instructions we will destroy any hope of keeping Germany alive.' To which the Führer responded: 'If we lose this war, Speer, then the German people are as good as lost; failure means they don't deserve to exist.' "

A clear question played across Meckerle's face, but Buback could not bring himself to answer it. *Is he trying to provoke me?* Buback's head spun; *is he testing me? What does he want?* After a moment of silence the giant suddenly grinned.

"I know what's worrying you. No, I don't want your opinion; I'm simply giving you mine, at my own risk. I've had you thoroughly checked out and there wasn't any indication that you're a fanatic or a traitor. Your lack of party activity indicates that you joined to keep your job, one you thought would be honorable in any society. And your behavior leads me to believe that your highest goal is the survival of our people, whether or not they achieve what they aspired to. Anyway, if I had the slightest suspicion that you'd betray my confidence, I'd finish you off, Buback, once and for all."

He made his point by banging both fists down, shaking the solidly built desk. Then he relaxed into his armchair again and continued in an almost casual tone.

"The imperial minister and an overwhelming majority of those present at the following session decided to interpret Plan Nero (that's what someone called it) as a grave warning from the Führer, meant to galvanize the nation's heroic resistance. They resolved unanimously to carry out the order—what else could they decide, of course—but to modify its goals. The western imperial territories, whose loss is inevitable, will be handed over with minimal damages, so they can become the initial base for our people after the battles end. All forces and materials will be withdrawn to strategic areas of the center, where the new weapon will be launched. This territory will be defended to the last man, and in tactical retreats will be destroyed as the Führer requests. Because most of this area is within the Protectorate, the non-German nation and its economic base must be wiped out. Now do you see?"

"Yes," he said finally. "But I still don't understand what my role is."

"What you saw in Moravia was the beginning of this operation: one of the largest military movements of all time. Within a month it will be a stronghold capable of repulsing any attack. The eastern line alone will consist of two million soldiers; its nucleus will be the military command of General Field Marshal Schörner. I want to rule out in advance any possibility of internal resistance. And that's where you come in, Buback. We both know that only the Czech police are capable of organizing that sort of activity. We could, of course, take their light weapons away, but that would have a drastic effect on public order, again to our disadvantage. Those few thousand policemen know from experience how to fight and lead; each one of them could organize an attack on a smaller German unit and teach a hundred people how to fire a weapon. We'd have to round them up and possibly shoot them as a precaution, but in doing so we might set a Warsaw ghetto effect in motion—an uprising out of sheer despair. So, Buback, let Baroness von Pommeren continue to be a German foot in the Czech door, and you can be our Trojan horse. Keep your eyes and ears open and don't be afraid to ask for whatever help you need."

Immediately the images of apocalypse gave way to the memory of a shy girlish face.

Buback said, "I need the cooperation of the department dealing with black-market meat sales. The father of Beran's secretary has been imprisoned for an alleged violation of these rules. Leniency on our side would greatly simplify my job."

"I'll have Hinterpichler get in touch with you."

Buback felt tremendously relieved. His reaction amazed him. I must be in love with her, he admitted to himself finally; my God, I must really be . . . He stood up and said good-bye, hoping to leave before Meckerle got annoyed, but surprisingly the colonel was in no hurry to let him go. He scratched his shaved chin until it reddened.

"And . . . Buback . . . ," he spoke hesitantly, "do you think you could do me a personal favor?"

Buback had never been taken into Meckerle's confidence this way; unprepared, he stood motionless, with no idea how to react.

"But of course, Standartenführer," he managed to squeeze out just in time.

"There's a ball at German House today; you must know about it."

"No. . . ."

"It's not a real ball; they're forbidden till after the victory and we know and respect that. It's more like a sixth anniversary celebration of our occupation of Prague. The Castle has exceptionally permitted us a few dances, to lift the mood of our leaders and their wives. I invited a charming German artiste to accompany me a while ago, but as you know my wife escaped Dresden alive and has joined me here. Naturally I'll go to the ball with her, but I'd prefer not to insult or humiliate my . . . this sensitive woman. That's why I'd like to invite her to my table along with you as her . . . let's say her close friend."

"But I don't dance . . . ," Buback offered helplessly.

"She'll teach you fast enough. She even taught me."

He stood, showing Buback a figure sturdy as a Greek column. Then he extended his right hand aimiably.

"It's agreed, then. Eight o'clock; wear your dress uniform. I'll send my driver round; he knows everything."

"It's less than a year since my wife and child died . . . ," Buback objected again.

"Listen, in a war like this, different standards apply. It's high time you found someone to comfort you. But watch out!"

Meckerle released his painful grip and jokingly threatened Buback with a finger large enough to break an ordinary wrist.

"Not her. I'm the jealous type, all right?"

B y afternoon Morava knew all there was to know. It wasn't much. Any traces, if the killer had left them, had been completely obliterated by the fire and water. The little girl from the mezzanine still stuck by her water sprite; aside from the suitcase and the color she could not remember anything else. The victim's brother-in-law, whom he visited in the hospital, was still deep in shock; between torrents of tears he told them far less about the deceased than her neighbors did. The descriptions matched: a quiet, good-hearted woman who took exemplary care of her husband until his painful death and then touchingly revered his memory. She lived modestly on his pension, probably with support from his brother. Apparently he was the only person who had visited the two of them and later the widow alone. There was a substantial chain lock on the door. The mystery was why she too, just like the baroness, had let her murderer in. Did she know him? Impossible! He must inspire trust. How? Of course! The suitcase. Was he a traveling salesman with goods in demand? Candles for air raids? Household soap? Quality rye coffee? Some other article that vanished from the shops long ago? But why wouldn't the caretaker have remembered something as conspicuous as a large suitcase? Why hadn't the clothing's unusual color caught his attention, since he noticed the man's unusual pronunciation? And the serious little girl showed no signs of having a wild imagination. The autopsy confirmed beyond a doubt that it was the same perpetrator. Why, then, were there so many different indicators? Had he deliberately changed his appearance? So, this was no primitive on the rampage; there was a mind behind it. Then his method of killing must have a deeper meaning. Is it a symbol? Of what? A message? What sort?

Even before Morava's return from Brno, Beran had assigned two more men to him: Šebesta and Marek, experienced sleuths who were not at all offended to be working under a youth their sons' age. They shared Beran's good opinion of him and, in their time, had voluntarily chosen careers as "sniffing dogs," because they enjoyed working in the field and had no desire to learn German. They quickly reconstructed the daily habits and routes of Barbora Pospíchalová. On the last day of her life she had gone to the post office to deposit part of her pension; at the butcher's she had bought sausage worth a quarter of her month's rations, and at the grocery store she had arranged for lentils on her allotment and elderberry wine, procured for a special occasion. Her husband's brother was coming the next day, she had told the shopkeeper with unusual animation. Just before noon she had taken her bed linens to be pressed and bought a bunch of cowslips, which they later found in a small vase at the cemetery. According to the sexton she went there every other day, sometimes more often.

No one had noticed when she returned home. Because of the fire, the exact time of her death could not be determined; she must have had several hours to let her murderer in (assuming she did not bring him back with her—and the possibility remained that she had). The origin of the fire was a further question mark. Had it been set deliberately? Then why had this crazy man taken such care with the baroness to make an altar of death and this time destroyed his work? Maybe it had not turned out the way he'd expected?

That afternoon they assembled, crossed out, rewrote, and rerefined both texts, for public and selective distribution. For the latter Morava more or less copied out of his notebook his first, raw impressions from the embankment.

At five in the afternoon he gave his report to Buback first. The co-operativeness that had replaced the German's earlier primness on their trip seemed to have evaporated; he was practically sleepwalking. Finally Buback said he agreed with the suggestion in principle, but they would go over it together in detail the next day; now he had to leave.

As Morava walked past Jitka to Beran, he managed to surprise her in the anteroom while she was on the telephone. He bent toward her and blew gently on her hair from behind, but when she quickly swiveled toward him he saw alarm on her face instead of a smile. She covered the mouthpiece.

"Jan, stop it," she whispered forcefully.

She was apparently dictating some statistical data to the presidium about office supplies—quite absurd as the apocalypse approached!—and in the meanwhile Beran returned. He read through each version carefully twice and gave them his blessing. Buback's delay meant their publication and distribution would have to wait a day, which disappointed him.

"Let's hope the murderer isn't conceited to boot," Beran remarked gloomily. "If he's trying to send the world a message, we may be torturing him with this silence. He might strike again immediately to get the word out."

"Then why did he burn the last one to cinders?"

"The fire definitely started near the stove; he might not have closed it all the way."

"So what else can we do?"

Beran fixed him with questioning eyes.

"You're a Christian, aren't you?"

"Yes . . . Czech Brethren. . . ."

"Then you can definitely do more than I can as an agnostic: pray. Sadly enough, Morava, the toughest hours in this job are dealing with maniacs like this one. He has to continue in this game until he makes the fatal mistake that betrays him. All we can do is wait; wait and not despair."

He went with Beran to pick up the mail from Jitka, and so Morava only found out what had scared his beloved so badly as they came out late that evening onto Bartolomějská Street.

"Buback came to see me."

"Will he help your father?"

"He didn't say . . ."

"So what did he want?"

"He invited me . . ."

Morava halted, confused.

"What?"

Shadows moved across the darkening Národní Avenue. The trams and cars acridly belching wood gas had narrow cats-eyes scraped from their blued-out headlights. They stood face to face and could barely see each other.

"He invited me to dinner," she finished.

"When?"

"Tomorrow."

"Where?"

"He said he'd pick me up if I liked."

"And you said . . . ?"

"I said yes . . ."

He knew it was the only possible answer, and he also knew it was good; after all, he himself had arranged this opportunity for her. For Jitka? Now he was not so sure; maybe it was for Buback? His heart rose into his throat and so, for the first time, he knew what it was like to be horribly jealous.

"Was that wrong?" she asked timidly.

"No." He brushed it off bravely. "Buback is a German, Gestapo even, and I barely know him, but I don't think he's an extortionist or a rapist. When he told me that a bomb had killed his wife and daughter, there was no hatred in it, just grief. That surprised me. I'd say he'll help your father."

They still stood on the corner of the narrow street, although they were both going the same way.

"I'm still afraid . . ."

Morava was too, but as the man it was his job to provide solace.

He clasped his palms behind her back, pressed her close, and tried to talk himself into believing it.

"War or no war, German or not, even evil has to stop somewhere; that's why God made people like you, Jitka, whom no one would ever dare harm."

Like evil itself howling with rage at how little he appreciated its omnipotence, sirens suddenly began to wail across the city. The closest, right above their heads, deafened them. The tram shadows stopped, and human ones hurried forward. Holding hands, the two young Czechs set off at a slow pace back to the air-raid shelter in the police complex, as alone as lovers on an evening stroll.

The air-raid siren nipped Buback's problem in the bud. Before they even got to dance, he offered Marleen Baumann his arm and instead of leading her to the floor took her down to the cellar. Everyone politely made way for Meckerle and his spouse; they sailed to the steps as if in an air bubble while the other two moved elbow to elbow in a pack toward the mouth of the funnel. Fortunately the ominous hum of bomber squadrons did not materialize, and the crowd's nervousness did not grow into panic. He could just imagine the ladies' hysterics; most of them had never felt the daily breath of war.

The woman beside him seemed made of sterner stuff. When he called for her at the relatively modern apartment house in Prague's New Town, where Meckerle's driver took him before picking up his boss, her appearance surprised him. She was not much shorter than he—the pants of her close-fitting suit showed her long legs to good advantage—but she seemed dainty, not only in body. Her face as well was unusually long and thin, accentuated by blond hair combed straight back over her ears, contrary to the current fashion, and caught at the nape in a short ponytail. He was intrigued by her reaction when he said he was honored to accompany her in the place of Colonel Meckerle. Without raising an eyebrow, she answered, "That's both gallant and prudent on his part. Dancing with me seems to exhaust him."

The driver apparently knew her well, so they limited themselves to pleasantries. He knew no more about her when he presented her to the Meckerles; but he did catch himself admiring how easily and naturally she behaved when being introduced to her lover. So what, he thought, trying to quash an absurd feeling of sympathy; she's just playing a role.

The giant's wife, whom Buback was also seeing for the first time (she was huge and square like a dish cupboard), seemed like a real shrew, probably the only person on this earth who knew how to keep Meckerle in line. From that perspective he understood his superior's choice of a mistress; she could hardly have presented a greater contrast. As the companion of an important colleague—which was how Meckerle introduced Buback—Marleen Baumann aroused no suspicions, and Meckerle's spouse accepted her with relative affability.

While real champagne was being poured for some of the more important tables, the giantess continued her laments about the loss of their Dresden villa and her complaints about the drabness of life in Prague. None of them could get a word in edgewise. Mrs. Meckerle seemed to forget completely about the other woman's existence until after the state secretary's short yet interminable speech toasting the Führer as creator of the Protectorate, when the first notes of a waltz sounded. Rising from her seat before her husband could ask for the dance, she turned to Marleen.

"Shall we take the boys out for a spin, then?"

The next second, with no warning, the sirens announced an air raid. The horrifying memory of February fourteenth and the sudden bomb explosions was still fresh. Even this group, with numerous experienced soldiers, was not immune to it as the crush of the crowd inched toward an illusion of safety. A proverbial deathly quiet reigned, broken only by the shuffling of soles. The bodily warmth of this mass in a heated building led to a greenhouse effect. Sweat stood out on the men's foreheads; powder trickled down the women's cheeks.

Buback at first led his date to clear a path for her. After a while he felt the throng push her sharply against his back, and managed by turning around to get her in front of him. She realized that he was trying to make room for her to breathe, and gratefully turned her head back toward him.

"Thanks. . . ."

A better reward was the pleasantly bitter scent of her hair, and he buried his head in it.

The bombs had not yet begun to fall, and they maneuvered fairly quickly into the narrowest part of the flow to the head of the stairs, which led them down to an extensive complex of shelters. The spacious cellars of German House were furnished with relatively comfortable benches, and it turned out—when after the shock of heat there came a gust of cool air—that the climate was pleasant down there as well. Following the militia's orders, they pressed onward, passing a cellar alcove restricted to VIPs; towering above the others in a gray haze was Meckerle, talking to State Secretary Frank. Buback was suddenly glad that his boss had not noticed them.

He and Marleen Baumann ended up among unfamiliar couples in a cozy corner, where there was only seating for two. There she thanked him again.

"You were both polite and skilled. What a shame we didn't get to dance; you must be good on the ballroom floor."

"Don't be sorry," he said directly. "I'm sure I would have disappointed you."

"You don't dance?" she asked, surprised. "I wouldn't have thought it of you."

For the second time in twenty-four hours he repeated the fact that he had suppressed for months in the vain hope that what went unsaid might not be true.

"I lost my family in an air raid last year."

And then he added quite superfluously: "I don't feel ready for dancing yet." He gazed into her gray eyes and saw there the same sympathy that had so surprised him yesterday in the young Czech.

"Please accept my condolences, Herr Buback. You have no idea how well I understand. My parents and brothers perished in the first raid on Hamburg. A stroke of bad luck that both my brothers were on leave at the same time. I lost my husband last year in the retreat from East Prussia. But as opposed to you, I've lost the strength to mourn. It's not just that as a woman, I can't allow myself to; to be honest, I didn't really feel like it. With him, at least . . ."

She gestured with her head in the direction where her expansive lover was taking cover with his wife and the cream of party and government society. Then she fell silent, rooting energetically through her handbag until she found a gold ladies' cigarette case and a matching lighter. She offered him the box.

"It's not allowed down here," he said, drawing her attention to a notice on the wall.

"But they"—once again that sharp motion toward the leaders' sanctuary—"they were smoking."

"Quod licit Iovi . . . Fine for the brasses, but not for the masses," he translated freely.

She swore softly like a man, threw the items back in her bag, and glanced around the cellar. This was his first opportunity to really look at her. What he saw surprised him. Why would a beast so powerful that even his equals trembled before him choose precisely this one—out of all the young German women running around Prague? And was she young? In the darkened entranceway of her building, in the half-lit car, even in the ballroom where she sat next to him, her slenderness helped her pass as a young girl. The bright light of the shelter, however, mercilessly revealed the truth. Thirty? Thirty-five? Even more? The energy of her every movement spoke against it.

In any case, she was the exact opposite of the Germanic ideal of womanhood as portrayed by the Freie Körperkultur. But she was equally un-like his Hilde and the Prague girl he had invited tomorrow . . . where indeed? And what would he say to the girl once they had covered her father's case? Would he invite her home? How would she react? And how should he behave? If she agrees? If she refuses?

As he pondered these questions, he must have been staring intently at Marleen Baumann, who brought him back to the present with an unexpected question.

"You take me for a better sort of whore, don't you? If not for a worse sort?"

Put on the spot, he stammered a confused protest. Surprisingly it satisfied her.

"I'm glad to hear it. You see, I'd been alone for so long. I find most German men repulsive. At least he"—again she nodded her chin in that direction, and Buback sensed that she was avoiding his name and title—"isn't a gutless ass-kisser."

She gave a gruff laugh, which matched her dainty appearance as poorly as her vocabulary did. In fact, her whole face, as he could now see up close, was a collection of disturbing details. Her dove-colored eyes sat strikingly far from one another; eyebrows rising from the bridge of a large nose drooped to the outer edges of her face in an arc reminiscent of clown's makeup. She had a long chin, a forehead that was too high, and very narrow lips set quite deep beneath her nose, which further increased the sharpness of her profile when she stopped speaking. Suddenly he noticed an oblique line falling from her left earlobe almost across her whole throat; how did he miss it earlier? Oh, of course! She had probably covered it with powder. This wrinkle or scar of a hard-to-distinguish shade between light green and pale yellow indicated a secret.

As if reading his last unspoken thought, she said: "Anyone who hasn't seen me in a year doesn't recognize me, Herr Buback. In the course of a few days I lost my reason for living and came to know every kind of depravity on earth. When I realized that I could not kill myself—because more than anything I fear my own death—I learned to survive. I can lie so perfectly that even you would believe me if I wanted you to."

"Why don't you want me to?" he asked her, purely to keep the conversation going; he was completely captivated by his new discovery. Yes, her whole face was disturbingly mysterious; as soon as she spoke she changed beyond belief. Her lips became her dominant feature, suddenly so full that they surrounded him, and all her apparent defects coalesced at once into an image far from "beautiful" in the ordinary sense but nonetheless provocatively attractive.

Erwin Buback now knew why his boss kept her. That face was omnipresent; you could not overlook it nor, apparently, forget it.

"Why don't I want you to?" she repeated, and laughed again. "Apparently I trust you."

"What did I do to deserve that?"

"As long as fate lets them exist, men only half as interesting as you," she said to his face without a speck of coquetry, "can live in the present moment, here in our twilight of the gods, day by day, night by night. But you've stayed faithful to your old loves. I admire it all the more for being incapable of it myself."

He remembered the young Czech woman again, but he did not have the strength or at the moment any reason to correct her. Instead, he gladly acceded to her next request, and began to talk about his wife and daughter. She listened to him attentively, her palms planted firmly on the bench, and he soon noticed the burden of his grief lightening and dispersing slowly into his own words, melding painful facts into comforting memories.

The Allied squadrons crisscrossing the Protectorate held them in the cellar until almost midnight. When the all clear sounded, a thoroughly bored Meckerle had to go off to bed with his wife, who had developed a headache in the cellar air. He managed to pay his respects to his mistress and convey to Buback that his personal chauffeur would return for them. Although the party was starting to gain steam again, both of them understood what the message meant. When later he kissed her hand at the car door and she realized that he was not coming with her, she used the curtain of sound from the motors and voices to ask a further unexpected question.

"Would you be interested in meeting again, when I have time?"

"No," he answered forthrightly. "The colonel made it clear that was out of the question."

"I'm not his property," she announced flatly. "I'm no one's, not anymore. I'm a free spirit. If some day you feel ready to listen to me the way I listened to you today, you know where to find me. And don't worry, our number one spy won't find out."

During the whole trip home on foot—an impulse he'd suddenly succumbed to—Buback found himself unable to concentrate. He felt torn asunder: He belonged to his old love, as he headed towards new hope, but out of the blue he had found a strange affinity with this unknown creature, who had captured the heart of the Protectorate's third-in-command.

H edvika Horáková found a friend at the graveyard. For three months she had stood alone, twice a week, at the grave of her spouse, killed by a toppled crane during the Totaleinsatz—the total deployment—in Essen. Then, one February day, a fresh hole greeted her from nearby. The next day it had been filled in, and she found a sister in grief sobbing over it.

They hit it off right away. On the fourteenth of February, Marta Pavlátová had been making lunch for her husband, who was on the afternoon shift at the Pragovka factory. As usual, he was hanging around the kitchen getting on her nerves, so she chased him off to the grocery store on the opposite corner for their potato rations. From the kitchen's second-floor window she could see him leaving the store with a full string bag, when all of a sudden a giant invisible hand picked her up and carried her across the apartment; the weight of her body smashed open the door into the hallway and landed her with a blow against the door onto the staircase.

When she managed to stand up and scramble back into the kitchen, the view from the dusty window opened onto a completely unfamiliar street. The grocery store building was split in two; its left half had collapsed into the small square. Only afterward did she notice that the rag doll lying in the center of it was wearing her husband's pants and sweater.

Hedvika's tragedy was a hundred days older; she could lend Marta courage. Both were twenty-seven; both had waited to start a family until after the war and were now left alone. They thanked fate that they had met. Hedvika sewed at home; the cinema owner had taken Marta on as an usher. For the moment, they had no reason or desire to look for new partners. Every Wednesday and Saturday before noon they would meet at the Vyšehrad cemetery, which was roughly the same distance for both of them—Marta from Pankrác and Hedvika from Emauzy—clean up the gravesites, and set off along the ramparts of the old castle. They would stroll around the accessible portions, taking in the panorama of their native city, which was pulling free from winter's grip just as slowly and unhurriedly as spring approached.

Then they would head back to one house or the other, depending on whose turn it was to prepare lunch. Over the meal they would talk about what had happened to them, and try to guess when and how the war would end—and what they would do then. They soon admitted to each other that their husbands had disappointed them. They honored the memory of the departed, but believed that once freedom came, a new and better chapter of their lives as women would then begin.

Today they had met as usual, Marta still in black, Hedvika—who simply could not stand the color anymore—in long beige slacks and a quilted bodice, with a kerchief tied around the top of her head. This time they set off for Pankrác, where at Marta's a rare treat awaited them: potato pasta with poppyseeds.

She had barely begun to cook it, adding the rabbit lard sparingly, when the doorbell rang. Marta's husband had worked the night shift every third week; at his wife's request he had equipped the door with a solid chain lock. Now it allowed her to open the door without fear. She spotted an unknown man in a smallish winter coat, unbuttoned to reveal a mouse-colored suit. In one hand he held the stuffed briefcase of an office worker; with the other he raised a flattened hat.

"Excuse me for disturbing you," he said politely, "but I was told that I might find Mrs. Horáková here."

"Yes, of course. . . ."

Although only a month had passed since they met, it did not surprise Marta to find someone asking after her friend here. Out of habitual caution she left the chain hitched and called into the kitchen.

"Hedvika, there's a man here looking for you. . . ."

Even the other woman was not too surprised; she too, in the short time they had known each other, had started thinking of her friend's house as home. She came into the entrance hall, and the man through the slit in the door raise his hat again.

"Mrs. Horáková?"

"Yes. . . ."

"I'm sorry to drop in on you like this, but it's in your interest. Your husband perished in the February air raid, didn't he?"

"No! There's been a mistake."

His hand, which was just replacing the hat, suddenly shook severely. It seemed to both women that he was about to faint.

"That was my husband," Marta exclaimed, "Radomír Pavlát."

"My husband, Ludvík Horák," Hedvika added, "lost his life last year during the Totaleinsatz in the Reich."

The visitor immediately calmed down.

"I must just have mixed up the names, then; I do apologize. As it happens, it concerns both of you. The offices of the Protectorate will be paying the families of air-raid and Totaleinsatz casualties a lump-sum compensation. I'm distributing questionnaires that must be filled out and signed. When they sent me here, I never thought I'd be able to take care of both you ladies."

"Why don't you come in?" Marta offered, and pushed the door to, so she could unhook the chain.

"But who sent you here?" Hedvika suddenly wondered. "I don't think anyone in my building knew—"

The man was already in the apartment and slammed the door behind him. His free hand suddenly held a long, thin knife.

"One word out of you," he hissed, "and I'll cut your throats."

At first glance Lieutenant Colonel Hinterpichler was a lover of good drink, better suited to lederhosen than a buttoned-up uniform. As head of the anti–black market and economic sabotage division, he had apparently been appropriately instructed by Meckerle. Hinterpichler passed his assistant the sheet of paper where Buback had written the name and address of Jitka's father (obtained from Beran that morning by telephone), and ordered the man to connect him immediately with the head of the appropriate office.

He offered Buback a cognac, which he claimed was an old French variety just seized from a black marketeer, and for a few minutes made small talk with him as if they were old chums in a pub. Finally one of the phones on his desk rang. Like an actor finishing his coffee and stepping onstage to play a sovereign, he instantly modified his voice and demeanor. Suddenly he was every inch a high functionary of the forces everyone feared so greatly, including their own employees.

Having demonstrated his authority, he listened silently to his subordinate in Moravia. The gold pen in his hand hung poised over the paper. Finally he asked a question.

"How is he physically? Can he stand a few knocks?"

Shortly thereafter he nodded contentedly and made his pronouncement.

"Slap him around a bit, but don't overdo it. Then stick him with a heavy fine and let him go. Heil Hitler."

He replaced the handset and, back behind the curtains, was jovial again, giving Buback a conspiratorial wink.

"A bit of a drubbing will squelch any suspicions that we've recruited him as an informer; that's what you want, isn't it?"

He grudgingly admitted that it was; he just did not know how he would explain it to the man's daughter. He stood up, so as not to put his discomfort on display.

"Thank you, Obersturmbannführer; it will make my work considerably easier."

"It's nothing, really," Hinterpichler grinned smugly. "Pig slaughtering is probably part of the local culture; we'd have to hang all of them. Better to punish a few randomly and keep it under control that way."

Back in his old office Buback breathed deeply in and out a few times, but could not calm down. Getting angry at himself helped; it was an old habit that had pulled him through many a life crisis. Have I lost my mind? Why am I behaving like an adolescent? He had the switchboard put him through to the Czech criminal police and instantly heard her voice (what was so special about it? Yes! Now he knew: She always sounded like she was just waking up).

"Buback here," he managed to say impersonally. "Is this Miss Modrá?"

"Yes. . . ."

"You were kind enough to accept my invitation for dinner tonight."

"Yes . . ."

"Would half past seven suit you?"

"Yes . . ."

"Where shall I pick you up?"

He noted the address and closed the conversation as officially as he had begun it.

"Please inform Mr. Morava that I expect him in my office at Bredovská Street as soon as possible."

He hung up none the wiser about what he was after that evening. Having no other work at the moment to distract his attention, he continued to fret over it.

He had no illusions that any normal Czech woman would, given the current situation, fall in love with a German, much less a Gestapo agent (she would certainly think he was one, and he was not allowed to disabuse her of the notion). And he was almost a quarter-century older than her—easily enough to be her father. He probed deeper, asking himself what led him to hope against hope, and realized what it was. In these five years of war he had met countless people in extreme situations, and more than once had seen relationships develop that would be completely unthinkable under normal conditions.

After all, the situation in the Protectorate could (and apparently would) become so dire overnight that the father's savior might well become the daughter's only protection as well. He could even remove her from Bartolomějská before Meckerle's strike against the Prague police—which he would help prepare.

But, for God's sake, how should he behave tonight? This Czech twin of his Hilde, just like her predecessor, lowered her eyes every time he entered. What if he tried to overcome that shyness in a stroke, as he'd done in his first life in Dresden . . . ?

He cut short his musings when Beran's boy entered. Buback had pretended to have desk duty here today, as if he had to explain why they were not meeting in his office at Bartolomějská Street. This ploy made him even angrier at himself, so he was not particularly pleasant to Morava, which irritated him further. It's a vicious circle; discipline, Erwin. He concentrated on the official announcements Morava had provided him with, and saw that the drafts were fine. Approving both texts without changes, he ordered Kroloff to arrange for the publication of the shorter one tomorrow in all the German papers across the Protectorate.

With this they were done, but the kid remained seated. Earlier he had conducted himself in a calm, efficient manner, but now his eyes searched Buback's face with a tense expression.

"Is there something else?" Buback queried.

The Czech shook his head and stood up awkwardly, but before he took his leave and turned toward the door his face flushed red. What was on his mind? Another request for help? Then why didn't he say so? Meckerle had basically given him a green light; he could help in other matters as well, as long as the Gestapo's magnanimity didn't become too obvious. The more personally he could intervene on behalf of Jitka Modrá, the happier Buback would be to work toward the success of his mission.

Remembering her diverted his thoughts again down that same channel with an insistence that almost frightened him. How could this be? A month ago only Hilde had existed for him; even dead, she had filled his life and blocked even the slightest flicker of other emotions.

He felt it again that evening, as the girl appeared beneath the blinded lantern in front of her house, on a suburban street his driver had spent ages searching for in the darkened city.

Her placid beauty (he could describe it no other way) was even more vivid in the near-darkness; her eternally sleepy voice moved him, though she was merely explaining that she had not been waiting long; no, she had just come outside, because it occurred to her they'd have trouble finding the house. He opened the rear right door for her and then got in on the other side. What sort of rare perfume was she wearing, he almost asked, before he realized that it was the smell of soap.

Of course, he did not intend to take her to German House, although they could have eaten there without ration coupons. He opted instead for Repre, visited mainly by the few Czechs who could afford it (collaborators, he thought with a certain malicious glee, who'd bet on the wrong horse). He remembered the famous turn-of-the-century restaurant from his childhood, when he had eaten New Year's and Easter meals there with his real mother. Just after his return to Prague he had come here to jog his memories of her; it had still made him feel sentimental, but inside it had been empty and deserted as a burgled home.

But not now, not now. Beneath the restaurant's glowing chandeliers, he led the girl in the long black skirt and white blouse to their reserved table, and the tension that had gripped him since morning blossomed into a feeling he had not had in months: joy, so strong it caught at his throat. He was grateful when the headwaiter—who could hold up both ends of a conversation—stepped in. The girl had no special requests, so he recommended the Vienna sliced sirloin tips for both of them. However, she flatly refused Buback's ration coupons and pulled out her own.

The ritual seemed doubly absurd in a fancy establishment: the headwaiter pulled scissors from the tail of his frock-coat and cut off squares representing decagrams of meat, flour, and fat. Buback squirmed at how much smaller the Czech rations were than his. Either it seemed natural to her or too awkward to mention; she carefully placed the remaining tickets into separate compartments in her plastic purse, clasped her hands on the table, and turned her great brown eyes on his with an unspoken question.

"Gnädiges Fräulein," he then said, "I took the liberty of looking into your father's case; I'm interested in the well-being of the Czech police, since we're cooperating so closely. I can assure you that his only punishment will be a fine and that he'll soon be released. However, to be completely honest with you, I could not prevent them from.... They didn't exactly handle him with kid gloves, I regret to say. What's important is that nothing more will happen to him."

"My father is strong," she said simply.

"Anyway," he added, as if to excuse Hinterpichler's idea, "now no one will suspect him of buying his way out with a relatively mild punishment."

"No one in our town would ever think that."

He admired that directness in her; it did not strike him as haughty. When she was sure of something, she expressed it in the simplest possible way. This too he had only ever experienced with Hilde.

"Thank you, Herr Oberkriminalrat," she added.

He took a step toward intimacy.

"Do you think you could forget about that title?"

She flashed him a heartfelt smile.

"Thank you, Herr Buback."

"Erwin...."

She nodded.

"I know."

He did not insist and tried instead to draw her gently into a conversation that might bring them closer. In decent German she told him about her family and her youth—as she said with her still childlike lisp—in a land where several languages met; her description matched the one he had heard two days earlier as they drove through that very countryside.

"So you're from the same area as Mr. Morava?"

"Yes...," she answered more shyly than usual. "In peacetime we would undoubtedly have met a long time ago at socials; the war saw to it that we only met here, in Prague. He even speaks the same way; there's a lot of Slovak in our dialect."

For a couple of seconds he weighed addressing her now in Czech, so her speech could leave its narrow channel of foreign words and fill in his picture of her personality. Immediately he rejected the idea. He was acting like a college student smitten by a first crush!

The food interrupted Buback, letting him marvel at her long fingers holding the silverware with an unusual grace, at the small mouth, which barely moved as she ate; at the slight tilt of her head toward her left shoulder, causing her hair to cast an artful shadow on her right temple. Involuntarily he remembered Marleen Baumann's dramatic lines, arousing an anticipation of revolutionary acts, while this face radiated spiritual equilibrium, the sort that brings peace and happiness. I can't keep up this act for long, he realized; I'll end up telling her the truth.

And why not? Why not try it? What was he risking except a polite refusal? Wouldn't he lose far more if he let this opportunity slide by? Why not transform intent into action?

I don't know how it happened, my dear young lady; I know it goes against all the rules of this age, but in spite of it I love you. I've loved only once in my life, but my feelings were all the stronger for it; I loved my wife until the moment she died, and afterward as well—I thought that a love like that left no room for another. Then I saw you and from that moment I've known that her death made my love for you even deeper and stronger. I truly believe that she's sent you to me, and I implore you: overcome the revulsion you feel for me, a German. Hear me out, as a man who has never knowingly harmed another and who has tried amid the madness to maintain an island of justice. As proof I'll put an end to this charade by speaking to you in your native language, which is mine as well. What do you say?

He must have been staring silently at her with such intentness that she finally asked, "Is something wrong?"

The question tore him from his musings. Confusion filled her eyes. He had no idea how long his reverie had lasted. In the meantime, she had finished eating. He placed his silver on his half-full plate and tried to gain time for a good-faith effort.

"I'm sorry. . . . Would you like some dessert?"

She looked him straight in the eye again when she answered.

"No, thank you. It was very kind of you to invite me for such a nice dinner with such good news, but it's late already. My fiancé would worry."

D id you say who it was?" Morava interrupted her tensely.
     She shook her head. "That was enough; he called the waiter over immediately."

He forced himself to laugh.

"I guess everyone falls in love with you."

"Jan!"

He wanted to hug her, but for once she would not let him. He saw that Buback was still uppermost in her mind, and it irritated him.

"You served it to him straight up, and in spite of that he still drove you right home, kissed your hand, and said good night, everything as it should be; why let it eat at you?"

"What if he leaves my dad in jail . . . ?"

"He's not the extortionist type. No, I think your father's coming home."

"I don't know why I told him," she continued to fret. "He'll find out it's you in no time."

"So? Fortunately that's not a capital offense yet."

"He could harm you some other way."

He tried to reassure himself, so he could reassure her as well. "Jitka, my love, there's a decent chance he has other plans for me, which don't allow for personal revenge."

"What kind?"

He decided to risk letting her in on Beran's suspicions.

"And therefore it's entirely possible," he said, finishing his brief summary, "that his interest in you is part of the game as well."

Up till now she had been nodding sympathetically, but this point she rejected.

"That's not the way it's played, Jan. After all, he didn't say anything; he just looked. And he was completely lost . . . You're right, though, that's his business, and I'll just act normally. But please, watch out for yourself!"

They both heard a car approaching that caught their attention as it braked out front. Jitka jumped up, horrified.

"It's him!"

Her fear galvanized him. "Then I'll get the door."

She slipped around the kitchen table and whispered despairingly, "Go upstairs, I can manage him. Please!"

The bell rang.

"There's no point," he objected. "He'll hear me."

"He knows I'm not single. But he doesn't have to know who my fiancé is just yet. Don't worry, I just don't see any reason . . . Run along, I can handle it!"

The doorbell rang again.

"Hello," called a familiar voice. "Hello, hello!"

They both went to open it. The superintendent had eyes only for Morava.

"Am I glad you're here. I couldn't track Buback down. Grab your notebook and give her a kiss good night. He's done it again—twice."

K roloff sent an envelope with the news to be stuck under Erwin Buback's door early that evening, but the chief inspector had not returned.

When the door of the suburban house swung shut behind Jitka Modrá, he had the same feeling as last year, when an unfamiliar voice impersonally informed him that he was now alone in the world. It was neither despair nor regret; instead, he felt his old emptiness fill him again. He examined himself coolly as if from outside. Yes, this was his true, unretouched, unaltered state: solitude of body and soul. How had he let himself be swayed by such absurd feelings?

However, he could not return to his post-Antwerp method of survival. Something fundamental in him had changed. He had no desire to mope over a glass in the German House bar and go home to his impersonal one-room apartment. A strong need, buried these last twenty years, awoke in him. Dismissing his driver on Wenceslas Square, he strode energetically across the empty city center. He gave the top bell a long ring despite the risk that she might have company. It was a while before a tired voice answered.

"Yes?"

"Erwin Buback," he announced, sounding more decisive than he felt. "May I come up?"

"Of course," she said, just as abruptly. "One moment."

A minute later a key wrapped in newsprint landed next to him on the sidewalk.

By the time the elevator delivered him up to the top floor of the 1930s building, she looked ready for an evening on the town in her shaggy white dressing gown. The door of the cozy attic apartment closed behind him.

"So, the great Meckerle's jealousy no longer makes you quake in your boots?" she asked.

He decided to be frank. "I didn't come to sleep with you."

"Fabulous." She laughed. "I've always longed for a girlfriend."

Her miraculous appearance was quickly explained. She had just returned, exhausted, from a trip to the German troops; her troupe of opera singers performed operetta tunes for them every day, and she had not yet removed her makeup. He drained a bottle of champagne practically on his own, as if dying of thirst. When she realized he was absorbed in his own problems, she opened another one (apparently from the colonel's reserves), put some wild American music on the gramophone, and excused herself to go shower.

He felt each swallow electrify him like the galvanized strips of tin his chemistry professor had once given him to hold. The emptiness inside him warmed and became more tolerable, and he stopped seeing himself from outside. Even his exacting and intractable brain, which never stopped thinking, was beguiled by the bubbles; he turned off time and space and simply existed, like a pleasantly sated animal. Only his fingers moved, lifting the bottle regularly, filling the goblet and raising it to his lips.

He did not even speak when she came out of the bathroom in her terry robe, removed the old record from the gramophone, opened a new bottle, and lit one cigarette after another from a short pearl holder, putting on album after album of music forbidden in the Reich as the product of inferior races. Despite the wail of saxophones, he must have fallen asleep for a while; when he awoke it was quiet, and she was trying to remove his jacket.

"I'm sorry," she said, "please feel free to make yourself comfortable and stay. Our lord and leader is temporarily out of the picture. Total house arrest."

He slowly began to regain consciousness.

"Thank you, Marleen, but I'd better not complicate your life any further."

"First of all, Marleen is my stage name. The director of our group hoped it would remind people of Lili the whore from that hit song; I'm an ordinary German Gretchen. Second, even if his wife weren't around, he has no idea I'm here today; we were supposed to spend the night in Karlsbad. And third, I'll complicate my life if it pleases me to do so, which you definitely shouldn't take as an attempt to seduce you. I just thought you needed a bit of company today."

He shivered with a kind of shame.

"Lord knows I do. . . ."

"When you want to sleep, I'll make you up a bed."

He had no strength to protest. After a hot shower that tired him further, he put on his white undershirt again and his shorts, and wrapped a bath towel around his waist to seem more fully dressed. She greeted his appearance with a hearty laugh.

"A chastity belt? I have seen a naked man before, once."

Soon after, he lay on a narrow couch in the living room–kitchen, staring into the darkness. Complete calm reigned in the building and the yard out back, but he was as hopelessly alert as in broad daylight. Now! Now it will come, he was sure; first all his own wounds would open before his eyes, and then the abyss where his people's fateful piper had resolved to lure their entire nation.

At that moment he knew for sure that the glorious secret weapon was nothing more than a final deadly lie—a bluff, a boast, a dodge, a trap—base deception and trickery meant to prolong for another few weeks this twilight of the idols. The ones who fell for it would obey Hitler's monstrous order, transforming their homeland into a desert that would never support life again, much less support all those thousands of young Germans freezing in the pre-spring night in the south Moravian woods—and all of them together were doomed to rack and ruin, just as he was; he would consider himself lucky if they merely shot him without torturing him first.

Why wait around? He had lost all the ties that force a man to live for others' sake. The only remaining reason for his existence was to snoop around the Czech police force, which would influence the course of the war about as much as a swarm of mosquitoes influences the weather. Why not do the one thing that was within his power, since he actually had the means . . . ?

He'd left his pistol at home, but the solitude of this attic apartment would be the perfect place!

He got up, turned on the light, and managed to open the kitchen door noiselessly. Grete Baumann's forehead was creased in sleep, and her chin was propped against her hand; she looked as if she were deep in thought. He left the door ajar, and in the scattered beam of light he searched for the hanger with his dark suit on it. As he returned to the kitchen on tiptoes, he looked over at her one last time and found her eyes open.

"Would you like to come in?" she asked.

"Yes, I would. . . ."

He stripped off his underclothes and she lifted the blanket. She was naked and drew him close with no overtures or ceremony.

When he clasped Grete in his arms, it was like barriers collapsing. He became his old unrestrained self once more, the one Hilde had tamed with her tenderness, and his long abstinence made him even more passionate.

He felt his life depended on their love.

And he realized that Grete was opening every corner of herself to him.

Morning found them in a lovers' competition over who could give the other more and better pleasure; they were acrid and ashen from physical exhaustion but, aware that this night would never be repeated, they neither were able nor wanted to break apart.

Hour after hour they barely spoke; occasionally he heard her call weakly, "Oh, ja!" or "Oh, Gott!" but if he said anything himself, he did not notice.

At seven the alarm clock went off. They were so engrossed in each other that moments went by before she flung her hand over her head to turn it off.

"Sorry," she said hoarsely, "got to catch the tour. . . ."

"And I've got to get to work. . . ."

"Good thing I'm in a chorus."

"Good thing I have subordinates."

She returned from the bathroom a few short minutes later, dressed, coiffed, and made up. He was further impressed.

"You're like a soldier."

"I'm a wartime lover."

When he came out of the bathroom the scent of strong Dutch cocoa, like he had not had since childhood, wafted from the table. She held her cup to her mouth with both hands, but did not drink, merely shook her head thoughtfully.

He felt uneasy. "What's happened?"

"Something very strange. As soon as I find the words for it, I'll tell you."

S HE had praised him. Yes, he should be proud! What a great idea, having them tape EACH OTHER'S mouths and bind EACH OTHER'S legs! Except AGAIN there was NOTHING in the papers.

By now he was sure he wasn't hallucinating. He already had FOUR OF THEM in the cellar behind the ice blocks. So why the silence?

At the same time, something told him they were CLOSE TO BREAKING. He would just have to do it OVER AND OVER AGAIN!

This time he settled on a Sunday, so he could vanish without being noticed. There would be lots of people there, but it might help him to blend in; he'd manage as he managed WITH THE REST.

The third day, when he had already lost hope, he found what he was looking for.

"Beware of the sadist!" warned a small but unmissable headline. "Several brutal murders have been committed in Prague; the victims were single women who let the murderer into their apartments. The unknown assailant then sadistically slaughtered and disfigured the corpses without robbing them. The police are looking for a perpetrator and a motive, and ask the populace to take note of all suspicious persons. Women, especially those living alone, are cautioned not to admit anyone they do not know well. Information, anonymous and otherwise, will be accepted at any police station in the Protectorate."

He was quite satisfied. Especially pleasing was their admission that he was NOT A BURGLAR. And the knowledge that he could finally take a well-deserved rest before CONTINUING ON SCHEDULE.

On Easter, bombs fell on Prague for the second time. Again it was broad daylight, but this time their targets were factory complexes outside the city center. Because of the holiday, human losses were low, although the buildings were largely reduced to ruins.

"A clean job," Beran remarked as they returned from their survey. "Or maybe just a tiny bit dirty."

Morava did not understand.

"Two years ago," the superintendent explained, "it might have shortened the war by a month. But at this point I have to wonder if this isn't the first volley of a postwar rivalry."

"But they're allies."

"Morava, Morava, dear little Morava, when this war ends, take care your world doesn't collapse around you. You're a homicide detective and a Czech, so you're living in a dream world if you think good always fights against evil. Now, I lived twenty years in a relatively good country—I mean the old Czechoslovak Republic—and I can assure you that sometimes it turns your stomach all the same."

Morava could not see it.

"But now that the Nazis have lost the Ruhr Basin and Silesia, only the Czech factories can rearm them."

"That's true too," Beran exhaled. "And anyway youth is entitled to its hopes. As for us older folk, our skepticism probably just leads to capitulation. So let's hear it."

They were at the station already and back on the topic of their own work.

"So far we have had four hundred twelve calls about suspects, mostly through our office. About half of them we've eliminated as groundless or misleading; the rest are under investigation. Especially those in Moravia; the Russian advance on Vienna may cut them off soon."

"Any fresh trails?"

"So far all cold ones; everyone named had an airtight alibi on at least some of the dates. But information is still coming in; it's surprising, but even in abnormal times like these people are quick to notice deviants of all sorts. Or to invent them."

"Such as?"

"Turning in lusty ladies' men for stealing their wives."

"Aha. Has Buback come up with anything?"

"He confirmed that Hunyady, the Gypsy, died in a work camp, and Thaler—the butcher and Henlein's man—is apparently working where he is supposed to be in the Reich. We can be sure our colleagues in Brno didn't get hold of the right man."

"Apropos of Brno," the superintendent remembered, "is there anything new with Jitka's father? I haven't seen her yet today."

"I'm sorry; I meant to tell you. She took today off. There was a telegram last night telling her to expect a phone call at the main post office, but she's been down there since morning. Her father is already home, we hope."

"That's good news. Congratulations to you as well."

As he said it he raised his eyes queryingly and Morava as usual shook his head; so far there were no signs of other activities on Buback's part.

"We're both happy, but a bit afraid of how our parents will manage if there's a battle."

"As if we know how we'll fare here. They might get lucky and find the front whips past them like a hurricane; we'll be the unfortunate ones if Prague is conquered bit by bit, like a fortress. It's in the hands of fate. Or God, in your case. Anything else?"

Finally there was something Morava was on top of.

"I think it's safe to call him a widow killer. And it occurred to Jitka that maybe he prowls the cemetery. He might count on them leading him home, where they're probably alone. Say he claims to sell gravestones or something. . . ."

Beran picked up the train of thought.

"And the four deceased husbands are buried . . ."

"All at Vyšehrad!"

"Which you should have under surveillance immediately."

"There have been two people there since this morning. I'm going straight from here to meet them, so we can set up our surveillance."

"Good work, Morava!" It was the first time in a while Beran had praised him, and a feeling of bliss wafted over the young detective, although this rare feather belonged in Jitka's cap. "Look smart and hop to it."

A cold wind lashed the intermittent rain at the cemetery; there had been two or three women all told since morning and not a single man. The pair had had plenty of time to talk tactics. The problem was that there were three entrances. Lebeda, a greenhorn Morava had conscripted in desperation, suggested that they simply close two of them off. The other two warned him in unison that it was the best way to scare the murderer off to another venue. No, they'd have to spend a portion of their lives here as sweepers, stonelayers, gardeners, beggars, or the bereaved in mourning. They had no choice but to deputize the sexton, who would be sure to notice a repeat visitor. Before doing so, Morava verified that the tubby fellow had been digging graves with an assistant on the days of the murders; otherwise the sexton himself would have become a suspect.

He returned to Bartolomějská to send a third man out to the cemetery and set two shifts for the next day. Then he called Buback at Bredovská Street and learned he was back in his Czech office. The German had not appeared at Bartolomějská Street since his odd supper with Jitka; was he waiting until her father was released? Morava knocked and opened the door.

The chief inspector was poring over a mountain of papers. When he spotted Morava he started, as if caught at something.

"What is all this?" he snarled at him without a greeting.

Morava had no idea.

"Can I have a look?"

Buback shoved the papers toward him. Morava recognized them.

"I ordered that you be sent copies of all the reports that came in from our appeal—"

"And where are the translations?"

So that's why he's upset? Mistake!

"My fault, I'll put someone on it right away."

But who? he thought despairingly; it'll take three people a week to get through it. . . . To his surprise the German calmed down as quickly as he had flared up.

"That's not necessary. You don't have the men to spare. Give me one person who can summarize the most important ones for me orally."

Who can figure this guy out? Morava mused, but a weight lifted from him. He informed Buback about the steps they had just taken, and then sprang a request on him. Only German offices could authorize the installation of telephone lines. They needed one in the sexton's tiny workroom, so they could call for reinforcements in an emergency.

"I'll see to it," Buback announced curtly.

"Your translator will be here in fifteen minutes," Morava promised him again as he left, and it occurred to him that he owed the man more than that. "Miss Modrá is probably on the phone right now with her father. I'd like to thank you for that as well."

"Then you're in the wrong place," Buback cut him off. "I told you the Reich is a government of law, and it expects in return that the Protectorate police, above all, will not waver in their respect of that law."

"Understandably so," Morava assured him and left.

Get as far from that guy as possible, he thought. Suddenly he believed Jitka when she said Buback could destroy him as effortlessly as he had helped her.

She must have waited so long at the post office that it wasn't worth coming in to work, but why hadn't she at least called?

Impatiently he sorted through the new reports, arranged a translator for the German, and stopped by the cemetery to ask his men for their first impressions. He was pleased that it took a long time to find them;

even in this cramped space they had already learned how to make themselves nearly invisible.

At home, the smell of Jitka's maddeningly delicious cabbage cakes and a bouquet of tulips, as dear and rare as meat these days, welcomed him.

"So Papa's home," he said joyfully, swinging her around in the air.

"Grandpa, you mean," she corrected him.

"How's that?"

"You'll be the papa now," she said, slipping into their south Moravian dialect. "Watch out or you'll shake the baby right out of me, lover boy!"

APRIL

Jana Kavanová walked home from the funeral smiling. Beneath her black stockings and black ankle boots the bright green grass struggled up between the cobblestones; runners of woodbine wound about the fortress ramparts, their leaves slowly unfolding, and the sky over the moat of the street was amethyst blue and free of airplanes, as it had been for weeks. A feeling of complete happiness suffused her, so strong that she felt ashamed.

Her older sister had just buried her beloved husband. Jana had left her up at the graveside and hurried home to the embrace of her young lover. She could—and would—comfort her sister tomorrow, the day after, and all the days to come, but she would only have Robert today. Prague was swarming with Gestapo agents; it was too risky for him to stay. She had made the arrangements; tomorrow he would be taken on borrowed documents to a place where he could wait out the end of the war safely.

Jana, almost thirty, had met Robert two months before in the shelter beneath Prague's main rail station. A tall fellow in a clearance-troops overcoat, he gallantly offered her the rare gift of a cigarette. His voice was deep, and in the emergency lighting he looked like her contemporary. She had already accepted his invitation to meet that evening when she learned that he was a newly deployed seventh-year gymnasium student. She kept her word, however, and had not regretted it.

He ended up at her place that evening. The majority of pubs and cafés were closed and the rest seemed hollow and empty: either there were no menus for the customers, or no food for the cooks, or no appetite for the food. Back at the statue of Saint Wenceslas, still the meeting place for young Prague—and God knows Jana didn't feel old!—she boldly invited him to her apartment for tea with real rum. She could always send him home to his mother, she rationalized to herself. However, as it turned out, he was no child; she warmed to him more and more, and when they had finished the rum (without any tea), she was happy for him to stay.

I'm certainly not his first, she thought jealously, when she saw how skillful he was. Still, she had not slept with anyone for a good six months, since her most recent disastrous fling, and this kid was only a temporary distraction, anyway. Eventually she would find the right man, maybe after the war when the better-quality ones came home from the army. So she gave herself to him without a second thought.

Apparently he took to her as well. He confessed that he'd never been with such a . . . mature woman. He chose the word carefully and it stung her, but at the same time she felt appreciated. After that he came to see her every night and painted a humorous picture for her of his aunt and guardian's mounting disapproval. Then, in mid-March, he had learned that in two days his whole class was leaving for northern Moravia.

The Protectorate's eighth-year gymnasium students had long since been deployed at hard labor around the Reich; the seventh-years were now assigned to build the defensive line against the anticipated Russian offensive. Gangs of eighteen-year-olds were to do the excavating under the supervision of German guards. Families of deserters would be threatened with punitive measures. Robert therefore went.

As they agreed, she tagged along that morning, twenty yards behind him—too young to hug him like the other mothers, too old to join the girls accompanying their boyfriends. The truck with its benches trundled off and dissolved in her tears. She knew then that this was not just a passing fling; Robert had truly become her lover.

For a month she heard nothing from him. Her initial despair gradually abated as she stubbornly pieced together information from every possible source. Finally she could not bear the burden of her love alone, and confided in her sister. It surprised and comforted her when her sister emphatically told Jana not to worry about the age difference; she was happy just to see Jana happy.

Leaving early today had been her sister's idea. Her older sibling had fallen in love with and married a man twice her age, knowing she would soon be more of a nurse than a wife. But she loved him even then and cared for him for many years. Four days ago he simply did not wake up. Only then did Jana hear her sister wail that her life had lost all meaning.

Despite this, her sister ordered her to go straight home from the funeral. She was the only one who knew that Robert was momentarily hiding at Jana's. As the Soviet cannonade swept across the northeast past Ostrava, the Nazis' deviousness grew worse and worse; there were fearful rumors that in their desperation the Germans were planning to send the Czech students out in front of the tanks as human shields. His classmates were afraid to flee, so Robert risked it alone.

Two days' hard march brought him to Olomouc. Even hitchhiking, he'd seen his luck hold; a truck driver put him in a sick deliveryman's seat, and took him all the way to Prague. Their first night together he and Jana made love until morning. The following day she visited Robert's aunt. The woman was overjoyed to hear the news, and promised to arrange safe transfer and shelter for her nephew until the end of the war.

So this would be their last night together for who knew how long, and Jana was grateful that her sister had not asked her to give up a minute of their limited time. At the graveside, she thought fondly of her dear brother-in-law, cast a handful of dirt on the coffin, gave her sister a heartfelt kiss, and set off toward the tram. Death was instantly forgotten, and Jana was filled with that joyful longing that had been with her for three days, ever since she let Robert in and he knelt, exhausted, on the threshold and pressed his head into her lap.

The tram conductor asked if she had a ticket, and Jana returned abruptly from her thoughts of Robert to the outside world. As she paid she noticed a postman with a bulging bag. Why did he seem so familiar? The fog began to clear from her brain. Hadn't he passed her on the way from the cemetery? But if he'd been going uphill, how did he end up here?

She put him out of her mind and spent the rest of the trip to Smíchov laying her plans. Of course, Robert couldn't come to Prague from the country, but why shouldn't she visit him on Sundays? The trains still ran, albeit with delays, despite the air raids. She wasn't afraid of them anyway; love was her armor.

As she quietly unlocked the door, her heart was in her throat. She crossed the entrance hall on tiptoes and silently opened the bedroom door. Robert lay naked on the bed, breathing deeply. Yes, he was a man, but in sleep his boyishness showed through. She gazed at him, lost in adoration, and in that moment believed that despite the difference in their ages, nothing could separate them.

The doorbell made her jump. Who could it be? The police? Or maybe the Gestapo? Impossible, she snapped at herself; no one had any idea he was here, aside from his aunt and her sister, and they would never betray him. Feeling more confident, she returned to the apartment door and boldly asked, "Who's there?"

"Special delivery," the answer came back.

She remembered the man in the blue cape, swollen by the fat bag underneath it, and had to laugh: she and her postman had taken the same tram here. Or would it be a different carrier? Probably! She opened the door.

It was him.

They still kept to their unspoken agreement: the terrors and horrors of their work would not cross the door of their tiny and uncertain refuge. The need for peace and quiet ran deep in their blood.

Both Jitka and Jan had grown up in families that were a world unto themselves, and had spent their childhoods in an atmosphere of gruff tenderness. Just north of Moravia's vineyards, nature seemed to have run out of the gifts she had been so profligate with farther south. Here she coddled no one. Economy was everything, starting with food. Children handed down shoes and clothing until the oft-mended uppers and fabrics gave out.

Caresses, not sweets or presents, were the only signs of affection for the youngest offspring—and those often hurt, since hardened calluses covered their parents' palms. And when that same hand punished them—as it occasionally and reluctantly did—its traces were visible on the skin for days afterward. However, one thing neither Jan nor Jitka could ever remember was a conscious injustice. Once, when Jan was beaten instead of the true culprit (a stable boy who had blamed a broken jug on him and was later found out), his mother knelt before him and kissed the hand she had just thrashed.

Jan and Jitka first spotted each other in Beran's anteroom. It was just before his promotion to assistant detective; she had arrived under the work exchange, a Nazi order that uprooted young people from their native villages, breaking the ties that might lead them into the Resistance. The very first words they exchanged brought them closer together: their south Moravian accents marked them as clearly as a scent identifies a flower. Their deeply ingrained modesty did not, of course, permit them to show their interest. It took them a year to get farther than "good morning" and until recently they had addressed each other formally, but their warm smiles—his as gentle as hers—confirmed they shared a common temperament.

Their meeting as lovers on the day the bombs reached Prague was therefore natural—and practically foreordained.

He never doubted they would stay together afterward, nor did he need to ask; it was further proof of the link their shared roots had forged. Young couples can have trouble adapting to sudden communality and often falter on it, unable to overcome the selfishness of differing habits, but from the first time Jitka and Jan woke up together, their common language smoothed over the minor differences in their characters. Their opinions and needs merged; they became in truth "one soul—one body."

When they boarded the tram at the long-closed National Theater, the working day with all its filth was simply forgotten, as if they were never going to return. At home they cleaned and cooked together, discovering new stories that mapped out the part of their lives when, incredibly enough, they had not known each other, and in love they learned more about one another. This time of innocence would end each morning as Jan awoke. Holding Jitka close in his embrace, he would let his brain get to work.

Today, exceptionally, his mind was already racing before bedtime. In her second month of pregnancy Jitka felt worse than ever before. Her frequent indisposition made her tired during the day; lethargy dulled her appetite and her ensuing weakness made her stomach more irritable. It was a vicious circle that accelerated as time went on. Beran spared her as much as he could; he even suggested that she take sick leave, but she refused.

"Then I would really fall apart. It's work that's holding me together right now."

Morava knew she did not want to leave him alone with his string of failures, and in return he arranged something to look forward to: Saturday, April twenty-eighth, would be their wedding in Jitka's hometown church, and he had already filed the applications. Both families had agreed by letter that if the front moved dramatically before then, they would marry in Prague, in a civil ceremony; it was unthinkable that Jitka should remain single as their child grew inside her.

That day became a magic date for him. He had learned from Beran that a good detective always sets a deadline for cracking the case, even if the deadline was only a personal one. Now the repeated newspaper announcement and the confidential information they had sent had brought in a stream of warnings and reports, and it was up to him to solve it in time. He had no doubt that the butcher was planning to strike again, and this time he wanted to be quicker.

The killer, he felt, was already in his closely woven web, and Morava's greatest fear was that some accident of fate would let the man slip through a slack loop. Although his most experienced people were reviewing the reports as they came in (so long as none of them were busy directing the graveyard operation), he tried at least to have a look at all of them. In doing so he realized he had come to rely on Buback as well.

At a certain point—actually, since his mysterious dinner with Jitka—the German had begun to cooperate enthusiastically and with impressive results. During their daily consultations, Morava noticed that the chief inspector was fingering the same sort of suspects he was. One time he mentioned it and had the impression his overseer was even pleased.

Today, Jitka had fallen asleep as soon as they arrived home. Morava opened his briefcase and removed the materials he had prudently smuggled with him. Making his way quietly down to the kitchen, he spread the new leads across the table like playing cards. In about fifty cases, his intuition had coincided with Buback's: half a hundred fates marked by a predilection for perversion. Almost none of the fellows (all were men) had cropped up on the criminal register, and the few who had were down for minor offenses: three petty thefts, one drunken vandalism, and one slight injury.

The public servants they had contacted were deeply shaken by the detailed description of the murders. They had taken pains to observe their patients, clients, guests, neighbors, and other people who they sensed might harbor traces of exceptional if hidden brutality. A good half of the reports concerned repeated mistreatment of women, children, and animals. The majority took place behind closed doors at home, and therefore had been classified, albeit with some sense of discomfort, as private affairs.

A slew of the men were barroom brawlers, prone to brutalize other pub customers over a difference of opinion, a game, or just because they were too drunk to care. A couple of cases mentioned torture, and the witnesses belatedly reproached themselves for not having the courage to step in. In the end all were concluded by settling the score somehow, with the participants agreeing to hush up the affair.

For obvious reasons the rape cases interested Morava most. In some, women were tied up and subjected to sadistic assaults. It amazed him how many serious offenses like these went unpunished, because the victims either let themselves be bought off or did not dare to press charges for fear of retribution. He marked as "urgent" the case of one barber who, according to the examining surgeon's report, had sliced into his unwilling lover's breasts, but later prevailed on his victim to change her statement, apparently compensating her financially as well.

The remaining reports did not fit any one profile: there were exhibitionists, sodomites, voyeurs, and other deviants indulging their aggressive whims. Under the Nazis, unlawful firearms possession by a Czech usually meant death by firing squad, so knives were now the weapon of choice.

A few unclear reports were left over. Instead of containing direct leads, they were requests for consultations. None of them sounded urgent enough to require immediate action; Morava saw them as fallbacks in case the other trails led nowhere. For example, there was one note requesting the police to kindly visit the rectory in the north Bohemian town of Klášterec u Teplic. It concerned the disappearance of a picture of Saint Reparata, which was later returned by the thief.

Morava shook his head and resolved to give the newcomers on his team a little lecture about concentration at work. On the sheet he noted that it should be remanded to the appropriate department. Then he pored over the sorted piles and tried to put himself in the killer's place the way Beran had taught him to.

Why is he doing it? So consistently and painstakingly? Why the fixed order, even with a double murder? Where did he find this secret rite, one never before seen or heard in this country? Could it be from somewhere else? Only the excised heart reminded him of Inca rituals.

The one thing that continually nagged at him, and he repressed it with revulsion, was the method and the vessels the killer used—all startlingly similar to those of the Moravian zabijačka. . . .

It was past midnight when, his skin burning from an icy shower, he crawled under their eiderdown slowly and quietly, so as not to wake Jitka.

"I'm not sleeping," she said.

"Did I wake you?"

"No, I couldn't fall asleep."

Morava was immediately worried. "Is something wrong?"

"No. . . ."

"So why, then?"

"I'm angry at myself for wanting it . . . our child. . . ."

She was turned away from him as she said it, and he sat sharply up, turned on the light, and leaned over her to see into her eyes.

"Jitka, please! Look at me."

Her eyelids were scrunched up in pain, and she shook her head.

"But we both wanted . . . we both want it, Jitka."

"It's always the woman, though. I really only wanted it because I was worried about you."

"Well, so?"

"I should have been thinking of the child. It's so defenseless."

He managed at least to turn her toward him. Even in their mutual solitude he whispered to her.

"It's in the safest possible place: inside you. And I'm right here."

"But what if one day you're not? Look how useless I am."

"It'll be over soon. You read our mothers' letters: they were sick up till the third month, then it vanished. Remember?"

She was not comforted; instead she turned away from him and her heaving shoulders told him she was crying. He was at a loss.

"Come on, Jitka! Please?"

"No, Jan . . . This is no world to bring a child into. . . ."

It was the first time their thoughts and feelings had diverged, and the change was sudden and dramatic. Stubbornly he sought the words that would convince her.

"It never has been a good world. The pages of your family Bible testify to that. But it's been better, and it will be again. Who would have believed three years ago that truth would win out? And now we can almost touch it. It may be a few more months, but the Reich will collapse, it's in the air, as inevitable as spring; even Roosevelt's death can't change that. Peace will come, freedom will return, and our child will live in both of them."

She said something; he didn't immediately understand.

"What?"

"But so will that monster! Catch him, Jan! He frightens me more than Hitler does. . . ."

Grete stepped into the bathroom as Buback began his soak in the tub. He had not heard her arrive over the din of the water and was all the happier to see her. Buback never knew for sure when and if she would come. After his first night with her, the longing to be back with her had never abated, despite his fatigue. He felt sure he had never had and could never have a better lover. However, a nagging feeling of impropriety held him back: Meckerle had entrusted her to him, counting on Buback to behave decently. But did that extend to covering up Meckerle's infidelities . . . ?

Just before midnight, his body had resolved his debate with his heart. Resolutely he left the German House bar and set off to see her. When he rang the bell he did not even have the chance to say his name before her voice broke in: "Where are you?"

This time she was wrapped in the white bath towel he had worn the day before; it emphasized the length of her arms and legs.

"What have you come to tell me?" she asked before he could speak. "That you betrayed his confidence? Or even mine?"

"No," he admitted. "Just that it was pure rapture with you."

"Aha. . . . So then, Buback," she said, addressing him as a man would, dispensing, as he would soon find out, once and for all with his Christian name, "if you want to keep me, then grant me three wishes, as the old custom goes. One: no watches. It's bad enough that I have to be on time once a day. Two: I want to tell you the truth. I've been lying my whole life, playing a role, and before I die—which these days might be anytime—I'd like to find out what in me is real and what's a lie. And the third one you can discover on your own, since you're something of a detective."

Then she opened the white material like a curtain.

Encouraged by the way she gave herself to him again, he tried afterward to draw her closer as he used to with Hilde. However, the intensity of her resistance contradicted the passion preceding it. Although he owned her completely when she was in his embrace, he lost her entirely the moment she was dressed. Her estrangement took place with miraculous speed. She hardened like plaster of paris, he thought, and mentioned it to her: did she push him out of her mind before he even left her sight?

She hated good-byes, she explained, and had decided that sorrow and disappointment would never rule her again; she'd seen too much of them already, *finito!* At the best possible moment, she would snap down the shade and hold it there until she was sure the joy would stay with her. How did she know? he asked. The way a bat knows, she laughed; she had learned to sense unhappiness and deception even in the dark, and to veer around them.

"Space, Buback! I hate walls; I have to feel space around me."

He understood that freedom was fresh air for her. Without it she would choke; she fought for it fiercely, like a drowning woman. Did she want to see him tomorrow? And how could he find out today? Maybe he should stop watching his watch and find out for himself when the time came! Would she take his extra set of keys? Why not, unless he needed them for another woman. . . .

Her "truth telling" was even more disconcerting. Soon she began to lay out her life story for him, loading one cigarette after another into her holder like ammunition clips. Her first lover at fifteen, a dancer only three years older, who held on for over ten years; it was a long, happy young love, Hansel and Gretchen, that would have lived on into friendship in old age, except for Martin Siegel. Like the actor? Buback asked, surprised. Yes, the very one.

Siegel, the darling of Hamburg's female stars, suddenly fixed his gaze upon her, a novice. Hans shook with rage. On his twenty-fifth birthday she did not have a present for him. "I'll cut Siegel off," she promised, as a consolation prize. The oldest trick in the book, she now laughed; the famous thespian behaved just as Meckerle would years later. Instead of consoling himself with the next in line, he would not let go.

Siegel rewarded her coldness with heightened attention; in a short while it changed to outright wooing. Passionate poems soon accompanied the flowers; he found her slenderness captivating. Bemused, she read them to Hans and was surprised to see how jealous they made him. Why was he so upset? she objected; Siegel was thirty years her senior, an old man. But if it bothered him that much, she realized, then why didn't Hans marry her? They'd send the artist a wedding announcement and if he still wouldn't leave her alone, Hans could challenge him to a duel.

Hastily conceived, eagerly accepted by Hans and carried through by both of them with youthful verve. True, an insultingly extravagant bouquet arrived from Martin Siegel, but with a disarming note. He apologized for pestering her; now he knew her true feelings, and he wished the couple a long and happy life together. At once, she admitted, she felt disappointed that the game was over: it was she who had been defeated. When, two years later, the film weekly *Ufy* gave detailed coverage of Siegel's spectacular marriage to a beautiful young Berlin actress, envy entered the fray as well. Now she knew for sure that her Hans needed precisely those thirty extra years to treat her the way a man should. Her love for him was no longer young or happy; in fact, it wasn't even love anymore. It was then she began to deceive him.

Over the years, many men had vied for her favor; now their time had come. She found a new game: men, she learned, fell head over heels in love with her. She managed to convince each of them that he was her chosen lover, while his competitors were no more than a pretext. If she had learned anything perfectly, it was how to pretend passion and to lie. Let Buback beware! For none of these men had been able to give her the pleasure she faked so expertly.

Then she met Martin again.

This time he came to Hamburg on tour, and she fretted over how to behave. Avoid him? Confront him? He solved the problem for her. When he spotted her, he came over and greeted her affably, as if they were close friends. He asked if he could invite the two of them to dinner. And she lied to him, saying Hans was not in town, but she would gladly join him. Martin was staying, of course, in the luxurious Hotel Atlantic; they feasted on lobsters with French wine, and then he returned to their old story. He hadn't been able to accept her refusal at the time; he could laugh at it now, but she had been the first woman to turn him down at fifty. For two years he was devastated, until fortunately he met Ursula. She was Grete's age, and that helped him get over it.

She laughed along with him, but felt miserable. Suddenly all the time she had wasted with Hans hit her full force—she could have spent it with this enchanting man, whose skin was just like Hans's, and his eyes even younger! Soon the hotel carriage would come to take her home; she nearly wept at the thought.

Once they had explained everything to each other, he asked if he could invite her to his suite afterward. There was champagne on ice waiting for him there every evening. In the elevator she decided to be his lover.

"And this fellow I had written off three years earlier as an old man was the first to bring me to a climax and keep me there all night—like you, Buback. . . . Why do you look so embarrassed when I praise you? Come make love to me instead."

He was only too glad to obey, but her past was beginning to affect him. Why? Hard to be sure, but he felt a strong urge to keep his own a secret. Once, he confessed the short but strong burst of feeling he had had for the Czech girl. The restaurant fiasco had done him more good than harm, he declared, because it broke down his defenses and led him from an imaginary lover to a real one. She laughed.

"So I was a consolation prize! I'll make you pay! You'll never have me again!"

He took it as a joke, but when he tried to make love to her again, she crossed her thighs and locked them together. He tried to overpower her; after all, he was sixty pounds heavier and had wrestled. But she thrashed about in his grip; he could not grab her hands or open her legs. He could not even roll her onto her back, because she would wriggle deftly from side to side. Gasping for breath, he talked to her, begged her, warned her he would hurt her. Just before he crossed the line into brute violence, he gave up. His week of euphoria over, he lapsed into a deep depression. He remembered the men she had teased and led on, and felt sure she had written him off for good. Had she gone back to Meckerle? After all, she hadn't shown up the night before. . . . Silently he released his grip so she could get up. Instead he was suddenly in her embrace.

"Come on! Make love to me. Buback! More than ever!"

Much later, when she seemed far more passionate about her cigarette than about him, he dared to ask why his truth, in contrast to hers, had deserved punishment.

"Your fateful love was Hilde; mine was Martin. The rest of them don't belong here."

Another thing confused him. It could happen at any time, except when making love—they could be listening to music, eating a meal, or just talking. Suddenly, she seemed to back away from him. A strange, bitter smile would appear on her face, and her mood would change as abruptly as the fickle weather of Sylt, where warm stillness gave way in seconds to an icy gale. When he mentioned it, she snapped irritably that nothing was wrong; she wasn't moody, just thinking! After all, she couldn't giggle at his every comment like an imbecile. If he wanted to stay with her—which was up to him—he should stop trying to force her to explain things and learn to deal with her as she was.

He asked himself why he should bother with the whims of this woman, when their only connection was a mutual need to dull the pain of irreplaceable loss. He got his answer one night when she failed to show up. Although it was his first chance at a good night's sleep in days, he stared for hours into the darkness and tried to conjure up the sound of quick footsteps on the side staircase. With Hilde he had been a good husband; with Grete he was a complete man again. But he didn't feel like much of a man at the moment. There was no point in drawing it out: if she wouldn't explain why she stood him up, he would end it.

But the next night, when she ran up the stairs to his door, his need overwhelmed everything else. And when she hungrily kissed him like before, he lost his desire to ask the question. So she continued to come or sometimes not to come, when she supposedly wanted to be alone, and when she came, she drank, smoked, talked, and made love to him even more insistently. Then, by the time he returned from the shower she was asleep again, as if deep in thought, chin propped on the back of her hand.

Today, he dived into the bathtub, not knowing if he would see Grete or not, and took stock of their time together. He had known her less than thirty days, and yet she had altered the very fabric of his existence. She lent it meaning, he admitted; she gave him a goal, even if for now it was only to wait for her.

Like before in Dresden, in the days of his professional innocence, he studied the reports of potential widow killers on a daily basis. First he would listen as the translators summarized them for him, then later, with the office door locked, he would read the Czech originals over in detail. He consulted with Morava and his group as to what was and was not worthy of investigation, and meanwhile, diligently and unfalteringly as a barometer, measured the pressure and temperature in the ranks of the Czech police. This morning for the first time he would be able to satisfy Meckerle's curiosity.

"If there's a rebellion, the Czechs' trump card will apparently be the radio, Standartenführer."

"No kidding," his boss snorted in contempt. "Now there's an idea. Radio's been a target since the day it was invented."

"I don't mean the Protectorate radio station; a couple of tanks and a round of grenades will take care of it. I mean the city radio station."

"And what's that?"

"The central office for civil air-raid defense under the Prague police. Besides the sirens, it can patch through to all the public loudspeakers in the city."

"Wouldn't one tank and a single regiment be more than enough?"

"For the office, yes. I'd assume the Czechs are clever enough to broadcast by telephone from any local switchboard."

"Aha," Meckerle mused. "So what then? Cut the connections?"

"We could turn them off from the main post office, but then we'd be risking our own people's lives; we don't have a separate warning system."

The giant leaned forward in his chair and thumped his elbows down onto the table, which indicated he expected his subordinate to make a suggestion.

"So, then."

"With your permission I'll ask our technicians and their Czech colleagues to check the state of the equipment across the entire city grid. Our agent will be there to map out all the stations. Then he'll hand over a precise plan to the SS officer you designate, who will put together units that can occupy or decommission all the radio transmitters at once when the time comes."

Meckerle sank back into the armchair.

"Dictate the order. Have it brought to me for my signature."

Buback snapped to attention.

"Permission to leave, Standartenführer."

"No . . ." His boss visibly wavered before finally deciding. "Do me one personal favor, if you would. Take this note to . . . you know."

"Yes," he said, hoping that he wasn't blushing. "Should I wait for a reply?"

His oversized boss looked as pleased as a child.

"Great idea, Buback! Thank you!"

"Silly idea, Buback!" said Grete, freshly returned from a performance. Balancing on the edge of the bathtub, she skimmed through the letter.

"Sorry," he said humbly. "Somehow I thought it might divert any suspicions he had—"

"He's got other problems at the moment," she retorted. "He's under suspicion himself."

An image flashed through his mind: the conversation about that secret meeting of high-placed Reich chieftains, which had de facto contravened the Führer's orders.

"Who suspects him, and why?" he asked tensely.

"His wife. Because of me. That's the reason I have so much time for you."

"But for God's sake, how did she find out?"

Grete tossed the paper away, stood up, and began to undress gracefully, a warm smile on her face.

"From me, love. I wrote her an anonymous letter. Now, let me into the tub."

As always he read the daily papers on the night train. STILL NOTH-ING! Meanwhile, for three long days they'd been going on about how the American president's sudden death would disrupt the Western alliance with the Bolsheviks. He didn't know much about politics, but was sure this was empty talk. The Reich was on its back, like a beetle that's been kicked over. He grinned at the thought of a street full of Krauts, their boots scrabbling in the air.

He felt himself CALMING DOWN, although home was still more than an hour away. He was alone in the compartment; the majority of travelers were commuters who had debarked by the time they reached Beroun. No one boarded the train there for Plzeň; it was almost midnight. Despite the shock he had gotten, he WASN'T TIRED. Not in the least! He was content.

I'M REACHING MY STRIDE!

There was no denying he'd made some nearly fatal mistakes. That whore was the worst one yet. He'd latched onto her by the cemetery as she hurried off to satisfy her lust. She was quiet as a mouse, the way she'd retreated so obediently, cowering with the knife at her throat. Then she did something he hadn't expected. She threw open a door. Through it he could see a bed.

"Robert!" she shouted, and jerked away from his hand with such force that he dropped his knife. At the same time a man emerged from under the featherbed, naked but amazingly tall and with good biceps.

He broke out in a sweat; panic crippled him and drowned out everything else. Fortunately, it gave him time to realize the guy had no idea what was happening. Meanwhile, the woman, in an awkward retreat, tripped over the low footboard and fell on her back.

That was enough to allow him to bend down, grab the haft of his knife just below the long, thin blade, and then just stab. He reached the man's heart in the first blow. It took three, maybe four for the woman; he didn't count them. He managed to kill her even before the man's body collapsed across hers. Interestingly enough, neither of them screamed.

He made sure he was in no danger from either of them and then sat down beside them on the bed. Eventually he caught his breath and stopped perspiring. All the while, he muttered curses at himself. Why did he lose his head so often? Where did the soldier in him go? He used to keep his cool even under fire. He'd have to get back on track. . . .

On the other hand . . . how could he have known she'd already have a new stud in the bedroom?

He looked at the dead man's face now and realized it wasn't that of an adult. The height and broad shoulders were deceptive; the face was almost childlike, unmarked by great tragedies or passions. Suddenly he felt sorry.

THAT WASN'T WHAT I PLANNED!

This was a depraved relationship, and the boy was clearly the victim; that was why he was PUNISHING THEM. And he would not stop . . .

UNTIL I WIPE THEM OUT!

A while later he threw off the cape and put down his postman's bag. Methodically he proceeded through his task. The unfortunate boy he laid out in the bed, covering him up to his chest with the featherbed, unstained side up. He closed the boy's panicked eyes so that it looked as if he were still asleep.

As he put the cursed SOUL into his satchel next to the unused straps, he decided to change his appearance again. Someone might wonder why an unfamiliar postman had been in the building so long. Then he remembered the caretaker on the embankment, still the only person to have gotten a good look at him. Maybe he should stop by today? No, not worth the risk; they might be watching.

I WILL GET HIM, ONE OF THESE DAYS!

After a short search he found a ball of hemp rope. He turned the cape inside out, wrapped the satchel in it, and tied it up, crisscrossing it with the twine into a shapeless bundle like the ones carried by countless Eastern refugees wandering across the Protectorate. He could not change his postman's pants, but the boy's jacket, with the sleeves turned up, obscured its origins.

As usual, he met no one in the building and felt sure the passersby outside were paying no attention.

As he finished his paper in the train, he was more interested in what they would say about him tomorrow than about the course of the war after Roosevelt's death. However, he was sure of one thing: the decay of morality had spread so far—he'd witnessed it personally today—that he had to change his plans.

I'll punish them EVERY WEEK!

Once again he felt an unpleasant tingling as he got off in Plzeň. Recently, food inspections had become more frequent on trains from the countryside. He hadn't yet met one on an express from Prague. Fortunately the platform was empty. And anyway, he grinned to himself, what could be so interesting about a single solitary PIG HEART?

B etween lovemaking and her stories they sipped champagne; right at the beginning she'd hauled three cases of it over in a taxi, Meckerle's entire stock. He set up a military storehouse at my place, she said mockingly, and Buback did not dare to ask the next logical question.

She was sitting on the bed again, hugging her knees, wrapped in a large white towel as usual. He realized from the beginning that she was obsessed with cleanliness; she showered several times a night, and taught him to do the same. How had she done it near the front? he'd asked. She always chose lovers with running water, of course! And during the retreat? Suddenly she turned ashen.

"I told you I'd rather die than talk about that."

He would have been glad to be finished for the night; the role of confessor, hearing the details of her love life, was mentally exhausting. He did feel honored, but at times her directness seemed almost cruel. She evidently wanted to emphasize the casual nature of their relationship, but why so bluntly? That night she seemed determined to finish the story whose beginning he already knew.

Grete managed to make Martin Siegel fall in love with her a second time and after a short tempestuous affair he even divorced on her account. Her own marriage had a catastrophic ending: amiable Hans, who up till the last believed he and Grete would reconcile, fell under a subway train on the way back from family court. She could only guess as to whether it was an accident or suicide—it happened while she was riding up the escalator. She was so in love with Martin, though, that this shameful tragedy affected her far less than the sudden change she saw in her relationship with Martin.

The banal story's sudden change into drama managed to raise Buback's weary eyelids.

"What change? Did he find someone else?"

"No, that wasn't it. During our whole time together he never deceived me, not once. But I was the last in a line of conquests that always ended with him returning to his true love, the theater. I should have seen how easy it was to pry him away from his wife—it was more like I set her free. When he was learning and playing a big part, it was as if I didn't exist. Othello and Mercurio occupied him far more than any passing fling could; a woman I could have buried, like any other competitor. Martin, that fantastic lover, stopped needing to make love when he was with me. Fleeced a second time! And what's worse, I was still just his mistress; 'we've both had our marriages already,' he'd say, 'haven't we, darling?' "

Then war broke out for real. Actors of Martin's caliber did not have to enlist so long as they joined troupes entertaining German soldiers behind the front lines. Grete forced him to arrange for her to go as well, singing in a group with the depressing name *Freudenkiste*—"Box o' Joy." She thought that, removed from the surroundings where he was king, he would come to appreciate her presence. They could return to their starting point, those rapturous nights in Hamburg. The director of the group, however, soon struck Martin's modest handful of famous monologues, which had been his substitute for performing the classics; they bored the soldiers. Instead, he was condemned to recite trite little verses, meant to give men who used traveling whorehouses for sex an analogous replacement for emotions.

Martin was unbearable. Because he couldn't punish that Nazi, she said—lighting a new cigarette while Buback rubbed his eyes quickly, so she wouldn't see—he tormented her instead. He must have known how she longed for him and he must have wanted her himself at times, but he had an inhuman self-control; crawling into bed, he would turn away from her and fall asleep without so much as a good night.

Desperate and vengeful, what else could she do but have an affair—but with whom? Even after days of bathing in the Lido, the soldiers and officers currently recuperating in Rome after their Sicilian battles stank of God knows what, most likely death. And she would rather have died than sleep with a troupe member. Then she saw her chance.

After a performance for their Italian allies, she received a bouquet of roses. A calling card in it requested her to accept a supper invitation: they could meet at the Hotel Dei Principi, a chauffeur was waiting outside in a silver Lancia—*cordialemente*, Gianfranco Bossi. Ordinarily she would have refused, if Martin had not remarked that she ought to go; this might just be the supermale who could finally slake her nymphomania. She changed and went.

The driver in livery delivered her to the doorman, the doorman took her to the concierge, the concierge brought her personally to the head-waiter. She ended up at a table where a slender, dark man with un-believably green eyes rose to greet her; he could have been thirty or fifty. If she would like, he said, kissing her hand, they could take dinner together here. With her consent, of course, he would be pleased to invite her for dinner at his home. She liked what she saw, and, furious at Martin, she accepted.

Home, she continued raptly, as if seeing it once again, was in an old palace filled with servants, whose silence reminded her of ghosts: a scene from a film, with silver, candles, the music of a hidden quartet. And after a feast like that, there would have to be a canopied bed. . . . Was she boring him, she asked Buback. Of course not, he said swiftly, for fear of being left alone the next evening.

The Italian remained virtually silent; he ran the dinner with gestures of his handsome fingers. She did the talking: about Hamburg and Ber-lin, about books and the theater, ever more intrigued to know how this man, evidently an aristocrat, would negotiate the next bend in the road toward their evident goal.

He did it quite differently than she expected. At a certain point he stood up, walked over, helped her pull out her chair, and offered her his arm. Then he led her out past the entrance hall to the door of the palace, where the blacked-out vehicle was waiting to take her back.

He invited her night after night, four evenings running; only the food and music changed. Once the last cup had vanished from the table, the music disappeared as well. From the hallway, the sounds of a small fountain burbled into the dining room. He no longer moved, just gazed at her. Confused, she spun the conversation onward alone, until he rose from the table.

They had two days remaining in Rome when it dawned on her: the moment silence descended, she fell quiet as well. They looked at each other mutely for several long minutes.

He knew she was leaving in two days' time he remarked suddenly; he would return to Sicily the next day. But the Allies are there already, she replied, shocked. Oh really, he smiled; what's the difference, a change might be nice. He would like her to accompany him. As? As his betrothed.

She was flabbergasted. But she was here with her husband!

The Italian was apparently well informed. The actor wasn't really her husband, though, was he? No, not officially; they hadn't felt it necessary to formalize things, but she had been with him several years already. So why did he let her go out at night with a stranger? If she were Sicilian, her brothers would have killed him long ago. He meant his offer seriously and would prove it by confiding in her: he was a member of an old noble family here on a secret military mission. Couldn't she stay here with him? Early tomorrow he'd arrange for her luggage and documents.

No, she said, no, she was truly sorry. No tonight or no forever? he asked. He is my fate, she whispered. Only death can release us. In a rush of emotion she then asked if he would like her to stay tonight, at least. He nodded almost solemnly and led her up a marble staircase and along hallways with ancestral portraits; the palace was desolate— and then there it was, the canopied bed, and she felt an indescribable gratitude to him for the way he had exalted her and confirmed her uniqueness. She had never made love more passionately—to be precise, she corrected herself, she had never pretended passion more expertly.

Before she began to get dressed, the Italian made a cross of kisses on her mouth, breasts, and lap.

At home she woke Martin. She repeated everything that was said in the dining room and waited to hear what he would say. And he . . . even now she swallowed angrily and fumbled for another cigarette— he congratulated her and asked if she needed help packing.

"And I began to hit him, Buback! I hit and kicked him. Until it hurt me just as much. I was punishing part of myself in him too. For the fact that together we killed such a perfect love. He defended himself; he was strong, so he quickly got me in a lock on the ground. Except that I can't be tamed, you know that. I spat, scratched, even bit him.

He howled, and I was sure he'd wound me too. But suddenly he let me up, opened himself to my blows and whispered, Thank you, thank you, until I screamed furiously, for what? And he said: for still caring that much. At that I burst into tears. And then we made love till morning like in Hamburg."

Early the next morning the chauffeur woke her; he had brought a ring from the Sicilian. A large diamond was set in platinum between two emeralds the color of his eyes. She knew it cost more than all the money she had ever earned. For the few minutes she held it in her hand, she felt the way she had always longed to feel: the chosen one among women. Then she showed it to Martin and sent it back.

As if this last memory exhausted her more than her whole life story, she laid her forehead on her knees. Buback's tiredness, meanwhile, had completely fallen away.

"Why?"

"What do you mean, why?"

"Why did you return the ring? It's not as if you deceived him. On the contrary . . ."

And then he realized he was jealous of both the Italian and the actor.

"That's odd. . . ." She shook her head.

"What's odd?"

"Martin asked the same thing. Typical that you'd ask as well."

"Why is it typical?"

She yawned, threw off her towel, and slipped under the quilt, without even a longing glance at the bathroom.

"Think about it, Buback. Or sleep on it; with you it amounts to the same thing. Good night, love."

The woman's newly widowed sister found the corpses. Despite their ghastly appearance, she kept her head; instead of fainting or raising an alarm, she relocked the apartment and went down to the police.

Jan Morava, accompanied by all the free men in his group (and by Buback) was for once able to arrive on the scene of the crime first and secure the evidence. Soon Beran arrived, called by a pale Jitka out of his latest useless meeting with Police Commissioner Rajner, who was agonizing over how long to keep serving the occupying powers.

The three men on duty yesterday at the graveyard were there too. Šebesta remembered the murdered woman well; he had seen her hurry off through the side gate toward the embankment. He swore solemnly that no one had been following her, and Morava spotted a gaping hole in his net: the murderer would have taken Jana Kavanová for a widow by her clothing, even outside the cemetery.

Jana's sister cleared up the mystery of the dead youth. His flight from the trenches could no longer harm anyone.

The perpetrator had as usual chosen a time for his attack when men were away at work, children at school, and women at the stove. According to the witnesses, only the garbagemen, coalmen, a policeman, and a postman had come down the street since morning. These testified to seeing only a pair of housewives. Once again the unidentified killer had left no trace. He appeared and then vanished into thin air.

Morava had to summon all his strength to keep on track. Outwardly he seemed fine, but inside he was in utter despair. There was one person, however, who did notice. When the German finally left to inform his office, the superintendent clapped his adjutant on the shoulder.

"Take me along with you."

Morava was so crestfallen that he fell speechless. He waited, suffering, for Beran to say the inevitable words. Halfway across the bridge from Újezd to Národní Avenue, the superintendent turned to the driver.

"Stop here, Litera. We're going for a little walk."

Morava saw the driver cast a sympathetic glance his way. He followed the superintendent down the stairs to Střelecký Island like a condemned man. At the bottom, Beran strode along the path for a while in silence, stopping finally at an old oak. He ran two fingers along a slender twig sprouting from it that was dusted with miniature greenery.

"Nice progress since last time, don't you think?"

Of course, Beran did not expect an answer; he understood his companion's mind was elsewhere.

"You know what I'm going to say, don't you? I have to say it, though. Yes, I'm taking this case away from you."

Morava must have been the very picture of misfortune.

"Don't act like you've been betrayed and abandoned, Morava," Beran snapped irritably. "You did nothing you shouldn't have and everything you should have. Personally I can't find fault with you, because I'm no idiot. We're hunting a treacherous predator. For now he has the upper hand, but you've set a ring of hunters on his trail, and the noose will eventually tighten around him, as long as he keeps to his habits. At the moment yes, the murderer is fixated on widows and the Vyšehrad cemetery. I wanted to tell you clearly, face-to-face, that you have no reason to criticize yourself. I'm taking over the case so that they won't ask for your head; Rajner is scared out of his wits and is looking for a sacrificial lamb."

Morava found his tongue.

"And you think you're a better target because your surname means 'ram'?"

"He won't touch me, because he knows the whole operation would shut down without me. They executed my potential replacement, and the next best person would be you."

Morava stared, dumbfounded, at the man who had just demoted him and then paid him the very compliment he'd desperately longed for.

"Yes, Morava, I sense a talent in you, the same kind—all modesty aside—that I once had. And you're just as tenacious. There are dogs who won't let go of their prey even if you swing them round in the air by their legs. You'll get that monster!"

"But how, if I'm not—"

"I don't have the time to reinvent the wheel, and fortunately I don't need to. I will officially conduct the meetings of the investigative team, but will always ask you first, one on one, how to do so."

"But—"

"Don't try to make my life any harder than it is already, or yours any easier. In public I'm taking responsibility away from you, but in private you will run things for me. Now, listen closely. I'm convening the team for two this afternoon to take charge myself. Fifteen minutes before that I want you to give me a precise plan of action and tomorrow's task roster—for everyone, including yourself. Take two more laps around the island to clear your head; in the meanwhile I'll inform Rajner and the Germans."

As he left, he turned around once more.

"You can let your beloved in on our little secret this evening. Just so she doesn't think she's marrying a good-for-nothing."

As directed, Morava set off around the sandy oval, trying to make sense of his public fall and private resurrection. He knew he had not made any mistakes, but also that this meant precious little. One of Beran's first pearls of wisdom, which Morava had written into his notebook, was that a seasoned detective had to do more than just what was necessary; he had to think one step further.

He felt sure the superintendent would want a fresh idea from him at a quarter to two. A new, more urgent message for the newspapers? He doubted strongly that widows would read it. A further appeal to a wider circle of specialists, maybe with a photograph of one of the horrid death altars? He remembered Beran's solemn warning. Reinforced surveillance of the cemetery? He knew the team was stretched to its limit; the criminal police could barely keep up as it was. Stretch them any thinner, and Prague would become a playground for thieves, robbers, and "ordinary" murderers.

He rounded the tip of the island for the second time. Leaning against a tree, he looked out across the water. Charles Bridge, the castle—this scene always raised his spirits, but now he barely noticed it. The worst thing, he admitted to himself, was that he had lost his spark, lost the thread, couldn't even concentrate; he caught himself thinking in turns about his mother, Jitka, their child—treasures the war would threaten far more than the widow killer ever could.

A long object slid into the corner of his vision; a barge drifted down the Vltava, with a solitary fisherman and two rods attached to the stern. Slowly and silently it floated down toward the nearby weir as a weak wind carried the rumble of falling water off toward the Old Town bank.

Morava knew how deceptive an idyll like this could be. Since their

March expedition to Moravia, the images of a powerful German army massing to the east had never left him. He sensed that despite all the defeats of the past two years, there was enough destructive strength in those soldiers to turn the Protectorate into a vast wasteland. In the upcoming conflict of responsibilities, how come he hadn't chosen his personal ones? Why wasn't he on one of those final trains right now, bringing his mother back here? Why hadn't he found her and Jitka's parents a place to rent long ago, maybe with farmers outside Prague? Was it the unholy sum it would cost? And what was he saving for, if not to protect his own family? Why hadn't he refused Beran right off?

Out of solidarity with him? Should it take precedence over solidarity with his family? Or out of fear for himself? But Beran had seen to that when he claimed the case as his own cross to bear. So then? Had Morava's gloomy craft become so crucial to him that he would risk endangering his loved ones for it?

Yes, he answered himself, but not for the sake of his career. Catch that monster, Jitka had told him; he frightens me more than Hitler does. He understood what she meant. Adolf Hitler was the product of a deranged nation's political will, horrible but explicable, and therefore defeatable. The unknown and unpredictable widow slaughterer stripped the thin veneer of civilization from mankind and threatened to return humanity to its savage prehistory.

The fisherman rowed closer; he lifted both lines from the water, opened an old can, and spindled wriggling earthworms on the hooks. Then he flung his arm wide and the floats whistled down between the dinghy and the shore. The man in the boat waved to him, but Morava just stared dumbly back.

He had his idea.

All the heads of department marched into Meckerle's office. They ran out of chairs; the assistants brought more in from the anteroom and the hallway as well. There was no food, no one thought to light a cigarette, nobody spoke, everyone sat clenched as stiff as a ramrod. A puppet theater, Buback thought to himself. It seemed inconceivable to him, but not long ago he had been one of those figurines.

Yes, Grete had freed him from servitude to the war. True, it was their unceasing and unflagging lovemaking that bound them together—interrupted by her stories, which merged with his deliriously exhausted dreams—but he realized that at some point he had dropped out of this society of soldiers, and now he was hers alone.

Had she truly freed him? Or had she deprived him of his foundations, his sources of equilibrium? She had exposed him—for better or worse—to emotions and passions; had she also transformed him into an animal, unprincipled, unwilling, and probably even incapable of defending an ideal?

But without her, without the woman who had stepped unexpectedly into Hilde's shoes, what sort of ideals would he have to defend? The ones that had deformed German culture so completely? Weren't the murderers sitting here today all the more monstrous for the fact that they massacred innocent victims left and right from the comfort of their desks, often by telephone? Without moving his neck he surveyed them in his peripheral vision, face by face. Was he the same as them? Probably not, so long as it seemed more important to him that he spend the next night with Grete.

The way she had detached him from Hilde was a more serious matter. A month ago, he had convinced himself that his dead wife had sent him the Czech girl as her own reincarnation, to cure his loneliness. Now he felt equally sure that she would not approve of Grete; Hilde would have found the actress's emotionally turbulent life contemptible. After all, it even bothered him. But why? Hadn't he become part of it?

The colonel appeared in the doorway, and all present snapped to attention. Meckerle whipped his right hand into the German salute and simultaneously motioned them to sit down. Then, as if he were alone in the office, he began to study the papers in the folder an assistant had just placed on his desk.

Buback remembered he had a letter for Meckerle in his breast pocket, and felt a new pang. Why had she left the colonel, anyway? And had she, in fact? What was she writing him about? The benefits of her relationship with Meckerle were evident; surely it was only a matter of time before the rift was healed and he, Buback, would become another of her episodes, one that would not even yield a good story. Advance nostalgia overwhelmed him.

"Gentlemen!" Meckerle slammed the leather binder shut with an audible crack. "The final battle has begun. Last night the whole eastern front shifted, from the Balkans to the Baltic. Vienna has fallen, and it seems the main defensive line on the Oder has been broken. There is no doubt that the main goal of the offensive is Berlin."

The meeting's participants neither moved nor breathed. Everyone except Buback seemed to know already. Had Grete's wiles even dulled his interest in the final days of the Reich (which might be his own as well)? Maybe it was time for him to loosen Grete's grip before she became a drug he couldn't give up.

"From this day forward," Meckerle pronounced, "the military leaders are following the Führer's strategic plan. Our goal is the defense of Bohemia and Bavaria as the launching point for our final victory. Mitte's army units have enough men, military machinery, munitions, and fuel to fulfill this historic task. Our job here is to insure absolute tranquillity behind the front lines. We will not declare martial law, as it might provoke the more militant domestic elements to resistance; nevertheless, it is in force from now on. Every act of sabotage or incitement hostile to the Reich—whether directed against soldiers or civilians—must be nipped in the bud, suppressed, and punished with Draconian severity."

A blow. This time everyone twitched. Meckerle's elbows had again come down on the tables. Buback's stomach cramped. Yes, no wonder Grete liked this Tarzan. . . . He regained control when his brain came to his aid. The Empire was dying, and he was jealous! Of a blabbering Gestapo agent and a woman whose life creed was infidelity!

"I want to warn all of you—and you must warn your subordinates as well—that a line of troops lies between us and the western front. Many will find this situation tempting, but anyone suspected of desertion will be swiftly sentenced in court to death by hanging. With no pardons! Prague is the primary railway and highway center of Bohemia, and we will defend it if necessary, even at the cost of its total annihilation. Why should it fare better than our lovely Dresden did?"

Buback remembered how Meckerle and his wife had described the destruction of their villa. A few hours later, the mysterious woman who sat next to him that night turned his life upside down. Wasn't it time for him to become his own master again, before his freedom became a new sort of slavery?

Before he could think this assertion through, he was dragged into the sudden motions and sharp noises all around him. Force of habit catapulted him out of his chair along with the rest, who were hastening to flee Meckerle's office. He moved along with the flow; having missed Meckerle's last sentence completely, he had no idea what the order was. Then he heard it again.

"You stay, Mr. Buback."

The head of the Prague Gestapo occasionally respected Buback's civilian status and addressed him according to the old ways.

"Your order, Standartenführer," Buback responded.

"Did you give her my letter?"

The last officer was closing the door behind him; the two of them were left alone. His boss mostly seemed embarrassed.

"Of course. . . ."

Buback reached into his pocket and dug out the answer she had written that morning while he was shaving. He felt like the worst sort of liar.

And that too was her fault.

He handed over the envelope, resolving to end this awkward comedy.

"Permission to leave, sir."

"Wait a minute."

Meckerle ripped open the envelope and read the letter standing up. Buback's mind raced. What should he say if Meckerle asks about her? That he sees her from time to time? Where, when, and how? God, why hadn't they at least agreed on the details, if she was going to keep up the deception? The giant raised his eyes. Buback saw surprise.

"Did she let you read it?"

"No."

"That's just like her . . . damned like her. Have a seat."

Once again he brought over the bottle of cognac and the rounded glasses single-handedly, and poured them almost to the rim.

"Cheers!"

The colonel drank half his glass in one gulp and then bemusedly scratched his head some more at Buback, as if he could not quite place who he was. The detective drank cautiously, looking in vain for a hint of what was going through his boss's head. Meckerle gave a bitter laugh.

"Messengers like you used to be thrown to the wolves; thank Lady Luck that you're living in a civilized country."

A brave assertion, Buback thought; Germany hasn't done very well on that count. He wanted to see what would come next.

"She's given me the sack."

No . . . !

"She writes that she's cutting me loose, because my behavior is insulting. Even though I explained that some idiot wrote my wife about her, and that I'm looking for a solution."

Hmm . . . maybe the murderer could help . . . ?

"She says that naturally, under the circumstances, she'll find someone else."

Meckerle lightly swirled the remains of the viscous liquid in his goblet, stared at the letter, and melancholically nodded.

"And do you know what the strangest thing is?"

Here it comes, Buback thought. Why had she put him in such an impossible situation?

"The strangest thing," the giant answered himself, "is that I feel relieved. I do! I've always been lucky with women, but she was a colossal mistake, do you believe me?"

Buback did not respond, but no response was needed; Meckerle had to talk through this to get it off his chest.

"Before she chased me down—and she did the chasing, that cunning beast!—I noticed her in the troupe. She looked like a schoolgirl in a bunch of Brunhildes, but I sensed she'd be a passion bomb. Before she was firmly in the saddle—and yes, eventually she was—she'd heat me up white-hot, but wouldn't give it to me, the vixen; every German in Prague knew I was sleeping with her, only I wasn't. Till she got the apartment keys. And then it happened. . . ."

He waved his hands and fell into a reverie.

"The first time was sensational. Like drumfire!"

By now Buback's stomach was definitely hurting.

"But then it was over. A fish."

"Fish?" Buback repeated involuntarily.

"A Pisces. By sign and by nature—a spoiled kitten. In public, by my side, she'd make eyes at everyone and anyone until I . . . well, I was mad with jealousy. Then back in the apartment she was a wet rag. Each time I had to prove myself again, or so she said. She smoked exclusively Egyptians, drank champagne like it was going out of style, listened only to that crazy nigger music, which I'd get for ungodly sums from Switzerland, and wanted her feet massaged every evening. Yes, she turned me into a masseur. It was unbelievable the way she pushed me around. When she disliked something I did—and often she wouldn't even tell me what, I was supposed to guess—she'd turn into an icicle."

It was too much for Buback to accept.

"I know it's hard to believe," Meckerle continued. "Pretty soon I had to ask myself: Why do I keep her, especially in this city, where all I have to do is . . ."

He snapped his fingers loudly.

"But each time I wanted to slam the door behind me, she'd sense it a moment earlier and find a way to make me stay on. She's a truly fateful woman, Buback, a femme fatale. The glow that tempts you to love her is real, but then she expects the same in return. With me she finally realized that she would always be third: after my work and my wife. So she held me like a hostage until she could find the man who'd give her what she lacked. . . ."

The head of the Gestapo sighed. "That bitch! That goddamned bitch! And I can't even destroy her, that beautiful little bitch!"

He downed the rest of the cognac.

"Or you, Buback. . . ."

His gaze pierced the detective, sharp as an interrogation. As chills and hot flushes raced through him, Buback decided silence was still the wisest option. Meckerle raised the hand with the letter in it.

"That's right, she presents you as my replacement. Handpicked, with my own stamp of approval. Because she guessed—correctly—how furious I would have been if my men had reported you to me. Of course it makes my blood boil, but . . ."

He rose, towering over Buback, and angrily shred the paper into tiny pieces.

"Get the hell out of here! Go hunt that pervert with your Czechs, snoop around in their drawers, and stay out of my sight. Heil Hitler!"

M orava ran into Bartolomějská Street breathless, but in time to catch Beran before he sent off his message.

"Mr. Beran," he pleaded, "I know you want to cover for me, but please, hold off for a while. This is a demanding plan; it'll be hard for you to find time for it."

When he finished his brief explanation, he heard the words that made his heart soar.

"Good work, Morava."

A minute before two, Chief Inspector Buback arrived with today's interpreter; now they had a political quorum as well. They were all there, even the Vyšehrad team, and Jitka was taking notes.

"Bait!" Morava announced to the assembled men. "We'll throw it to him day in, day out, until he bites. And then we'll reel him in."

In his typical style, he laid it out for them, point by point.

Point A: Tomorrow, in a convenient free spot in the Vyšehrad cemetery, a false grave would be installed, where the technicians would place a marker with the name of a newly deceased man.

Point B: An apartment under the same name would be designated appropriately close to the cemetery.

Point C: Several female volunteers would be chosen from the ranks of the Prague police staff to play the role of a grieving widow who visits the cemetery twice daily.

Point D: During her visits, the apartment would be occupied by two men, armed with pistols.

Point E: The "widow on shift" would not lock the front door, and if someone rang or knocked, she would call from the kitchen that it was open.

Point F: As soon as the perpetrator entered the kitchen, he would be seized and disarmed by the hidden policemen.

Morava snapped his notebook shut.

"Of course, we will continue to review any reports that come in, but this trap should be flawless. There must be a compelling reason behind the killer's routine, since so far it has outweighed the risks he's taken. We have good reason to think he'll take the bait. If any of you have a lady colleague in mind, please bring her to me."

He turned to the German.

"Does the chief inspector have any objections or comments?"

When it was translated, Buback shook his head.

Morava then opened his notebook again and read out the roster of tasks.

"Any questions?" he asked in closing.

The technician in charge of the grave plaque spoke up.

"What about the name on the grave?"

"Whatever occurs to you."

"Nothing occurs to me," the man insisted.

"How about Jan Morava?"

He noticed Jitka's sudden start and tried to reassure her.

"Superstition says grave owners live the longest."

The technician had already written it down.

"Where will we find an apartment?" Šebesta wanted to know.

Morava's eyes once again met Jitka's, this time questioningly. It buoyed him to see her nod back immediately.

"Jitka Modrá rents a room in a house in Kavčí Hory that fits the requirements quite well. The owners are away from Prague; if they return, we'll show that it's in the public interest and possibly pay them."

The technician wrote down the address for the plaque on the door.

"Anything else?"

The team already looked like runners crouched at the starting line. Beran, however, spoke up for the first time in that half hour.

"Be sure to tell your lady colleagues the whole truth: We'll give them the best protection we can, but at certain points the murderer will be closer to them than any assistance we can give, and his behavior might unexpectedly change. Any women who volunteer in spite of this will immediately be elevated to a higher service grade, but they must be aware that they are voluntarily exposing themselves to a degree of risk. I'll want to speak with all of them personally at four as well."

These three sentences instantly deflated their hunters' euphoria. They dispersed in a pensive mood. Beran asked Buback to remain behind with Morava. He dismissed the interpreter and led the discussion in German.

"Herr Oberkriminalrat," he said to Buback, "I'd like to personally convey to you some information I'm sending to the police commissioner. The case of the widow killer will continue to fall under the jurisdiction of Assistant Detective Morava, but all his activities—including this most recent one—have been cleared with me, and I am therefore responsible for them."

"I will pass it on," the German said, and added unexpectedly, "along with the fact that I approve of the plan. In this phase I will continue to be at your disposal in my office here."

As he and Morava proceeded through the anteroom, where Jitka was alone at her desk again, he stopped and asked her, "How is your father doing?"

It was the first time Buback had spoken to her since their dinner together, and Jitka, surprised, stood up as if reciting in school.

"Danke. . . ."

"Please, sit down. Is everything all right?"

"Nothing happened to him. . . . Almost nothing," she added in her forthright way, "just a couple of bruises. . . ."

"I'm sorry about that."

"Oh," she replied quickly, as if approving the deed, "they weren't the first ones he's gotten. And at least he survived. We're all very grateful to you."

"Good," said Buback a bit absentmindedly, "very good. Well then, good luck. To you, your family, and your fiancé. Who is it, by the way?"

Morava could sense Jitka's unease at having deceived the German. Hesitantly she answered, "The assistant detective . . ."

When Buback still seemed puzzled, she pointed at Morava.

The German stared, flabbergasted, first at him, then at her and back at him. For the first time they could remember, he laughed out loud.

"Oh, no! Oh, no!"

He took her by the left hand and him by the right, and shook both their hands simultaneously. The warmth of his response seemed completely sincere.

"My heartiest congratulations! My heartiest congratulations!"

With that he let go and left them, still laughing. Morava and Jitka were equally dumbfounded.

What has happened to him? Morava wondered.

He knew there was no way to find out, so he gave Jitka a kiss and set off on his way. The rest of the day did not go nearly as well; later that afternoon in Beran's office a dejected Morava had little good news to report.

"At your suggestion, Mr. Beran, we gave briefings in all our departments, but not a single female employee volunteered."

"That's not surprising," said his superior, "but they're not the only women in Prague, after all, are they?"

"No," Morava sighed, "but where can we look? We need some sort of assurance. . . ."

"Relatives of the victims," Beran suggested. "The last one had a sister, maybe the other ones did as well. Or jailers; there's a few sharp girls among them."

"Actresses. . . ." The German surprised them again.

"But of course," Beran concurred. "Morava, put your men on it."

"I sent them home," Morava confessed, deflated. "They haven't had a good night's sleep in a week."

Before Beran could rebuke him, Jitka walked in through the open door.

"Tomorrow I'll go, Mr. Beran," she announced simply. "It's my house and Jan will certainly protect me best, don't you think?"

S he sat, wrapped again in a large white bath sheet, legs crossed beneath her in his only armchair, laughing her head off as he told her about his conversation with Meckerle.

"Don't you know *Hamlet*?"

"I remember it vaguely from school . . ."

"They send him to France with a letter requesting his execution."

"Is that what you wanted?"

"Come on, love! Big Mecky explained it himself, didn't he?"

"What?"

"He had to learn about you from me, and in your presence, no less. He's proud—as I'd expected—but he does have some sense. He'd been wondering what to do with me anyway."

"He tried to tell me something of the sort."

"You mean he confided in you?"

Buback attempted to reproduce in his own words Meckerle's description of her as a femme fatale and his regret that he couldn't destroy either of them.

"I'm inclined to believe it," she remarked. "He'd never had it like that before, so he should be grateful."

She said it quite matter-of-factly, as if they were talking about the weather, and Buback once again felt how deeply it pained him.

"Like what?" he managed nonetheless to ask.

"Come on, you saw his wife. If you want to know a man, look at his spouse. He tried to impress me by bragging about his mistresses, but I saw one of them and that confirmed it: yet another peasant. I taught him what royal lovemaking is."

Buback felt worse and worse but still could not stop this new confession. He wanted finally to understand completely whom she chose and how, so he could find the strength to end their relationship.

"I don't understand. He told me you were uncommunicative and chilly. Like a fish."

"You're joking. Were you that open with each other? That should have pleased you, shouldn't it? That you know a different me?"

"I was more surprised than anything. And now you tell me that he—"

"What don't you understand? After all, I admitted, he did impress me a bit. So I gave him the opportunity to find himself through me. Don't let his appearance fool you; he's not much of a lover. I taught him that in bed, rank, weight, age, and responsibility don't matter. With me—and only with me—he learned that there's more to love-making than a bit of grunting and thrusting. I stimulated his imagination, because I didn't fuss over him. Instead, I made him win my favor on his own."

Buback was so visibly upset that she suddenly turned petulant.

"What's wrong? Aren't you pleased I've decided to sleep only with you?"

"You know I am!"

She let the bath sheet drop past her chest and hips.

"So then, love, what are you waiting for?"

Two hours later, she was resting again in utter self-surrender, her head on his "wing," as she called his shoulder, her right leg beneath his knees and her left on his belly. In this tangle of limbs, she began to describe how she and Meckerle had met. She'd recuperated a bit in Berlin after that horrible retreat through Prussia . . . but she didn't want to and wasn't going to talk about that. Through connections she'd gotten herself assigned to peaceful Prague. After her first appearance in the German Theater's troupe, two Viennese petty officers were waiting for her afterward by the back door, offering her an evening out. She had already learned from her colleagues who the master of Prague was. They would have to ask Colonel Meckerle, she told the two of them with a frosty smile and they disappeared into the darkness.

She used the same answer on subsequent days to more and more new suitors. Theater fans followed the troupe's membership closely, and apparently she was unmissable. As interest rose so did ranks; soon she was rebuffing generals' aides-de-camp with the same line. As she had anticipated, she said cheerfully to Buback, a month later Meckerle personally appeared in the auditorium. During the intermission, she— and not the soloists of the *Magic Flute*—was invited secretly to his box so he could ask her if it was true she had linked herself to him.

She asked for his pardon; having lived through war and personal hell in the East, she wanted to stay clear of these heartless meddlers, she said. The imperial protector and the state secretary did not look like the type to have mistresses, so she had decided unilaterally to put herself under the protection of the third most powerful man in the Protectorate. That swelled his head a bit, of course, and not only his head, she laughed gruffly. When she guiltily promised him that she'd stop immediately, he relented and gave her permission to continue.

Then she cut off the confidences until, as she said, he was in rut. On principle, she refused to meet with him in his apartment or a hotel, because she knew full well that he absolutely could not visit her in the German artists' dormitory. Anyway, she hated the place, because living there marked her as just another a dime-a-dozen troupe member. It was true, though, she admitted to Buback; she was a dancer, had never studied singing, and still did not know how to read music. She had been accepted into the first troupe for Martin's sake, so she could accompany him. Only later did it become clear that she had more talent than many of the trained singers.

She had correctly calculated, she continued during her next cigarette—which she managed to find, settle in its holder, light, and tap on the rim of an empty glass without changing position—that here in Prague, only Meckerle could raise her from the abyss to the heights she'd scaled five years earlier with Martin in Berlin. Once again she would be admired and envied for catching the biggest fish in the pond (then, a star of the stage; now, a warlord).

Meckerle, she said, returning immediately to the story, procured a suitable apartment for her as she had expected. To thank him, she presented him there with a feast for the senses. Not a real one, of course, but a perfect replica, she assured Buback, as if this would comfort him. She'd done it so that, for once in his life, he'd have some inkling of what it could be like. After that he would have to get there on his own. Did Buback understand?

She finished her cigarette, wound her slender hands about his head, and kissed him passionately again. He was happy to hold her, but her merciless tale had been depressingly similar to Meckerle's. For the first time since he had known her—for the first time in his life, really—he felt he was about to explode. She really was a better sort of whore! But then for God's sake, why had she chosen him?

He knew that if he asked, she would be packed and gone in five minutes, never to return, and the emptiness that would remain after her flooded over him almost physically.

Only a bullet could fill that gap.

He swallowed his shout so forcibly that his Adam's apple must have moved. Instead, he asked a question.

"So why risk his anger now?"

"First of all, there won't be any," she announced convincingly. "You should have realized that today. He knows he got what he deserved. Most likely he's hoping that he'll win me back. And second? Figure it out for yourself, Buback; you have a splendid imagination in bed, but in other areas it's sadly lacking. Use the opportunity while it lasts."

An hour later she was again lying blessedly in his arms. She still could not sleep and would not let him drift off either.

"Now it's your turn to talk," she ordered him, "but not about women. I don't want to hear that you've ever had anyone else."

"But you—" he finally objected.

"I want you to know me as I am," she interrupted.

"So then why do you refuse to know me?"

"Why, why, why! Why don't you tell me what you do? As a child I thought policemen protected the world. So what do you protect now that the world's coming to an end?"

His work was the one thing that had always upset Hilde. She was constantly afraid for him, and they had tacitly agreed he would not speak about it to her. Now he tried, and surprised himself: His description of the case of the widow killer was brief and dramatic. Grete even sat up in excitement, hugged her knees with her elbows, and propped her childlike breasts on them (for a week now she had insisted that with his help they were finally starting to grow). She was listening so intently that she even forgot to light another cigarette.

When he finished the most recent episode, in which Beran's secretary insisted on serving as the decoy, Grete asked, "Is she your lotus flower?"

"Please don't get angry again," he pleaded panicking.

"I'm not angry. It's an act of womanly solidarity. And I'm surprised you didn't offer me the chance."

"Where did that come from?"

"She's helping her fiancé; why can't I help you, love? I'll never make a good wife, let alone a good widow, but surely I can play one as well as your little goddess, don't you think? But you'll have to let me go to sleep earlier. Not tonight, though; not tonight. . . . Remember how that first morning you asked me what had happened? Well, here's what it was: Your sex touched my soul."

Morava was getting to know a new Jitka. Where had that touching shyness gone that made him long to protect her unto death? Now he could only see it in her as she slept. It was as if incipient motherhood had brought out features rooted deep in her bloodline, which had survived centuries of catastrophes wreaked by mankind and nature in that wide-open land.

He often felt that despite his enthusiastic embrace of city life, he was still a part of that natural landscape, even though he had only spent his childhood there. At certain points, especially crises, he found an inner strength that was not his own. Then he would always remember the strange exhilaration he had felt at his grandfather's and father's deathbeds. Even today he did not dare to express it—it seemed too odd—but he believed that at the time some immortal part of their being had passed over to him.

The family smithy, as renovations revealed, had burned down at least twice during the Swedish or Turkish wars. Even the anvil was no more than fifty years old. No one knew where the previous ones had gone, along with the bones of all the local blacksmiths, since only the last three Moravas rested in the town cemetery. Once, while digging, they found a horseshoe, which might have hung over the entrance at some point. It appeared to bear the date 1621 (a tragic year for the Bohemian and Moravian nations), thus proving the existence of at least thirteen generations of blacksmiths on that spot.

The closely written leaves of Jitka's family Bible suggested that they had lived a few steeples away for at least as long. In her family, the women held sway, since according to records the imperial and royal press-gangs had taken most of their men and never returned them.

What Morava now saw in Jitka seemed to be the reincarnation of her female ancestors. It was as if his future wife had in the course of several weeks taken on the combined strength of all of them.

When she overheard the men's conversation in Beran's office and stepped in to offer herself as human bait, Morava had counted on the superintendent's refusal. Beran did try to dissuade her, but stopped short of forbidding her once he had heard her out.

"Gentlemen," she addressed them in German, and Morava could not shake the feeling that she was playing for Buback's support, "you knew the risks, and yet you decided to find a woman who would come forward in the interest of the cause. I'd hate to think you'd be less concerned for another woman than you would for me. Therefore I have to assume you'll give your consent."

You're expecting a child, he thought, but did not dare say it aloud. Buback's presence still discomforted him, even after his unexpectedly warm congratulations. As if in response, Jitka said, "It's not as if I want to make a career of this; once you find someone else, I'll stop, or we can alternate. You can count on me tomorrow, though, so start making preparations."

Beran shrugged, Buback was silent, and Morava had to give in. He set to work even more intently on the details of his plan. It had to run at least twice daily, and at any time and place the unknown butcher might take the bait. That night he tested the most dangerous scene in the kitchen with Jitka, confirming for himself what she had known from the start: This trap could not fail.

As soon as his people gathered at the cemetery the next day, he ran a test. Jitka stood over the false burial site in the light April rain, dressed in a rubber raincoat; they were still hunting for black clothes and a mackintosh for her. The technicians and the sexton had placed the grave on one of the side paths, just like the ones where the murderer had snared his victims. The baby of the group, Jetel, played the killer; he followed her at a distance without even noticing that Šebesta kept him constantly in view from a safe remove. The slow walk home took Jitka nearly fifteen minutes. Once there, she opened the door with two pronounced turns of the key, emphasizing her solitude to the stalker.

When Jetel rang, he heard her answer that the door was open. Entering the unfamiliar hallway, he looked around. To his left he saw stairs leading up, and to the right three doors, the farthest a crack open.

"Where are you?" he now called out, as most people would have done in that situation.

"I'm in the kitchen," Jitka responded. "Come on back!"

He took about a dozen steps and from the foot of the staircase glanced into the kitchen. Jitka stood at a large dining table, her back to him; she was pouring milk at the stove.

"One moment," she said. "It's almost ready for you, Mr. Roubal."

Jetel drew his ruler, which they had armed him with instead of a knife, looked through the door again, and quickly crossed the threshold. Instantly he found himself in a lock from behind that immobilized him.

"Good work, Jitka; good work, gentlemen," Beran said a moment later, satisfied.

Pinning Jetel were Morava and Matlák, the former freestyle wrestling champion of the St. Matthew's Day carnival. Buback followed a step behind. The four of them had been packed into the dark alcove under the steps, and Jetel had not even noticed them. Less than a minute later, Šebesta, their last piece of insurance, barged in.

They thanked the somewhat shaken young man and evaluated the trial run. It had been a success. Even Morava was relieved to see that everything ran like clockwork and his dear decoy was in practically no danger. Still, he tried once more to dissuade her from her decision. As the others discussed the incident, he reminded her in lowered tones, "You're not feeling well, after all . . ."

As if she had expected this objection, she answered just as quietly, "Both our mothers were right; I felt fine this morning when I got up. Maybe I needed this mission to stop me from being so preoccupied with myself. Believe me, it'll be good for the little one as well."

As had happened several times recently, the German then surprised them with an offer.

"The Reich's criminal police will not be mere observers in this task. Miss Modrá will share the role, on my authority, with Marleen Baumann, a member of the traveling German Theater of Prague who is willing to take part every second or third day."

He then disappeared in his official car to return in half an hour with a creature everyone at first took for a young girl. However, a second close look told them otherwise. Marleen Baumann's type always baffled Morava—he was still a country boy when it came to the fair sex—but he was grateful to her for bearing part of Jitka's cross, and she flew through the test just as successfully. The few necessary Czech phrases she committed swiftly to memory, pronouncing them with an accent, but comprehensibly.

When Buback took her back, the remaining Czechs convened around the table for a last consultation.

"Children," the superintendant began, once he had asked for a cup of the nettle tea Jitka had laid in last summer, "there are five—including the Brno woman possibly six—dead women and one young man, who was an accidental bystander. Our experience from the prewar years gives us hope that the compulsions driving this monster will work the same way next time. But since he has left so few traces behind so far, you must be on your guard constantly. We are dealing with an exceptional criminal intelligence. Never underestimate him, not even for a moment, or you will cause a tragedy, and this time, we will be the victims. The ladies helping us aren't the only ones in danger; anyone the murderer thinks is in his way is at risk. He will kill him without hesitation, just as he killed that boy."

For now, they left Jitka at home and found a rental shop which could round out her widow's wardrobe. Morava returned with Beran to Number Four and quickly ran through all the investigations. Every suspect had a reliable alibi for most of the dates in question. He pulled some newly arrived reports for further investigation and came across a second note from the Klášterec priest requesting that they contact him about a stolen and returned (so what's the problem then?) picture of a saint with the exceedingly odd name of Reparata.

He had the novice Jetel walk the letter down to the appropriate department, and on a whim stopped in at Buback's office. When the German unlocked the door for him—these days he always kept it locked—Morava requested a short consultation and was amicably let in.

He wanted to thank Herr Oberkriminalrat for the moral and material support he had given the whole group—and especially him—in the last few days. Would it be possible to expand their cooperation? Morava saw, for example, that there was no interpreter present; had they failed to honor the agreement? Should he go over today's reports personally with Mr. Buback?

No, Buback countered quickly, the translator was perfectly adequate. As Morava could see—the German pointed to the carefully stacked sheaf on the desk—he had finished with this lot and unfortunately had come to the same conclusion: The murderer had managed to steer clear of their net. It seemed, he mused (and Morava silently agreed with him), that it was precisely his inconspicuousness that made the widow killer a continuing danger: He was a dime-a-dozen type trying to make himself stand out. A baited trap did seem the most effective of ineffective methods.

Morava asked him to convey his thanks to Mrs. Baumann. Given the reaction of the female workers in the police department, he thought it was brave of her to volunteer. Of course, his gratitude had a purely personal motive as well, he admitted, since she was sharing the risk with his fiancée.

"Believe me, I know what you mean," Buback said, closing the conversation. "After all, Mrs. Baumann is my close friend."

"I just don't know what to think about him anymore," Morava reported to Jitka that evening, shaking his head. "I do believe Beran that Buback has other reasons for being in our department; a month ago I even feared him at times, but I don't think his sincerity is entirely false. Any thoughts?"

"You said it yourself."

"What?"

"A month ago he was alone; now he isn't."

"The phrase 'close friend' doesn't have to mean . . ."

"I saw the way she looked at him this morning."

"How was that?"

"Like this."

Jitka's adoring gaze warmed him, but only briefly.

"Meanwhile he looked here and there, just the way you do when other people are around."

"Wait a minute, what are you trying—"

"Come on, Jan! Men are naturally ashamed to show their feelings in public. In any case, this Marleen has decided he's hers. And in his loneliness, he's taken a step in her direction, whether he knows it or not."

All the while she gazed at him with her big brown eyes until he could no longer stand it and went around the kitchen table to kiss her. Then he asked her a favor: "For God's sake, take off those widow's garments. I'll be crazy with fear every time anyway. If it works out, I'll come guard you personally along with Matlák. But be awfully careful, my darling!"

"Don't worry. You'll protect me, and God will protect both of us; what could possibly happen?"

Kroloff's behavior was merely the most graphic example of Buback's fall from grace in the department. The skeletal figure had clearly noticed that at a certain point—after his confrontation with Buback, in fact—the colonel stopped calling personally and began sending all his messages through Kroloff.

Now Kroloff relayed another one: Buback was to report immediately to the head of the SS special units. The tone in his voice betrayed his glee at his superior's evident humiliation. The detective could see that Kroloff had never truly reconciled himself to the way he had been shunted aside since Buback's arrival; Buback sensed a rancor in him that at the first opportunity would erupt into revenge.

He forced himself to react casually, accepting the order and Kroloff's behavior with apparent indifference. The mental discipline he had learned as an interrogator came as naturally to him as the multiplication tables. He pulled on his overcoat and directed Kroloff with a short glance to open the door for him as always. Then he turned around.

"Kroloff?"

"Yes . . . ?"

"Tell the colonel I said thanks for the fish."

He watched the skeleton's jaw drop, and hid his grin. Would Kroloff convey the message? And what about Meckerle? Would he swallow it, or explode? Grete insisted that despite all his bad qualities, the giant did feel a need to preserve his masculine honor. However, these were purely personal problems of the chief's own making; there was nothing honorable about disgracing Buback publicly. It was high time the colonel realized who he was dealing with. Buback was, after all, a specialist; technically, he answered not to Prague but to Berlin.

His defiance grew stronger when the SS officer led him into the room on the second floor of the former Czech law faculty. Judging by the spaciousness and mahogany paneling, it had been the office of at least a university rector. Instead of standing up or motioning him to sit down, the pockmarked SS major snapped out his right hand in a greeting.

"Heil Hitler! Your orders were to determine and report locations from which the Prague police might direct a rebellion against the great German Reich. Is this correct?"

Buback knew the type. He would have to put a stop to this arrogance straightaway or the man would wipe the floor with him. After all, Buback's borrowed rank made them equals. He put his hand on the nearest chair.

"May I?" he asked as he pulled it up to the table. Without waiting for a response, he sat down face-to-face with the major.

The scarred face twitched, but that was all.

"You are correct," Buback affirmed, "and my report, as I see, is in front of you."

The SS man knew he had met his master; he changed his tone.

"We have worked out a plan of action that will let us occupy communications hubs and potential foci of resistance within two hours of an alert. You are to give me crucial information on when we should put it into effect. Tomorrow, today, yesterday even?"

Now he whinnied, displaying a mouth tiled with gold.

"I warned the colonel," Buback said, "that shutting down the city radio station prematurely will prevent us from warning the German population of air raids and passing on other information important for their survival."

"We don't intend to destroy the machinery," his opponent objected, "just get the Czech workers out. Our men can broadcast in German."

"And do you have twenty free radio technicians?"

"If we occupy the central office, one person can do it, right? Or two, to allow for bathroom breaks."

"The Czechs can broadcast from any of the nineteen local stations."

"We'll lock and guard all of them."

"But we should be using them to direct emergency operations; otherwise they'll be totally crippled."

"Fine, we'll take forty technicians from some regiment or other."

"And forty translators, so they can figure out what's going on?"

The SS man grappled with this.

"You're saying we should let them stab us in the back?"

"An uprising doesn't come out of nowhere, Major—you know, by the way, that we have the same rank!—an uprising spreads, and it will take at least a couple of hours before things get out of hand. This country is thoroughly occupied and we have a powerful presence in Prague, both in the police and with the army. We couldn't possibly miss the first signals. If you're really capable of striking within two hours, we should wait. Otherwise we might bring an avalanche down on ourselves for no good reason. Will you take responsibility for this decision?"

Scarface was on the defensive again.

"Will you take responsibility for seeing we're informed in time?"

"Yes."

Buback felt confident of this; yesterday he could feel how much closer Grete's offer had brought him to the Czech policemen. And he knew them well enough to spot any suspicious behavior.

The commander of the special units asked him a couple of routine questions about the Prague police's weaponry. Assured it was a risible quantity of closely controlled pistols and rifles that were not worth the price of a politically damaging raid, he released Buback, even shaking his hand.

176

Buback then skipped lunch and headed straight back to Bartolomějská Street to find out for himself—and for Grete—how the first
hunt had gone. Morava excitedly told him how he had hidden under
the staircase for the first time. He described the tension that seized
him when he heard the keys and steps, caught sight of Jitka's black
boots over the kitchen threshold and then the endless seconds where
the pounding of his heart drowned everything else out. How much
worse it must be for her, the young detective sighed.

To his horror, he recounted, the door handle clicked a second time.
He and Matlák instinctually seized each others' hands in a painful grip,
each hoping to prevent the other from giving the game away prematurely. The shuffling footsteps approached, and he fought the temptation to step straight out, so powerful was his fear of missing his
chance.

"Hello," the visitor then called out, "it's me, Šebesta. Not a single
man at the graveyard or on the way here."

Jitka decided to set out right away for a second round and then
again that afternoon.

"She's right," Grete said that evening. "In for a penny, in for a
pound. I'm going at least twice tomorrow; we don't leave for the
Beneschau SS garrison until four."

Before heading home to find her, Buback had had the newly arrived
reports translated for him. Of course, he could read them far faster
than the day's interpreter could stammer through them, but he had a
game to play and found that in any case he paid closer attention that
way. The repeated message from the Klášterec priest caught his eye as
well. Had it been dealt with, he asked; yes, he heard, it had been passed
back to their colleagues in Burglary and Robbery.

Sitting in the small wicker armchair by the bathtub, he told Grete
about his day's experiences. He realized with a shock that he was betraying official and military secrets with conveyer-belt speed to a
woman he had known less than a month. Her daily ritual mesmerized
him: Each evening, she rinsed off her exhaustion by holding the
showerhead motionless with both hands just over her head, and the
water ran down her body like a fountain pouring over a statue. He
never ceased to wonder at the unbelievable femininity of her slender

body, and later at the inexhaustible energy she could unleash as they made love.

She washed him clean of the stains the day left behind; she freed him from the horrible war and his work without enslaving him to new needs, the way he had feared at first. How can I fall for her so completely, and still feel so free? He did not understand, but soon he stopped thinking, period, and enthusiastically lost himself in her over and over, until it was the only thing that gave his life meaning.

Hunger regularly hit her after midnight, and he could not open the cans of military rations fast enough; mornings he would make her cocoa at the signal of her fluttering eyelids or, when he could not wait for her, he left it in a thermos. Gradually he took on other functions in her life, things he had never done when married: he kept her diary, picked up their grocery rations, and took care of the laundry. His reward was the childish pleasure of her whimpers as she slowly roused herself in the mornings.

"You're the best, Buback, because you never wake me or pressure me . . ."

She made up for their lovemaking hours with a sleep that was strenuous in its intensity, while he thanked his age and military training for keeping him alert during the day. Today, however, after her midnight snack, she did not take him into her arms again.

"Let's be good tonight," she decided. "Tomorrow I want to be a widow that shark will sense from halfway across Prague!"

When a Werkschutzer ordered him to report immediately to the building director, he was rattled. Was it a TRAP? Would THEY be waiting for him? The fat man with a pistol under his paunch, however, showed no inclination to accompany him upstairs, and as he went up the service staircase his pulse surprisingly slowed. He was all the more devastated when Marek—as always, without even a greeting or an introduction—thrust a new task at him.

"The Luftschutz has decided to enlarge our shelter, in case there are more air raids on Plzeň. See that it's taken care of."

"Who's it for? We're not even open; there's room for all the staff as is."

The theater had been closed for two years now. The actors were weaving bast wrappings for grenades, the stagehands had been conscripted in the Totaleinsatz mobilization and only a half dozen rejects and cripples were left to ensure that the building did not leak, the pipes did not burst, and the sets and costumes were not eaten by moths before better times came. He was one of those who stayed, partly thanks to his old head wound, but also because he was skilled and extraordinarily intelligent for an ordinary laborer.

"They say there may be fighting in Plzeň, so we need a public shelter for three hundred people. Get a team together and clear it out."

He could only think of one thing.

Where will I put my souls?

"Can we leave at least a few lumps of ice down there? Once it gets warmer the beer'll be swill."

For a year now the theater canteen had been open to the public, partially offsetting the lack of ticket receipts. Pensioners especially were lured by the chance of getting some horsemeat stew alongside their still passable pilsner without needing to dig into their meager ration coupons. Marek dismissed the suggestion with a wave of his hand.

"I've tried that already, of course. They just said that starting Monday they'll take ten thousand for each day we delay. And what's more, they could imprison me for sabotage. So beer or no beer, take it out to the canal-side courtyard."

Four days left until Monday. And he had no time tomorrow. To-morrow makes a week! An idea came to him in his hour of need.

"Easy as one, two, three! Before then I'll try to visit a couple of pubs, see if someone'll buy it from us. If not, we'll do the job Sunday."

By then there'll be a sixth one! And he'd have time to think where to put them. He willed Marek to nod.

"Fine, try it. But on Monday the cellar'd better be empty and clean as a whistle—it's up to you, you hear?"

Without even a dismissal his boss bent back over his files.

Cheapskate, he thought on his way out. If only you knew! Still, he was grateful the man had unknowingly given him the opportunity to disappear the whole next day. He'd forget about buyers for the ice, take two slabs back to his own cellar, and secure his treasures for at least another two months.

He realized that the sixth one was still beating in some sinner's breast, and broke out in an excited sweat at the thought:

THIS TIME TOMORROW IT WILL BE MINE!

What should he go as? He remembered the Werkschutzer.

But wasn't it time to change cemeteries? Through the veil of years he saw HER showing him the graves of their national heroes. Someday you'll lie here, my little Tony, respected by our whole nation. . . . Well, maybe ONE MORE TIME!

Slowly but surely Morava calmed down. Jitka had three shifts behind her already, as they'd had to note in their record book, during which she made the trip from Vyšehrad to Kavčí Hory seven times. Buback's girlfriend had alternated with her; she'd played the bait (as she called it) four times all told.

Neither the women nor their guards had noticed even the slightest sign of interest. The men appearing at the cemetery were for the most part older widowers; many they recognized after a couple of days as regular visitors of their wives' graves.

One day, a hale and hearty forty-year-old newcomer caused a commotion. He was so evidently interested in Jitka that all three watchers simultaneously latched onto him as he traipsed behind the girl at a dangerously short remove. Šebesta, who was in charge in an emergency, finally decided there was no danger of attack just yet if the perpetrator was after his usual goal.

The man, who politely addressed Jitka after a short while, turned out to be a stonemason from Kolín near Prague who was looking for customers. He had noticed, he explained, that her grave lacked a fitting stone; he had a wide assortment at home and would give her a good price. He showed no interest in accompanying her back, but just to be sure they brought him in and, with Morava's aid, presented the horrified man to the caretaker on the embankment. The old man was surprisingly sure that he had never seen the stonemason, and later the suspect produced airtight alibis for all the dates in question.

Five unsuccessful days brought nonetheless one encouraging result: The five policemen—three on the street and two in the house—calmed down and learned to work together.

"If he makes a move, we've got him," Morava announced cautiously to Beran, who had requested a report each time "the hook was cast," as he said.

"Just so you don't get too comfortable," he said to Morava, explaining his unwearying interest in the operation. "I have to keep reminding you that he'll appear right when your attention wanders. And Morava: I assume you're following the rules just as strictly when the German woman's on shift."

He saw the red seep into the adjunct's face, and immediately soothed him.

"Forgive me; that was out of place. At least you see that even old age is no guarantee against stupidity. I was thinking about her disadvantage, not knowing Czech."

Of course, Morava took the warning seriously enough to visit Buback again about Marleen Baumann.

"Thank you for your consideration," the German said. "Grete—that's her real name, by the way—is aware of the problem. In an emergency she'll rely on voice intonation to figure out what's happening. She thinks she's quick enough to manage it."

"Please tell her that I admire her. We'd like—my fiancée and I—to invite her—and you too, of course—to dinner sometime. . . ."

What am I saying, he wondered belatedly.

Buback could not conceal his surprise.

"Aren't Germans risky guests for you these days?"

"Well yes, that's true . . . ," Buback had said exactly what Morava was thinking, but the Czech's resolve did not fail him. "Except since they're both putting their lives on the line, they should get to know each other a bit. And we're part of it as well. . . ."

"I'll pass it on," Buback said after a short pause. "In any case, thank you again. By the way, she's quite fond of your fiancée . . . as am I. . . ."

Then his eyes slid quickly to his watch.

"Will you excuse me? I still have some work to do. Grete is on duty at the cemetery tomorrow and Sunday; would some time after that suit you?"

"I'll pass it on," Morava repeated, for a change.

They parted with a hearty handshake. What had caused this shift, he wondered on his way back to the office. The two women, he realized; mine and his. Strange, very strange. Can ordinary human sympathy really scale these moats and barriers?

With this thought fresh in his mind he went to see Jitka. Beran was at another senseless meeting with Rajner and had sent her home, saying she had done her share. Jitka, however, refused to see her "two spring strolls" as a full day's work.

"I wouldn't be doing myself any favors, anyway," she explained to the superintendent. "You'd make such a mess of the paperwork that I'd have to come in Sundays to sort things out."

When she heard Morava's embarrassed confession how in her name he invited Buback and Grete to her house, she was quick to respond.

"They're the enemy, no doubt about that. Their nation has caused mankind so much suffering that they have to accept part of the blame. But in a couple of months they'll be defeated, and there'll still be fifty million of them. And what then? My papa once tried to imagine how he'd behave if he met a German on the street after the war. 'Out of my way, German,' he wanted to say; 'sidewalks are for human beings.' I don't believe he's changed, even after what just happened to him. Now, I don't know about Buback—by the way, he's started to behave quite decently—but his Grete doesn't seem to have anything in common with the Nazis other than their German ancestry."

"Except people"—he could not help saying it—"might say we're collaborators."

"Yes." She nodded seriously. "And after all, it's possible they both have other motives, like *he* said." She pointed toward Beran's office. "But what if they're just people who have finally come to their senses? What if they're seriously trying to atone for their sins? Should we reject them just because we're afraid of being slandered or mistakenly fingered? We'll just watch what we say."

From the hallway Superintendent Hlavatý stepped in. A couple of years earlier he had been one of Morava's first instructors. His department was theft, and he was the bane of Prague's pickpockets.

"Hello, Jitka; hello, Morava," he addressed them both before turning to the detective. "Why do you keep shoving that stolen saint at me? The picture was returned a long time ago and criminal charges retracted."

"Sorry about that," Morava said guiltily. "I didn't know what to do with it, and the priest had written twice already. . . ."

"He didn't get your announcement, by any chance? I mean the description of that deviant?"

"We did send it to priests." Jitka now turned to Morava as well.

He still could not see the point.

"But what does it have in common with—"

"I had no idea"—Hlavatý winked at him, as if preparing him for an excellent joke—"so I had a word with my experts. The Romans supposedly disemboweled Saint Reparata alive, and cut off her head and breasts. Her heart, however, escaped in the shape of a white dove."

"Oh my God . . . ," Morava breathed. "Oh my God!"

Before leaving for home with Jitka, he first called the emergency number Buback had given him. He left a message for the German that a fresh trail had been found, and Assistant Detective Morava would be waiting the next morning to hear when and where to pick him up.

In the house at Kavčí Hory he heated pots of water for Jitka's bath. When he had poured the fifth and last one into the battered enamel tub, he retired to the kitchen while Jitka undressed and plunged in; with the exception of the moment when she had asked to bear his child, she was still too shy to be naked around him.

Afterward he brought in the kitchen stool and sat down, half turned away from her. They decided to put off the wedding, gossip or no gossip, until this hunt—and maybe even the war itself—was over, and then they dreamed together in a confidential half-whisper of the things that awaited them in ten, twenty, and many more years. For a short while neither the monstrous murderer nor the fiery steam-roller of war that had separated them from their loved ones (may the Lord protect them) could threaten them.

They prayed once more together, aloud, for themselves, their family, and their child who was there with them. In their attic bed their conversation gradually slackened and grew quieter, until, overcome by fatigue and hopes, they fell asleep in each others' arms almost simultaneously, he with his chin in her hair, she as if nursing, her mouth at his breast.

A hillock with a church, rectory, and cemetery hid the market town of Klášterec from their view, bulging out of the north Bohemian plain as if it had been artistically inserted there to soften the dramatic backdrop of extinct volcano cones. The parish priest and his cook, an older woman, seemed to step right from the pages of a color calendar, from their rounded bellies to their rosy cheeks. He was close to sixty and spoke passable German; Morava did not have to translate.

The two policemen wanted to see the picture first. The priest unlocked the church with a large key, drawing it forth from his cassock, where it hung around his neck. God's tabernacle in Klášterec was not especially beautiful or luxurious and spoke of a land neither wealthy nor pious. The only adornments on the walls were the Stations of the Cross, garishly cheap and vulgar in execution. Seeing their searching glances, the priest explained that they would find Saint Reparata in the sacristy.

"It's the only valuable item we have, but it hung there even before it was temporarily lost. Right after the death of the baron who bequeathed it to us, some of the parents requested we hang it where their children wouldn't see it."

They understood as soon as they saw the picture. The baroque painter had rendered in oil with shocking accuracy what Superintendent Beran had scrupled to show the public at large. In front of them was essentially the same altar of death the widow killer left at the scene of the crime, albeit with a classical backdrop. The tortured saint had both breasts cut off and her intestines were being wound on a windlass. The artist had added to this a snow-white dove flying from the bloody wound below the severed head.

Morava's eyes met Buback's in mute awe. The explanation was here in front of them. They would need the priest, however, to interpret it for them.

"Father," Morava began, once the vicar had poured them some quite decent coffee back at the rectory and it was clear the German was letting him take the initiative, "I apologize for not understanding your message right away. I'm not a Catholic, and the point of it escaped me. It's highly probable that the man who has so far tortured six women to death was inspired by this work. You wrote us that it was lost and then returned; please tell us more about this."

The old man had seemed quite eager when he first saw them, but now he seemed equally hesitant. His hands were folded; the balls of his fingers pressed against his knuckles until his nails and skin turned white.

"The theft occurred before the war . . . if you can call it a theft. When the man in question returned the picture personally, he asked me to believe he'd only borrowed it."

"Which man in question?" Morava asked almost casually.

The priest did not fall for the snare.

"If you'd permit me, I'd like to describe the whole episode for you first. . . ."

Morava nodded, even though it required superhuman self-restraint to put off the moment when they would learn the man's name.

"I knew him because—" The priest once again halted and looked for the right words. "Well, let's just say I knew him well. He was a brave and pious man who had one single but fundamental problem: He could never escape the clutches of his domineering mother. His father—her partner—left her before he was born. What hurt her most of all was that he took up with a much older widow."

Yes! Morava was already sure: It's our man! He glanced fleetingly at the German, but Buback still wore the impersonal mask of disinterested officialdom.

"I'm not an expert on women's minds"—the priest opened his childishly chubby hands apologetically—"but from experience I know that women like that make their child—especially if it's a man—the single focus of their lives, their so-called alpha and omega. He's supposed to restore her trampled honor, become a sort of avenging knight for her."

Very accurate, Morava thought admiringly; it fits like a glove. If only he'd tell us already who it is!

"The son's attempt to break free began successfully. He enlisted in the new Czechoslovak Army; he had a promising career ahead of him. However, he suffered a severe concussion on the Hungarian border after a grenade explosion. He was discharged and remained dependent on his mother until almost forty. Then, for the first time, he met a girl when he was out of town on his own. It was a passing acquaintance on a train; no normal man would have attached any significance to it, but he was so inexperienced that he did exactly that. She too was a recent widow, still in black, and unfortunately she gave him her address."

"Was she from Brno?" Morava blurted out.

"Yes," the cleric said, stunned. "How did you know?"

"Please continue."

"He finally confessed his love-at-first-sight to his mother, who was enraged at the thought of losing him to a widow. She tried to make him see the vileness of it—creatures still in mourning who stole honest women's husbands and sons. She reminded him about his father, whose lover abandoned him soon after, driving him to suicide. She wished the fate of Reparata on those widows. For the first time, though, he found the courage to stand up to her and leave. Unfortunately it was for a love he had dreamed up out of thin air."

"She wasn't alone," Morava guessed.

"Unfortunately, on that evening she was. And when a man she didn't even recognize asked for her hand at the front door, she mocked him. . . ."

The priest flushed and fell silent. He seemed to be fighting himself as to whether or not to continue. This time Buback spoke.

"Did he confess to you that he'd killed her as well?"

"Yes . . . ," the priest whispered in a rasp, "he did . . . didn't he. . . ."

"And when did he—"

"Two years later. Our country was already occupied—" He halted and glanced fearfully at Buback. "I mean taken under the Reich's protection. . . ."

The German smiled understandingly.

"He appeared out of the blue as a voice in the confessional. 'Father,'

I heard, without even recognizing him, 'I've leaned your picture against the door to the sacristy.' Then he told me this story in detail. . . ." Sweat broke out on the cleric's forehead. "An awful story—that he had punished her, for his mother's sake as well, just as the executioners punished that poor martyr. . . . I didn't know what to say, much less what to do. . . ."

It was as if he were lost in his memories; both detectives ceased to exist for him. They all sat motionless for several long seconds before Buback sensibly asked, "And finally you . . . ?"

"The confessional was stifling; I ran out and over to him. . . ."

"To whom?" Morava tried.

The narrator was present in space, but not in time.

"I locked the church and dragged him and the package into the sacristy. He looked the same as always: vigorous, keen. His problem wasn't at all obvious, except for a certain shyness toward women; I was probably the only one who knew about it, from confession. . . ."

He halted, as if he'd said something inappropriate, and was once again back with them.

"He said he didn't tell his mother, of course, but when she was hit by a car and died, she must have found out up there, because she praised him and urged him to continue his work of purification. And he told me all of this as if it were a perfectly everyday occurrence. Yes, I thought just what you're thinking now: the grenade wound. I begged him to see a doctor. He shouted and got so angry that it frightened me. As a priest, he said, I should believe in life after death, and anyway, he'd come to confess, not to turn himself in; why didn't I just send him to the police? All I could do was refuse him absolution until he could tell me that he deeply regretted his deed and would never again spill blood. He kissed my hand silently and went. . . . I never heard of him again, nor of any horrors like the ones he told me about. In time I convinced myself that this picture of ours had conjured up a monstrous fantasy in him, and therefore he returned it to us . . . until the local policeman brought me the news. . . ."

"Father," Morava addressed him once he realized the man had finally finished, "we're deeply indebted to you for this information, because—and I'm convinced of it—it frees us from the darkness.

We've been looking for a needle in a haystack, and now we know where it is. Or we will know, once you tell us his identity. He knew the picture. Does he come from around here?"

The old man's hands shook.

"That's the thing . . . that's my problem. I've lived with it ever since. My church is consecrated to Saint Jan Nepomuk, who was tortured rather than betray the secrets of the holy confessional. . . ."

"Excuse me, sir." Morava could no longer contain his outrage. "This is a fanatical killer you're talking about—a butcher of defenseless women. If you'd come forward to the police earlier, you could have saved six lives."

"I know," he wheezed like an asthmatic. "I know, gentlemen, and this is my mortal sin, which I will answer for one day. But surely you can understand I don't want to compound it—"

Before Morava could boil over, the German interceded in a calm voice.

"In cases such as these, won't the church grant some sort of dispensation?"

"I'd have to request it . . . ," the priest responded.

"Why didn't you do it long ago?"

The cleric was struggling to undo his collar, but his fingers would not obey him.

"I guess . . . out of shame that a holy picture could lead someone to such a monstrous act. . . . Could you please open the window?"

Morava stood up to grant his request, but remained merciless.

"So why are you telling us now?"

"Those horrible murders. . . . How could I live with it . . . ?"

"And how will you live with what he does next? If we don't catch him in time, he'll do it again soon. The conditions are perfect for it."

"Yes . . . yes. . . ."

He's having a stroke, Morava realized, his heart in his throat, but he did not feel even an ounce of compassion, only a powerless rage that that human animal would wreak further havoc, unpunished and unrecognized. The crisp April air streamed into the room, but the priest's face had turned the color of ashes.

"Your Reverence," Buback spoke almost soothingly, playing the time-honored role of "good cop," the carrot to Morava's stick, "do you think you could ask for that dispensation today from your diocese? I'm sure they'd be glad—"

At that the priest of Klášterec truly fainted. Neither of the policemen managed to catch him as he fell. They summoned the housekeeper, who calmly sat down, crossing her bowling-pin legs by his head and placing it on her lap. Gently she slapped his cheeks.

"Venda! My little Venoušek! Don't worry about it, you had no choice!"

A scene from a mediocre anticlerical farce, Buback thought to himself, but quickly realized his error. The housekeeper turned out to be the priest's sister, who had come to work here after her husband died. She told Buback that her sorely tried brother had asked her whether he should go to the police or not, but had not even told her that the murderer and the thief were one and the same.

They helped move the priest, who soon came around, into the bedroom, and then had to bow to her insistence that they leave him in peace today. He had high blood pressure, she insisted, and further disturbance could strain his heart; they could probe more later. Of course, she was right, and so they agreed with her over the remains of their now cold coffee that they would come again tomorrow, either to take him to the diocese or bring someone from there to him.

On the way back they were mostly silent; both knew that it was pointless to talk until the next day. The younger man, sitting beside Buback in the back seat, was obviously suffering from a deep depression. Buback could certainly sympathize: Grete was today's bait. Her spontaneous offer and his efforts to insure the trap was safe had made him assume she found it an exciting role, and nothing more. Only early this morning had she confessed that each time she walked through the cemetery gates she could feel her backside clench—she showed him her closed fist—this tight!

"Come on, why?" He tried to reassure her. "You know how thoroughly we've tested the scenario."

"Too thoroughly, if anything." She grimaced. "What if this show doesn't run the way you've written it?"

"He's the one who wrote it—five times already," he objected. "They all opened the door themselves. You won't even come into contact with him."

"You don't think so? I hope you're right."

"Then there are still two men inside with pistols."

Grete freed herself from his embrace and went to light up. Sitting in her favorite position—knees against her chest—she exhaled the smoke and laughed awkwardly.

"Today I imagined that for some reason they weren't there."

"You have a sick imagination," he rebuked her, and was instantly afraid he had insulted her.

"Forgive me. It was silly and mean of me to take it for granted. It never occurred to me what must be going through your head. I'm an idiot."

"No! You're wonderful both as a lover and a person. You really have only one flaw."

"Which is?"

"Oh, love, I told you before: think it over."

Now Buback turned to his companion. Their driver, Litera, knew barely enough German to say Gootin tock or Owf weeder zane, so he did not worry about him understanding.

"Mr. Morava," he said, addressing him as a civilian, "does your fiancée ever feel frightened as she plays the widow?"

Surprise reflected from his neighbor's face.

"I was just thinking about that."

"So she does, then."

"I don't know. She says not, but maybe she just wants to reassure me. Does Mrs. Baumann?"

"Today she told me she's afraid the safeguards will fail."

"How could they?" Morava was uneasy again.

"I'm with you; I don't think they can. Anyway, she let it pass."

Buback remembered how, and was filled with joy at the thought that tonight he would hold her in his arms again.

"Still, I've got three people to worry for," the Czech said. "We're expecting a child, you see...."

Buback was amazed. How could they do this? An apocalypse was coming, and these two were having a baby right in the middle of it. With Jitka promenading herself every other day as bait for a murderer? He gazed into the young, tense face and was surprised how deeply touched he was by another man's problems.

"When?" he asked, so he would not just be staring.

"By all the signs, just before Christmas."

Sometime between today and Christmas—probably sooner rather than later—the battle of battles would take place. Did the boy have any idea? And what did he expect from it personally? Why not ask him? He could answer as he liked.

"Do you think it'll be born in peacetime?"

The Czech stared right back at him.

"Yes."

"Any feeling how the war will end?"

"Yes."

"Do you want to tell me?"

"Yes," his neighbor repeated for the third time. "I think the Reich will collapse fairly soon."

"And aren't you afraid it might be disastrous for your people? They say dying horses kick the hardest."

In return he got an unexpected counterquestion.

"Don't you want to live?"

"Of course I do," he said without thinking, and again remembered Grete at night.

"Well, I think it threatens Germans more than Czechs. You're the only German I know to any degree, but you can't be the only one who feels that way. I'm counting on people like you to prevent it."

"Aha . . . but how?"

"By capitulating in time, how else?"

Morava expressed this without the slightest embarrassment or hesitation. Buback was at a loss for words.

"Do you really trust me that much?"

"Yes."

"Why?"

"Sometimes a person just has to decide. And I've decided to believe you."

"But why?"

The Czech was ready with an answer; he seemed firmly convinced of what he was saying.

"My fiancée—actually, she's already really my wife, it's just we haven't gotten married yet on account of the war—she says that a man's partner is a reflection that doesn't lie. Both she and I are very fond of Mrs. Baumann."

"Aha. . . ."

He could not think of anything better, but what was there to say anyway? His Germany was locked in a life-or-death battle, and what was the Czech's sympathy worth, anyway, if he didn't even bother to hide his allegiance to the enemy?

"His" Germany! Yes, unfortunately so.

In his mind's eye he saw Hilde in the Franconian vineyards and once again heard her question: Wasn't it the Führer who had lost touch with his people rather than the other way around? At the time—not all that long ago—Buback had babbled confidently about the iron will of all Germans. Today remorse stung him as he realized that hers could not have been the only voice in the wilderness. After all, it anticipated his own doubts as well. And Grete? Was it just the natural cynicism of a generation come of age in wartime that made her avoid any mention of it? Was her obsession with passion and love a woman's only way of resisting this type of Germanness?

Buback had broken off the conversation after leading it down a figurative blind alley. Now the car approached an actual one. A large sign directed drivers to turn off the main road for a detour. They had used it this morning on the way from Prague, arcing around the forbidden zone where, as the signs cautioned, guards would shoot without warning.

"Tell him to go straight," Buback ordered on a sudden impulse.

Morava immediately translated it, but Litera stopped the car.

"Is he crazy?" the driver asked in Czech.

The assistant detective translated it as a polite question: Could they really do so?

"Tell him to go," Buback repeated. "I'll deal with it; it'll save us half an hour."

He assumed both Czechs had some idea what hid behind the walls of the Theresienstadt fortress and former army base. At the stone gates, a barrier and men in SS uniforms stopped them. They studied Buback's document much more closely than the military police had done that March in Moravia, and demanded the police IDs of both Czechs as well, but finally let them pass without a word.

The road led into streets that at first glance looked almost normal. The only surprising details were the barrackslike appearance of the buildings and the throngs of people that immediately surrounded the car. Buback had been through here quickly once before, investigating a case last winter: the deputy commander of the so-called Lesser Fortress had been robbing other officers. Thanks to Buback, he disappeared into a chain gang out east. That time too Buback had only driven through the fortified city, but the images of the strange anthill were unpleasantly fixed in his memory.

During their visit no one had attempted to explain to either him or his deputy Rattinger whether this was a permanent population or not, whether this was a practice run or a test of how Jews would get along in the victorious Reich, or whether this was just a way station on a journey somewhere else. No information was forthcoming, not even a hint, and asking questions was a violation of military secrecy.

From comments heard here and there in the Gestapo building, he had nonetheless formed his own picture. The most logical one seemed to be— and his first cursory visit to Theresienstadt confirmed him in this belief— that the Jews had been resettled in this way here and there, primarily in the East, where they had always been more common. It therefore shocked him when Grete laughed rudely at his recent mention of it.

"Buback! Are you really that naive, or that cunning?"

"What are you trying to tell me?" he asked, stunned.

"Nothing at all. If you're that cunning, I don't need to tell you anything, and in the other case I don't want to deprive Germany of its last lotus flower. I'll admit, I'm an ostrich with my head in the sand."

Nothing could persuade her to explain herself, and for the first time he had the impression that she did not completely trust him.

For God's sake, it wasn't as if Himmler's executioners were really liquidating them, as he'd heard in those anonymous rumors that refused to die! Of all the things his lover had offered him since that first night, her joyous levity fascinated him most. His early bad experiences taught him to avoid disrupting Grete's now continuous sunny weather, so he swallowed her mockery this time as well. The day before yesterday he had heard a reliable report in Bredovská Street that a Red Cross mission led by Count Bernadotte of Sweden was operating in this very ghetto. It confirmed his cautious optimism: Otherwise they'd never let in a prominent neutral power, which could report any crimes they found to the world. However, he decided not to mention it to Grete. . . .

As opposed to his last visit, the winter coats, blankets, and rags of various origins that protected their wearers from the cold had vanished from the streets, as had the infamous yellow stars. Neither did they see a single German uniform. The Jews—for Jews they clearly were—plied their trades, bought and sold, but also kept the peace. Even an exacting Swedish eye could hardly find fault with this picture, so why did he find it even more disturbing now than last time?

The answer was obvious: Suddenly he was seeing it through the eyes of the two astounded Czechs. The crowd fell silent, doffed their hats, and pressed to the side of the road at the mere sight of three civilians in a car—only the threat of imminent death could strike this sort of dread into people's hearts. Yes, Hilde had sensed the truth and Grete probably knew it directly from Meckerle. But simpleminded little Erwin had stayed faithful till the bitter end, the slave of a regime embodying the very opposite of the values he thought he had spent his life serving.

He was so deeply depressed that his companions sensed something was wrong. Why had he treated them to this spectacle, which he was supposed to hide from them? The human mobs suddenly ended at the exit gates. The guards let them pass without notice and the car rolled past the ramparts of the Lesser Fortress and out into the open countryside. Suddenly he knew why he had done it. He turned to Morava.

"I want you to know that I don't agree with that."

And when his neighbor did not respond, he added, "Take it as a confidence, in return for yours."

They did not speak the rest of the way back to Prague. He had no idea what the two Czechs were thinking, but felt relieved anyway. At last he had done and said what he should have a long time ago.

He caught himself thinking intently about Grete again. What did she mean to him? For some reason he couldn't see in her the one thing he'd wanted so desperately from the Czech girl: a future. But what was so strange about that? It was probably why Grete did not want to hear his story. Only the present could link a man and woman whose destinies and personalities were so different; a deeper feeling and a more serious relationship would cost them both too much. Wasn't it significant that neither had thought to ask the other what to do if the unthinkable happened? A volcano could erupt under them any day now, and they had not even discussed where and how they'd find each other afterward.

"Where to?" the driver asked in Czech, and Morava repeated it in German.

The car was approaching downtown Prague. Buback glanced at his watch. Past two. Grete was finished with widowhood for today, and was probably catching a nap before the afternoon trip out to the troops. He'd see her later, he was sure of that: She no longer missed a day.

"I'll go with you," he decided. "Let's contact the diocese right away, so we don't waste time tomorrow."

The surprise at Bartolomějská Street hit Buback harder than Morava. A chain of SS forces had closed off the road. Their car was immediately surrounded by heavily armed giants and they were ordered to leave the vehicle. He pulled out his papers again.

"What's happening here?"

The corporal lowered his weapon and clicked his heels.

"Raid on the Czech police."

"When did it start?"

"Once the workday was under way."

Buback's throat closed up. Grete's nightmare!

"Come on," he shouted at his companions. "Quickly! To Kavčí Hory!"

He kept running, even when he rattled and gasped for breath and his blood threatened to burst his arteries; he swerved from street to street, always heading downward, seeing no one behind him, meeting no one, and still in the back of his mind loomed the fear that they would catch him. Idiot, I'm an idiot! The words echoed in his ears, idiot, idiot, IDIOT!

Why didn't the whore's walk tip him off, that strange walk, too slow for such a young woman; why didn't the location of the house, that street ending in a steep craggy slope, make him think twice; why didn't the unlocked door and the way she called "come in" warn him off?

Half a dozen chickens in his roaster had spoiled him, made him overconfident; without a moment's hesitation he'd walked in, convinced this would be the easiest catch of all—and meanwhile he'd practically put his head under the blade!

When he finally looked into her face from the kitchen threshold, he realized immediately she'd been waiting for him, that she must have known, that she'd led him here TO BE TRAPPED! Then it happened again: He froze, seized up, and turned to stone in the kitchen doorway, knowing their strong hands were about to grab him.

He knew that DEATH HAD COME for him, and just like the last time, when the grenades had fallen all around him, he felt anger seeping into his fear. IS THIS WHAT YOU WANTED, MOTHER?

Then a miracle happened.

Fear crept into her eyes, the sort he was used to seeing.

Their plan had clearly gone wrong. . . .

"He's here," she screamed, "he's here! Where are you?"

Instantly he came to, pulled his knife from the sheath, and sprang at her.

AT LEAST I'LL GET YOU!

She did better than he had counted on. As she fled around the table, she grabbed a porcelain vase with flowers in it and hurled it at the window with such force that it broke through both the inside and outside panes.

SO THEY'RE WAITING OUTSIDE!

Before he dealt with them he had to silence her. Otherwise he wouldn't be safe for long.

Don't let her distract you! He leaped back to the kitchen doors, cutting off her escape, and stabbed her in the back. She fell instantly as if cut down.

ONE DOWN!

His brain was still working. From the kitchen door he spied a dark alcove under the stairs and nipped into it a fraction of a second before someone ran in off the street.

A moment later he spied the back of a man bent over the woman. The man's right hand curled round a pistol. Time for a risky move.

As he jumped he swung wide and buried the long knife up to the hilt beneath the man's left shoulder blade.

The other twisted around and in doing so almost pried open his hand; still, he managed to get the knife out of the man's back and stab him a second time right in the heart.

TWO DOWN! WHAT NEXT?

He had no idea how many of them were still left, but now he had a pistol too, which he easily ripped from the man's enfeebled palm. He felt sure he was still a pretty good shot.

THANK YOU, MR. POLICEMAN!

A look at the two of them told him they'd cause him no trouble. No regrets on account of the policeman. Shame, though, that he'd have to leave THAT NASTY DOVE.

His pistol drawn, he looked carefully out the doors the kid had not closed onto the street.

NO ONE, NOWHERE!

He went out slowly, hiding the weapon under a hat that had fallen off the dead man's head. He felt relieved when he reached the first cross-street where he could head downhill. The hat he simply tossed aside; it didn't go with the canvas overcoat of the Werkschutz. A gust of wind blew it alongside him for a while until he changed its direction with a kick. He shoved the pistol into the front pocket of his pants, but it was uncomfortable there, so finally he moved it and the knife to his briefcase (a miracle he hadn't left it there in the confusion). Now he was trotting along the surprisingly deserted street that linked up with the riverside road below. He was puffing like a steam engine; it was a good thing he heard the car coming.

The squeal of tires racing up around the curves wasn't a normal sound for this corner of the city. He halted, rooted to the spot, and looked wildly around for cover. There were no passageways between the houses, the garbage cans would not hide him, and it was a good hundred yards to the sparse copse beyond. Once again he improvised. He sauntered off downhill along the sidewalk, suppressing with all his might the ragged heaving of his chest as his lungs gasped for breath.

Suddenly a car loomed up in front of him. He caught sight of three men in civilian garb inside, but the way they roared past betrayed what they were after. He managed to pull out his handkerchief in time and pretended to blow his nose so they wouldn't see his face, but once again he felt his strength ebbing away.

He was sure this was a HUGE TRAP they had laid for him. Today he'd escaped it by a hair, but now they were drawing the net closed and he had no idea how tight it was. The fact that the car hadn't stopped didn't mean there weren't more waiting below, and here he was, caught in this treacherous, craggy defile like a cork in a bottle.

WHAT NEXT?

He certainly couldn't go back, so he trudged on aimlessly. His evident exhaustion made him as conspicuous as an autumn bumblebee. And as his conviction grew that SHE HAD BETRAYED HIM, he turned, after years of silence, back to HIM.

You above all know I WAS ONLY FOLLOWING HER ORDERS. I wanted to IMPROVE YOUR KINGDOM, not destroy it; save me and I swear I WILL NEVER DO IT AGAIN, and that I'll serve you AS YOU COMMAND ME TO!

In answer he heard a ringing sound.

The tram terminus lay before him. The empty vehicle's driver was urging him to hurry.

M orava knew they were in an awful mess, but the first thing he
felt was relief: Grete Baumann was at the cemetery today. His
Jitka was protected by that very same impenetrable cordon of SS men.
How absurd!

He knew he ought to be ashamed of himself, so he tried to feel some
of the anguish of the man sitting next to him. It was evident in Buback's
face, and he did not even try to hide it.

They barreled along the embankment; Litera overtook other cars
whenever he could. Once Morava could think again, their panic
seemed unreasonable. He tried to calm his companion.

"Mr. Buback! It would have to be an awful coincidence for him to
strike today of all days."

The German gave no reaction; his eyes remained fixed on the pavement in front of him, as if concentrating could increase their speed.

"And Šebesta would have gone after her; the three of them were
supposed to start their shifts there."

At this Buback finally nodded weakly and fell silent. He did not
move or speak again until Litera veered full speed into the narrow
street that led from the tram terminus up to Kavčí Hory. The turn
threw him across the seat into Morava.

"I know . . . ," he said, and shrank back into his corner.

Morava thought of his recent conversation with Jitka. So he loves
her too, he realized; he wouldn't be so worried about a passing acquaintance. In the end, that wave of fear will join him to her. Jitka will
be pleased. . . .

Careening through a short, sparse wood that stretched along the
rocky hillsides toward Pankrác, they reentered the city they had barely
left. The street here was lined with low buildings; originally temporary
workers' houses from more prosperous times, their term of service had
been extended when the Depression hit. The car jolted over the bumpy
cobblestones. They passed a solitary pedestrian, plodding down to the
tram lines below; just then Morava and Buback had to brace themselves
to avoid being thrown together.

They swayed even further around the next curve, when Litera
swerved around an item near the edge of the roadway. A hat, Morava
thought, surprised; what was it doing there? He instantly put it out of

his head as they turned into their street. Then he almost yelped in pain as he felt Buback's nails dig into his wrist.

Litera was already braking by a large glistening puddle. For a moment all three of them looked at the shards of glass and porcelain, scattered amid the carnations. . . . From me, Morava realized.

They scrambled out of the vehicle.

The chief inspector was unbelievably fast and managed to enter the house first.

It was already clear that the unthinkable, impossible, and inhuman coincidence had come to pass.

A corpse in a checkered suit slumped from the kitchen into the hall. Šebesta's glassy eyes stared wide at the ceiling.

Morava saw the blood suddenly drain from Buback's face. Like the priest, he remembered.

Has he lost his second love as well? What a horrible fate!

They stepped over the dead body and were in the kitchen.

Between the door and the table lay Jitka.

B uback put his experience from past German retreats to use. The girl was alive; the wound must have barely missed her heart. They had to get her on the operating table as soon as possible.

While her fiancé applied mouth-to-mouth resuscitation, he and Litera removed the sideboard's narrow door.

Using it as a stretcher they carried her out to the street and gently laid her on the back seat of the vehicle.

The young Czech squeezed himself into the narrow gap next to her, rubbed her pale cheeks, and willed her to live.

Litera drove like a madman again; they made it to General Hospital in under a quarter hour.

As they took Jitka Modrá away, Buback allowed himself to stroke her hand. It was warm.

"She'll live," he said to the Czech, as if trying to persuade himself as well. "She will live!"

The youth nodded absently and without a word followed the orderlies off.

Buback arranged for Šebesta's body to be removed. Then Litera drove him back to Bredovská Street. As he got out, he instructed the driver: "Return to the hospital and remain there at Mr. Morava's disposition. Don't go back to headquarters yet; they'll just detain you. I'll call the superintendent."

He couldn't possibly have understood me, Buback realized a bit later, but by then he had already raced into the colonel's anteroom, stormed past the adjutant there, entered Meckerle's office, and slammed the door behind him.

The giant sat awkwardly half-hunched in his chair, with a pained expression on his face. At the sight of Buback he practically cringed, as if expecting his subordinate to hit him.

"It's all right . . . ," he said weakly. "Calm down, man, nothing happened to her."

"You call that nothing? She's fighting for her life!"

Meckerle abruptly stood up and winced even more, holding his right hand over his crotch as if he had a terrible pain there.

"Grete . . . ?"

"Fortunately not! But only because she switched shifts," Buback shouted into his face. "We had him, he ran right into our trap, except our ambush wasn't there. As a result, he severely wounded the other woman and killed a policeman. And got away! Who ordered the blockade of the Czech headquarters?"

"I did."

"And why?"

The colonel was rapidly regaining control; if he had any pain, his anger drowned it out.

"I explained that at the last meeting, and it was clear to everyone, except possibly you. Fuck you and your murderer; you're not up to the job I gave you!"

"You approved my report."

"Which blocked the SS special units from doing their job."

"They won't find any weapons there unless they plant them. Now we've thrown away the advantage of surprise—all for a couple of pistols and rifles that were already registered!"

Meckerle was himself again. Now he'll let me have it, Buback thought, seeing the familiar crimson vein throbbing at his temple.

"I'm the one who decides what the right time is. And what's more, I didn't appreciate your cheek in thanking me for the fish. You're getting too big for your breeches, Buback. Dismissed! I'll inform you shortly of your new posting."

Buback turned and marched out of the room, pressing his lips closed. Any more slips would just hasten his descent. No, Meckerle had not yet formally ousted him from his post. He had a couple of hours left to catch that murderous beast.

Just to be sure, he avoided his office and went straight to the head of dispatching. Bureaucratic inertia got him a jeep on forty-eight-hour loan with an armed soldier at the wheel.

On the way he stopped at home, expecting to find an explanation. Inside he found a note.

"They came here to pick me up; an unexpected special engagement, they say. M. apparently gave them your address. Will stop at J's, see if she'll step in. Take care, love. G."

He turned the page over and wrote on the back side.

"Your nightmare came true. He found her alone and badly wounded her. I'm going after him, I hope. B."

And then added: "I was horribly afraid it was you!"

M orava held Jitka's right hand as it lay beside her body. It was still moist and his thumb fearfully tracked the weak, slow pulse in the vein of her wrist.

The surgeon who had operated on her came back and measured her pulse and temperature. He had done what he could, he explained: a pneumothorax and stitches. Her blood was still flowing bright red from the drainage shunts.

Morava finally dared to ask the question that had been torturing him for hours.

"And the child . . . ?"

"Will survive if she does," the doctor said, and left.

Was he trying to encourage him or prepare him for the worst?

He drew hope from the expression on her face. Instead of horror, he saw a glimmer of the shy smile that had captured him forever at their first meeting.

Forever?

My beloved, my beloved, stay!

God, how could you do this?

A t the end of the platform the abandoned concrete piping seemed to grow out of the bushes rather than vice versa. Sidling up to it, he pretended to be urinating in secret and placed his briefcase inside one of the pipes. He'd risked enough today!

He was the first one here and would have to wait; as usual he read the newspaper. As the front withdrew, the German units had deserted Brno. Il Duce Benito Mussolini had been treacherously ambushed by partisans, then shot and hung by his legs from a gasoline pump. From his battle headquarters in Berlin, the Führer and Reich chancellor had commended the members of the Hitlerjugend.

He stared at the picture of the children in their oversized military raincoats: A man with a demented expression was pinning Iron Crosses on them. In his mind, however, he saw other pictures: The eyes of that whore shining with fear, and the surprise of that cop as he ambushed him.

The train picked up speed, clattering down the battered rail ties. The carriages emptied out as Prague receded and filled up again as they approached Plzeň. Near Rokycany they braked with a crazed screech. A whistle shattered the air. With detached reserve he watched his fellow travelers rush out of the carriage and across the plowed field to a nearby copse.

He knew that train passengers often died in buzz-bomb attacks, but he remained seated, with his newspaper open. A sudden decision strengthened his will.

I will survive it!

And then i will never fear again!

The airplane motor roared nearby, a machine gun barked, and there was a loud hissing.

Despite this he did not budge, and was richly rewarded: The engineer fooled the attacker by loosing a geyser of steam to indicate they had been hit.

When the passengers returned, they showered the cool-headed reader with admiration. He merely shrugged his shoulders, although inside he was rejoicing.

Once and for all!

At the Plzeň train station he finally fell into the clutches of the food inspectors and thankfully could show them empty hands. His worries happily behind him, he was about to jump off the tram at the theater stop when he spotted a long white shape emerging from the side gates.

They're carrying out the ice!

New passengers pushed him against the rear windows as they boarded; from there he watched his colleagues unnoticed as they lifted the gleaming beams onto the back of a truck.

They sold it themselves!

He couldn't tell how far they had gotten, but it didn't matter. There was no way to stop them from finishing the job.

And then they'll find them!

At first they probably wouldn't realize what they'd found, but someone would undoubtedly get curious and refuse to leave well enough alone.

And then they'll find me!

The conductor tugged the bell strap, the tram screeched off, and the theater receded into the distance.

He realized he couldn't go home either; they might be waiting for him. And he had no one else on this earth except her. His sulk evaporated, and he implored her to help him again.

Where should i go?

———

The priest managed to disappear from the garden before they arrived, but Buback had sharp eyes. When the housekeeper tried to convince him her brother had not budged from his bed since morning, he pointed at the two small hoes in the half-raked vegetable patch. To make a suitable impression, he had taken the driver with him up to the rectory; the man's black uniform and accompanying giant pistol had the desired effect. She sat them down in the parlor, and in a few minutes the cleric arrived. He was nervous but seemed even firmer in his conviction than before.

Buback began the attack without delay.

"My young colleague—the Czech fellow I was here with this morning—had a wife, and was expecting a child with her. Three hours ago, she and another person became the latest victims of the murderer you are concealing. Yes, I said 'concealing'; you can't deny that you're personally responsible for what could be three unnecessary deaths. Your Saint Jan Nepomuk kept the secrets of the confessional at his own expense, while you let others pay with their lives. I'm ordering you to reveal everything you know, dispensation or no, about the man who confessed to the Brno murder."

He wanted to threaten the man with imprisonment, but could not imagine what he would do with him. Bartolomějská Street was out of commission for now, and taking him to Bredovská, the heart of the enemy's camp, could bring on a stroke. His speech and his escort, however, were enough for the man's sister.

"Venda," she beseeched him, "you've got to tell them!"

Buback seized the opportunity. "What's his name? How old is he? Where does he live? What does he do? I won't rest easy—and neither will you—as long as he's free, so out with it!"

The housekeeper, no longer the meek little mouse, now showed herself to be the real ruler of this small household.

"Come on, Venda, tell him! Would God hide a villain like that? Why claim that right for yourself in His name?"

As if that decided it, the priest cast an almost thankful glance at her, turned to Buback, and poured forth a sentence he clearly knew by heart.

"Antonín Rypl, born 27 May 1900 in Brno, nationality: Czech;

marital status: single; trained as a heating mechanic, then as a soldier; temporarily on an invalid's pension after a war injury; employed here in Klášterec the last four years before the war as a sexton while his mother was a cook; mentioned during his visit in 1940 that he'd been living in Plzeň since her death. . . . That's all I know. . . ."

Buback wrote it all down and stood up so sharply that his escort automatically reached for his pistol. The detective nodded to him that everything was in order, but did allow himself a parting shot.

"Before you start your repentance for violating the sacrament of confession, why not do something more useful: pray that the young woman and her child survive."

Outside he ordered the driver: "To Plzeň!"

A t some point during the evening—Morava had lost track of time—Beran appeared in the hospital room. The bags under his eyes were heavier than usual; today more than ever he looked like an old Saint Bernard. He did not ask about Jitka; he must have spoken with the doctors himself. Standing motionless behind Morava's chair, he sadly observed the girl, her hand tightly clasped in the young detective's. Then he gently clapped him on the shoulder.

"Come with me for a moment. . . ."

Morava seemed eager to obey, as if this experienced and wise man, his teacher, advisor, and second father, could make sure that their beloved Jitka returned from death's door. The superintendent took him by the arm and silently led him down the hall into another room. On a conference table in the doctor's office stood Beran's personal thermos, the one Jitka filled over and over with fresh rye coffee.

As if reading his thoughts, his boss said, "Unfortunately I made this myself, but it's better than nothing. You have to get something into your stomach."

Like the mysterious old man in fairy tales, he unwrapped some baked dumplings from a small sack.

"Matlák's morning snack. He lost his appetite during the raid and is sending them over as . . . well, just because, what can I say? Eat."

"I can't," Morava blurted.

"You have to. I've arranged for you to stay here; this bed is at your disposal, try to nap from time to time when your head feels heavy. And eat."

Obediently he bit into the dough, chewed, but could not taste the filling. He froze and looked up at Beran.

"And it was my idea. . . ."

"It was, and you did an excellent job. If it hadn't been for the SS you'd have won."

Then the superintendent did something no one had ever seen him do before. He stroked Morava's head.

"Buback says hello," he continued, practical as ever. "A strange man. He apologized on the phone for the Germans; he had no idea about the raid. The priest gave him the name. Rypl. Antonín Rypl. Buback is in Plzeň and hopes he'll find him. Eat. . . ."

"Why?" He spat the word out in his hopeless misery.

"What, why? Eat to stay alive."

"But if she dies, I don't want to live!"

"I thought you believed in God."

"How can I believe in God if she dies?"

Beran's hands rested on his shoulders.

"I can't tell you that, kid. I'm not a believer. But every once in a while I force evil to a standoff, and that gives me a higher purpose. Maybe it seems I know more about life than you, but right now, next to you, I feel like a schoolchild. I'm alone because I never dared link my fate to anyone else's. I felt less vulnerable that way, and stronger. But today, by your standards, I'm a poor man. You suffer because you love in a way I never have, and that makes you more experienced than I am. And it'll make you even stronger in your fight against evil. Eat; now you just need to eat, to make it through."

Morava obediently bit into the dough again, even though the dumpling was salty with his tears.

"Good work, Morava," Beran praised him, "good work, good work."

It was long since dark and noticeably cooler; he cursed himself for choosing a thin overcoat today. On the other hand, it made him blend in; these coats were popular in Plzeň, and both office staff and the Škoda factory workers wore them.

Worst of all, since February he'd been taking his own success for granted. Today he'd only taken enough money for the train and lunch. He hadn't eaten, but even so he could barely afford the ticket back to Prague.

AND WHAT THEN?

During his years in Plzeň he had lost contact completely with the rest of his family, who had always been suspicious of the almost matrimonial relationship between mother and son. He greeted everyone here in his building politely, and at work they all acknowledged how handy he was, but aside from HER he had never found another kindred soul.

SHE WAS THE ONLY ONE WHO EVER LOVED ME!

His intoxicating successes these past few weeks had clouded his reason. The distance between himself and the rest of the world had become proof of his own superiority. Now, at the end of the vicious circle, he stood shivering and hungry at the train station again, and an old fact hit him with renewed force.

I'M ALONE!

What he still had, he realized, was a knack for self-preservation, which had saved him this morning in Prague. And he still had his luck, he remembered; without it he would have walked blindly into his own destruction.

SO THERE IS SOMETHING!

He was amazed how little it took to shake him free. And he knew where his strength came from. How awful he'd been this morning, cursing HER memory as he fled!

MOTHER, FORGIVE ME!

Now he knew what to do. He bought a ticket to Prague from the sleepy cashier. If they weren't waiting for him here, they'd hardly be waiting there.

AND FROM THERE I'LL MANAGE!

At the documents division of the Plzeň police they gave Buback everything he needed in a few minutes. If Germans have taught mankind one thing, he thought bitterly, it's how to track civilians.

From there he called Superintendent Beran. He learned that the raid had ended ingloriously shortly after noon. Not a single extra weapon was found on Prague police premises.

Buback informed Beran where he could find Jitka, Morava, and Litera and requested that he tell the assistant detective he was still on the trail. The superintendent then had a word with the Plzeň police, which they correctly interpreted as orders.

Eight men in two cars formed a small convoy; in between them Buback rode alone with his SS escort. He decided not to bring in the local Gestapo, in case they decided to report the expedition to Prague; what if Meckerle sent Rattinger or even Kroloff here after him?

On his way to catch the murderer who'd almost killed Jitka Modrá, Buback read through the man's extensive card file. As a seventeen-year-old apprentice Antonín Rypl had been found unfit for service in the Austrian Army, but a year later was accepted as a volunteer for the new Czechoslovak forces. When the doctors' board questioned the sudden change in his health, he explained that his mother had made him drink a coal brew to keep him off the front. He thus fell right into a smaller war; as a new recruit, he was sent to cleanse southern Slovakia of Hungarians. He was seriously wounded in action and was granted a temporary pension. Later he worked in his native Brno at a large heating installation firm until it closed during the Depression. After several years apparently spent living on support or off his mother, the Klášterec rectory hired him as a sexton. When war broke out in 1939, he moved to Plzeň and found work as a stoker and janitor at the city theater.

They opened the garret of the apartment building on Pražská Street without any trouble. Inside, it was as clean and orderly as a military sitting room. Or the bedroom of an exemplary little boy, Buback thought. A large photo of a woman approximately forty years old hung on the far wall. The deeply carved features spoke of severity, but certainly not coldness. She must have been an extraordinarily passionate woman! When she was photographed, she fixed her eyes right on the lens—so her son would never be able to escape her gaze? Buback could imagine how here, through this picture, Rypl had begun to talk to her. . . .

Their search revealed nothing. They left an ambush team behind and continued on to the theater; in the meanwhile the local police had surrounded it. The business manager sent for Rypl, but no one had seen him since early that morning. He then took Buback and his escort to the furnace room; it had been closed since February, when the German military hospital had requisitioned their remaining supply of coke fuel. There too there was perfect order in the desk and the tin locker, and not even the slightest clue.

On the way upstairs they had to stop and press against the wall of the staircase as two technicians dragged the last dripping slice of ice past them.

A third man followed them rather perplexedly, carrying five small frozen objects wrapped in wax paper.

M orava mechanically finished the dumplings without tasting them; he drank the coffee, forgetting to sweeten it. The bed went unused. As soon as Beran left he returned to Jitka's bed, holding her motionless hand and silently watching the nurses and doctors go just as mutely to and fro. He did not ask. He knew that they would tell him if there were any good news.

They came more frequently now with injections, and her breathing became still louder and more ragged. Morava felt himself swimming up out of a shocked numbness; his grief seemed almost a physical ache. Yes, Beran had been right; his suffering was as great as his love for her. But he could not imagine surviving her, or more importantly, wanting to.

At the thought of her death, the whole long life they had dreamed about together the night before was suddenly, unexpectedly, and irrevocably cut short, and none of its possible replacements could hold a candle to the project they had embarked on together. What would he do then? Redouble his fight against evil, as his mentor expected?

But how, when he'd already lost the decisive battle? Evil would laugh as he mourned her.

At moments an intolerable pain twisted his heart and stomach. He tried to staunch this new hopelessness, willing himself to the faith he had always used since childhood to quell his fear of death. For minutes at a time he would emerge from his gloom; surely Jitka could not resist his stare, and any moment now would open her eyes. As soon as it happened, he would easily pull her back among the living.

However, her eyes remained shut and her face began to change, as if once again she were facing unimaginable horrors. He returned to the question that had oppressed him since Beran's departure.

Why, in all this time, hadn't he asked God for help?

Because, he admitted, for the first time he was angry with Him. If this was punishment for his sins, then why Jitka and not him? Or was it a test of his humility? In which a pure creature, carrying a child untouched by sin, would meet a cruel death?

The certainties he had grown up with now left him. Doubt filled the void.

Maybe there is no God. What a frightening thought.

Or what's worse: maybe God exists, and would let Jitka and their child die, leaving him alive.

I don't want a God like that!

Inwardly he flinched. Would this bring His wrath down on them? Then his resolve hardened: it was the only way to save her.

If He were as just and loving as the Scriptures said, He would be appalled by what was happening and save her.

Three faithfully devoted sheep, or none at all. He would have to decide for Himself.

At the height of his agitation, Morava fell asleep on his uncomfortable chair.

S HE WAS STILL WITH HIM!
Only SHE could have led that guy to his compartment, of all the ones in the almost empty train.

The little fellow was looking for a match to light his cigarette, but failing to score one, he stayed on for a chat.

When he spoke, it was one long salvo of insults against the Reich and its Führer.

At first he thought this half-pint had to be a provocateur, but soon he came around. This was no stool pigeon, just a person who, after six years, had had enough.

IT'S STARTING TO BREAK!

At first he listened, then grunted his assent, and after a while they were talking heart-to-heart; he felt himself being drawn in, and waited for HER sign. Finally it came. Light filled the cabin, like a ray from heaven.

He saw his old sergeant, Králík, giving him the thumbs-up as he had done on the Brno shooting range.

I'M A SOLDIER, AFTER ALL!

He remembered the incident on the bombarded train.

AND I HAVE NERVES OF STEEL!

AND IMAGINATION!

Immediately, he confided to the guy in strictest confidence who he really was. The story was so convincing that he believed it himself. With his military background, it was easy to create the impression that he was still active in the now-illegal Czechoslovak Army.

By the end of the trip, the runt was bursting with pride. After all, he was sitting in the same compartment as a real parachutist, just back from England!

At Smíchov station, he pulled the contents of his bag out of the concrete pipe in the guy's presence, dispelling any remaining doubts. Of course, he was taking a risk, even there on the deserted railway platform, but now he was sure he was back on track.

HER HAND PROTECTS ME!

His old army pistol clinched the deal. The guy—naive beyond his years!—enthusiastically promised to hide him in his own home.

THANKS, MOTHER!

Jitka Modrá died at exactly five A.M., and with her died what would have been her child.

The firm grasp of a man's hand accompanied her on her journey into oblivion.

Jan Morava slept soundly through it, waking only later to Erwin Buback's sympathetic hug.

The sun had just peered over the crown of the nearby hill, silhouetting the stadiums against the morning sky, when the car pulled up outside the house.

Buback could hear the music even over the noise of the motor. A raucous melody split the air, one that supposedly had the whole American army grooving wildly on the dance floors. It was the Glenn Miller Orchestra playing boogie-woogie; Grete seemed to think this Miller fellow was some sort of god.

The young driver in the cap with skull and crossbones listened carefully. When his eyes met Buback's, he smiled almost conspiratorially.

Throwing custom and protocol to the winds, Buback slipped the driver a fifty-mark note. The SS agent took it as calmly as a waiter would a tip.

Now I know the war is ending! The thought pleased Buback, but he immediately remembered the living man and the dead woman he had just left. Evil, however, goes on. . . .

The staff car vanished around the curve below. Upstairs, the noise went on unchecked, a testimony to the gradual depopulation of Little Berlin. However, as he rummaged for his keys on the sidewalk, the house's front door opened, revealing the judge. Dressed already, at this early hour? No. The man's unshaven cheeks suggested that he had not yet gone to bed.

"There's no need to go around the back, Herr Oberkriminalrat, come this way. . . ."

From up close he confirmed that the radiogram Grete had recently moved to his place was even louder here than outside. Evidently it was now set to its highest volume. He realized it had undoubtedly kept the judge up, but he did not feel the slightest desire to apologize.

"Thank you, but I'm used to it by now."

"What are you going to do," the judge wailed after him in despair.

Buback tried to imagine how many anguished howls this pitiful, sleepy figure had caused, screams torn from the throats of countless men and women before the bullet or blade reached its mark. He responded with barely disguised glee. "Apparently, we're going to dance."

On a volcano, he thought, climbing the winding back stairs that shook with the syncopations of degenerate music. As he pressed down the door handle, it flooded over him as if he had opened the sluice gates.

Grete half lay, half sat on the bed in black ski pants and a black T-shirt; its long sleeves gripped and further flattened her chest. One hand clutched a cigarette holder, the other curled around a glass; all around her were stains and cigarette butts from an overflowing ashtray. Her eyes were unfocused; she was so engulfed in the melody, humming along wordlessly with it, that it took several seconds for her to realize he was home. First she smiled dreamily at him, then flung away the holder, cigarette, and glass, and, jumping up, threw her arms around his neck.

"The bastard croaked," she exulted, "bit the dust!"

And so he learned of the death of Adolf Hitler, who supposedly fell in the defense of Berlin.

Once she cooled down a bit, he extinguished the smoking carpet and prevailed on her to turn down the gramophone—not because of the judge (who had no power anymore), but so that they could hear each other speak. She listened to his story so intently that all the alcohol seemed to evaporate from her completely; her gray-green irises stared at him without blinking, like the eyes of a beast of prey. When he reached the part where they found the dead policeman and the wounded Jitka, she interrupted him with a shout.

"No! That son of a bitch saved me?"

She was clearly still tipsy; forgetting about his story, she launched directly into her own. There hadn't been any performance, she said, pointing to her morning message still lying there with his afternoon postscript. That son of a bitch, she repeated, that pig Meckerle had her brought over like a cheap whore to a hotel outside Prague, one she knew the officers used as a high-class flophouse, but she didn't realize what was happening even when the unfamiliar driver took her to the suite and told her to wait there for her colleagues and wardrobe, until she entered the bedroom ("stupid cow," she fumed), where the colonel was waiting for her ("naked, the swine!") in a state of drunken anticipation; he locked the door and threatened to rip off her clothes if she wouldn't undress herself, and that really made her blood boil: She grabbed him, threw him down on the bed, and then went from his head to his chest past his belly down to his lap, and then . . .

"I bit him as hard as I could!" she grinned. "Right in his stiff dick!"

She said he'd let out a dreadful scream; he must have thought she'd bitten it off, she continued, shaking with laughter, but he wasn't even bleeding, and when she thought he'd regained enough strength to beat her to death . . .

"Then I started to shriek; I never knew I could make such a loud noise, and he was so terrified that he just fled, naked, in a panic."

Buback remembered Meckerle's painful grimaces that afternoon and marveled that he had escaped his superior's office alive.

Leaving the hotel room, Grete had gone down to the reception desk, where they pretended they had never seen her before. No, they didn't know what happened to the car that brought her, and there were none available, but she'd certainly have no problem hitching a ride along the road with a German officer. By the time someone finally stopped, she had practically walked back to Prague.

"But it was worth it to hear that the bastard of Berlin had snuffed it."

And she nearly paid the officer back with a slap when he tried to force his way upstairs with her.

" 'To grieve together,' he suggested; not a bad-looking guy, but with one basic flaw: He wasn't you."

And then she had waited, longing impatiently for him, reading his message over and over, shaken by the fact that she could have been the murderer's victim.

Now she bent forward, stretched out her hands to him and pulled him toward her.

"Love! My love! Where were you all my life? Why did you let me wait and lie for so long?"

She held his head in her outstretched arms and then pulled him close, covering his forehead, temples, eyes, and chin with almost child-like kisses.

He held her and wished it would never end. Slowly he felt their passion dissolve into tenderness.

"Come to me," she whispered after a long while. "I want you so much! No, wait. . . ."

She slipped away from him to the gramophone, where the record crackled at the end of the last track. She replaced it and then stopped short.

"How is she? You must be sick to death of my interruptions."

He took off his jacket and unbuttoned his shirt.

"She's dead."

"I'm sorry?"

"She died an hour ago."

He sat down on the bed and everything he had been through since that morning suddenly hit him.

Grete stood motionless. She glanced at the gramophone as if she could see and feel on her body the slow, heavy melody she had chosen for their lovemaking. When the piano and percussion began their variations, she lifted both hands and swayed into the rhythm. Her supple arms drooped to the floor and encircled the lamp overhead. Then her long legs joined in, and the slender figure in black seemed to fill the entire space.

It was as if the music were dictating thoughts to Grete, and her motions turned them into words of sorrow and hope.

As he watched her, captivated, his sorrow and revulsion dissolved. Two unbelievable gifts of fate shone brightly above the filth and blood of the miserable world.

He was alive.

And he had her.

She stopped and knelt down at his side.

"And why were you so horribly afraid when you thought it was me?"

"Suddenly I realized I loved you. . . ."

"Oh, Buback! Now you really are perfect!"

MAY

The little guy protected and threatened him at the same time. On the train, his bold openness had brought them together, but even at home he would not shut up. He was sure to tell his foreman at the locomotive depot in Beroun that he was hiding a parachutist. If he didn't spill it to the other railwaymen himself, his boss would see to that. By evening some informer would know, and that night they'd seize him.

From the frying pan into the fire. MURDERER OR SPY? THE BLADE OR THE BULLET?

The warmed-over potato stew tasted of bad beer, but at least it filled his empty stomach; he chewed and listened to the tripe that his host served up.

"Give this to your signaler," the runt was whispering urgently. "No, don't tell me where he is, we'll all get together for a drink once it's over, but the train schedules for the Protectorate could help the Allies considerably, couldn't they?"

He realized swearing this man to silence would be useless. The runt would promise, but wouldn't obey. This was a man who longed to live an interesting life, and finally his dream had come true—except it would be wasted without spectators.

Even so, he felt calmer already. The situation still wasn't rosy, but he had averted the catastrophe facing him in Plzeň. And now he had time to think what came next, before the half-pint set off for work.

FIRST I HAVE TO GET TO KNOW HIM.

In case I need to stay a while: Inquire how he lives, what his habits are, his acquaintances, friends, who visits him, why and when.

His host's temperament made it easy. Despite the late hour the guy kept talking, questions or no. He longed desperately to engrave himself on the memory and heart of his unexpected guest, who had accepted him into the Resistance.

The story matched the storyteller. It was primitive. In an hour he was sure.

I KNOW EVERYTHING ABOUT HIM.

Karel Malina lived alone but carried on with his married neighbor, who—he winked knowingly—cleaned for him and fed him for free. Her husband was also a railway engineer who slept every other night in a different city, leaving Malina to warm his bed. Everything was taken care of; Malina was snug as a bug in a rug.

So, THE WOMAN NEXT DOOR!

He knew, he told the runt, that for his own safety, Malina would need to watch his tongue. However, if Malina was going to hide him till the coup, he would have to mention the arrangement to his neighbor.

The guy shone with bliss.

Of course Malina couldn't introduce them—parachutists need to keep a low profile—but he should tell her what was going on. That way she wouldn't worry if she didn't see her neighbor around for a few days, because . . . yes! He'd make Malina his contact with his signaler.

Now the guy nearly squealed with bliss.

Once Malina told her in the morning, he should come back to report how she took it, and then as usual set off for work. By the time he returned home, the first report, based on the information he'd given, would be ready. That evening they'd flesh it out and the next day Malina would fake illness to arrange its dispatch. From there they'd have to see.

The half-pint was in seventh heaven. He gave his guest his own bed and went to sleep in the bathroom, where he fit comfortably in the tub.

When he was alone in bed at last, in the quiet and the dark at the end of that crazy day, a single image occupied his mind: The slab of ice moving out of the cellar. What would happen when the hearts melted?

WILL THE DOVE-SOULS FLY OUT?

Nonsense, logic told him in those final moments; he'd killed them dead, time to forget about them. . . . Now he felt with every fiber of his being that another task was calling him. . . . But what was it?

He plunged into sleep like water.

Finally, at the tail end of the night after the day the world got rid of Hitler, Grete fell asleep, or more accurately fainted from exhaustion. Buback remained lying beside her, his senses aglow but his mind strangely clear, knowing that for the first time he was feeling the responsibility of love.

In his first life he and Hilde had been young and Germany had been different. Back then, values that had grown and matured since their bloody birth in the French Revolution still ruled. Hilde had imparted them to Heidi and Buback had guarded the laws that kept them safe. The generation that grew up during the Great War, and then Germany's civil war, was firmly convinced that a battered and wise mankind would never put itself through hell like that again.

Even the prosperity following the Führer's rise seemed to confirm this. New job creation schemes had instantly wiped out unemployment and given the Reich—among other things—the world's most modern highway system, proof for many that an authoritarian government sometimes helps a nation more than parliaments full of idle, chattering humanists.

When Hitler built a massive army to defend the German miracle from an envious outside world, he placed love for homeland above love for individuals. Even Buback, who tried to be an instrument of useful ideas, could not control his family's life. Its destiny was determined by the war, which played with his loves like a cat plays with mice, luring them into the idyllic land of vineyards to smite them with its paw.

Those endless seconds yesterday afternoon, when he thought the murderer had killed Grete, shook Buback's emotions down to the very core of his being. Until that moment Grete was just what she had said: a wartime lover, linked to him by loneliness and a sudden flame of passion meant to cremate the dead in both of them. The threat of losing her opened a new dimension inside him. An icy emptiness surrounded him, as if he'd stepped across death's threshold while he was still alive. And when he found the other woman was the victim, he felt an almost inhumanly cruel relief.

He had instantly regained control, trying to support the young Czech with his burden. Still, Buback was still deeply grateful that this time fate had passed over him. If Jitka Modrá had given him the hope that even after Hilde he might love again, Grete Baumann had fulfilled it.

He now knew that he was not here to participate in this dirty and hopeless war any longer, but rather to protect his love and lead her to safety. But how . . . ?

The man who woke at five A.M. at the bedside of a dead Jitka Modrá was a completely different Jan Morava than the one who fell asleep beside her while she was still alive.

His nighttime despair and his contention with God were gone. He helped the nurses wash her and dress her in a clean white shirt, accompanied her on the stretcher to the pathology lab, kissed her on her still-warm lips, and then waited for an hour like an errand boy in a hallway reeking of disinfectant before he was permitted to see the examination results.

"Death from hemorrhaging into the mediastinum after a puncture wound to the aorta."

Litera, who discovered him there, was the first person caught off guard. Before he could express his sympathy, Morava reeled off his plan for the day's excursions, as if this were a morning strategy session after an ordinary night.

His other colleagues in the department found a man unchanged in appearance and demeanor from the day before. He returned their sympathetic handshakes just the way he would have at daily meetings; anyone who dared to express condolences got at most a nod.

The women at Bartolomějská, confirmed in their rejection of Operation Decoy, were especially shocked. Could this sorry young man really be that insensitive? The men were marginally impressed by his self-control, but it still seemed unnatural to them.

Morava understood what was happening. During that short nap by her bed, he had died along with Jitka. She had then sent him back to the living world to complete his task. During this temporary resurrection, he had resolved not to let anything impede his work.

Maybe it was the combined spiritual strength of all his ancestors, forged by unending blows of fate, that so mercifully numbed him. Otherwise, he knew, he would have gone mad.

He would have cried like a child, howled like a beast, stopped eating, given up sleeping; soon he would have set off aimlessly, half awake, half asleep, down the dark streets of a city ever closer to the front until, heedless of warnings, he would probably have been shot by German guards.

Instead, he resolved to forget that for three months there had been a woman he fell asleep and woke up with, constantly conscious of their child growing inside her, and decided to be only what he had been before: a criminal detective investigating the murders of Maruška Kubílková of Brno, Elisabeth, Baroness of Pomerania, Barbora Pospíchalová, Hedvika Horáková, Marta Pavlátová, Jana Kavanová, Robert Jonáš, František Šebesta, and Jitka Modrá.

He waited for Beran in his anteroom as if there had never been a third person there.

"Since we now know his identity," he began with no preamble, "we can disband the special team. But I'd like to direct the investigation, and I want to start in Plzeň."

"Shouldn't you get some sleep?"

"I've slept three months away already. I have to catch up."

At first he didn't know where he was. He felt refreshed, but all around was deepest darkness. Gradually he collected his thoughts until he could stand and grope his way to the blackout shades. A murky light passed listlessly through the dirty window and curtain. He thought of the neighbor who did the cleaning. Apparently she spent more time on the bed than in the rest of the apartment, except he couldn't really imagine them . . .

He remembered the ferociousness with which his host had spoken about the Germans, soldiers and civilians alike, servants of the Reich sent to Prague and those who had been here for generations. From "exclude them" he'd progressed to "expel them" and then "exterminate them," and he always added, "no exceptions!"

KRAUTS FOR HIM ARE LIKE THOSE WHORES FOR ME!

This discovery fascinated him. He had to learn more. The empty bathroom didn't surprise him; the guy would certainly have snuck out through the living room so as not to wake him up. But the empty kitchen made his blood run cold. He tore into the front hall in his underwear and pressed the apartment door handle down. Locked. He dashed to the window. Mezzanine, at least six meters of sheer wall.

SO, A TRAP!

Once again that awful feebleness overpowered him, the one he thought he had banished the day before on the strafed train; he could thank HER for it. As a child he'd developed it when he'd been IN UNLOVE. "Unlove" was HER worst punishment; SHE wouldn't speak to him and would look right through him, as if he were thin air. He felt so abandoned, so humiliated that . . . he almost . . . hated HER! Once he'd grown up, he confessed this to HER, and SHE was horrified that she'd made him feel that way. SHE never did it after that, but he never got rid of the reaction; in a crisis it would always sneak up on him and make the situation even worse.

WHAT NOW?

He realized in a panic that the guy was a provocateur and had gone to denounce him. At least he had time to break out and disappear! With shaking hands he put on his shirt and pants and prowled around the small apartment like a hunting dog until he sniffed out what he was looking for: A hatchet lay behind the top-fed wood stove. He slipped it under the handle of the front door and got ready to pry it open when he heard steps and the clink of keys. Fully on guard again, he sprang into the corner, where the open door would conceal him, raised the ax above his head, and waited.

The runt saw him and stopped dead in his tracks. His usual bovine smile turned to a desperate grimace, and he dropped his keys and string bag on the ground (fortunately there were only potatoes and bread in it).

"You ass!" his guest exploded as soon as he had slammed the door with his foot. "Didn't you have orders?"

"I just . . . I thought. . . ." He pointed pitifully at the floor. "I thought I'd make you—"

"You entered my unit of your own free will; you'll follow my orders to the letter! How was I to know you weren't a traitor?"

Only now did he feel the pistol pressing against him in his pocket. Why was he waving an ax around when he could just as easily have shot? Shooting's like riding a bicycle, Sergeant Králík had always said; you never forget how!

"I almost split your skull open so I wouldn't alert the whole house!"

"Forgive me. . . . I'll never, ever . . . I swear . . . !"

The half-pint was sincerely devastated. He brewed some rye coffee, and dutifully repeated what he could and could not tell his neighbor before going over.

"One more thing," he asked the little man at the last moment. "Does she have your keys?"

"Yeah, she does."

"Then get them back! I want to be sure no one comes in except you while I'm here."

"Right, got it!"

When the door slammed shut, he began to sip the hot liquid carefully and reflect in peace.

WHAT WILL I DO WITH HIM?

H e had never written with lipstick on a mirror before. "Love," he began, "my greates—" The softened stick snapped. He looked at his uncompleted confession and was still amazed at how much had changed in him since yesterday. Although he had barely slept, a shower refreshed him completely; his brain was like a letter knife, smoothly opening problem after problem until it reached a solution.

He had to retain his post at all costs. And at no cost could he give up his official contacts with the Czech police. In an emergency they were the only ones who could protect Grete—and him as well.

There was no point sticking his head in the sand and waiting until Meckerle had it pulled out for him. He went straight to Bredovská. After all, he had been right, and the colonel must see that. Would Meckerle punish Buback out of sheer jealousy as the water rose around the two of them? With Hitler's death the precariously balanced upside-down pyramid of the Third Reich had come crashing down. Who had seized the highest office; who held in his hands the fate of the German nation, the life and death of millions? Was it the mysteriously vanished Goebbels? Admiral Dönitz, brandishing a supposed last will and testament from the Führer? Or Reichmarschall Göring, who was supposedly exposed in it as a traitor?

Each of them, as Meckerle must know, was a potential protector for Buback. But even the light of the Protectorate's former polestars paled before the brilliance of another contender. Although only a guest in this region, and until recently almost unknown, he commanded the million-strong mass of soldiers which now threatened to overflow their ever-contracting territory like dough rising in a bowl.

Buback had once learned to play poker. In the days when confessions had to be extracted without torture, Dresden detectives had used it to train in their craft, leading shysters down a false trail. One after the other, they showed how to bluff suggestively—for instance, that a criminal's coconspirators had long since confessed. Today, for the first time, Buback would use this skill to deceive his superior.

He entered his office, slamming the door open, contrary to habit. Kroloff, in the anteroom, snapped to attention even more furiously than usual. By the time a sign of defiance appeared in his eyes, he had lost his chance.

"Get me Schörner's adjutant, on the double! Move it, man!"

His commanding tone and the rank of the man he was calling made a deep impression on Kroloff, who was eagerness itself as he reached for the receiver.

Buback leaned back into the armchair and waited. He was convinced that a call from the Prague Gestapo headquarters would not go unanswered—correctly, as it turned out.

"Oberstleutnant Gruner. What can I do for you, Herr Kamerad?"

"Did Lieutenant General Richard von Pommeren serve with you?"

"Confirmed. But if you're looking for him, you're in the wrong place. He fell at the start of the Russian campaign."

"It's not about him, it's about his spouse, who was brutally murdered in Prague. I've identified the killer with the help of the local detectives and now just need to catch him. Attempts are being made on our side to call off the operation, under the rationale that von Pommeren was not a notable military figure. Is your superior interested in having me see this through?"

"I'm surprised you need to ask. The field marshal is firmly convinced that the army is the last guarantor of German law and order. The opinion you have conveyed to me, whoever its author might be, is insulting and politically aberrant. Without even asking I can tell you that you should—no, you must—continue."

"Thank you, Herr Kamerad," Buback said, using the National Socialist title for the first time in his life. "In that case I request that you phone my superior immediately, so I'll have a free hand for continued cooperation with the Protectorate police."

"Let me take it down. His name?"

"Standartenführer Meckerle."

"Christian name?"

"Hubertus. . . ." Buback remembered.

"No! Hubertus the Great! He was the head clerk at my bank at home. And no doubt will be again some day. I'll call him straightaway. Heil . . ."

Pause. And then, in sincere confusion:

"What do we say from now on?"

When Buback dropped in at his Czech office to pick up his hat and raincoat, Beran turned to Morava in surprise.

"Could I have been wrong? What could interest him more than the situation in this building? Not the case, certainly? Keep his nose to the grindstone; it'd be damned awkward having him around here when we have our own collaborators to watch. Best of luck, but if things heat up in the meantime, back to me on the double!"

He dismissed Morava without further explanation, wordlessly squeezing both his shoulders.

On the way to Plzeň, Buback informed Morava—as if nothing had happened in the meanwhile—about everything he had learned since yesterday.

"I've had a couple of cases in my career where we uncovered what could be termed a ritual. The perpetrators picked a ceremonial method of killing, out of a conviction that they were acting in a higher interest. This is clearly Rypl's case; he became his mother's instrument of revenge. Maybe Rypl believes he's ridding the world of trash, and that's why he's not a depressive maniac, the sort that give themselves away. His coworkers and neighbors in the building described him as quite a pleasant person. Most of those women opened their doors to him trustingly. His shy inconspicuousness and serious demeanor will no doubt continue to cover his tracks."

They were in Plzeň just after noon and began by combing Rypl's apartment again, looking for a portrait better than the five-year-old photo from his identity card application. After his mother's death he had evidently had no one to take pictures for; they found absolutely nothing.

Then Morava assembled the entire theater staff and had them rack their brains. In vain. No, Rypl hadn't gone to parties, when they were still permitted, nor had he gone on staff days out; no one had ever made up a staff photo album, or taken pictures at meetings, certainly not!

Buback spoke into the silence that followed.

"Was he ever in a performance?"

"No!" The manager dismissed this idea. "After all, he was a stoker and a jani—Wait a minute!"

He headed for the program archives, but before he had plowed through them the others remembered as well: To earn some extra money, Rypl had played a walk-on role as a servant just before the Czech theaters had been closed. A photo was found; it was sharp and those present agreed that it captured Rypl's current likeness quite faithfully.

Two hours later, Plzeň policemen had spread out across the city with photos reproduced by the local criminal section. Working from a plan they drew up quickly with Morava, they covered the various crucial points at which the suspect could have been spotted. Meanwhile, the Werkschutz log at the theater door showed that on the days murders were committed this year, Rypl had been either on vacation or supposedly running errands, but he always left and returned at times corresponding to train arrivals and departures.

"Why not yesterday?" Morava racked his brains. "Or did he come back and was warned? How? By whom?"

Buback was comparing the times as well.

"The ice," he guessed. "He saw them carrying out the ice and figured they'd find the hearts."

An hour later the supposition was confirmed by the conductor from the tram that had passed the theater yesterday. A bit later they had two witnesses, who recognized the picture: It was the man with nerves of steel, who sat through a bomb raid in the train without putting down his newspaper. Finally the railway ticket agent on the evening shift confirmed that a traveler he had previously seen only in the morning had yesterday quite exceptionally bought a ticket on the last train to Prague.

"So, back again," Morava ordered. "The needle has returned to the haystack."

"To Bartolomějská?" Litera asked.

"No, home."

He realized two pairs of eyes were fixed on him, and for a moment despair overwhelmed him as he thought of the other half of his body and soul freezing in one of Pathology's sliding drawers. Then awareness of his obligation resurfaced and sheathed him in its armor, protecting him from hurtful memories and thoughts. He checked that he had his old keys and specified: "Back to the dormitory."

They rode back silently and swiftly. Their side of the road was empty, while an uninterrupted column of military vehicles dappled generously with staff cars and moving vans rolled westward toward them from Prague.

The yellowed centers of the blue-painted headlights passed by Morava, as indolent as the eyes of giant cats.

J udges!" Grete snorted contemptuously. "They judged humanity, but didn't quite manage to hang all of it, so now they're fleeing its revenge. Your neighbor, for instance, took to his heels as soon as it got dark, like a criminal. So, downstairs to his stores, love; we've drunk our reserves and I'm thirsty."

"I don't have the keys," Buback responded confusedly.

"And don't tell me: You're a man of the law! Except this isn't robbery; it was all stolen goods to begin with. Doesn't matter, I'll go myself. These might be the last treats we get."

In the end, of course, he accompanied her down and broke the back-door window with his elbow. Then they reached in and turned the key from inside. The open, half-empty cupboards and half-full drawers bore witness to a hasty departure. The judge either had not been a drinker or had taken the remaining alcohol with him. However, they found unbelievable riches in the icebox and the pantry: a hunk of Swiss Emmenthal, a slab of bacon, sardines, and nuts. Behind the teapot they finally discovered a bottle of English rum and two packs of American cigarettes. Buback shook his head. What a mockery of their insistence that all right-thinking Germans should hate the products of enemy civilizations!

They made themselves some grog with the rum and hot water, and their tension slackened; after the second glass they were pleasantly relaxed.

"Love," she said, returning to her theme, "how long do you intend to stay here on this Titanic? Everyone's already in the lifeboats."

"Not everyone. A couple of people think once you've made your bed you should lie in it."

"What bed did you make," she flared at him. "You hunted criminals and murderers."

"Wasn't it you who pointed out that I let the biggest ones go unpunished? You were right; I even applauded them! Just last year I ruined my last visit with Hilde in an argument where I took the Führer's side against her."

She grinned bitterly.

"I'm a fine one to lecture you. I fought my battles in the bedroom. Buback, how could an entire nation fall so far so fast?"

"An epidemic of obedience. The greatest scourge of mankind. A couple of people think up a recipe for a happy future and shout it so loud and long that all the lost souls take up the cause. The careerists follow. And suddenly they're a force that no longer clamors and offers; instead they demand and direct. Disobedience is punished, obedience rewarded: An easy choice for the average person."

"And then comes the bill."

"Yes. And once again it's time to pay."

"But haven't the two of us paid enough, love? Don't we have the right to get off the boat? Except it's harder for you than for me, I guess; the military police are waiting for you."

"That's not the issue. . . . What bothers me more is that suddenly I don't know what honor is and what's disgrace."

"Can we stop the riddles? I'm not in the mood just now."

"Schörner intends to turn Prague into a fortress."

"Then it's high time to turn tail like the jackass downstairs. We both know what happens to fortresses. And you were assigned here; why can't you go back?"

"To where?"

"For God's sake," she snapped, "couldn't you think of something and arrange it?"

"Grete, you've had this German guilt far longer and harder than I have. Maybe I can mitigate it."

"You!"

"I was born in Prague. And it's the last city in central Europe whose beauty is still intact."

"And you're going to save it!"

"Calm down! Listen to me. I'm working with the Czechs, after all. I could warn them in time."

She stopped short. Her aggressiveness ceased; the thought intrigued her.

"So do it."

It's not real till you say it, he chanted to himself for the last time, but now there was no way out.

"No matter what language you speak, that's called treason, Grete."

"Aha . . . and who are you betraying?"

"Well . . ."

Now he stopped short.

"Your homeland, maybe," she snapped. "That lunatic and his henchmen betrayed it a long time ago. Their secret weapon was a con game for the softheaded from day one, and you'll excuse me, but they've made a fuckup of the war—how long do you intend to keep this up, Buback?"

He felt awkward, but couldn't not say it.

"I took an oath."

"Loyalty to Führer and the Reich, right? But he's stone dead and the Reich's practically fallen apart. Anything else you'd like to die for? Or anyone? Maybe you'd care to show your devotion to the Nibelungen, to have the honor of falling in battle for Schörner and Meckerle? Now that's what I call a disgrace! Disgrace? Try stupidity!"

She poured herself a nearly full glass of rum and topped it off with boiling water.

"If you think you can prevent those sons of bitches from destroying this city too, then you should tell this Morava of yours what you know; you made him out to be a decent person, and he looks it, but there's got to be some give-and-take!"

He did not understand. She bristled again.

"Do you need me to point out the obvious? We're in a lion's den. All Prague knows this is the German quarter, and believe me, the lions will come—excuse me, did I say lions? More like hyenas!— as soon as they sense Germany is flat on its back. And for them you're Gestapo and I'm a Kraut whore; there'll be no mercy for us. My love, why leave me hanging here? Do you want me to end up like those widows?"

He was shocked by the thought.

"Why would you—?"

"The murderers' holiday is already starting, love. They're flying in, converging on the feast like bugs on a lamp; the killing is never better than when your nation has its moment in the spotlight, and Germany is proof of it." Then she spoke calmly and practically, as he'd never heard her before.

"I'm a silly woman and can't understand how a man of your position can and should act in this situation. But I'm depending on you to find a way to save us both in time. At the very least your Czechs owe me something."

As if reading his furtive thought, she continued.

"It was fate's doing, not mine, that she died; her death isn't on my conscience, nor should it be on yours. Good night."

She suddenly rose and headed for the bathroom.

"I want to hold you," he said.

"Not today. Your weakness is catching. I need your strength, so I'll have to hold off. I'd rather go home, but he might be there, so let me stay, but pretend I'm not here."

He bounced up so quickly that he was able to block her way.

"Grete! Everyone has the right to weak moments. And that's what the other person is—"

"Don't count on it," she said brusquely. "I have to be strong when I'm alone. When we're together, it's your job. That's why I love you."

G et up, Jan!" Jitka said. "Enough sleep; time to go to work." He could sense the touch of her face, which had moved next to his, but he did not want to open his eyes; those morning visits with her in the unknown reaches of sleep were now the most important moments of his life. He had no idea how he could have ever woken up alone and spent whole days without knowing they would fall asleep that night together. "Jan," Jitka called again, "time to get up, beloved; today's a big day for you!" He pretended he was sound asleep, so she would use her tender wiles, brushing lips against lips and blowing on his closed eyelids. Instead, she said despairingly, "Jan, enough already; go find that monster—he did kill me, you know!"

He blinked. On the night table was a daily calendar, frozen in time at February 14. The woman he had escorted home and stayed with ever since was dead, and he was hugging his mother's old featherbed in his dormitory room near Number Four. He stood up, so as to be entirely awake before hopelessness hit, did a couple of stretches, and let the cold shower pound into him. By the time he had finished brewing his mother's rose-hip tea, his defensive armor had closed around him again, impervious to thoughts of the body in the dark icebox.

He was in her service and had to fulfill the task she had set him; then he'd see what happened.

He got only Matlák and Jetel for his plan and was satisfied. He didn't see Beran or even look for him. Most of his colleagues, who would normally have been around, were absent. Even a simpleton could tell that the brain stem of the Czech police was securing itself against the danger of another attack.

He realized that he had not seen a single German uniform on his way over. He had seen the film *The Invisible Man* several times before the war, and it always gave him goose bumps. The Germans, hidden behind the walls of former schools, universities, dormitories, and hotels now serving as barracks and offices, were suddenly more malevolent than they had been in full view. It reminded him of the stony plain above his village, where what appeared to be an innocent heap of brushwood would in the blink of an eye become a tangle of attacking vipers. Prague now seemed much the same way.

He therefore agreed at once when Buback offered to come along; the German could vouch for them in any confrontations with his countrymen.

The four of them formed a chain as each train arrived from Plzeň, and questioned all the passengers. Most knew each other by sight from traveling to and from work. No one knew the man in the policemen's photograph.

Between trains Morava sat on a bench beneath the roof of the first platform and stared straight ahead. The others left him alone, and he tried to distract himself by fixing his thoughts on the insignificant. He calculated the length and height of the buildings opposite, counted the crossties in his vision, concentratedly followed the crooked flight path of one of the birds in a flock circling above the station.

At noon the others brought him bread with some kind of spread, in the evening a warm potato pancake; after the last train they took him off to sleep and brought him back before the first one the next morning. All of this he sensed as if in a dream, one he left only when another train arrived from Plzeň. And no one, not one passenger, recognized that face.

"It's the same people as yesterday," Matlák said near evening.

Morava could see that himself. Rumors of the hunt for the widow killer had spread. When they saw the four men with photographs, the passengers would shake their heads or hands, and the men were stung by the first sharp retorts: Why were they still hanging around doing nothing? By now even that killer must know where they were. But Morava never raised an eyebrow or doubted his decision. The first thing Beran had taught him was patience.

That evening it paid off.

It was the novice Jetel who excitedly brought over an older man returning from his shift at the Beroun locomotive depot. Yes, he confirmed, he remembered the man well; on Sunday he had seen him waiting for the night tram with his coworker Karel Malina. He himself had waited behind a tree, because Malina was a well-known motor mouth. He'd been glad enough to be rid of him on the train; Malina had gone to look for matches and never came back. At the last moment, the railway worker had boarded the rear car of the tram and dozed all the way to the last stop. No, he didn't know where Malina lived; surely the police could find out?

Malina's other potential acquaintances had long since left the station. The only thing left to do today was follow up the lead. There were eleven Karel Malinas in Prague. When Morava began to plot a route for visiting them, Buback raised his first objection.

"It's quite late and we could start a panic. They'll think it's the Gestapo."

He stared in surprise at the German.

"Yes," he said, "you're right, thanks. Good night."

In his room, it seemed he barely closed and opened his eyes only to find it was morning. He broke through the horrible moment of awakening when she died for him again, and set off on the trail of her murderer. As a good morning, Matlák and Jetel announced that only the German newspapers had published Rypl's picture. The Czech papers had objected, saying that the Gestapo had used this method a few times already to try to catch Resistance workers; they could not risk taking the Germans' bait in the eleventh hour.

As they left, Morava noticed a further gesture from Buback: he let the lanky Matlák have the front seat instead of himself, so he would not be cramped in the back of the car. Matlák took advantage of the language barrier to make a biting comment in Czech. "So they've finally decided they have enough 'living space'."

At the depot they easily obtained Malina's Prague address. Alarmingly, the repairman had not shown up for work yesterday or today, and had not notified them why. The personnel department clerk added that, sadly enough, this was a common occurrence these days; people find a thousand excuses, and this was probably just the beginning.

For Buback's sake Morava conducted the conversation in German, and the clerk in his shirtsleeves suddenly wagged his finger at the liaison officer, like an old-fashioned teacher lecturing an unruly pupil.

"You promised Europe order, and you leave behind havoc and anarchy!"

B uback knew the four Czechs were waiting to see what he would say to this bold reproach.

He looked briefly from one face to the next, ending with the clerk's.

"If an individual can apologize for a whole nation, then I hereby do so."

No one said anything to that, and he was glad when Morava gave the order to leave. On the way back to the car he overheard another of Matlák's sotto voce comments to Jetel.

"Is he that decent or just chicken?"

Yes, he admitted, it was a good question; was he, an insignificant German, truly convinced he bore all his nation's guilt on his shoulders, or had Grete's "give-and-take" infected him? Was he simply a better sort of opportunist, abandoning ship in a slightly more genteel fashion than the bosses who fled with their loot?

After all, he'd only needed one thing all his life: self-respect!

Buback mused on this on the way back to Prague, as the driver and his companion boldly compared notes in Czech on the illegal radio stations' war reports. What he was doing now made him the lowest sort of stool pigeon, if for no other reason than that Morava had trusted him. It was wrong to continue deceiving him. But how could he end the deception? And should he really give up his last and only advantage in this godforsaken posting?

On the way through a small town halfway to Prague, the Czech contingent suddenly fell silent and stared in the same direction. A man stood on a ladder in front of a pub with a bucket hung at his side, painting over the sign WARME UND KALTE KÜCHE, BIER, WEIN, LIMON-ADEN with circular strokes of his brush. The meaning of this spectacle evaded Buback, and they had already turned the corner when he understood: The man was not getting rid of all the lettering, only the German phrases. And he was not doing it surreptitiously by night, but in broad daylight, in full view of the German soldiers passing constantly through on the main road.

An SS man taking a tip; a clerk admonishing a Gestapo agent for destroying Europe; and a man with a bucket of lime—the first three visible cracks in the facade of the Third Reich. It reminded Buback of the time during the retreat from Belgium when he had watched the military engineers destroy a bridge. After the blast it rose upward along its whole length and seemed to hang in the air for an unbelievably long time before it hurtled into the water, disintegrating into a thousand pieces. He felt that all Germany was now in that deceptive state of elevation preceding collapse, and would carry both him and the woman depending on him down with it.

"Excuse me," Morava's voice broke in. "I have to work out with my colleagues what we're doing next."

He nodded, knowing that the majority of men from the Prague criminal police had formally passed the required examination in German, but like Litera could not hold a conversation; for ordinary workers the Reich offices had had to turn a blind eye to keep the Protectorate government functioning at all.

"Whether he's hiding there or not," Morava began in Czech, "he has Šebesta's pistol, and yours were taken in the raid."

Angular Matlák turned toward the back and waved a powerful paw dismissively.

"That's all right."

"Don't overestimate your bare hands."

"They're not bare."

"What do you mean . . . ?"

Now Jetel grinned as well.

"They left us our gun permits, so we dug into the old reserves, as the super—"

"That's enough!" Morava warned them almost casually.

He doesn't trust me, Buback realized, noticing only now that his companions' jackets bulged gently. So they've opened the secret cache! Meckerle had sensed it, while they'd managed to lead Buback away from it from February till now. But maybe he'd let them succeed. Had he already given up the Germans' war when he got to know Jitka Modrá and the young man beside him? The Czechs' brief conversation yielded one important fact. Morava had not disappointed him; even

238

his own people, the Czechs, knew he was a "lotus flower" incapable of deceit, so for safety's sake they had isolated him from all information. How should he treat his relationship with Morava and the whole confounded situation now, after his last conversation with Grete?

He never finished the thought. They had come to a halt in front of a house that stood out like a poor relation in this well-to-do neighborhood, which bore the name Královské Vinohrady—"Royal Vineyards." On the crumbling facade of the late-twenties apartment building was a barely legible stucco sign: RAILWAY HOUSE.

The lady caretaker, clucking like a chicken at the police's arrival, informed them in one long sentence that the man they were looking for lived on the third floor, number fourteen; was orderly and friendly; paid her, without arguing, to unlock his door when he forgot his key; and was a bachelor, so the wife of his friend Mr. Kratina in number fifteen looked after him, cleaning and doing his laundry. No, she herself hadn't seen Mr. Malina since Sunday and didn't know the man in the picture.

The card on the apartment door read MALINA and was handsomely executed in prewar style, with India ink. Morava motioned to his subordinates to wait on the stairs below the landing. Buback understood he was worried about the peephole, and retreated. He watched Morava expertly press his ear to the door before ringing, to catch any possible reaction, but the building was too noisy. Two more rings and still no reaction; Morava stepped over to the neighboring apartment.

An attractive forty-year-old woman opened the door in her apron; she looked feisty, but the foursome made an impression on her. Like a schoolchild called on in class, she answered them in complete sentences. Mr. Malina? Yes, she knew Mr. Malina; she earned some money helping him with the housework. The keys to his apartment? She only picked up the keys to his apartment on Wednesdays, she didn't want to be responsible for someone else's home these days, she's sure they understood why. Yesterday? Yesterday she saw Mr. Malina when she returned the keys to him; he'd mentioned he might go see his mother. Where? She didn't know where, maybe Kladno, west of Prague . . . or was it Kolín, to the east? Someone else in the apartment? No, there was no one else in the apartment; she'd been there to clean, after all!

When Morava began to translate for Buback, the German could not help noticing that the woman was trembling with nervousness. As a Czech she was certainly within her rights to do so. Involuntarily her eyes strayed over to him; she averted them instantly and turned back to the assistant detective.

"Sir, he ... Karel ... I mean Mr. Malina sometimes talked too much, but he wasn't the type to get involved in anything, especially anything political!"

"He wouldn't have let anyone stay over here, by any chance?" Morava asked.

"I would have known!"

"Just so we understand each other: I'm asking in his own interest. We're looking for a man he was seen with the day before yesterday, that evening at the train station. The man is most probably a murderer we've been tracking; he could easily kill Mr. Malina as well."

"Do you really believe I'd want that on my conscience!"

She's got something with him, Buback sensed. Morava was apparently thinking the same thing.

"Listen to me, then," he said, giving her Rypl's photograph. "As soon as he returns, send him immediately—day or night—to number four, Bartolomějská Street; my name is Morava. If he did meet this man, he has to tell me everything he knows. You're sure you've never seen him?"

"No!" she said plainly and convincingly, as if a huge weight had been lifted from her. "As God is my witness, on the lives of everyone I love, never!"

It was all worked out and rehearsed in advance. For two long days he'd done nothing besides listen to the building. He heard the steps of four men on the staircase at that odd hour and was at the door in his rubber-soled shoes before they rang. SHE had taught him to plan for the worst: Life stinks, Tony; it's always got more lousy tricks up its sleeve! The runt had probably opened his big mouth on his morning grocery run and now someone had blown his cover.

After Malina returned from his neighbor's, he had forced the terrified runt to bind his own legs at gunpoint with the straps. The poor half-pint still believed that his disobedience had aroused the parachutist's suspicions, and swore up and down that he was a true patriot. Obediently he put his hands behind his back, so he could be more easily tied up, and even nodded appreciatively when told that the Resistance hero would have to secure him temporarily; of course, he would release his host with honor as soon as it was possible.

When it came down to it, this motor mouth posed a real danger to him. Now that he'd resolved to take revenge on the Krauts he had THE RIGHT TO A TACTICAL DECEPTION.

He explained his reasoning to the half-pint quite convincingly. After a while Malina stopped squirming and resigned himself to his unpleasant fate, lying bound and gagged in the bathtub bed he had made for himself the day before. During the day the bathroom door was unlocked, and he was allowed to signal with a muffled knock that he needed facilities or food. Eventually the half-pint's hunger passed. At least we'll save on food, his captor thought; for the moment there was nowhere else to go and supplies were running low. At night he locked the bathroom so he could sleep in safety. If you even think about knocking on the wall to your neighbor . . . He had left the sentence unfinished and put his long, slender knife up to the guy's throat.

It was strange that now, when the only thing keeping him safe was the thin wooden panel of the door, his heart wasn't even racing or his knees knocking! In the space of a few dozen hours, something had happened to him in that apartment, and it was evidently connected with his NEW MISSION. But there was something else, something he had automatically grabbed at home and hidden to use later as bait, and now, as he felt it, it brought back the best moments of his life.

THE PISTOL.

He could still remember the marvelous happiness he'd felt on the Brno shooting range. In 1919 he had joined a regiment of fresh recruits for the brand-new Czechoslovak Army. SHE tried to derail his application, but failed: he was absolutely healthy, and greenhorns were just cannon fodder anyway.

Seasoned legionnaires from France led the exercises; they worked the recruits so mercilessly that he had no time for homesickness during the day, and evenings he simply collapsed from exhaustion. The Hungarian invasion of Slovakia made time of the essence. On the seventh day they marched over to sharpshooting, and that was where it happened. He was the only one in his unit to hit all the targets and was singled out in the orders for his unforeseen talent. He had never been the center of attention before. It was no surprise that he now set his sights on the army.

I'LL BE A SOLDIER!

The soldiers at the front sensed it. He was the only rookie they didn't mess with; on the contrary, a week later when he repeated his achievement in a mock battle, the feared Sergeant Králík invited him to the canteen for a beer. He should sign up for Slovakia, the sergeant urged him; it would undoubtedly be the last war for a long time and that was when military careers were made. He'd return as a noncommissioned officer and would be set for life.

After all those years with HER he was so utterly unprepared for this opportunity that he hesitated. No need to worry, Králík said; he sensed something in the boy that makes a soldier a soldier. What? Well, what else: A TASTE FOR KILLING!

He froze. He did not understand where he, a fragile and unsure loner nicknamed "mama's boy," could have gotten it from, but at that moment he knew for sure that Králík was right.

I HAVE IT!

AND I WANT TO BE MYSELF!

He rushed into battle like it was a hunt; he literally shook with longing to score a hit. The Hungarians abandoned Komárno, on the Slovak side of the river, of their own accord; the battle in the streets was almost over. The rest of the day they spent huddled on the banks of the Danube in grenade-launcher fire, pulling the wounded out. When they were just about to storm the Hungarians, the last grenade landed and IT WAS ALL OVER.

He had had no place to go from the hospital except back to HER.

That taste suddenly resurfaced after almost twenty years, but by then he was guided BY THE PICTURE. It had captivated him so completely in the country church that he had remained there largely for its sake.

When he left, he had to take it with him, since he knew it was the PROTOTYPE.

He had that taste, that old taste for shooting, again today, as beyond the doors the trap closed around him. He listened to the Czech-German conversation outside: Someone had seen him with that guy. With his pistol in hand he felt confident. If that whore had the keys, or if they broke through the door, half a round would take all of them out, and no one else would stand in his way.

Then he heard the neighbor's oath, and even though it was the result of his own cleverness, he was still a bit disappointed. Still, there was no need to stir up extra difficulties for himself. Not when the hunt for Germans was just beginning!

SO NEXT TIME!

Once the woman had returned to the apartment and he heard the men's footsteps on the staircase, he went quietly through the kitchen and bedroom into the bathroom to see if the guy had wet his pants in disappointment.

M y love," Grete welcomed him home as he opened the apartment door, "they want to evacuate all of us."

He had been expecting this pronouncement for almost a week now as various institutions vanished from Prague on a daily basis, but had not dared to think it through. Even if Grete had a definite destination, the likelihood of their meeting again was minimal. Once the fiery column had rolled past, telephones and post offices would no longer exist, and millions of homeless would wander across a devastated Germany like nomads. And as for himself, he knew he'd already decided inside; it was the only way to avoid complete disgrace in his own and her eyes as well. If that was his path, then his fate lay with the stars.

"Where to?" he asked, just to say something, and tried not to show how upset he was.

"Somewhere in Tyrolia."

"And there?"

"All troupes of the German Theater are to be housed there temporarily until we can return here."

"They said that!"

"Yes," she sneered. "Theater Director Kuhnke appeared personally to assure us that starting next season we'll be playing in Prague as usual."

"And what does it really mean?"

"He wants to cut and run, but can't do it without us, so he'll pretend it's to protect the flower of imperial art for better days. He'll shove us into some flea-ridden barracks and get his own fat ass over to Switzerland; his brother works at the embassy there."

"You think."

"Everyone thinks."

"And what do the others want to do?"

"Go, of course! Who wants to wait till it breaks? Come on, love, we talked this through two days ago. From there it'll be clear what to do next."

He could see in the distance that bridge blown off its foundations, hanging deceptively in the air.

"Yes. It's coming soon. The only question is who'll start it."

"Exactly."

She fell silent and looked inquisitively and inquiringly at him. He gathered his strength.

"I hope you'll go," he said.

"You want me to?"

"Yes."

"Ah . . . that's interesting."

"Why so?"

"You mentioned something a while back about loving me."

"Yes!"

"So that's no longer the case?"

He could not let her get away with that.

"If I love you, how can I want you to stay? I want you to live, I want to have a reason to survive this. Once the battle starts, I could probably find you a hiding place, but I could hardly stay with you."

"I know," she said.

244

"Well, then."

He felt the emptiness begin to open inside him, but kept his face and voice expressionless, so as not to evoke her sympathy. But why? Why not admit that without her he would be alone with the war, and his life would lose all meaning? Or should he give up this messianic complex of personal guilt and go with her? She was right: he was alone at work; he could issue his own marching orders.

"So you love me," she said before he could speak again.

"Yes."

"And you'll let me leave."

He steeled himself.

"Yes."

"Well, that's good."

"What?"

"That you love me so much."

He did not know what to say to this. He felt like he was slowly losing her; every word he said sounded weak or false. This was to be his punishment; could there be a worse one? His nation had visited immeasurable sorrows on the world, and he was sacrificing his personal happiness to redeem them. He wanted to know everything, quickly.

"When will it be?"

"This evening at six, suitcases packed, at the theater. Departure is precisely at seven."

He looked perplexedly at his watch.

"But it's eight. . . ."

"I know," she said. "You see, I love you too. So why should you die here alone?"

Jitka's funeral took place the morning of Saturday, May fifth.

Jan Morava had barely left the dormitory on Konviktská Street when he sensed a new mood in the air. Once again the city's temper had completely changed. An almost awkward enthusiasm replaced the fear that had gripped it since the February air raids. Most of the German signs had disappeared. The stragglers removing the remaining few did not worry about appearances; they simply crossed out the German words with two strokes of a brush dipped in lime or paint.

This time it was the Czech police closing off the entrance to Bartolomějská Street. They looked quite exotic. For the first time in years, they wore their black helmets and officers' belts with pistols and carried rifles. These men were clearly from another district, but they amiably waved him through without checking his documents; they must have known him from occasional contact with his office. Morava had only come in to announce that he intended to continue his search after the funeral, and was surprised when Beran told him that they would go to the cemetery together.

"I've made the arrangements," he said. "I'll just change quickly, and you should put on a uniform too; it's important we all be seen today. And Morava," he called after him, "pick up a pistol as well."

For the first time in two years, since his promotion to assistant detective, he pulled his uniform down from the top shelf of the office wardrobe. The years of disuse showed. When he met the superintendent again they couldn't help smiling. With training, Morava's shoulders had grown, and his sleeves barely fit. Beran had lost weight in the bustle of the last few months and his shirt swam on him. Their holsters weighed them down; they kept wanting to cinch them up. The high cap with its badge crimped Morava's head and settled on Beran's ears. On top of this they smelled of naphthalene.

"Well, how-dee-doo!" a similarly dressed Litera summed them up. "One look at us and the Germans will pee in their pants and lay down their arms!"

That was his first and last joke for the day. They rode silently through Prague, watching the city painstakingly transform itself from a German metropolis into a Czech one, and trying not to dwell on the reason for their trip. This hysterical rush, Morava mused, was like trying to erase the traces of your own deeds, as if overnight the city could expunge— or at least will itself to forget—six years of meek acceptance too often verging on active collaboration.

The Czech activity had caught the Germans' attention. Heavily reinforced military patrols were everywhere. Today they walked in threes or fours instead of in twos, and hand grenades with long hafts now jutted from their belts.

"Hey hey!" Litera pointed at a trio they passed underneath the railroad bridge.

The German army had always flaunted its orderliness and discipline in the occupied territories, but the cigarettes stuck in the corners of the soldiers' mouths were a far cry from that image. For experienced warriors, apparently, Prague was already on the frontlines.

They reached the crown of the steep street alongside the Vyšehrad ramparts and rumbled across the cobblestones to the church by the cemetery. There Beran surprised Morava for the second time that day.

"I got one for you, too," he said, while Litera opened the trunk and removed two bouquets and a small wreath.

FOR JITKA FROM JAN—FOR JITKA FROM V. B.—FOR JITKA FROM EVERYONE said the ribbons. Red, white, and blue, they were the colors of the Czech flag, which until now had been strictly forbidden.

"Everyone wanted to come," the superintendent explained, "but I'm sure you'll understand I couldn't allow that, so I'm here both in a personal capacity and for them."

Beran had arranged the simple ceremony after a short conversation with Morava on Wednesday. He had unsentimentally ordered that under no circumstances must it run late or exceed fifteen minutes. The police technician removed the decoy tablet with the name JAN MORAVA from the gravesite where the murderer had taken the star-crossed bait, and replaced it with a real one:

JITKA MODRÁ

The sexton and a vicar from the Evangelical Church of the Savior were waiting at the graveside. Next to them was a simple wooden coffin resting on planks. In a few sentences the vicar said a farewell for her parents and relatives, who were cut off from Prague by the front. Then he read the Lord's Prayer, and for the first time Morava neither moved his lips nor even said it to himself.

Even now he could only think about the man he was after. How to find him now? Prague was coming to a boil, like a cauldron whose lid dances as the water threatens to spill over. The Czech newspapermen, overcome at the eleventh hour by sympathy for the Resistance, kept sanctimoniously refusing to publish the murderer's picture. Morava had made a thousand copies of Rypl's photograph, but only a few policemen in Prague had one, and they were already preoccupied, waiting to see whether the Germans would attack them again, this time more savagely, or whether they themselves would suddenly be forced to attack the Germans. Where could a man hide if he apparently had no relatives or friends here? And who would harbor a strange man at great risk to himself when it could still be a Gestapo trap? Unless ... unless ... unless he thought he was hiding Rypl from the Germans!

Yes, if people who had called the Germans valued customers yesterday could turn about and publicly erase all the German signs today, wouldn't someone who desperately wanted an alibi be tempted to hide a supposed ... what? Maybe a persecuted patriot? But then it could be a whole family covering for him, or a whole building. Rypl wouldn't even have to set foot outside.

In that case, the key character was this Malina. The murderer had almost certainly left the train station with him. Why should they accept the neighbor's statement that he went to visit his mother and that there was no one in the apartment? No, he'd have it opened today on orders. . . . He almost turned to Litera so as to be off without delay, when a movement disrupted his thoughts.

Four men in well-worn dark clothes skillfully tightened and then loosened the straps. The coffin began to descend into the grave he had designed himself and adorned with his own name, only to place his wife and unborn child into it. Just at that moment Jitka seemed to be physically present by him; he could see the shyness of her brown eyes beneath their lids, smell the country milkiness of her skin, feel her fingers, knuckles, elbows, sides, breasts.

For a moment that numb silence in his soul threatened to rip wide open; he nearly sank to his knees and wept bitterly, almost jumped into the pit to huddle on the wooden lid. He felt someone's palm clasp his arm. It was Beran, guiding him to the lip of the grave. Together they threw a handful of earth on the coffin. And afterward, as he strode off down the grave-lined path toward the car, he heard a quiet voice behind him.

"Good work, Morava!"

Beran continued in the vehicle from the front seat.

"Today you'll have to interrupt your investigation and be my personal adjutant for a day. I've become a commander in my old age. The Germans were right to hang that bogeyman Buback around our necks, you know."

"Why didn't you even hint to me that—"

"You're not made for deception, or so I felt. I wanted you to keep your credibility. Jitka was all I needed."

"She knew?"

"Of course. She was my right-hand man. I had to order her not to breathe a word to you until I gave permission."

Grief wrung Jan Morava's heart again; he'd barely begun to know the girl now buried deep in the stony soil.

"Live in the future, my good friend," Beran said knowingly. "Your life is only beginning, even though you may think it's already ended. May she have a long life inside you. Do you know how to use it?"

With no transition he nodded at Morava's holster and pistol.

"No," the younger man answered, complying with the change of subject. "I started right when Rajner lowered the number of employees approved to carry weapons."

"Aha. Well, now we're raising it again. Take it out of the holster and look straight ahead."

He obeyed and examined the piece of steel as if it were an unfamiliar animal. Beran leaned over from the front seat, took the weapon and demonstrated.

"This is how you remove and replace the magazine. This is how you take the safety off and put it on. We won't take it apart now. And then you just squeeze this. Try it."

Morava obediently slid the magazine out and back in, flipped the safety off and then squeezed the trigger.

A deafening shot rang out and the interior of the vehicle filled with acrid dust.

Litera, shaken, careened onto the fortunately deserted sidewalk.

They stopped.

Morava blushed and stared at the upholstery of the front seat. A small black hole had appeared in it.

Beran bent over and picked up the cartridge, which had flown off to one side and rebounded to land on the floor.

"That was my stupid mistake," he finally said. "At least you won't forget that there's one in the barrel. And never to point it at people. Ugh, what a fright!"

L ove," Grete said, "you're going I don't know where, and all I can do is cross my fingers for you. But when you're doing I don't know what, don't forget there's someone waiting for you who needs you. Just so you'll remember to stay alive and not go belly-up."

First Buback needed to stop at the central office. There he checked that his full powers were still in force; apparently Schörner's star was still at its zenith. However, the commanders' assembly, which had seemed so promising, was unlike anything he had ever seen before in that building. All the former masters of the world (as Grete had nicknamed them) and their flunkies were nervously chain-smoking and acting slightly demented. The colonel was still in a meeting at the Castle with K. H. Frank. The two of them were trying to contact Fleet Admiral Dönitz; as the Führer's replacement, Dönitz would give them clear instructions on the course of the war and would resolve the jurisdictional dispute in the Protectorate, where overnight Mitte's army seemed to have seized control. Buback heard the wildest rumors around him, and his head spun: which should he take seriously and pass on to the Czechs, if he truly wanted to make a difference? Finally Meckerle's aide-de-camp entered.

"Achtung! Der Gruppenführer!"

Everyone flew to their feet; there were a few seconds of tension— which lieutenant general had Berlin dispatched here from the remainders of the Reich?—and then surprise. In marched the old familiar colonel.

For the first time there was no Heil Hitler. Meckerle motioned them to sit with a sharp flap of his hand and curtly advised them that Dönitz himself had just promoted him. Then he laid out in just five minutes what Buback needed to know. Measures for a military occupation of Prague were to be implemented immediately. At noon, units stationed around the city would begin to secure strategic points, and that night the army vanguard would arrive. The latter would crush any resistance and secure the city, so that elite divisions and troops could use it as a transit point before the Russian pincers closed in on them from the north and south. They had chosen a time when employees of large firms would be headed homeward for Sunday, and most Czechs would be busy in their gardens. General Vlasov's corps of former Russian war prisoners was pressing toward the capital of the Protectorate, and this complicated the situation even further. The Russians all faced charges of high treason at home, and they were wreaking havoc with the Germans' plans by trying to break through to the advancing American army ahead of the Soviets.

"This will all be clarified in a new political doctrine which has just been decoded," Meckerle finished. "It will be announced in a secret order at fourteen hundred hours. Dismissed!"

He disappeared without a good-bye. Buback, who sensed that they would be served up more fantasies and hot air that afternoon, already knew enough. Old dog or no, he could still learn a few new tricks; he would betray a regime he had sworn allegiance to, in order to uphold values that every normal, feeling person held dear.

His first reward was a dangerous surprise. While central Prague still seemed to be firmly in German hands, he met armed Czechs as soon as he turned off Národní Avenue. They were policemen, true, but their number and weaponry indicated that the Reich had not sent them here. His German caused a sharp change in their behavior.

"Hands behind your head!" said the sergeant in charge.

He obeyed and calmly looked on as they frisked him and studied his papers, which proved him to be a member of the Reich's criminal police force with the rank of chief inspector. A moment before the Czech, Buback noticed for the first time a round stamp placed there in Bredovská Street when he took up his post: GEHEIME STAATSPOLIZEI PRAG.

"Gestapo!" said the commander of the security line, more in amazement than anger, but instantly Buback was among enemies. He had seen this sudden eruption of hatred in the other occupied cities he had hastily left, and knew where it would probably end. Guardians of public order, who spent years in the Germans' pay suppressing their countrymen's resistance, were often the first to take revenge on their old masters, either to avenge their former powerlessness or to secure their jobs under the new regime.

"Can we rough him up a bit?" asked an aggressive, pasty-faced kid.

"I'm a criminal detective and am cooperating with your colleague Morava from Number Four," Buback said to the man who had called him Gestapo, trying not to betray any reaction to the Czech words.

"Don't know him," snapped the sergeant.

"He's an assistant detective—"

"A spy!" chipped in another policeman. "He'll tell them we have guns and they'll send the tanks in!"

"No chance. Teplý! Votava!"

"Here!"

The new men surrounded Buback with practiced ease.

"Take him to Number Four. And if he's lying, put him behind bars!"

"Why not just take him down to the cellar and bump him off?" the pasty face said.

Buback fixed his eyes on the sergeant's; keep your fingers crossed, Grete, he thought superstitiously.

"I need to see Superintendent Beran," he requested firmly. "I'm working with him."

This name made an impact. He could see that they all knew it.

"Take him over there," the sergeant ordered the two men, who had meanwhile locked elbows with Buback. "Make sure nothing happens to him until they find the superintendent. And if he's feeding us a line, then do what you want with him."

There were more surprises in store for Morava. The car did not return to the police complex on Bartolomějská. Instead, Litera swung off Na Perštýně Street into Husova Street and from there into a long, dark alleyway. They alighted in a small courtyard beneath the sign COLLIERY; the German equivalent was, of course, freshly painted out. A couple of grubby men smoking on overturned tubs greeted Beran like an old friend.

"Josef, you wait here," the superintendent said to Litera. First names? With his driver? Suddenly Morava's familiar world seemed utterly foreign.

"And you're with me," Beran called out to him.

They entered an office where two policemen sat with rifles and car-tridge pouches. The men hastily stood, but Beran nodded for them to sit and headed down into the basement. From the firm's giant wood and coal storerooms they slipped through a newly made hole in the wall into a small cellar for tenants. Wooden crosspieces divided the area into cells; the last one was open and empty, and an opening at the back led into the neighboring building.

In the next cellar, several policemen were unpacking weapons and ammunition from crates, carefully cleaning the rifles and standing them in rows against the walls, and placing the boxed cartridges and hand grenades on boards laid across sawhorses. The men took no no-tice of the arrivals, and Beran strode past them without looking around. Morava's surprise grew. Was there another Prague, another police force, another Beran he knew nothing about?

Apparently so, for suddenly they were in an extensive vault with a Gothic ceiling, full of people in police uniforms and civilian garb; there must have been thirty of them in various corners and from various divisions. Morava recognized the faces of his department's technicians. At the sight of the superintendent their conversations gradually trailed off, and in a few seconds silence had descended.

"How does it work?" Beran asked.

"So far we've only tried gramophone music," volunteered Veselý, who on the surface ran the telephone and telegraph exchanges, point-ing at an antique machine with a horn, "but they've confirmed that it comes out all over Prague. Now they're checking the backup stations in Vinohrady and Nusle; once they're done, we can start whenever we want."

"Good work," said Beran, "very good. Is Brunát here?"

"Hej!" affirmed the bearded sixtyish superintendent of the transit police, in the one word of Slovak left him after his prewar service in Slovakia. He had just appeared through a tunnel from the basement opposite. "Here's the council's resolution."

Morava realized that a system of tunnels and escape routes must have been prepared in all the police buildings on Bartolomějská.

Beran read over the paper and then addressed the crowd in a steely voice.

"Colleagues, up till now we have introduced you into Resistance activities gradually and sparingly, so as not to needlessly threaten our conspiracy. All of you here enjoy my confidence and that of my friend Brunát, and we have now pledged our loyalty to a new political organization: the Czech National Council, which is the temporary representative of the Czechoslovak government, located for the moment in liberated Košice. In accordance with its resolution, I hereby absolve you of all obligations arising from professional oaths taken to the occupiers. The Czech police is the best organized and best armed civilian group—albeit modestly so—and has therefore been entrusted with a crucial task: to ensure the transfer of power with as few casualties as possible, protecting our people and our town. Now that peace is in sight, we cannot let Prague meet the fate of Europe's other cities, a fate it has so far been spared. We are not to mount a headstrong, all-out attack—we don't have the resources for it—but to engage in strategic and principled confrontation backed by careful use of force. There are as many possible variations as moves in a chess game; therefore we have decided not to commit ourselves to any in advance, and instead to retain flexibility of planning and reaction. The first announcement inaugurating our regular city radio broadcasts"—here he waved the paper in the air—"contains an appeal for calm, order, and reason that will be welcomed by the Germans. However, word combinations in the text contain hidden instructions to our neighborhood offices and primary Resistance groups, who will begin the immediate, unobtrusive isolation of German units and offices located directly in the capital.

Gentlemen, good luck with your instructions and I'll see you at thirteen hundred hours, when we begin."

He gave the exact time, and thirty men synchronized their watches.

"Brunát, Morava," the superintendent called, and when both had come over he added in a low voice, "time for the three of us to give Rajner what he's got coming."

"You have an urgent visitor," Brunát informed him.

"Who?"

"Your German inspector is here with an escort."

"Gestapo?" Beran said warily.

"No need to worry. Our men brought him in. They assumed he was Gestapo; only the fact that he asked for you saved him."

"What does he want?"

"To speak with you or Morava; he supposedly has news that can't wait."

"When did he arrive?"

"Not fifteen minutes ago."

"Him first, then," the superintendent said, picking up the pace. "Where is he?"

"You assigned him an office, didn't you?"

A thousand arrests made, but his first time arrested! Buback grinned, but did not feel like laughing. He sat at his old, familiar desk, its surface covered with carefully arranged reports on the widow killer. The one very basic difference was that now the key, turned twice in the lock for extra security, was in the far side of the keyhole.

He had no one to call, but tried the telephone anyway. Of course they had disconnected it; they weren't amateurs. At least he felt safer here than he had with those policemen, whose patriotism had begun to affect their judgment.

The Rubicon! Caesar's fateful river came suddenly to mind. Now Buback was about to cross his own, and he knew that nothing would be the same afterward. He'd gone too far to stop or turn back, though, so he simply cleared his mind and waited. Soon thereafter, the key turned in the lock and the superintendent and his assistant entered. With them was an unfamiliar man who reminded him of an old but still powerful lion.

"Good morning," Beran said in the same tone he had always used. "I heard you wanted to speak with us. This is my colleague Brunát; he and I have been temporarily entrusted with running the Czech police."

"Nice to meet you," said the lion, amiably baring his formidable teeth. "I might add that the former commissioner doesn't yet know of his good fortune."

Thus inspired and emboldened, Buback stepped out and over the imaginary river.

"Gentlemen, you may think I'm a coward betraying his own people out of fear, but I'd rather you believe that than prolong this war any longer and multiply its victims. Anyway, you, Mr. Morava, said you were betting there were Germans who would try to stop the worst from happening."

"That's right," the young Czech affirmed.

Buback reeled off Meckerle's information almost word for word. As he did so he felt his tension slacken, and as he finished, a feeling of calm settled on him. It was behind him, and he was past it. For the first time in years—maybe for the first time in his life—he was at peace, as both a German and a human, because he had suppressed his Germanity for humanity's sake.

Both older men exchanged a long glance.

"I'll inform the council immediately," the second said and thereupon vanished.

"We're very grateful to you, Mr. Buback," Beran said, "and personally I think it took great courage. Will you stay in contact with us?"

"I'll try. My assignment to cooperate with Mr. Morava is still in force. Of course, it's linked with another task: ascertaining the plans of the Czech police."

"I can't imagine you discovered much."

He decided to be forthright.

"No, not much."

"I simplified your job by not telling Mr. Morava."

Buback felt glad that at least he'd been right about the kid.

"I did not go to the funeral of Mr. Morava's wife," he said, "because today my participation would have seemed inappropriate in the extreme. However, his behavior and hers as well contributed to a change in my views, and led my companion and me to try to redeem at least some small part of Germany's guilt. I'd like to continue, as long as a higher power doesn't interfere to prevent it."

"Herr Oberkriminalrat . . . ," Beran said, weighing every word, "risk for risk. I'll give you a pass to confirm your cooperation with us in the investigation. We'll be grateful for any further news. What can we do for you?"

He had understood Grete's "give-and-take."

"How about assistance for someone else who helped you at great personal risk?"

"You mean Mrs. Baumann?"

"Yes. Her theater has gone to American territory, but she refused to leave—on my account. At the moment she's in my apartment in the neighborhood they call Little Berlin. I'm afraid what might happen to her there once emotions start to run high."

"I'd be worried too." Beran nodded glumly. "And we're certainly in her debt. You can take her in our car, if you can manage your own people on the way. But where will you go?"

"That I don't know," Buback confessed. "Our homes and families are gone."

He realized he was asking them for the impossible. Grete and he, like all Germans, were at the mercy of fate.

The superintendent seemed to feel the same way. At a loss for words, he glanced over at his adjutant.

The young man drew a key from his pocket.

"She'll recognize it," he told Buback. "It's the key to the house. I don't know if she can stand the idea; I moved out rather than go back. If she can, then take her there. And stay there yourself, if you like. The owners won't come back till the front's passed through; until then, only the two of us will know you're there. And we'll keep looking for a way out."

Buback was deeply moved. How would he have acted if their roles were reversed, he wondered. The only proper way to thank them, he felt, was to reveal his final lie.

"Gentlemen, I have a secret advantage over you; it's the reason I was put here. But your generosity compels me to give it up."

Then, finally, he broke into their common native tongue.

"Umím česky—I speak Czech. Please forgive me!"

The commissioner's office was just around the corner, so Beran, Brunát, and Morava walked over, but at times it was more like elbowing through a crowd. Bartolomějska Street was swarming with officers, all hurrying to and fro and saluting the two police chiefs. Morava kept shaking his head until the superintendent asked him why.

"All those cops running off at the mouth with Buback around. . . ."

"Whatever he heard, he heard. In the end he did what he did. Maybe hearing those rumors helped."

"The whole time he was deceiving us. . . ."

"A military stratagem. And beautifully executed, I have to admit. I never even suspected."

"Except you made sure I didn't know anything."

"Except for that," Beran conceded with a smile.

Then they plunged into the corner building. The secretary transmitted their request for an interview. They waited silently for a few minutes; this was Rajner's way of demonstrating his rank. Once admitted, they greeted him respectfully, took their seats, and were asked the reason for the audience. Only then did Beran request that the police commissioner formally step down.

Everything went so tactfully and the superintendent phrased his request so politely that at first Rajner completely missed its significance. Once he had heard it for the second time, his forehead broke out in sweat.

"Who . . . whom did . . . what were you . . . ," he stammered.

Morava knew the others had caught that whiff of fear as well.

"I'm authorized by the Czech National Council," Beran explained to him matter-of-factly. "Brunát and I have been temporarily named to your post, with the responsibilities divided between us."

Rajner tried to object.

"I don't even know this council of yours!"

"It's a new organ appointed by the legal government of the reconstituted Czechoslovak Republic—which you once swore allegiance to."

"And the Germans . . . Did they agree to this?"

"When they learn about it, they'll probably welcome it. At least they'll have someone to negotiate a capitulation with."

"But gentlemen . . ." Rajner's voice almost cracked into a falsetto. "They have a huge advantage in numbers and strength! They'll turn Prague to dust and ashes; is that what you want?"

"Actually," Brunát said, stepping into the fray, "that's what we're trying to prevent. First of all, we can offer them an orderly retreat from the city. We'll make sure they're not attacked, and that it's not attractive for them to attack. But just in case, we've taken measures. So you'd better get over to the interim internment wing, where we'll be keeping collaborators until the courts can get to them."

The door flew open and Rajner's secretary ran in.

"Mr. Commissioner, sir! Turn on the radio!"

She did not notice the mood in the room at all and ran around the table to turn on the huge superheterodyne herself. The magic green eye was soon fully open and an excited voice filled the room, accompanied by distant gunfire.

". . . are murdering our people! I repeat: We call on the Czech police and all former soldiers, come immediately to the aid of the Czech radio; the Germans here are murdering our people! I repeat . . ."

"Morava!" Beran bellowed. "Captain Sucharda's team is waiting at the garage. Go with them; you can translate and serve as my representative. Try for a truce, but first and foremost save those people and the studios. We won't get all the city loudspeakers working; we'll have to blanket Bohemia with our broadcasts. And Morava!" he called after him through the door. "Have them form up and send out more teams. If there aren't enough cars, they can commandeer trams!"

The last thing Morava saw as he closed the door was Rajner's frozen, waxy face.

He got to Sucharda in three minutes, and shortly thereafter fifteen men with carbines were jumping into the bed of a small truck driven by the garage manager, Tetera. Morava had to admit that once they had fastened their helmets beneath their chins, they looked quite imposing. He squeezed into the cabin behind Sucharda, and the vehicle pulled out of the courtyard and turned right. Through the open windows they heard dull thuds and curses; a few of the men in back must have fallen over like bowling pins.

Národní Avenue had changed. Any building not already flying Czech flags was unfurling them from the windows. For six long years under the Nazis, displaying red, white, and blue together had constituted a serious offense; where, Morava wondered, had they hidden those mountains of material? Crowds of people coursed along the sidewalks as if it were a national holiday, with tricolors in their lapels; who had made them so quickly? Groups sang; snatches of the former republic's national anthem flew by. The truck full of armed Czech policemen was warmly greeted all along its path. The men up top were infected by the general enthusiasm and shouted back that classic Czech greeting from a generation before, when they had first shaken off the Hapsburgs.

"Nazdaaaaaaaar!"

Rypl might be waving to us too, Morava thought, but immediately turned his attention to the captain. Sucharda had been in constant telephone contact with colleagues who were unobtrusively monitoring the numbers of German guards at the radio station. At around eleven-thirty, however, a motorcycle detachment of SS forces sneaked into the courtyard so quietly that they managed to occupy the first through third floors of the building where the announcers' offices and the technical equipment were located. Fortunately, Sucharda smirked, some clever fellow had hit on the idea of unscrewing all the directional signs and nameplates from doors, so the Germans were wandering around like Hansel and Gretel in the Black Forest.

"We've got to get past them and block off the broadcasting studios."

When they turned onto Wenceslas Square it was as if they were suddenly in another time. The long, wide street was quiet and empty. They spotted the reason instantly. Starting at the intersection with Jindřišská Street and Vodičkova Street, a half dozen firing posts zigzagged up the square toward the National Museum, each manned by a trio of Wehrmacht soldiers. One lay on the pavement gripping the handle of a heavy machine gun, the second knelt next to him with the ammunition belt, and the third stood ready to give orders to shoot.

The garage manager slowed down.

"Should I turn around?" he asked huskily.

A tense silence descended on the back of the truck.

"Sir, the rifles—"

Morava did not need to finish. Sucharda was already bawling an order through the tiny window into the truck bed.

"Hide your guns!"

A prolonged clattering noise indicated that the carbines had landed on the floor.

"Halt!"

The truck hovered in the middle of the intersection about thirty yards from the first machine gunners' nest. Its leader, an older German lieutenant and a reservist, by the look of it, had one hand threateningly raised. The police captain nudged Morava out of the truck with his shoulder so he himself could exit, and set off toward him. He saluted as he walked and barked over his shoulder at his guide.

"Translate for me! The security division of the Czech police asks permission to proceed through to assist in defending the radio building."

The German was tremendously nervous; they could feel his isolation, a foreigner in the heart of an enemy city. Morava added pleadingly: "Let us through, sir; we want as many people as possible to survive this war. Not just ours; yours too!"

He could see the same wish in the eyes of both young gunners, and the lieutenant seemed to sense this; it probably matched what he was hoping as well.

"Weiterfahren!" he ordered them onward a bit louder than necessary, and cupped his hands to his mouth to inform the other stations.

"Let the Czech police through!"

Sucharda waved, and the truck moved forward.

"Don't stop!" the captain warned the garage manager. He and Morava each jumped on the cabin step and held on by the window.

"Danke, Herr Leutnant. Viel Glück!" Morava wished him.

He hoped the German wouldn't decide to examine the truck more carefully; the small arsenal might seem provocative.

They passed the remaining gunners' nests at a leisurely pace, so as not to provoke a panicked reaction; at any point they could have been mown down. However, Morava felt more like an officer reviewing the anxious, frightened German troops, who were clearly reluctant to throw away their lives on the brink of peace. The policemen rolled uphill past them and heard the noise of battle.

"Morava!" Sucharda shouted at him across the roof of the cabin. "Let's try the same number again. Men!" He called to the back of the truck. "Coats off, and wrap your rifles in them; don't let the Germans see them till they have to."

It was a bizarre sight: Fifteen men in helmets removing their long coats and fighting centrifugal force as the truck took the curve past the museum. Behind the concrete wall above the Vinohrady tunnel a couple of crouching men gave them a warning sign, but the excitable Tetera hit the gas instead. At Sucharda's "Stop!" he braked sharply in front of the main entrance to the radio building, which was covered in rolls of barbed wire.

"Morava, let's go! Men, get down!"

Behind him he could hear the thuds, snorts, and wheezes of the policemen, pressing the rifles wrapped in coats to their chests; he saluted for the first time in his life at two SS men, armed to the teeth, who nearly filled the entranceway with their bodies. Had he used the correct hand? A shudder ran through him.

"Grüss Gott," he heard himself bellow at them in a tone of voice he couldn't stand in others. "We're the Protectorate police reinforcements here to defend the German employees!"

Miraculously the guards stepped aside for the handful of trotting men; uniforms, even foreign ones, still had an impact, and Morava's curt announcement had made the right impression.

The garage manager disappeared in his truck around the corner.

"Follow me!" Sucharda ordered from the front and headed across a spacious hall where Germans stood frozen in surprise, facing the staircase. "Third floor, left and to the back, where the announcers' offices are!"

He himself stopped at the foot of the stairs and slapped his men on the backside like sheep as they ran past. One of the last ones stumbled and dropped his bundle; the carabine fell out of the man's coat and clattered down the stairs.

A major standing right opposite Sucharda was the first to realize what had happened; he ripped his pistol from its holster.

"Scheisst doch!" he roared at the others. "Shoot! It's an invasion!"

He fired at Sucharda at point-blank range and hit him in the forehead; the captain keeled over like a felled tree.

Jitka, Morava wondered, is this all real or is it a new dream? And if it's real, will I see you soon in our new home? He ducked, picked up the fallen rifle, and ran after his men in a hail of bullets that buzzed past him and opened dozens of small craters in the ceiling and walls.

P otatoes were coming out his ears, but he kept eating them, because he knew:

I HAVE TO BE STRONG!

For five nights he'd slept lightly so he'd hear them coming, and now he'd take a new leap into the unknown; it was too risky to stay. So he tucked into the food like a fattened goose and listened with one ear to the murmur of the radio connecting him to the outside world. Suddenly a melody practically bowled him over. It was the famous Sokol march, the anthem of the most patriotic Czech society, which had been outlawed the first day of the German invasion. Its message flew over airwaves censored till now by the occupiers, exhorting the occupied nation to move forward "with lion's strength on falcon's wings."

Before he had time to wonder, the song was interrupted, and a voice cut through the ether. Now it sounded agitated, almost like a different person from the familiar announcer who had read out the correct time just a moment before, twelve-thirty—but ONLY IN CZECH, he realized belatedly!

"We call on the Czech police and all former soldiers: Come immediately to the aid of the Czech radio! The Germans are murdering our people!"

Along with it he heard a thumping he recognized as distant gunfire. The announcer repeated the call a second and a third time before he understood.

THEY'RE CALLING ME!

His hour had come, bringing him a NEW TASK, just the way he'd known it would that night in the train. Why just punish a few lusty hussies when there was an entire GUILTY NATION out there! He'd seen the Czechs' and Moravians' hour of glory once already, when he was fighting the Hungarians. Now once again his time had come, freeing him from his self-imposed imprisonment. With an iron will he scarfed down the rest of the potatoes.

I'M A SOLDIER AGAIN!

He pulled on the leather coat he liked the best from the wardrobe; to his surprise it fit him (did it belong to the cuckold next door?) and the pocket would hold his pistol. With an ear to the outside door he listened to the house's murmurings to choose the right time for his exit. Suddenly he remembered.

THE GUY!

The decent thing would be to tell him he was leaving, thank him, and give him his freedom, so he could take off the straps. . . . The straps! The shorter two around the guy's ankles were from his first schoolbag, a present from HER; the longer ones, binding his arms up to the shoulders, were a memento of Šimonek and Bárečka, two angora goats he'd loved taking out to pasture. These strips of leather were scraps from the bootmaker's workshop next door that SHE had used to make the shopping bags she sold. Now that the SOULS were gone, the straps and his beloved knife were the only witnesses to an important stage in his life, as he stood on the threshold of an even more important one.

He entered the bathroom. The half-pint rattled as he slept; the gag interfered with his breathing.

Wasn't it awfully strange the way that runt had found him in the train? The way he'd risked his life to hide a parachutist in his home? Maybe the half-pint had something up his sleeve; maybe only his own presence of mind had foiled the guy's plot. He didn't have time to think it through, and so he followed his instincts again. . . .

Afterward he carefully cleaned his knife, wound the long straps at his sides like an outlaw's belt, and stuck the short ones into his pockets. He closed the door noiselessly, turning the key as the bolt reached the jamb so the neighbor wouldn't hear when it clicked shut. Once again he met no one in the building. Doubtless they were all glued to their radios, listening to the battle.

I'M GOING TO FIGHT!

There were no trams, but it wasn't far; he alternated quick walking and slow trotting—the "Indian run," she'd called it a long time ago. "I'll teach you everything he should have taught you, Tony, so no one will ever know you didn't have a father. . . ."

From Saint Ludmila's onward he could definitely hear gunfire. Clumps of people had positioned themselves anxiously and defiantly within reach of the buildings' front doors. At the Vinohrady Theater he came across his first fighters: a few men, mostly around twenty-five, dressed as the historical moment had caught them, one in a tram driver's uniform, the others in overalls or civilian clothes, wearing hats they had no place to leave. They had two hunting rifles between them and kept a respectful distance from the corner of the sloping street.

"What's happening?" he asked them.

"The radio's down there," one man said excitedly.

"So?"

"There's a side entrance. I know how to get to the studios; I'm a sound technician."

"So what are we waiting for?"

"A Kraut's hiding behind the garbage cans," one of the two hunters retorted, "and he keeps firing at us."

Rypl, called Sergeant Králík from the depths of time; bob and weave the way I taught you and take that Hungarian down. If you've forgotten how, you're done for.

Just like in Komárno, he pulled out his pistol and released the safety.

"Don't be a fool," said the tram driver. "He got two of ours already."

"Once I take him out," he told them all, "follow me fast!"

He lay flat on the ground, and then, lightning-fast, he stuck his head out and pulled it back. He had not lost his talent: The picture of the street was as clear in his mind as a photo in a frame, including the two motionless bodies and three garbage cans down by the radio station. Three doorways and an alley separated him from them. He retreated in the direction he'd come, diagonally across the roadway, until he could just see the first entranceway in the cross-street. They must have thought he'd given up, but all he needed was a running start.

He worked up enough speed that he hit the alcove of the doors opposite before the German could fire. No skill, he realized gratefully. Now he'll be aiming at the middle of the street. He waited for the man's hand to stiffen up a bit, took a deep breath, and hurtled toward the next house on his side. A shot cracked, but too late. His ragged breathing grew calm and he readied himself for the lookout trick again. The soldier had been firing through the chink between the garbage cans, and at some point he would have left the man's angle of vision. So? Careful . . . head out, then back! And now he was sure: To hit him, the soldier had to straighten up and make himself a target. Still, the German had the advantage of a rifle against a pistol, which couldn't aim precisely at this distance.

He hesitated. Because no one was covering him, he had to risk another leap forward into the alley or rot there until they picked him off; if the Germans sent a small counteroffensive from the building it might come sooner than he thought.

MOTHER, SAVE ME!

Her response came immediately.

I CAN TAKE CARE OF MYSELF!

He threw caution to the wind; racing out along the side of the building near the garbage cans, he deliberately squeezed the trigger, trying to hit the chink between them: one, two, three, four, shit in your pants, Kraut, and stay back there, or you might just knock me off, five, six—then he reached the life-saving alley, spitting distance from the garbage cans, and suddenly he wasn't running but flying through the air; dropping his gun, he splayed onto the concrete like a frog. Was he hit? No. Immediately he realized what had brought him down: he had tripped over a corpse without a face. The hand grenade that had opened these gaping holes in the alley walls had probably blown it off.

Why had he left those six whores' faces on? Shouldn't he have cut out their likenesses as well as their hearts? It could have been his own contribution to the inspirational PICTURE. Wait . . . maybe what he'd just tripped over was a SIGN meant for him. He ignored the German—let his nerves jangle for a while—and rummaged in the man's clothing. There was an identity card unscathed in the breast pocket. Tensely he unfolded it and swallowed with gratitude: The faded picture showed a middle-aged man with average features, easily interchangeable with half of mankind.

INCLUDING ME!

He shoved his own papers into the man's pocket and repeated his new name to himself.

LUDVÍK ROUBÍNEK.

Now he turned with renewed interest to the enemy. Pressed against the alley wall closest to the German he glimpsed the corner uphill where he had started. Those chicken-shits still didn't dare come after him. But he didn't need them; actually, he'd rather take care of the German himself and just hoped the Kraut wouldn't run away like the Hungarians did at Komárno.

He HAD THAT TASTE again and intended to satisfy it. He called out to his prey.

"You there!"

The air vibrated with the shots and detonations still resounding from the radio building. He shouted louder, and in German.

"Sie dort!"

No answer.

"Your men won't help you. They're surrounded. Give up!"

Silence, humming with the nearby battle.

"I have a grenade; I'll count to three. Put your weapon on the trash can, or it's all over. Don't be a fool and you'll live to tell the tale. One . . . two . . ."

MOTHER, HELP ME, don't let him call my bluff!

Metal clanged against metal. A submachine gun lay on the garbage can, gently rocking on the bent top of the lid.

YOU'RE DIVINE! But what about him?

Two fiercely trembling hands appeared. Slowly a cap and then a head emerged. The haggard kid in the SS uniform might have been twenty. BUT HE'S A GERMAN, SHE said sternly. AND YOU'RE A CZECH!

Yes, yes! He raised the hand with the pistol and went as close as he could, until only the garbage can divided them. The barrel touched the gray-green cloth in the region of the heart. No, that would be too fast a death for a German pig. The soldier licked his lips, but did not move when the gun slid diagonally down to his belly.

He'd give him time.

TIME TO REPENT.

I was waiting till I knew it was you, love," Grete explained; he had been banging on the bolted door, but she would not open it until he began to call her name. "No, I'm not afraid, not in the least; I'm just a bit terrified, actually. But since you wanted me to go somewhere I wouldn't go, and I decided instead to be terrified by your side, I really can't complain. Tell me what's going on; suddenly the radio only speaks Czech!"

Litera had explained why as they were leaving.

"They're fighting over it."

"And that means . . ."

"Probably the beginning of the uprising. And maybe of the assault on Prague."

"Aha. And what about us?"

"I warned the Czechs, Grete. And I want to keep it up as long as I can."

"Good idea. What will they do for us in return?"

Her selfish directness made him doubt his reasons for changing sides again. She flared up at him as if reading his thoughts.

"Don't try to be Saint Erwin, love. Since you've decided to save yourself, save both of us in the bargain! Why should the only Germans to survive the war be the criminals?"

"Morava offered me an apartment," he responded. "The one where you and his wife . . . where it happened. Can you bear it there until we can see what comes next?"

"Will you stay with me?"

"I'll do everything I can to stop in for you at least once a day. . . ."

"Aha. . . ."

She sounded disappointed. He wondered disconsolately how to respond if she suggested escaping together again.

"When?" she asked instead.

"Right away!" he said, relieved. "Pack what you need and I'll bring all the groceries from the house."

"What do you need?"

"Some underwear."

Like a seasoned traveling artist she was ready before he was. They packed the baggage space with two suitcases of personal effects, two bags of food, and a rolled-up blanket in a fresh plaid cover with a pillow—after all, she opined, they couldn't sleep in the same one that poor girl . . .

Then he remembered his pistol.

On the threshold, she kissed him.

"May we never be less happy than we are now!"

As it turned out, they had left Little Berlin at the last possible moment. At the intersection below the last house a Wehrmacht truck in the hands of the insurgents had blocked the roadway except for a narrow passage. A man in the moth-eaten uniform of a former Czechoslovak Army first lieutenant was directing a handful of civilians with tricolors pinned on. All of them had rifles.

The police driver and car satisfied the lieutenant; he saluted Buback as well, who was sitting with Grete in the back. Down by Stromovka Park a German guard unit had surrendered a small arsenal, he told them; they'd found a pile of guns there. They'd been sent here to comb through the villas, checking for any treacherous "werewolves"— German storm troopers—who might be hiding there.

"Take care," Litera advised him. "The criminals will be right behind the war heroes. Everything's public property now."

"I'm no policeman!" The first lieutenant seemed almost insulted.

"And our men aren't soldiers, but unlike you they're already in battle. Happy hunting."

He hit the gas and grinned at Buback like an ally.

"Mothballed soldiers!" Litera sniffed contemptuously. "We haven't seen the last of 'em."

On Mendel Bridge, where tar-paper signs had restored the Czech painter Mánes's name, the crew of a German light cannon tried to drive them back. Buback took care of it. He easily negotiated passage around the large-caliber machine gun at the National Theater.

Litera slowed down again at the railway bridge to let two city buses move aside; they were blocking riverside traffic and the way south to Vyšehrad. Prague seemed to be divided into Czech and German islands. On the former, celebration was giving way to resistance activities, while the latter were empty spaces guarded by jittery soldiers.

"I see we make a good pair," Litera said to Buback after his performance at the theater, "so long as we don't pull out the wrong piece of paper!"

Beran's apparent involvement and Buback's miraculously good Czech instilled in Litera a measure of goodwill toward the German, which was now growing into approval.

Grete was quiet as a mouse the whole trip, but the anxious grip of her fingers told him her true state of mind. At each control point he had to free himself from it forcibly, only to return tenderly afterward.

Only a few nights ago she had been amorous, uninhibited, an apparently superficial consumer of her own existence. In this dark hour, however, Grete's character seemed suddenly different, contradicting her own confessions. Now she would suffer all the more as he abandoned her to an unknown fate for an indeterminate time, but she did not use any of the feminine weapons arrayed at her beck and call to force him to the decision she must be hoping for. Or would she try it at the last moment?

They arrived. He could feel Grete tremble at the sight of the house. The kitchen windows had not been repaired, but someone had boarded them up, nailing the planks an inch apart, so there would be light inside during the day. Litera carried their baggage in alone. The two of them shouldn't be seen much in public, he said; there were only a couple of old geezers living around here, but just to be on the safe side! When he disappeared into the hall with the first load, Grete had her last chance.

Instead, however, she kept her grip on his fingers and stared motionlessly ahead. Once Litera had taken in the last bundle and was waiting inside to show her in, she kissed Buback gently on the lips and, surprisingly, made the sign of the cross on his forehead.

"Come back when you can, love. And ring or knock the fate theme: da da da dum . . . !"

How would he get back here? he wondered once she had disappeared into the house. And would he come back at all? The only thing he knew for sure was that he loved and admired her.

He and Litera retraced their journey. At the railway bridge two pot-bellied garbage trucks had joined the buses. Men in leather aprons were rolling heavy trash cans over from the nearby houses, but instead of feeding their contents to the metal stomachs, they made rows of them in front of the trucks. Litera stuck his head out the window.

"What's it going to be when it's finished?"

"City radio just urged people to set up barricades. The Germans are on their way from Benešov!"

Buback felt sure it was a consequence of his information—the first result of his betrayal . . . no! He remembered Grete's words: he had simply tried to mitigate the effects of a grand treason his people had perpetrated on . . . on his people, yes. . . . what was he anyway? A Czech, like his mother, or a German, like his father? Wasn't he a living example of the senselessness of nationalism? And therefore wasn't he predestined by his heritage to. . . .

A traffic policeman jumped out of the left bus and cut off his musings.

"You won't get through along the embankment: the Nazis are there and now they're shooting."

Litera squinted at his neighbor. Buback said in reply, "We've done well so far together. I'll cross the last German watchpoint with you, and once I've negotiated your way out, I'll go back to Bredovská Street on foot."

He saw the driver blink in shock.

"Tell Mr. Beran that I'm trying to talk to my supervisor, who was just promoted; I'm hoping he'll agree to proclaim Prague an open city they won't fight for. I'll try to get back with fresh news as soon as possible; could you ask the chief to inform your guard posts?"

"You're asking for trouble, Mr. Buback, do you know that?"

"Well, did you know I was born here, in Prague?"

They passed easily through several checkpoints on Czech-controlled territory, getting as far as Štěpánská Street, where the German-occupied city center began. From there on no one stopped them; the presence of an employee from the Gestapo building must have been relayed by field telephone. Buback rode with him as far as the boundary formed by a row of machine guns; now Litera would easily be able to draw a plan of the German defenses. Am I a spy on top of everything else? Buback wondered.

When they parted and the car disappeared in the direction of Národní Avenue, he set off back toward Bredovská to the sound of detonations carried down from the radio on the spring wind. What chance, he wondered, did a small cog like he have of influencing the workings of this huge machine?

J an Morava's first direct military involvement in the Second World War lasted all of a few long seconds. By the time he had reached the bend in the staircase in a hail of fire that miraculously missed him, the fifteen policemen ahead of him had used the element of surprise to clear the Germans from the main halls of the second and third floors. The occupiers were now stuck in the side hallways, preventing the Czechs from breaking through to the broadcast studios, wherever they were. The newcomers moved to secure what they held to the left, the right, upstairs, and downstairs. SS troops still held the fourth floor, which was the seat of the German directorate; at noon they had driven the first group of Czech policemen up to the top floors, where they were still contained.

In both mezzanines and the mouths of the corridors, barricades of desks and file cabinets were going up all around Morava, while he racked his brain. How could he achieve the main task Beran had set him: ending the fighting?

The modern 1930s building was like a labyrinth; its hundreds of locked doors, all missing their plaques, would have been a tricky puzzle under normal circumstances, let alone with ricocheting bullets whizzing past like crazed bees. He knew the Germans must still be searching for the source of the broadcasts, which were being heard across Bohemia. If they found them, brave announcers and technicians would die, and Germany would inflict a heavy moral defeat on a citizenry trying to atone for the national shame of the 1938 Munich capitulation. Morava understood: The fighting had to be stopped or resolved as soon as possible. With Sucharda dead, the young detective was now in charge.

Fortunately the city telephones were still working and the radio's switchboard had not been disconnected. The employees trapped there led him on all fours to a phone; a sniper was peppering the front of the building from an attic window opposite. They drew him a rough plan on the wooden tiles of the whole complex and a more precise map of the back wing where the broadcasts were coming from.

At Bartolomějská they either could not or would not bring Beran or Brunát to the telephone. Finally they got Superintendent Hlavatý, who had so brilliantly scented the widow killer's trail in the Klášterec priest's missive. He instantly grasped the urgency of the problem, and shortly thereafter Brunát's voice came on the line. On the advice of two editors, former reserve officers, Morava requested that he send another armed unit through the attics of neighboring houses and across the flat roofs. With this assistance, the men defending the upper floors and those down below could clear the Germans from the middle and then the base of the building.

The Germans in the middle had fortunately run out of grenades and lacked Panzerfausts; like the Czechs beneath them, they were cut off from supplies on the ground floor. The first side to obtain reinforcements would break the stalemate.

"I'll bring them personally," Brunát promised. "The radio's the key to everything now. But try to negotiate with the Germans; maybe they'll fold of their own accord."

"Depends whether Schörner's set out already," Morava replied. "How does it look?"

"For now it seems we're ahead by a hair. The city radio's sending out instructions on how to build barricades. Prague's starting to become impassable; I'm afraid it'll take us a while to get to you."

"Try the way we went: up Wenceslas Square past the Germans— yes, they're reserve officers and new recruits. If you wear police uniforms and formulate your request correctly, it gives them the option of saving their own skins without losing face."

"Wait, Jan. . . ." He heard Brunát give a muffled assent. "Beran says that in the name of the Czech National Council you're to meet with Thürmer, the German radio director. You can offer free passage for German employees and soldiers, but careful: no weapons, period. Break a leg; we'll be over in a jiffy to give them a good-bye kiss."

They crawled out of the threatened office to plot how and when to proceed, shouting at each other in the hallway against the noise of the battle. Morava picked the two who spoke the best German and were least afraid to negotiate with Thürmer. The apparently insurmountable problem of how to contact him was solved again by the telephone.

"The director will meet with you," his secretary responded after a short while, "if you'll stop shooting and cease your hostile broadcasts from this building for the duration of the negotiations."

Morava rejected the second condition. Thirty employees trapped unexpectedly by the turn of events were squashed with the policemen into a narrow space between the unreliable-looking wooden barriers. In a few cases, their nerves were in tatters.

"Why not call the studios and have them play music for a while," suggested a pitifully pale woman slumped weakly on the tiles, her back propped against the wall. "Everyone's heard the broadcast anyway, and we'll never get out of here unless—"

"Chin up, Andula!" a colleague interjected. Another employee added, "The Germans know they won't just be able to escape, not at any price; all of Prague is sharpening its knives for them."

Finally the German fire began to quiet down. The phone rang; the director was waiting for them. The negotiators should put their hands behind their heads; they would be searched on arrival.

Morava left his pistol and holster and proceeded to the steps. His footprints remained in the fine plaster dust just like in snow. He was the first to crawl over the office-furniture stockade. The maneuver required both hands, but he was not afraid.

"At least," he said to himself in a low voice, "I'll be with you sooner, my love."

W hen they finally ran up and showered him with praise for his amazing courage, he experienced a remarkable feeling.

I DID IT!

It made him even happier that this time he hadn't had to hide his deed; quite the opposite:

I CAN DO IT IN PUBLIC!

He was terribly sorry that SHE could not have seen it herself, but he was sure that SHE knew, if SHE hadn't in fact been leading him.

Even the boy with wire-rim glasses who hurried over from the garbage can couldn't spoil his mood.

"Sirs," he said in a trembling voice, "he's alive."

In their ensuing silence they heard a weak moan from outside.

"Let him enjoy it, then!" he answered the kid. "Like we enjoyed living with them for six years. Or do you feel sorry for him?"

"Stomach wounds are extremely painful. . . . You see, I'm studying to be a doctor, and—"

Before he could think of a way to regain his new admirers, a well-muscled man in overalls grinned at the kid.

"Then finish school and cure him! Or finish him off, once you have something to do it with. Personally, I wouldn't waste my ammunition on him. So what next?" The overalls turned to the group. "The evening's still young!"

And he felt everyone's eyes resting on him. They looked up to him the way he had once looked up to Sergeant Králík, he realized proudly.

I'M THE BEST ONE HERE!

It was time to consolidate his leadership.

According to the technician, the entrance by the garbage cans was thinly guarded because the Germans thought it only led down to the archives. But from there, he assured them, you could get upstairs to the broadcasting rooms where the calls for help were coming from.

He took one grenade along with the soldier's submachine gun, which naturally fell to him; the other grenade he gave to the man in overalls, who, he learned, had also been in the army. Both rifle owners followed them into the basement; after them came a couple of empty-handed men hoping to find some weapons as they went.

The hallway turned two corners and then brought them to a narrow staircase leading upward. They walked so slowly and quietly that they heard the steps and German voices approaching from above before the soldiers found them. Was it just a coincidence that once again he and his men were ideally positioned for an ambush? The archive was over-flowing with old tape recordings, and its hallways were lined with narrow shelving housing columns of round metal cases; here, just behind them, was an alcove they all fit into.

Rypl, his sergeant reminded him, in concrete your bullet will likely hit you on the rebound; a blade's your best bet. . . . After all, it was Králík who'd instructed him in the use of knives when they'd visited his brother's slaughterhouse. . . .

Today, however, he had another idea, his own. He motioned to his supporter to put his weapon down and, turning to the others, mimed grabbing someone by the throat.

There were two Germans, evidently convinced that the basement was still clear: Their submachine guns hung over their shoulders as they headed for the stairs to have a smoke. They had no chance against the half dozen or so men who suddenly fell on them. In a couple of seconds they felt their backs slam down on their gun barrels and gasped to find at least three Czechs kneeling over each of them.

He was crazy, he shuddered in retrospect, to jump on them practically empty-handed with a bunch of strange men; it could have back-fired badly. And yet here they lay, rank-and-file SS storm troopers, both wide-eyed rookies.

Yes, Mother, TODAY IS MY DAY!

"What should we do with them?" he asked the one who had taken his side; now the man showed his hands, large as shovels.

"Tie 'em up and guard 'em," the tram driver said. "There are rules about prisoners, aren't there?"

He knew them from even his own short war and momentarily considered using two of the straps girdling him—but would he definitely get them back? And after what happened to the poor runt who'd had to return them. . . . One thing was certain: They couldn't drag the Germans with them, nor could they leave them here with inexperienced guards. So he made his decision.

"Where's the toilet?" he said, turning to the man from the radio.

"We passed it as we came in."

He left his regiment by the steps, guarded by two newly acquired submachine guns, and nodded to his new ally. The Germans went in front of them, hands crossed high on their backs, the way Králík had taught him. The best way to stiffen them up, Rypl, as every schoolteacher knows! The archive toilets were hidden in a small side hall. Beyond the urinal was a stall with a toilet bowl; the yellowed door ended about a foot from the ceiling. It was perfect for his next idea.

"Hinein!" He pointed the gun muzzle at them. "Both of you, inside!"

They squeezed into the narrow space; the second one chuckled uneasily. He slammed the door behind them and asked his guide, "Is there anything to wedge the handle with?"

The man reached into a corner and grabbed a broom standing in a bucket with a rag. Deftly he propped it between the stall door and the wall. Did he already know? He looked so eager!

He nodded for him to go out into the hallway first, and eyeballed the size of the gap above the stall door. Then he pulled the pin from the grenade, silently counted to three, and hurled it into the stall. He heard a double scream, but he had already slammed the washroom door and pressed himself against the side wall.

The explosion jammed the door shut. Too bad. He would have liked to look. An admiring smile crossed his companion's face, and he made a further discovery.

I HAVE A FRIEND!

On the corner of Bredovská Street, which was guarded by two light storm-trooper tanks, Buback was assaulted by the pungent stench he had smelled during each post-Normandy retreat. In the courtyard, a huge pyre was burning; files with documents from various departments were heaped on it. Why, he wondered for the first time: Why burn the only proof that even in these infamous walls they had proceeded strictly according to regulation? Except that was the problem.

The German nation was not the only one ever to place its own interests above the legal norms of the civilized world. However, it seemed likely to be the first one condemned for applying its laws strictly and thoroughly, because *ius germanicum*, which allowed the death penalty for a critical word or a hook-shaped nose, had now thrown the greater part of a civilized continent back into the Dark Ages.

It had always consoled him that the paragraphs he enforced defended the time-honored values for which mankind created laws, even if they were part of that greater German legal code. He had been practically the only officer at all his previous postings who had not needed to cover his tracks. But was that enough to let him shrug off responsibility for what the burners were trying to hide?

What was his own part in his nation's guilt? Could the two be separated? And more importantly: Could Germany's guilt be redeemed? He kept trying to do just that, even though the Third Reich could still avoid total defeat, leaving *ius germanicum* the law of the victors. The newly announced German doctrine seemed to count on this possibility, at least in Kroloff's version. It took his breath away.

According to absolutely reliable sources, British prime minister Churchill and the new American president Truman were convinced that Stalin intended to establish Communist regimes in all the territories occupied by the Red Army, thus building a bridgehead that would let him quickly conquer the rest of Europe. The new German leadership planned to distance itself from the excesses of some SS units, which it would apparently disband, the skull head explained enthusi-astically—as if the Gestapo would go scot-free! They would then offer the Anglo-Americans a partial capitulation and an assurance that Ger-many would carry on the battle against the Bolsheviks.

Field Marshall Schörner had assumed the high command over German staff, central offices, and services in the area controlled by Mitte's armies, who would play a leading role in these plans. Certain persons had let the situation in Prague get temporarily out of hand; they would be punished and replaced. Lieutenant General Meckerle was sending his best men to provide political reinforcement in threat-ened areas. He, Kroloff, felt honored to be accompanying the chief inspector to Pankrác, a crucial neighborhood in the southeast of the city. There they would secure the beginning of the route that would let more than fifty thousand troops and their equipment leave Prague every day for the west.

Impossible, Buback marveled; they were sending him to Grete! Given the circumstances, he quickly reconciled himself to the change in plans. Anyway, he soon found out Meckerle was momentarily ab-sent, and Buback could learn far more in the field than the gossip and fairy tales he'd heard here.

"How will we get there?" he probed. "As far as I can tell, we only hold the city center."

"Armored transports will come for the authorized representatives," Kroloff announced. "The Czechs only have light weapons."

Among which is a Panzerfaust, Buback nearly said aloud. He would have to rely on Grete's cross.

They waited almost three hours for the escort vehicles. The column commander seemed on the verge of shooting himself as he described how they had wandered around and around in some suburb, because the Czechs had repositioned all the road signage, even swapping the street signs around; the Nazis' perfect maps were useless. Finally a German woman, a native of Prague, had saved them when she saw the convoy for the third time and had the courage to run out of her house, climb up to the cabin of his vehicle and guide them here.

On the way to Pankrác, Buback saw that what had been primitive barriers at noon were being continually, diligently, and painstakingly strengthened. However, the flotsam and jetsam from workshops, construction sites, and houses were no match for caterpillar vehicles. All along the route the Czechs fled into nearby buildings; the convoy met no opposition.

In crossing the deep gash called the Nusle Valley, Buback was reminded of how the city's topography would aid in its defense. Still, he knew the force that was preparing to strike, and could imagine the desolation it would leave in its wake. As they rose toward Pankrác, a rare panorama opened for a moment before them: to the left the towers of Vyšehrad, to the right the cupolas of Karlov, and beyond the river the distant Hradčany Castle, which seemed to hang in the air.

How odd: Although he had lived most of his life in Dresden, and its destruction had filled him with deep sadness, he accepted it as a higher form of justice, one gruesomely foreshadowed in the deaths of Hilde and Heidi. Now he felt sure: This war Germany had begun was immoral. It had bathed Europe in tears and blood, and his nation would be punished for it with the cruelest defeat in history—tragic, yet logical! Prague had been brutally violated six years ago; was it really possible she would be reduced to ruins now, when freedom and renewed dignity were just around the corner?

How strange it was! He had spent his early childhood in Prague, and had only a couple of fleeting, not to mention banal, memories of his life here; how could he feel more connected to this place than to the city where he had studied, worked, and loved, a city he had known far better? But he knew the answer: Something in the unconscious of the young child Erwin Buback had stirred his mind and heart and tied him inexplicably to this place. For years that "something" had been submerged beneath a flood of other sensations, but it did not disappear. It was still there, as strong as ever, and awoke again as soon as he returned: the language of his birth mother, forever his native tongue.

This did not quite make him a Czech, but he could not call himself a pure German either. So he was simply a native of Prague, heir to two and more cultures which for centuries had lived side by side, separate but not hostile. He must have had more of Prague in him than he realized, since both his Czech and German sides hoped with equal fervor that the splendid scene before him would be preserved for future generations.

So then, he was not a traitor, absolutely not. He was a redeemer of betrayal, destined by his heritage to help bring this destruction and murder to an end, so that Czechs and Germans in his native city could someday meet on the same sidewalk and greet each other with a tip of the hat. . . .

O nly the Praguers gave Brunát's reinforcements trouble on the way over. Encouraged by the radio defenders' example, they suddenly filled Wenceslas Square; the Germans lost interest in shooting, and seemed glad of the chance to withdraw to Bredovská Street with their skins intact. When the police finally got through, they reached the building by climbing across rooftops, and after a short battle drove the SS from the sixth to the fourth floor. The Germans attempted to break through past Morava to the main hall, but they did not succeed. The soldiers on the first floor were now hemmed in by Czech irregulars on the surrounding streets, and Director Thürmer was forced to open negotiations.

Thürmer was a shadow of the man who two hours earlier had shouted at them, pistol in hand; he clearly saw the situation (or, at the very least, his own personal case) as hopeless. He did not even mention retreating with weapons; instead he requested, or more accurately begged, for an escort to accompany the German employees and soldiers to the main train station, which was still occupied by the Wehrmacht. The commander of the SS forces in the hall agreed to the arrangement as well. Brunát took over command but did not release Morava.

"Once they leave the building, have it searched thoroughly, so they don't leave a Trojan horse in here—they'll certainly try to get the radio back by any means possible and we don't want to be stabbed from behind. And Morava: Get some systems in place right from the start. I know our countrymen: Soon thousands of radio station warriors will be demanding a reward for their services. Round up all the paper pushers and have them record everyone who's been here since twelve-thirty. And be sure to get a list of the dead; they'll start looking for them shortly. Then off to Beran; he needs you."

While two hours earlier everyone stuck at the radio had desperately wished to be as far as possible from that steel-and-concrete trap, now almost no one would leave the building. Despite the near-certainty that the Germans would be back, the Czechs were now eager and impatient; their long-awaited victory could come here, today.

Onlookers gawked at the battle sites, and the diligent cleared away the debris blocking passages. For safety's sake, the heroic announcers moved into a hurriedly equipped studio in an air-raid shelter. Doctors descended on the building, examining the lightly wounded on the spot, and sending the severely wounded off to various hospitals. The fallen were carried down to the courtyard.

This was where Morava stationed what seemed like the more reliable civilians, instructing them to secure the victims' personal belongings before the scavengers arrived. They did not believe anyone would take advantage of this historic moment, but promised him they would work in pairs, recording every detail.

A wild burst of fire in front of the building almost sent him scrambling outside, but it ended as quickly as it had begun; soon he learned that someone had tried to start a massacre of the departing Germans. Civilians kept bringing down more dead Czechs as they found them in various corners of the ravaged building, and he tried to wrap up all the tasks Brunát had set him as fast as he could, so that he could get back to Beran and then to his mission.

An hour later Morava was sure there were no Germans hiding in the building, and the snipers on the surrounding blocks had been taken care of. He returned to the courtyard. The fallen lay on thick curtains from the large music studio; at their feet were bundles made from canteen napkins, which held the contents of their pockets. Where possible, the personal effects of the deceased had been put back into the bags or briefcases they had been carrying when they were struck down. Morava promised to send a replacement over as soon as possible, took copies of the list, and went to report to Brunát.

On his way there, a woman in a beret, which looked odd against her gray pigtails, addressed him timidly. "Excuse me, officer ... my son ran over here at noon to help and hasn't come back; do you know if anything's happened to him ...?"

When he unfolded the papers he realized he could not give her a definite answer. He should have assigned someone to get a list of the wounded; now their relatives would have to wander from hospital to hospital. He could have kicked himself, but he hoped that at least he could rule out the worst for her.

"What's his name?"

"Richter. Rudolf Richter."

He looked but could not find the name.

"If it's any comfort, I have a list of the dead and ..."

He fell silent, staring at the name he had found in place of the woman's son.

"Rypl Antonín, b. 27 May 1900 in Brno, res. Plzeň."

Jitka! Could he have gotten off that easily?

The horror in the woman's eyes shook him out of his trance, and he quickly showed her that her son's name was not on the list. Then he hurried back to the courtyard. The dead man was number thirty-five and a bloody towel covered his head. Accustomed as he was to gruesome sights, he still shuddered when he lifted it. Only the back of the man's head remained; the front had been almost entirely shorn off.

He untied the bundle. The identity card! Agitatedly he unfolded it. The face from the Plzeň police document stared out at him.

But everything in Morava that made him a detective protested. Why, out of all the dead, had this particular one lost his face? Was it an incredible coincidence? Or a clever ruse?

He bent down, piled the rest of the personal items between the prewar corduroy trousers (Careful! We'll need the shoes and clothes to show Rypl's colleagues and neighbors!), and put one item after the other on the napkin. A comb. A nickel-plate watch. A key ring (important for identification)! A wallet. Contents? A couple of banknotes and change. A half-empty matchbox. No cigarettes. A child's fish-shaped penknife. A handkerchief. (Monogrammed? No. . . .)

Still, the bloodhoundlike stubbornness Beran had admired on their last stroll told Morava that this was not their man, and that the true owner of these documents could not be far away. So what was Morava doing here?

He persuaded a reliable-looking sergeant to leave the victory celebrations and arrange for corpse thirty-five and everything belonging with it to be sent over to Pathology. Then he rushed back to the building. He headed up to the top floor and circled the halls, sticking his head into each room. He continued this way from floor to floor, trying to use his one advantage: He knew his prey, but his quarry did not know its hunter. He did not stop until he was out on the street again.

There were hundreds of faces, but none belonged to Jitka's murderer.

The crowd's confidence grew from hour to hour. Finally they had seen their occupiers humiliated. Furthermore, a rumor was circulating that the Americans had sent a tank division east from Plzeň, which was due to reach Prague that night. Close to tears, Morava barely noticed them. Jitka, he's here, so close I could touch him, but he keeps slipping away.

He would go see Beran and request a change of plans. Uprising or no uprising, they couldn't let this monster go free.

On a hunch he turned to the closest cluster of onlookers and unfolded Rypl's documents.

"Gentlemen! This man is missing. Has anyone seen him?"

"That's him!" called a postman, his German helmet tied with a Czech tricolor like a hat with a bow, "the one who let 'em have it!"

One after another they told of a man with similar features who had fired into the throng of Germans granted free passage. According to their descriptions it was Brunát who stopped him.

"Mr. Superintendent," said a boy with wire-rimmed glasses, mistakenly elevating his rank, "I met him earlier; he's a moral degenerate who's turning the uprising into a slaughterhouse! He shoots prisoners through the stomach and blows them up with grenades."

"He called them right, though," the postman countered. "They were carrying concealed weapons."

Morava impatiently cut off the burgeoning argument with an urgent question.

"Where is he now?"

"He wasn't alone," said the bespectacled youth. "There were two guys with him. He said we were all cowards, and they'd go get themselves some jerries somewhere else."

Where? Where?? Where???

If he had his way, he would have run off, prowling the streets like a hunting dog, but he could feel the sharp tug of his professional leash. With a heavy heart he set off for Bartolomějská Street.

He and Ladislav, a stoker for the bakery firm Odkolek, understood each other from the first. Strangely enough, however, the others had disappeared by the time they returned from the washroom. Alone in the basement, of course, they had no chance of getting through, so they returned to the entrance. A pair of boot heels and toes now lay mute behind the garbage cans. The guns in the radio building were still quiet, but in the deadly silence the street seemed all the more menacing. Then two bullets struck the pavement. They hurled themselves to the ground next to the dead man and considered their options.

"Hello!" A cry rang out from the opposite side. They could see the outline of a man waving at them from the building's hallway.

"If you want to run out, I can spray them."

They exchanged glances, nodding to each other and then to him. Then they saw him raise his gun.

"I'll count to three. Ready! One! Two . . ."

The last word was lost in the gunfire; he covered the side wall of the radio building in a long burst. They galloped over, wheezing; it seemed the street would never end. They nearly knocked the gunner over. Then they all chuckled.

"Thanks!" he said.

"No fucking problem."

The stocky, balding man in a wildly checked pullover reeking of sweat grinned at them. Three ugly gaps broke his smile; he looked decrepit, although he could hardly be more than thirty.

"What's happening?" he asked the man.

"Zilch. Waiting for the Americans, they say. I thought it'd be different."

"How?"

"A chance to have some fun with the browncoats. I owe them."

"They knock your teeth out?" Ladislav inquired.

"Yeah. Deployed me to Düsseldorf in the Totaleinsatz. I was gettin' on real well with this German bitch. So they gave me this and the camps—for 'corrupting racial purity'—'cept then the Brits rolled in and threw the brig wide open. Couple of weeks I slept in ditches and ate last year's potatoes. Wouldn't mind a bit of Kraut, now."

"We made two of them into grenade stew," Ladislav bragged. "On the can! Shoulda flushed, y'know."

The grenade wasn't enough, he thought as he listened; you can't see it up close and it's too fast. Those son-of-a-bitch Germans deserve a drawn-out punishment, just like the widow whores. And suddenly he knew what it would be. The idea was . . .

ALL MINE!

And it was completely new. He made a mental note.

"Great!" The dental avenger was praising him. "Need another hand? Call me Lojza."

The stoker repeated what was clearly his favorite question: What next, since the evening was still young? Then the deathly silence outside ended. Individual shouts soon merged into a joyous noise. Both the side streets and the main road, where Czechs killed at the beginning of the battle now lay, were swarming with people.

He and his companions set off for the intersection. Above the front portal of the radio building, strips of white tablecloths and towels fluttered from the first and fourth floors. An excited throng had formed an arc at a respectful distance from the main entrance. Through the broken doors a curtain of smoke still hung behind the barbed-wire barricades. For several long minutes nothing happened. The Czechs' anticipation gave way to fear: Was it a trap? You could cut the silence with a knife; one shot, he felt, and hundreds of people would panic and flee.

Instead, a Czech policeman came out of the building, unstrapping his helmet and fingering a wayward lock of white hair. Then he picked up a megaphone.

"Citizens!" he rumbled. "The radio is ours. The Germans have capitulated."

Fear turned instantly to intoxication; the crowd went wild.

He and his two companions waited curiously.

The policeman waved his megaphone around for a while until the throng quieted down.

"They have ceased their resistance under the condition that all Germans, employees and soldiers, are offered free passage without weapons down to the main train station."

There were a few indignant shouts from the crowd.

"Citizens! This agreement was concluded at the behest of the Czech National Council. President Beneš has named a new Czechoslovak government, but until they can return here from Košice, which has already been liberated, the council is assuming control in Prague. We have been empowered to conduct similar negotiations with all German offices in the former Protectorate, first and foremost so that our beloved Prague can be spared the further ravages of war, and so that we can safeguard the fundamental human rights we will uphold again in the future!"

The cop was getting on his nerves more and more. Then he flinched when someone next to him whistled so loudly his ears rang. It was the balding Lojza, now shouting through cupped hands.

"Germans aren't humans!"

He clapped along with Lojza and a couple of bystanders. They began to chant.

"Germans aren't humans! Germans aren't humans!"

The white-haired man strode purposefully toward them, droning on through his megaphone.

"Masaryk, the founder of our state, taught us that humanitarian ideals do not admit the collective guilt of races or nations. These men were soldiers; they followed orders and in spite of them capitulated. We cannot change the decision of the Czech National—"

"Then they should fuck off!" Lojza shouted at him. "We shed blood and we want an eye for an eye!"

He almost laughed at Lojza for not saying "a tooth for a tooth," but it made him angry to see the policeman gaining the upper hand among the crowd. THOSE BASTARDS ARE LISTENING TO HIM!

At that the first of the Germans exited the building, flanked by Czech guards. The foursome of ashen women in front—probably secretaries—caused some confusion, but the male employees, marked by white bands on their sleeves, drew whistles of derision. Their escorters smiled, as if acknowledging the onlookers' annoyance, but implying the crowd must surely understand their position too.

Lojza was arguing wildly with the policeman; leaving them to their quarrel, he stepped forward to see better.

The soldiers had begun to come out. The orderly rows of men had neatly polished and buttoned their hated uniforms, and held their heads up as if on review. Their commander had made a mistake in thinking this would boost their morale; signs of defeat would have been more to their credit. Any feeble sympathy the onlookers might have had now disappeared.

Now, finally, there arose in him a strong, almost holy wrath against Germans, similar to the one his mother had instilled in him years ago against feminine infidelity.

Before anyone noticed, he raised his submachine gun, took aim so as not to threaten any of the Czechs, and began to squeeze the trigger. He heard another rifle at his side—must be Ladislav!—and in the corner of his eye saw Lojza fighting with the policeman.

The women shrieked, the whole transport dove against the pavement for cover, but shots rang out from it as well.

Those whore bastards had guns!

HE WAS RIGHT!

The irritable policeman with the wispy white hair immediately deflected his aim by shoving his gun barrel into the air, but in the ensuing chaos he had so many other problems that he was soon distracted; it was necessary to round the prisoners up again, look them over and send them and their dead away as fast as possible. The cop had managed, however, to infect a decent-sized group of people who instantly turned against the three gunners. Among them was the four-eyes who'd irritated him over by the garbage cans.

"Degenerate!" Now the kid was taunting him with this completely nonsensical word. "Go back to the nuthouse; this is a democratic revolution!"

You're the crazy one, he wanted to shout back; and a TRAITOR TO OUR CAUSE, who deserves the same treatment!

SHOULD I JUST BLOW HIM AWAY?

This time right in the heart, so as not to horrify the more delicate bystanders. . . . He quickly came to his senses. Many in the crowd were just as well armed as he was.

In addition he remembered that he had a new name, but the same old face. There were clouds of police swarming about; what if by coincidence . . . ?

"Men," he said to his companions, "the fun's over, anyway. The hell with these cowards; there are plenty of Krauts left in Prague."

M y love!" Grete said. "Oh, my love, finally! It's been forever since I saw you!"

Of course her time dragged, while his flew, it seemed only moments since he had left her at the house. In the meanwhile, however, yesterday's city had changed into a jungle which even the natives did not recognize.

The neighborhood called Pankrác, where he and Kroloff had been sent, was an exception; it was still firmly in German hands. A single barricade of derailed trams beneath the court building reminded them of the unrest; its builders had been driven down into the Nusle Valley. Immediately thereafter a merry-go-round of motorized watches went out, discouraging other potential barricaders.

Schörner's heavy tanks would turn Pankrác into an extensive operations base. From here they could roll over the barricades in the valley, opening a passage to the city center and onward to the west. Aside from sporadic fire from various directions, however, there was no noise at all, and even after twilight only advance men on motorcycles came through. They mentioned barricades sprouting in the villages and towns around Prague, saying the colonnades had had to detour around through fields. These could not have presented any real obstacles to such powerful equipment, and thus further rumors were born. The prevailing opinion was that the Americans were approaching, which made a German advance pointless. Kroloff eagerly spread that afternoon's news: In his imagination the Protectorate was to be the launching point for a future western alliance, including the Reich, against the hydra of Communism.

"And that's the secret weapon," he kept repeating, "the truly brilliant secret weapon the Führer providentially left us!"

The headquarters was filled with commanders from various lower units. They had nothing to do beside organizing patrols; there was no word from the approaching army and the Prague division just checked in every hour to ask what was new. Buback thought of Grete, alone and helpless. It gave him an idea for how the officers could usefully fill their time. There were thousands of German civilians in Prague; why not concentrate the ones in this corner of the city under military control, at least until the army could guarantee their safe passage out or their right to remain?

His idea did not strike anyone's fancy. None of the officers seemed eager to complicate his own life unless ordered to do so; not even Buback's authority as a Gestapo emissary helped. It was Kroloff who dealt the plan a final blow. The Führer's memory, he parroted, could be best honored by unflinching adherence to the principles of Total War. The German citizens of Prague had been offered the opportunity to arm themselves a long time ago. The ones who availed themselves of it must have realized that every German apartment here could become a fortress. The ones who failed to do so had only themselves to blame; they had cut themselves off from the fellowship of a brave warrior nation.

Buback reminded him about the German woman who had saved the armored transporters trapped in the web of suddenly nameless streets that afternoon. If any of her Czech neighbors had spotted her, she would pay dearly indeed. After all, they couldn't expect civilians in their apartments to behave like soldiers under fire, if only because they had no unified command or clear orders.

Aha, Kroloff trumpeted triumphantly, but a civilian evacuation would confirm the Czechs' false hope that the Reich was capitulating, and could provoke a real uprising—the recent attempts by extremists had fortunately been just a pale imitation. After all, they'd just learned that one airborne torpedo had put an end to the unfortunate episode with the radio!

Buback did not prolong the argument. Better to preserve his authority for a real crisis situation. He would have to meet with Morava or Beran again to warn them of the problem; the haunting image of a murderer's holiday, which Grete had used, was seared into his brain. Grete! He had to see her, to put his mind at ease.

Two highly unpleasant events put a temporary end to the confused discussion. The same Czech announcer who had recently been cut off in midword during the successful German air raid now unexpectedly resurfaced, apparently from a replacement studio. And the telephone stopped working in the local pub the German command had occupied. The Czechs therefore controlled the city switchboard. Buback seized the moment.

"You stay here as long as necessary," he ordered Kroloff. "I'll try to get to Bredovská. We've completed our mission, but I don't like the fact that we don't have orders covering various possible developments. What's important is not which of us is right, but what sort of general directives have been worked out in the meanwhile."

"They won't bring you back through at night, and there may already be more than one barricade in the valley."

Buback was amused to see Kroloff's earlier outbursts of toughness give way to fear.

"I realize that. The surest way back is on foot."

"But there's a curfew."

"All the better. I'll take an escort as far as our outpost sentries. On the other side I'll blend in in civilian garb."

"How will you get back tomorrow?"

"The same way, unless a corridor has been freed up by then. You should know, Kroloff, why I was transferred here: I'm originally from Prague."

The skull head was dubiousness incarnate, but as Buback's subordinate, he had to accept the decision. His superior had them fetch the headquarters' map of the district, which had the outposts marked. As he had assumed, the furthest was at the edge of Kavčí Hory, not far from the little house. Once there, he nodded to his escort and to the sentries sheltering themselves against the beginning rain, turned up his overcoat collar, and set off into the darkness.

He shoved his work papers into his right sock, on the inside of the ankle and then into his shoe; the pass from Beran he hid in his left one. Just in case, he took the safety off his pistol. Swiftly he strode down the empty streets with their low houses. He stopped next door to check he was truly alone, and only then approached the house and pressed the bell as she'd requested: three short rings and a long one. He was caught off guard when the door opened immediately; swiftly he reached for his gun, but then he smelled her perfume, felt her hands pulling him inside, and heard her whispering voice.

At his request, she locked the door in the dark, but she did not let go of him. Before he could speak again, she pulled rather than led him up to the attic, telling him what she had been through. For hours she hadn't been able to sleep, but neither could she wake up: Agitation followed exhaustion and then exhaustion overcame agitation again until she fell into a strange trance in which she could not move, but her visions seemed absolutely real. As if in a fever, she saw her whole life and finally her death, because suddenly she had become Jitka Modrá, who had so trustingly exchanged fates with her.

"Suddenly I was the one who was fatally wounded here, but I wasn't dead—you just couldn't see it, and I was there as you put me in the coffin and you didn't notice as I tried desperately to give you a sign, and then the lid slammed down and they banged the nails in and they picked me up and lowered me in and finally I managed to scream, just as the soil drummed down on the lid, so I made one last effort—I gathered all my strength and swung upright so forcefully the lid flew open and I tried to stand up in a hail of dirt, but I was too late, you see, it took away my breath and consciousness, and suddenly it's all over, but my head hurts and I'm standing at the door and you're ringing. . . . Where have you been so long, love?"

When he found out she had not eaten at all, he wanted to fetch her something from the stores in the cellar, but she went with him and would not let go of him, as if drawing energy from his touch, holding him by the hand even as he sliced the rock-hard bread and opened military tins of sausage and cheese. On the way upstairs his foot hit an empty gin bottle he had found in the judge's bathroom as they fled. He realized she had drunk it while waiting for him and then fallen asleep by the front door.

He forced her to eat and meanwhile decided to stay until morning; it would be easier and safer to get to the center during daylight anyway. When he undressed and lay down next to her, he felt for the first time that she was not interested in him as a man; she clung to him as if she were freezing and only animal warmth could save her.

He began to stroke her, slowly and lightly, with just the balls of his fingers, along her back, her shoulders, and as she gave in and opened herself to him, he moved along her elbows, thighs, feet, not missing a single spot on her body. He had never done this before, but he could feel how deeply it touched her, how her fear and agitation abated, how she gradually calmed down and her confidence returned.

"Ah, my sweetheart," she sighed, "this is even better than making love. . . ."

Then she took his hand and as shots rang out here and there in the distance, she suddenly took up her story again, like in the old days that now seemed so idyllic to him.

After Rome, where they finally reconciled thanks to the mysterious Sicilian, a nasty surprise awaited them in Berlin. Martin's former father-in-law, a high-placed Nazi, arranged their assignment to a theater touring the East Prussian frontlines. Although this was a part of the Reich, it was, under the circumstances, an extremely inhospitable place; the spectre of another Russian offensive hung over them constantly. The state of the German troops they performed for was ample evidence of what the Bolsheviks were like. These were no tanned sportsmen like in Italy, treating the war with the Anglo-Americans as a gentlemen's competition even after their recent defeats. The East Prussian soldiers, in spite of their youth, reminded them more of old men. There was no thought of volleyball or soccer, and neither did they laugh at the famous comedian in their troupe; at camp they mostly slept or stared lifelessly off into space.

For Martin, the environment and sterile, pseudo-artistic programs reeked of degradation and humiliation. It all depressed him so deeply that one day he wrote to Berlin for their Jester. Martin had never been one for dogs, Grete said, looking back through the twilight into another time, but this one had caught his fancy. An infatuated fan had given Jester to him one opening night, apparently in the hope it would open the door to Martin's private life for her. Grete was already ensconced there, but he kept the dog anyway. Jester was a delightful little mongrel—they found unmistakable features of at least five breeds in him—but he had inherited their best qualities, beginning with a rare good nature. He would draw his masters out of arguments—and Buback would just have to believe her—by laughing; yes, he would stretch his lips back just like a human until his teeth shone through, and grin and hoot with laughter. Who could resist him?

When Martin switched to doing tours and Grete was allowed to join him, his older sister was happy to take Jester home. Then they truly began to miss him. On each swing through Berlin they spent much of their time petting him; it was during their estrangement and Jester was the one thing that connected them. Her unused tenderness for Martin flowed through Jester, Grete said, as did his for her, or at least so he claimed later.

By the time they reached Köningsberg they no longer needed this service from him. The two of them were at the top of the world, their own personal Himalayas, as Grete called them (and here Buback finally felt that prick of jealousy again, reminding him of his humanity in that inhuman night), but she and Martin thought the sweet little animal would bring joy into the rest of their gloomy wartime existence. The single bright spot in the Prussian assignment was a spacious apartment in the house of a German teacher, who had worshipped Martin's films for years and still could not believe his luck in having the actor under his own roof.

That hot summer before the first evacuation—Buback felt her shudder inwardly again, but this time her storytelling calmed her—the post office and rail lines were still running, despite the air raids. They called Martin's sister, and had her send Jester in a small box with air holes, which they would pick up directly at the station. A vigorous dog who had been walked and fed should easily manage a seven-hour trip. His sister cried as she read off the train number to them.

The two of them were looking forward eagerly to his arrival; the little dog had become a sort of talisman for them, presaging their wild, crude world's return to its original state of innocence. Their disappointment and fear was all the greater when they did not find the package as advised in the baggage car. They were on their way to the station agent so he could telegraph back down the line when Grete— on a hunch!—stopped at another wagon where they were unloading huge wheeled iceboxes carrying meat, butter, and eggs for the army. With the guards' permission she went inside and immediately her eye lit on a small package with her address. In a trance, she carried it out and gave it to a pale Martin. Their fingers turned numb with cold. To this day she could see him holding the small bundle horizontally in both hands as he slowly tipped it: inside a dead weight slid back and forth.

They walked home silently, she said, shocked by this senseless, icy death. The creature who was supposed to bring them help had turned into a symbol of their own ruin. Neither of them had the courage to do the most natural thing: walk out past the town limits and bury the corpse. Bereft of reason, they brought the little coffin into their room and placed it on the table. The apartment was an oven in the afternoon sun, but they did not even open the window for a cross draft; instead, they sat broken-hearted at the table, helpless against this paralysis. It was like in the fairy tale, Grete said, where they all turned to stone until a miracle happened; she was sure that even three hours later they would never find the strength to get up and leave for the tour.

And then the miracle happened! They heard something like a hiccup from inside the box. Neither of them moved. When the sound came a second time, Grete saw Martin holding his breath to hear better; he looked as if he might suffocate, but now the wooden box trembled lightly and then shook with a blow, as if the object inside were scrabbling to get out. Martin let out a hiss; he flew into the front hall and returned from the kitchen with a wood axe. He pried sharply up; the lid instantly gave way and out flew a furry ball.

She had never seen anything like it, Grete marveled in this foreign house in an enemy city, as joyfully as if she were reliving this resurrection. Jester, restored from near-freezing by the room's intense heat, tore around the room like a crazy dog, across and back, up and down, flying over the furniture with huge leaps, running a third of the way up the wall before falling back to earth in a somersault, only to defy gravity again on the other side of the room.

"It was like an explosion of life. We just sat there, holding each others' hands awkwardly and watching his return from the dead: ten, twenty, maybe thirty minutes went by, and he ran, jumped, barked, pulled and gnawed at us; he couldn't get enough of this life, and we couldn't get over his boundless, unfreezable desire to live, which infected even us, consumed as we were by our ongoing destruction."

Grete smiled.

"It lasted until . . ."

Grete burst into tears.

It was grief, sudden and wild, and Buback realized that since he did not know its source, he could not console her with soothing platitudes. He just took her firmly in his arms, as if trying to prevent her from splitting wide open, and listened helplessly to her howls. As the sound weakened, his heart grew lighter; fortunately, even boundless despair eventually reaches the limits of our body and soul, and slowly blunts itself against them.

He said nothing, but began almost imperceptibly to rock her like a child. The sobs trailed off, her tense muscles loosened and slowly she relaxed. After a while she began to speak almost normally, as if beginning one of her many stories.

"The first retreat went fairly smoothly; the troupe set up camp and we went to walk Jester. We'd been on a horse-drawn cart all day; gas had to be saved for the army. A fire beyond the birch wood drew us over. It radiated a kind of serenity, and we completely forgot that border areas were strictly off-limits all over the Reich. Then we saw a strange group of soldiers, probably deserters, but it was too late. We tried to say hello and quickly turn around. But one of them had already picked Jester up and was playing with him. The dog gave him a smile, which made the rest of them laugh. And we laughed too; suddenly we weren't as anxious. Then the soldier said in bad German that he'd be good for soup. Martin nervously passed this off as a bad joke, but the man wouldn't let go of the dog; he held him in his left hand by the scruff of his neck. Martin tried to pull him away. And with his right hand the man pulled out a pistol and shot Martin through the temple. I saw his brain spatter. Then he threw Jester into the cauldron alive. The splash of boiling water scalded my face. I kicked off my boots and fled into the darkness, but went the wrong way. They chased me, but didn't catch me. I don't know how I survived that night. In the morning I left the forest. I found the remains of the campfire, but nothing else, not even a bone. Somehow I found my way to the road. Our camp was already gone. A military car stopped for me. It was carrying war correspondents; they had a lot of cognac. I drank and drank and told them jolly stories about the theater all the way to Berlin; it was like a dream. They roared with laughter. One of them fell in love with me and arranged to have me sent to Prague. And that's all I know. Now I have to sleep, love. But don't let go . . . !'"

She fell asleep instantly and he held her, motionless; from time to time his lips touched the fiery scar on her neck, as if it could heal her burned soul.

The staircase confirmed that he was deadly tired. Today it had no end, as if they were adding on floor after floor. At last he dragged himself wretchedly up the final flight. Suddenly he was on his guard. What was it? A sharp line of light beneath the door of his room. He was sure he'd turned it off. Most of the dormitory's residents were single policemen; none of them would enter his room. So who, then? Him, he realized! He must have been nearby when Morava had asked about him at the radio station, and had followed him back to Barto-lomějská. But how had he gotten the address? And most important: what now? Go back for reinforcements? And if the killer got away in the meantime? Then Morava remembered the pistol he'd fired that time in the car, almost killing Beran in the process. He pulled it out and carefully removed the safety catch. If he were right and Jitka's murderer was waiting for him, he would shoot once and only once, to kill. Wait. . . . did he really want to do that? Hadn't he taught his recruits what Beran had taught him and generations before him? Never let yourself believe you're the law; in all cases, gentlemen, you are its servants, and only it is sovereign! Behind the door, however lurked something only superficially human: it was pure Evil, and it mocked heaven by masquerading as a person in the presence of its victims. Could Beran's principles apply to it as well? No, he decided, if it were waiting there, he would kill it. His only responsibility was to do his best, despite his inexperience, to kill it straight off, so that it would not suffer the way its victims had. He inched the key into the lock bit by bit, so as not to make the slightest noise. With his finger on the trigger he slammed the door open and immediately dropped his gun hand to his side, horrified. His mother sat at a freshly-laid table, smiling back at him, her hands folded peacefully in her lap. Now her smile froze. Child, you frightened me, why all the hullabaloo? Mommy!—he unobtrusively hid the gun, which she fortunately hadn't noticed—what are you doing . . . ? Well, didn't you tell me to come if the war got too close? But, he stammered the Russians are already there . . . ! Yes, they came sooner than expected. So how did you get past the front . . . ? I don't know how, child, the main thing is I'm here; aren't you happy? Of course, mother, but . . . who opened the door for you? Who else, she laughed, you silly boy; your Jitka, of course!

Now he knew he was in the grip of a dream, but this deceptive condition was much nicer than full consciousness, which was gradually gaining a foothold. He tried to prolong the fantasy. Lying motionless, his eyes closed, he imagined the unrealized meeting of his life's two loves. He could see his mother's face and movements from his March visit: he called up images of Jitka from her last days and had a wonderful few moments when both of them were alive in his memory as if they'd known each other forever. For the first time since Jitka's death her memory did not tear at his soul. And if his mother was alive, as he felt with every fiber of his being, then he had at least one fixed star in his universe.

At that he remembered the horrible beginning of his dream and the beloved faces faded as quickly as a rainbow. He was back in the blood-stained present. But how could he catch Rypl now, when overnight the

298

killer had switched from widows to Germans and wrapped himself in the mantle of a patriot?

Morava could think of nothing else, even on the trip back from the radio to Bartolomějská yesterday. He had been there within a few minutes, since the city center was suddenly empty, as if everyone was celebrating at the station. However, by the time he reached the office, the revolutionaries had stopped broadcasting. A German turbine air-craft flying close above the roof had attacked the building in a daring raid; the torpedo plunged down precisely into the entrance hall, which Morava had just left. The explosion took many lives and disrupted telephone lines and broadcasting. Despite the chaos, the Czechs were working mightily to repair the transmitters and set up replacements, and Beran chased Morava straight back to prevent Brunát from broad-casting one particular proclamation, which he said could cause a split in the Czech National Council.

He had only recognized the white lion by his voice; a turban of bandages covered his mane. A piece of shrapnel had taken off a portion of Brunát's ear before ramming into a concrete column. The man who had been talking to the commander in the hall was killed on the spot. Brunát read Beran's paper, muttered something about pricks, and dis-appeared.

When he returned to Number Four, Beran finally called him to his old office for a report. He welcomed Morava in, saying he wanted a short break from all this soldiering. It was amazing how quickly his jovial old boss—despite a uniform he swam in like a scarecrow—had truly become a commander. Morava glossed quickly over his noon mission; it was old news. He described in detail how he had found Antonín Rypl's trail, and put forth his request.

"Sir, this isn't a personal vendetta, even if it could be seen that way...." They could both feel the emptiness of Jitka's abandoned desk through the open door behind them. "I'm concerned about the purity of our revolution; it was supposed to put an end to this sort of barbarity. According to witnesses, he's killed almost ten people since noon today: three sadistically and all of them without provocation, because they'd already surrendered. Anyone who says they were just Germans and brushes it off is making a terrible mistake. He keeps on murdering because he can get away with it. For some people he's a hero, and apparently he's found a few thugs with similar tendencies. And what if they become a murder squad? What'll they do once they run out of Germans? Turn on their fellow countrymen? Start on the collaborators, real and imagined? And who after that? Sir, we have plenty of men who are better than I am at messengering, interpreting, and capturing radio stations, but right now I'm probably the only one who can catch him. It's a point of honor for the police; he's a self-appointed executioner and we can't let him go free when peace comes."

He's looking past me at her chair; he can't turn me down! Morava felt sure he had won.

Beran stood up and went to close the door. Then, unusually, he sat down on his desktop and stared through Morava at the wall. The detective had never seen his boss this way.

"It's a point of honor for the police, if you're interested, to protect Prague from both the Germans and its own citizens," Beran began. "Using only our own modest forces we've met the demands of our political and military leaders: an impassable city, the Germans in it momentarily paralyzed. The sad thing is, the Czech delegation fell apart before they ever came together."

He saw that Morava did not understand.

"I think of myself as one of a dying breed of civil servants, who stood apart from factions so they could serve the community. I've been involved in this for weeks, as you know, and, in my neutrality, I've been more and more horrified at what I see. It was clear to both sides that an uprising would increase the chances that Prague would be destroyed, and it had no real military value given the massive front movements. But there was still a political value in deciding whether to rebel. The winning side will be the one that's best at anticipating the pious wishes of whichever Allied force ends up in control here. Finally, the democrats started it off; they bet on the Americans, encouraged by their quick advance, but now they've got the losing hand. At the moment the Communists hold the trumps, because the Western Allies have stopped outside Plzeň."

"No . . . !" A gasp escaped Morava.

"Yes. The Big Three have apparently decided that the Red Army will liberate Prague. I take it I don't have to tell you what the consequences will be."

"I had no idea," Morava admitted honestly. "When will they get here? It's just a hop from Dresden and Linz; those claws would cut Schörner off from the rest of the Reich and that would end the war."

"Remember the Warsaw and Slovak uprisings," Beran answered glumly. "They let them bleed to death."

"On purpose? But why?"

"A liberator never likes it when people free themselves first. They don't get the gratitude they need to stay in power."

Morava was shaken.

"So the Communists have renounced the uprising?"

"On the contrary. They're trying to seize control of it."

"How?"

"Very simply. They didn't start it, and now they're claiming they're obliged to salvage what they can. If it's successful they'll be the ones who give the Soviets the keys to Prague. If we're defeated, they'll claim the democrats are soldiers of fortune who are responsible for needless losses and damage. Today they blocked the decision to offer the Germans an unhindered retreat to the west in return for capitulation. Suddenly they were calling it a separate peace that would disappoint the Allies—read: the Soviets. As a result we'll be fighting a force that outguns us many times over."

"So it's a cynical game?"

"Why cynical? History proves that the worst atrocities are always committed by the keepers of a sacred truth, who truly believe in their mission. And that mission includes destroying all other truths—which, of course, are nothing but lies—along with anyone who supports them."

The telephone rang.

"Good to hear your voice." Beran sounded relieved. "When it hit I was really afraid for you. Yep, be right down."

He hung up and gave a sad grin.

"Brunát is supposed to bring me to the council meeting. More bull . . . bullyragging, apparently."

"I'll hold down the fort here."

"You'll do nothing of the sort; you're going to sleep. Have you forgotten what a day you've had?"

He remembered. His wife and child's funeral. And a bit of war. Suddenly an unbearable heaviness rolled over him. Beran took him by the arm almost tenderly.

"Get up, Jan . . . can I call you by your first name? I've been meaning to ask for a while, and I may not get the chance again. Get up and go lie down. You're absolutely right; the best thing you can do for your country is catch him. I'll give you Litera."

Then a listless stroll past Jitka's desk.

Then bed, and a fall into darkness.

Then the dream about Rypl, and his mother.

Then waking up with the picture of his mother and Jitka.

Now a sharp memory of his conversation with Beran.

And finally the hope that when he managed to fall back to sleep he would meet those two dear beings again.

Once they had cut a path through all the rubberneckers and cowards they found a skinny redhead tagging along, who had picked a Panzerfaust from the arsenal the Germans left.

" 'Scuse me, can I come with you? You're tough guys; you can make the Nazis swallow anything, hairs and all!"

"C'mon, you're not even fifteen yet," Lojza probed.

"Sure I am."

"Don't try it. If you wanna come, own up, we don't take liars."

"I will be in six months," he admitted, "but nothing fuckin' scares me."

"Your parents let you go?"

"Pop bit it and my mom can go fuck herself," he explained maturely. "She had her way I'd be wearing a skirt."

This caught his attention.

"You an only child?"

"Yeah. Why?"

"She ever beat you?"

"Like to see her try! She knows I'd send her flying."

He was confused.

"You'd hit her . . . ?"

"Why not? Not like I asked to be born. And I don't give a shit if I survive, either. So why should those fuckin' Nazis live? Well, can I come?"

"Why not," he said to the other two. "Maybe he'll learn a few new words too."

He would watch the boy. He had to figure out HOW HE GOT FREE FROM HER.

They were a scant two hundred yards uphill from the radio building when the crescendo of a motor caught their attention. At first he thought it was a tank and his eyes darted to the boy's Panzerfaust, but when he turned around, he saw an unusual-looking airplane appear above the buildings. A large cigar separated from it and dropped toward the ground. Immediately a detonation rolled past, so powerful that it shook the cobblestones beneath their feet. Lime-white dust rolled upward from the radio building, and tiny bits of concrete whizzed through the air toward them.

"Good fucking show!" the boy rejoiced. "That's what they get for taking the Nazis' side."

Everyone had to laugh at that.

Garlanded with guns, they trudged uphill along the main avenue side by side. The people hurrying downhill to help moved respectfully aside to let them pass. The fighters soon realized they would not have much fun that day. The citizens of Prague had gone crazy; their latest hobby seemed to be prying up and hauling around paving stones. Rain began to pour down, and in a wide area around the barricades the naked roadbed quickly changed into mud under the countless footfalls of their builders.

They were not dressed for this work.

"Where do we go for the night?" asked the youth, who had told them to call him Pepík.

"I'm from Brno," he said, half truthfully. "I don't have an apartment here."

Ladislav lived on the opposite—and therefore inaccessible—side of the city, Lojza had found a new guy at his girlfriend's, and there was no question of going to the boy's mother's. After a long while the caretaker on the embankment flashed through his mind. Why not finish him off and then stay there . . . ?

"For God's sake," Lojza said, lighting up, "there must be loads of empty apartments from the Germans. I know one that's pretty close, in fact. Belongs to the director of a glue factory—where I worked till the bastard handed me over to the Work Exchange. Everything that happened to me after that was his fault."

"What if they're still there?" Pepík inquired.

"Their bad luck. They kept a goat at their Vysočany plant and since I was the second watchman there, I brought them milk every day at noon. Twice I caught another guy in the apartment; I think my boss's wife sweet-talked her husband into bringing the milk himself in the evening, so he cut me loose. I'd like to kiss that whore's ass good-bye."

The intimately familiar word grabbed his attention. He approved.

The turn-of-the-century street far from the main avenues was trying to pretend it had nothing to do with the rebellion. No one reacted to the night bell. The bald man swore regretfully.

"The evening's still young. . . ." The stoker repeated what was evidently his only joke.

He did not want to give up so easily.

"We can open it. Anything handy?"

"Could always blow the fucker open with the Panzerfaust." The boy grinned.

No one even laughed. They were dragging an entire armory with them and it was useless. His years with the theater, however, had taught him that in a pinch anything would do. Now he remembered his knife. When he drew it out to its full length from the pouch tied around his body, Lojza whistled appreciatively.

"Nice poultry knife. You a butcher, by any chance?"

"No," he said, "but I like butchering."

The lock clicked on the first try. They lit matches. The apartment Lojza led them to took up the entire third floor. The doorplate had no name on it, understandably. They rang. Nothing. They gave a longer ring. From the depths of the apartment they could hear the bell. Still nothing.

"The blade?" the boy asked impatiently.

Then they heard a woman's footsteps: When she opened the door, chain in place, and he shoved his foot between the door leaves, he felt the excitement. It grew as Lojza tried to persuade her. Of course she should let them in; they'd been sent to protect her and she knew him, after all, he used to bring her milk from the factory . . .

"Ick habba eenen tseegenmilk haulen, gnaydigga frau . . ."

From then on, though, everything was different. Lojza and Ladislav played with her for an hour like cat and mouse; they let her change out of her nightgown and bathrobe into the clothes she'd wear to the assembly point for Germans; of course she could take her valuables with her. She outdid them in obligingness, and his mouth began to water when she poured a half liter of scrambled eggs into a pan.

Slowly she regained some color, repeating ad nauseam how grateful she was to Mr. Alois (as she called Lojza), because he was a personal acquaintance of theirs. Her husband must have been delayed over in Vysočany; Mr. Alois of all people knew how decently they'd both treated the Czechs.

He ate his fill, but otherwise kept quiet. Conversations with women weren't his specialty; after all, he'd only ever had one (that time in the train), and look how it had turned out. But what about HER? Wasn't SHE a woman too? How does it work, he began to wonder: are mothers women to their sons or not? SHE clearly had been, and such a strong one that he'd never had room in his life for another. The one time he'd been curious what he was missing, that woman had mocked him. He punished her on the spot, and since then he had either hated other women or simply ignored them. Now, for the first time, he could observe how men treated them and what they might want from them. Only his hellishly tight self-control stopped him from gaping open-mouthed like the boy.

They let her wash the dishes—so the Czechs who would come to live here, the bald one urged her, wouldn't think Germans were pigs—and then they all accompanied her as she went to make the bed. She continued to nod and obey them until Lojza gave her an almost friendly order to undress.

"Tsee dick aus!"

Once again she turned ashen and began to beg. He was very surprised that she chose him from among the four of them as her intercessor. Before he could react, Lojza's sharp slap silenced her.

"See this mess?" He bared his half-toothless gums at her. "That's your pig-husband's fault, for sending me to the Reich. So now you'll let us have some fun and we'll call it even. Agreed?"

She stood as if turned to stone, making not a sound. And her horrified eyes NEVER LEFT HIM. Why?

"We're not going to rape you," Lojza continued. "As Czechs we'd never stoop that low; but we could give you fifty on your backside, which is more what you deserve."

He pulled up his sweater and undid a thick belt. He cracked it with a whistling sound on the edge of the brass bed.

"You'll sleep at least a month on your stomach with a sore ass, guaranteed. Or is my first offer better? Might be more enjoyable. What do you say?"

He raised his hand again, but did not need to demonstrate any further. She began to undress as meekly as she had earlier cooked and washed.

He was excited now as well. He had never seen a woman naked before and the effect was even stronger amid three armed men. He found it disturbing, the way she kept looking at him when she WASN'T EVEN TIED UP.

"A gag!" he suggested.

"Why?" Lojza joked. "This way she can tell us who does it best."

"So she won't shout. . . ."

As if she'd understood the instruction, she let out a yelp, but a lot of water had gone under the bridge since that tart in Brno, and his skills had improved. In the twinkling of an eye he whipped out his handkerchief and stuffed it into her mouth, pushing her back onto the bed as he bent her legs. One hand held both hers in an iron grip, while the other fished under his coat for the straps. Then, with the help of the others, he tied all four limbs to the cornerposts of the bed. She lay stretched out like on a medieval rack, unable either to move or speak.

"You're a fucking grenade," Ladislav marveled belatedly.

"For that you can start her off!" Lojza offered appreciatively.

The boy just rolled his eyes and swallowed with excitement.

His cheeks flushed; he hoped no one would see it in the glow of the small night-lamp. He played for time, managing to laugh.

"She's your girl!"

"No problem," the bald man responded. "Anything for a friend."

It's crazy, the thought crossed his mind; it starts the same way. MY TWO MISSIONS HAVE MET!

"So help yourself," the stoker said, a bit impatiently.

He had already recovered and was ready.

"I'm sorry, but never with a German."

"No cunt stinks too bad for me." Lojza laughed toothlessly. "You don't wanna, then leave her; I'll start for old times' sake, gnaydigga frau."

He did not even take off his pants, just unbuttoned them, releasing an engorged member, and lay down on the German woman. For some time he moved up and down on her, grunted twice, and got up, satisfied, buttoning his fly.

"Take a number, step right up!"

Ladislav's turn lasted longer and involved much heavy breathing. At the end he let out a few sounds resembling moos.

He was careful not to let them notice how closely he was watching. And was that all, he marveled. For this people get married and divorced, love and hate each other? Then SHE had been right—a hundred times right!—to protect him from it. This, these funny jerking movements, was what was called passion? THEN MINE IS STRONGER!

It was the boy's turn. He wiggled oddly on the prone figure.

"What's wrong?" Ladislav inquired.

"I don't feel anything . . ."

The stoker bent over him with evident professional interest.

"Lemme see . . . it's not even up!"

"What the fuck am I gonna do?"

"Get off her." Ladislav chuckled. "You're impotent. Or a bugger."

"What's that?"

The toothless man, surprisingly, took pity on him.

"Leave the kid alone. Pepík, don't worry about it, you're still a bit too young. I say we leave her trussed like this until morning, gentlemen, and sack out somewhere else, there's loads of beds here. Before we go we can have some more for breakfast."

He leered at the boy.

"Maybe your willie'll grow overnight, then wham, bam! You might even want some too, Ludva."

He was still not used to the name Ludvík, much less to its nickname. And this boasting was starting to annoy him. Why did they think that was all there was to manhood? Even the youth would have sobered right up, if only he'd seen . . . But why not recruit the kid—or all of them—for his cause? Surely the world had never seen BIGGER WHORES THAN THE GERMANS?

And why was she still looking at him that way? Yes, she recognized him as her master!

"Once you've had your fun," he decided, "I'll show you what I do with a Kraut whore!"

He considered leaving while Grete was asleep, to spare both of them the good-byes. However, when he had made tea down in the kitchen and dipped his biscuit in it, he suddenly knew he couldn't disappear without at least kissing her for good luck.

As he had held her, sleeping, in the crook of his arms long into the night until he himself fell asleep, he realized why she attracted him more than his wife ever had. His conclusion was unfair but true: he had been Hilde's first; she had simply belonged to him, and never had any secrets from him. With Grete, the closer she supposedly brought them with her confession, the more mysterious she seemed. He had filled Hilde's entire life; in Grete's he was simply the latest man, or even one man too many. Sometimes he felt himself entirely superfluous.

He was wrong, she'd said once long ago (Long ago? They'd barely known each other seven weeks!), utterly wrong to make all his predecessors into rivals. You love once in your life, for your whole life, and that love simply takes on different names—but the final one is the sum and summit of them all, and that was him, as he knew full well; why brood over it?

He could not deny that he felt the same. As if he'd never loved anyone but her.

Anyway, why worry about it? Now the point was for both of them to stay alive.

He went back upstairs in his socks and tried to wake her by staring intently at her. She slept so deeply that finally he leaned over.

"My love . . . ," he whispered in her ear. "Do you hear me?"

She swam to the surface of consciousness remarkably quickly.

"Why did you wake me, Buback? You've never woken me before? Do you want to tell me you're staying with me?"

"No. . . ."

"Nor that you're taking me with you?"

"You know I can't."

"Then why? I could have not known for hours that you'd gone. That you'd left me in the lurch at the mercy of the first person to come. Maybe it'll even be your murderer. Murderers like to return to the scene of the crime, don't they?"

He was horrified.

"For God's sake, Grete. . . . I tried to explain to you . . ."

An ironic gleam appeared in her sleepy eyes.

"Now you've convinced me, love. Of course you explained it. And of course I'd rather see you than wake up here alone. Now go, for real, and leave me alone. I don't want to see you anymore."

"Grete—"

"I don't want to see you till I see you again!"

He collected his strength to leave.

"You'll have to lock up after me. . . ."

"Not now. Now I have you inside me and I don't feel so abandoned, so I'll try to sleep some more. Lock me in and keep the key. I won't be entertaining visitors today. Good-bye, love."

The bedclothes billowed. The last thing to register on his retina was the tiny flicker of a flame.

Grete's face, that battleground of despair and passion, stayed with him the whole way to Gestapo headquarters. No one noticed him; there was no gunfire, and the barricades had become social clubs, where people hashed and rehashed the possible developments while they waited for the Americans to arrive. Everywhere snatches of conversation told him people were convinced the war was over, at least in Prague.

He did not meet his own men until close to Bredovská, but even here Czechs living on "German" territory walked freely through. In the building he found the document burning was over and the drinking had begun. The collapse of Germany's self-declared millennial values and its leading characters was turning a national tragedy into a blood-stained burlesque. In his previous workplaces, a power elite directed by Berlin's mighty pen had managed to arrange an orderly withdrawal. Here the pen had snapped and the Gestapo had disintegrated into a frightened crowd of men arguing when and to whom they should surrender. To Buback's horror they were unanimous on one point: that all the prisoners in the underground bunkers should be liquidated first, so they could not inform on their interrogators.

Regardless of the state of their relationship, he had to speak to Meckerle immediately, and coincidentally he ran into his boss on the way. The newly minted lieutenant general was just leaving his ante-chamber; when he spotted Buback, he motioned to him with a finger and retreated back into his office. There he poured two large cognacs as he walked, drank his in a single gulp, and began to speak, standing.

"You were right, that SS moron's raid was a colossal failure, and then he slept right through that fiasco at the radio station. Prague is lost and I've given up on Schörner. Do you still have a direct line to the Prague police?"

Is it a trap? he considered hastily; is Meckerle after revenge? Does he want my confession so all he'll need is a quick field trial and an execution that's more like a dog slaying? But if Buback had been followed the day before, then saying no would only confirm his guilt. So he hedged his bet.

"Yes. Neither you nor Schörner withdrew your orders for cooperation."

"Perfect. If it amuses you, then keep looking for that deviant in this shambles, but help your countrymen while you're doing so."

For the first time, Meckerle gave that word preference over the Nazi term *kinsmen*.

"I'm happy to, assuming I can figure out how to proceed, and if it's in my power to do so."

"We need to get out of this trap, nothing more, nothing less, otherwise the Russians will sweep us up and put our backs to the wall. Yes, the western front has stopped. They could let us retreat toward it. We'll need our guns, of course—otherwise every kid we see will want to take a crack at us—but we'll give them up as soon as we see the first Yank."

No! Could this be his chance?

"And what are we offering?"

"Not to turn their baroque buildings into piles of rubble; what more could they ask for?"

"I don't think that will be enough. They have the upper hand."

"Probably so. What would you add?"

"Their people imprisoned in Pankrác. There's talk here of executing them."

"People are afraid the prisoners would want revenge."

Buback had an answer to this one.

"We'll give them the keys to the building once we've been allowed to leave."

"Done," the giant said without hesitation. "Move, then, and see to it."

Buback could not risk having the former bank clerk change his mind and overrule him.

"I request a written order."

"Have them write it up next door and hurry!"

Buback did not move.

"I have one further wish, Mr. Meckerle."

He deliberately neither phrased it as a question nor used his superior's title. It was a risk, to find out how far he could go with the lieutenant general.

"Speak."

Nothing more. So he'd mellowed.

"Have you already sent your wife home?"

The question hit the mark. Meckerle's answer was defensive.

"You know perfectly well I don't have a 'home.' They blasted my villa into smithereens."

"But she's left Prague."

Meckerle was starting to seethe, just like he used to.

"Yes. She's at her sister's in Bavaria. Is this an interrogation, Buback?"

"I think it's a man's first responsibility to take care of those close to him. In your position, all the German civilians in Prague should fall into that category."

There was still no outburst. Instead, the newly minted lieutenant general poured both of them another glass. But he did not drink; he was working up to a question.

"She's still here?"

"Yes."

"Where?"

"Last time you found out and practically had her abducted."

Once again he watched this powerful man practically drown in childish embarrassment.

"Well, all right. It's in the past. We all have our weak points; don't you? Anyway, she set matters straight right away. I should really lodge a complaint through you about excessive self-defense. . . . Keep your hiding place to yourself, but watch out for her; it'd be a shame to lose her."

"I can do that as long as the Czechs don't completely control the city. Then she and all the other Germans left will be at their mercy. There are recognized principles for dealing with soldiers that have to be upheld, even, more or less, in uprisings. But for civilians there's only a general declaration, and so far hatred has swept it aside each and every time. Yesterday, at a meeting in Pankrác, I suggested that we concentrate all civilian personnel under our protection; they'd certainly rather hang about the barracks on a hard floor than wait in their comfortable apartments until someone breaks down the door with an ax. Kroloff convinced the other officers that every German residence in Prague should become a fortress."

"Kroloff's a fanatic and a moron."

"Kroloff claimed to be quoting you."

"Now wait!" Meckerle was on the brink of exploding, but immediately regained control. "Until yesterday I had orders from the highest levels of the Reich to boost soldiers' and workers' morale at any price. But I depended on each of you using your own brain."

I've got to ride this one out in silence, Buback thought. The statement's author soon realized how absurd it sounded.

"Well, yes, all right. . . ." He sighed again. "We dug the spurs in; now we'll have to ride the horse till it throws us. You can convey your idea about the prisoners to the Czechs as my own offer. I'll have our civilians watched, but I can't promise much. Most of the city is no longer in our control, and to tell the truth I'm hoping none of our men get the bright idea to try to reconquer it; that would hurt us even more. Anyway, the Czechs have new allies. Vlasov's Russian division has moved toward Prague in the naive hope that they'll get a pardon from Stalin if they come to defend the Slavs against the Germans, even though it's shutting the door once the horses have left the stable. But don't tell the Czechs; it'll just puff them up. Let me make myself clear: The Reich is over, and the Protectorate no longer exists. I have no idea what Schörner's up to, and no inkling what's keeping Frank busy, but I know what I want. I've still got a good few thousand men armed to the teeth here in the city center whom the Czechs would be glad to get rid of because, well, why take the chance? I'm offering a nice little capitulation, one that'll be tolerable for both sides, in return for a retreat where we'll take all the remaining Germans with us. Pass it on to your cops, see to it they give us the green light, and save yourself and her."

He placed the glass firmly down, stalked off to his desk, and began to rummage through the drawers. Buback had the impression the hearing was at an end, and moved to leave.

"Wait!" Meckerle stopped him. "Does she have a way to defend herself when you're not around?"

"What do you mean?"

"I mean, did you at least leave her with a gun?"

"No . . . I don't think she'd know how—"

"What? You didn't know she was crazy about guns? I think one of her lovers got her interested in pistols. She even knew how to take mine apart; just to be sure, I always unloaded it. Wait. . . ."

Finally he found it. What he gave Buback was a small ladies' revolver with a handle of inlaid pearl.

"This little jewel, which makes perfectly good holes, was going to be a present for her. If it doesn't bother you, give it to her with my apology. She can shoot me with it later. That's all."

Buback could not think of anything better than to stick the thing in his pocket. From behind as he left he heard Meckerle say nostalgically, "Tell her I said hello . . . that pretty little bitch."

He felt another of the stabs inside which love used to scare war away.

While the photographer made more and more enlargements, Morava sat writing notes. He was taking the first five hundred prints out to Litera's car, wracking his brains over how to arrange transport around the shattered city without Buback's help, when he spotted him. The chief inspector was walking toward him from a controlled crossing point, waving at him like a friend arriving for a social get-together. From up close he did not seem as relaxed; he urgently requested a meeting with Beran.

The latter, now ensconced in Rajner's office, made time for him immediately and got hold of Brunát as well, whose turban had lost its snow-white color overnight. The injured man looked as if he'd been wandering the sewers, the former superintendent (now the other half of their commissionership) joked, and Brunát, to their surprise, confirmed it. He had been directing work on the sewage-main barricades, so they wouldn't find themselves—as he put it—with visitors up their asses.

Buback described the mood at the Gestapo and then went through

Meckerle's suggestions in detail; at that they sent him into the ante-chamber. After what Beran had said the night before, Morava would have expected him to be pleased at the disintegration of the unified German command, but the serious faces of both men told him there was a problem: The end of the war, in Prague and all over Bohemia, was sliding out of control.

He was even more shocked at the political problem presented by Vlasov's anticipated attack on his former allies. The outlaw Russian general was expected to turn on the Germans, a move that would greatly help the insurgents. According to Beran, an increasing faction within the council believed that any cooperation with Vlasov was tantamount to approving the Russian rebels' original motive for fighting against their native country.

The commanders from the city's southeastern edge were asking urgently for an explanation: Why couldn't they accept Vlasov's men as emergency protectors? They were exasperated to see the Germans' death grip closing around them, and made it clear how little these breaking and re-forming political ice floes interested them.

However, both commanders thought the suggested German retreat from the area around the main train station—a dangerous reinforcement source if Schörner should attack Prague—should be accepted as a local decision not affecting the Allied principle of total and unconditional capitulation.

Beran and Brunát therefore decided to recommend that the Czech National Council accept a political resolution to the situation.

And what about Vlasov? Beran claimed—and Brunát backed him on it—that the Russian would not want to attack unless necessary. Then he reached for the telephone.

"If the Germans attack you," he ordered someone, "Vlasov's people can fight alongside you; I'll take the heat for it."

In the meanwhile, Buback would wait there, the chiefs decided in conclusion; they would guard him against the ever-growing numbers of patriots who were trying to set a sharper tone at Bartolomějská. Several colleagues, supposedly led by the garage manager, had adorned themselves with armbands marked RG, calling themselves the Revolutionary Guards.

How strange, Morava thought. Tetera—nicknamed "Pretty Boy" for his skirt chasing—never let a word against the Germans pass his lips; they'd always watched their words in his presence. But the young detective had already noticed at the radio station how quickly the cowards became heroes. After all, the woman called Andula (who, at a critical moment, had asked them to heed the Germans' request to cease broadcasting distress calls) had become the first to compile a list of "radio station fighters."

Finally he had finished his tasks. As he left, he agreed with Buback on three times and places to meet (just in case) and picked up Litera and the car in the courtyard. After confirming with the operations officer that, excepting the center, Bubeneč and Pankrác, there were still contiguous bands of the city in Czech hands, he decided to wear his uniform so they would not be held up with constant identification checks. The others wanted to avoid Germans, but Morava now believed he might be able to reason with many of them. They could always ask to be taken to the Gestapo building; curiously, thanks to Buback, it might offer them the greatest degree of safety.

First they visited the caretaker. The house on the embankment was locked and they had almost given up ringing when unexpectedly something moved in the raised ground-floor window. The Germans had had guards here till Friday, he explained once he'd opened the door; yesterday they'd disappeared with a truckload of papers, so he was on his own. They still hadn't caught the murderer? No, Morava admitted, and now they couldn't even help the caretaker. Surely he could see what was afoot, so in future: Keep the door locked and don't open it! Still, they would like to test his memory once more.

In putting nine other photographs chosen randomly from the archive on the table along with Rypl's, he was satisfying the conscience Beran's training had drilled into him, rather than his intellect; he had long since ruled out the caretaker as a reliable witness. Instantly he realized his error.

The shock of the murder, the bombardment and his resulting shameful bowel trouble must have temporarily clouded the man's memory, but a few months' distance had refreshed it; the caretaker pointed without hesitation to Rypl.

Finally, a state's witness!

Could he move somewhere else for the meanwhile, Morava asked. Where, the man replied; the front would cut off his path to safety in eastern Bohemia any day now, and how would he get out of Prague, anyway? It occurred to Morava that he could requisition a guard for the man under the pretext of securing German secret offices; his boss had been right once again.

On the way over Morava had thought it strange he was fighting so hard for one witness while Rypl was conducting public executions. Or does murder stop being murder, legally, when the victim belongs to a stronger nation that forces its law on others through violence? And what does it mean when a new police force starts to form within the old one? Would the garage manager Tetera dare say he served the law better than Beran did? He persisted in his gloomy thoughts as they crossed a dozen or so barricades. Finally they were at the house where earlier he had come looking for Karel Malina, the Beroun depot employee.

"Take something we can pry with," he suggested to Litera.

He headed straight for the neighbor's bell. A bony man opened the door.

"Come in. Eliška's been expecting you."

She greeted the policemen. Her cheeks burned with repentance.

"Why didn't you tell us the truth?" Morava scolded her, although he was mainly angry at himself.

"You didn't have uniforms—"

"I showed you my documents!"

"But there was a German with you—"

"From the criminal police. He's helping us."

"How was I to know?"

"I told you clearly we were looking for a murderer."

Her husband had been studying Morava. Now he made a decision.

"Tell them. They don't look like provocateurs. And it's out in the open now anyway. What if something happened to Malina?"

"Karel . . ." She swallowed and corrected herself. "Mr. Malina came on Tuesday to tell me he was hiding a parachutist . . ."

No! Morava despaired; he'd been here—just one door away.

"...and that he'd be going away to meet the man's contacts, so he might be detained. He took his keys back; I had to swear not even to tell my husband."

"But you did tell him," he reproached them both.

"Only yesterday. I thought it was taking too long, and by now it seemed a bit strange . . ."

"Have you heard anything from next door?"

"No. But a cop could have a peek, couldn't he?"

"Not legally," he said, chafing at the impotence of old-fashioned laws. "We have to have authorization for forced entry. I don't know where I would get it in this situation, so I'll take responsibility for it myself. But I need both of you as witnesses for the opening, search, and closure of the apartment."

The engineer agreed for both of them. When Litera tried to pry the door open with a tire iron, the man brought a whole box of tools from his apartment and wedged a massive chisel in himself. At the second hammer blow the lock gave way. A stench hit them as if they'd opened a sewer.

It never ends, Morava thought, his heart sinking. Dumbly he exchanged a knowing glance with Litera, who no longer hid the pistol in his hand, and suggested to the woman, "Better stay here, ma'am. I'm afraid it won't be pleasant."

"Run along home, Eliška," her husband ordered.

Now the import of it hit her, but she could not obey. Collapsing against the staircase wall, she clutched her throat with her hands.

Piles of trash lay in the kitchen; an unmade bed and an open wardrobe greeted them in the bedroom. Morava pressed down on the last door handle, his hand wrapped—out of habit—in a handkerchief.

In the bathtub, on a checked blanket smeared with feces, lay a small man, dead less than twenty-four hours.

Jan Morava immediately remembered another body lying beneath a cover of soil and once again felt the touch of pure despair.

———

He was the first to wake up, thanks to his bladder. They had left the German woman overnight to "rest in peace," as the bald and toothless Lojza jokingly put it. There were plenty of other guest bedrooms in the extensive apartment, but his wariness had led him to choose a maid's chamber instead, where he could sleep alone and lock the door.

It was raining. Not hard, but persistently; in the misty morning the scrawny courtyard trees evoked the inhospitable mood of a chill winter's end. Here and there a pop resounded, as if someone nearby had smashed an inflated paper bag; it didn't sound at all like distant gunfire. The noises were so few and far between that suddenly he felt worried: maybe it was all over. THAT WOULD BE A SHAME!

Yesterday, he was sure, had been a milestone in his life just like the day he punished that floozy in Brno. With one difference: back then he had failed miserably, thanks to his own incompetence, and withdrawn into his shell for years; it took him from February until the black April day when they nearly caught him to crawl painfully out again. Still, since the uprising began yesterday he'd done better than he'd ever dreamed, and now he was awash in self-confidence, just like that rookie on the Brno shooting range years ago.

Most of all, he FELT GREAT. Although he had devotedly followed HER orders, he had always been prone to treacherous attacks of lethargy. Now he knew their source: society's hypocritical morality had forced him to hide. It called righteous purges a crime and had him pursued like a beast, hoping to wreak its sorry retribution on his neck. The same society, however, had now declared open season on its occupiers, and he was its tool of punishment.

I AM THE NATION!

On the way to the bathroom he gave the others a military wake-up call; before he could shower, he found them blinking sleepily in the kitchen. Real coffee (which they'd found here, of course) revived them, and Lojza remembered the German in the bedroom.

"Anyone like seconds?" he asked.

The boy turned red as he shook his head; clearly he was afraid of any further humiliation.

" 'Snot really my thing," the stoker admitted. "I have to feel a woman all around me."

"Well, I'll just jump on 'er for a second and then we're off," the bald man said. "Sure you don't want any, Ludva?"

This time he was ready.

"Actually I do," he said, "but once you're done, and my own way. Let me know."

When Lojza reported a short while later that he'd had his fun and was looking forward to the show, even the others could not hide their curiosity. The night had not been kind to the German; she certainly hadn't slept and the uncomfortable position had exhausted her perhaps even more than the men's lust. When all of them entered the room again, she did not even open her eyes.

"I know," Ladislav guessed. "You'll do her dressed, so you won't get dirty."

He grimaced ironically at the stoker.

"Look at me!" he ordered her in German, the way he had done to the baroness in February, and to the rest in Czech thereafter.

So she listened, and he once again saw in her eyes animal fear splintering into humble resignation, as if he were her only hope.

Suddenly he was hungry to SHOW THEM ALL OF IT. In the theater where he'd worked, he had never understood how a grown man could take satisfaction in performing, but now it was exactly what he longed for. Of course it was primarily the boy he wanted to see it, Pepík might be his first apprentice.

WATCH OUT!

A red light flashed in his brain. Was he really out of danger? Someone might recognize him and try to make him into a run-of-the-mill murderer. With one witness still at large (whom he couldn't forget), could he afford to hang three more around his neck, including an adolescent?

I'M NO FOOL!

After all, he could show them another way, similar, but a bit more ambiguous. He'd just neutralize that perfidious dove, where her depraved soul would try to hide!

He checked that her mouth was still well gagged, and placed the point of the knife beneath the nipple of her breast.

"This is how I do it," he said.

He began to press, gently but insistently. The sharp blade broke the skin, leaving only a red line. Her body tensed as far as the straps permitted; the sound that emerged from under the gag was more like a long brass tone with a mute.

Yes, now he was really aroused, truly aroused like a man who determines life and death, but his hand remained firm, pressing evenly on the haft even while the woman struggled ever more fiercely. Her eyes seemed to flow over, but so did those of the men, he noticed with satisfaction. No one breathed a word; motionless, they followed the slow plunge of steel into her breast.

Then, finally, his sense of touch told him the tip of the knife had reached her heart. Normally he stopped here to come back to it after he had finished the rest. He paused now as well, but only to release his fist for a moment and show them the blade stuck firmly in her flesh. The German had meanwhile closed her eyes; she was trying to escape, to flee from him in spirit.

The other three men were pale. He could not risk it; their wonder might turn into disgust. He grasped the handle again with his fingers and guided it in as deep as it would go. The body immediately slackened. He ripped out the knife, and to his surprise, there was not a drop of blood on the blade.

"What the . . . ," Lojza whispered.

That was all anyone said.

As he undid the straps to wrap them back around his waist, all of them solicitously helped him, one at each corner of the bed. Then it was he who used the stoker's joke:

"Well, the morning's still young!"

To dispel the shock, he had them count up their money. When he'd left the runt's yesterday for the radio station, he'd completely forgotten he was broke. Events had taken the other three unawares as well; the older two had a couple of crowns, the boy not a coin to his name. They searched the apartment, but the Germans had cleverly removed their marks and jewels to a safer place in the Reich. In the woman's purse they found a handful of crumpled Protectorate crowns; it would have to do for the time being.

"So what," he reassured them. "The harvest's just starting; we'll do our reaping somewhere else."

As they were putting on their guns in the entrance hall, the bell rang. His throat caught, but immediately he realized the advantage was on their side. He nodded to Ladislav and Lojza to stand with him opposite the front door, and to the youngest to go open it. The boy showed his cleverness; as soon as he had done so he dropped lightning-fast to the ground to give them clear aim.

The two men in front of them, one in a police uniform, the other in civilian clothes adorned with a helmet and bayonet, were suitably horrified.

With the reaction of his comrades to the bedroom scene, he felt confirmed as their leader.

"What do you want," he asked sharply.

The civilian could not stop shaking, but the uniformed man was not as green and quickly found his tongue.

"We're securing German apartments. And what are you looking for here?"

"Nothing. Quite the opposite. My friend had to pay back a debt." He turned to Lojza, who bared his gap-toothed jaw.

"So you're the council for the protection of Krauts," the bald man spat.

"We have no interest in protecting them," the policeman retorted. "Our job is to secure property and deliver the Germans with any necessary belongings to Girls' High School, where they will be concentrated for the meantime."

"Best this lady can hope for is concentration in a mass grave." Lojza laughed.

The man remained businesslike.

"I am required to uphold certain directives. The Red Cross will take charge of German civilians in Prague, according to international—"

"Where was your Red Cross when those pigs kicked out my teeth," Lojza shot back angrily.

"The newly resurrected Czechoslovak Republic will be a country of law. Private reprisals have no place here," the policeman insisted.

He knew the other three were waiting to see what he would say or do, and it made his blood boil to hear these platitudes again.

"This lady knew she was guilty. She committed suicide."

"How?" The pest would not be satisfied.

SHOULD I DEMONSTRATE ON THEM?

He suppressed the temptation. There might be more of them hiding here; only the STRUGGLE AGAINST THE KRAUTS could give him and his men a sacred mission, and he did not want to lose it.

Now the boy answered.

"She impaled herself on my knife," he announced. "The fucking whore tried to seduce me, and I showed it to her, like this, told her to get dressed, and suddenly she ran at me like a crazy woman. A second later it was all over."

"Where's the knife?"

"I was so scared I threw it out the window. It's somewhere in the vegetable patch."

"Are you making fun of me?"

"No." Now he cut the kid off. "And if necessary he'll have three witnesses right away."

The uniformed man could see he was on the losing side, but wanted to save face. He addressed the boy.

"Your papers."

"At home," Pepík said. "How could I know some Czech cop would want to see those fucking German papers?"

"If mine will be enough," he offered on a whim, "here."

The others gaped while he enjoyed watching the fool copy down Ludvík Roubínek's address. When the policeman wanted more names, though, he put an end to the comedy.

"One witness is enough for a Hitler whore; no one could care less about her. Enjoy playing Samaritans and detectives; we're going to join the fight."

The adventure had an unexpectedly pleasant finale. A large Mercedes stood in front of the house; it had Berlin plates, but Czechoslovak

flaglets adorned its windows. A handsome mustached man in an Af-
rikakorps cap with a tricolor pinned to it was slumped behind the
wheel.

OUR STRUGGLE DEMANDS TRANSPORTATION!

He did not bother checking with the others.

"You're waiting for your colleagues."

"Yeah. . . ." The driver perked up.

"You're to take us there first."

"Where . . . ?" He seemed doubtful.

"To Girls' High, of course. But we'll stop on the way for a stool
pigeon."

Interestingly enough, none of his men so much as opened their
mouths. He could sense why: Before they'd felt RESPECT for him, but
that German lady had infected them with her FEAR. He was quite satisfied with this development.

The chauffeur shrugged and started the engine.

"Whatever you want. Where to?"

"Can we get through to the Vltava?"

"For now."

Not much had changed in Prague overnight. The war was only an
occasional distant drumbeat, and the ants were still diligently hauling
paving stones to raise the barricades. There were more guns and unshaven men trying for a fighter's look.

He too was sprouting stubble; it had been stupid of him to shave at
the runt's house when he could have had a new face to go with his
new name. So, onward! From the front seat he laid out the plan. They
were after a caretaker who'd betrayed a Resistance contact man and a
parachutist to the Gestapo. He intended to get more information out
of the caretaker, but must not be recognized beforehand. The other
three would pick the man up and blindfold him. Than they'd all take
him down to the rafting yard and he'd put the pressure on him. If the
traitor confessed, they'd take him up to Girls' High with the other
Germans, where he belonged.

"And if not?" Lojza wondered.

He threw the bald man's line back at him.

"His bad luck."

Their target played dead for a few minutes. Just as they had decided there was no sense in ringing again, there was a flutter of dirty curtains as the old man tried to check inconspicuously who wanted him. The boy climbed up on the stoker's back and rapped on the high first-floor window. The caretaker's nerves failed him, and he went to let them in.

Shortly thereafter they led him out blindfolded; a woman passerby took it as she was supposed to and spat distastefully. As they crammed into the backseat with him, a foul stench filled the car. The confused driver crossed the intersection as ordered and turned down the ramp to the river's edge.

"Where are you taking me, sir?" the caretaker asked fearfully.

"Just a bit further," the stoker reassured him.

He observed the two streaks dribbling from under the kitchen towel that covered the man's eyes, and began to have doubts: Was he truly dangerous? The wretch had only seen him for a couple of seconds three months ago. He was a man, and a Czech.

HE WOULD GIVE HIM A CHANCE!

He ordered the driver to stop just short of the bridge's arch, and had the other three take the caretaker out. The booming echo of their steps frightened the man even more.

"What do you want from me?"

"We just need to ask a few questions," Lojza said.

He pondered how to arrange it so he'd be alone with the caretaker for a while. A sudden sound and movement gave him his chance. The starter sounded and the Mercedes began to crawl back up toward the embankment. The bald man was first to understand.

"He's giving us the slip!"

Without waiting, he tore off, the stoker and the boy behind him. Now the caretaker would get his chance.

"Take it off."

The trapped man relaxed a bit as he untied the rag with trembling fingers. His eyes squinted as they got used to the light again. A few paces away the car's motor had shut off; Ladislov and Lojza were arguing with the driver.

He asked the caretaker, "Do you know me?"

What he saw sufficed. The man before him began to shake his head when suddenly his face twitched. He was not clever enough to mask it; he froze in recognition.

NOTHING TO DO, THEN, BUT . . .

"Pepík!" he shouted at the car.

The boy ran over.

"Here!" He gave him a submachine gun, safety off. "He confessed. He's yours."

The excited Pepík almost dropped the Panzerfaust on the ground. For safety's sake he took it from the boy and set out toward the car stopped halfway up the slant of the embankment. Behind him he heard the caretaker's wheezing.

"Let me go! I'm a witness, he's a murderer, the police are protec—"

A long fusillade cut off the last syllable; the kid doesn't know what moderation is, he'll turn him into a sieve!

But he did not turn around, just slowed down to let the boy catch up before he reached the petrified group at the Mercedes. Wordlessly he exchanged Pepík's weapon for his own.

"Thanks, Mr. Ludvík," the boy said enthusiastically. "You can count on me!"

I n the two hours he spent in the police commissioner's office, Buback found the Czechs were having similar problems with the uprising: Things were not going smoothly, and skirmishes between local Resistance factions were hindering their struggle against the occupiers.

The military situation in Prague and the rest of Bohemia had not changed significantly overnight, but Buback knew it was just the calm before the storm. Right now the Germans were determined to wait for the Americans, but sooner or later that would give way to their fear of the Russians. And once that giant mass of frontline soldiers and war machines moved, it would pour like molten lava over everything in its path. The only way to prevent it was for the Czechs to open the barricades and let the Germans retreat westward, except that the Czechs could not get a political consensus on this point.

Forgotten in a corner of the antechamber as policemen, soldiers, and civilians ran in and out, Buback could overhear snatches of heated arguments and wondered whether Beran trusted him or was simply careless. Finally the new commissioner emerged and explained it himself.

"I don't think there's anyone else in Prague with as good a chance as you, Mr. Buback. That's why I want you to have a clear picture of us. You didn't get any military secrets here today, just an impression you can take back to your superiors. I'm hoping they won't react the way they've done at the front or in other occupied countries. The fighters in Prague don't take orders from us or any other centralized authority. All we can do here is try to bring some order to what's already happened, or what's happening now without our knowledge. But if the Germans preempt the council's decision by attacking, that fractiousness and unpredictability will work against them, because then they'll be at the mercy of each and every barricade commander. I'd caution you strongly against risking it."

Beran added that the Czech National Council was trying to contact the Košice government by radio, but they were not expecting a response before evening; there was no sense wasting Buback's time. A new letter of transit with a minor Czechification of his identity would open a path through Czech Prague for him. . . .

He took it and read his Czech name.

ERVÍN BUBÁK.

In the middle of the city the barricades were still up; the German guards were letting local residents past, and Buback got through with them on the way to and from Bredovská Street. He wrote the absent Meckerle a short but emphatic note and then set off for Grete with the lieutenant general's present. Ever since he got the pistol he had been berating himself for not thinking of it on his own. But how could he have known she was a crack shot?

Meanwhile, May turned rapidly into a dank autumn; it began to rain again and the temperature continued to drop. Yesterday's enthusiasm had evaporated from the streets. The long wait had divided Praguers into two camps. For one group, the war had ended, and they grumbled that the rest kept playing soldiers and tearing up the streets; who would fix things afterwards, and when? The others were busy fortifying and strengthening the barricades.

The dead-end street was devoid of life again; did anyone live here? This time he went straight to the door without stopping and confidently unlocked it; it seemed the least conspicuous entrance. He knocked their agreed signal inside on the wooden banister, but his heart leaped into his throat when Grete did not respond. He bounded up the stairs two at a time, all the while ruing leaving her alone in this murder-stained house.

"Grete!"

Silence. Would she too be lying on the floor just through the kitchen doors? He whirled in panic and might have injured himself on the steep steps if her muffled voice had not stopped him.

"My love . . . !"

She crawled out from beneath the bed like a small animal from its lair.

"If you didn't know I was here, you'd never find me, would you?"

She must have seen the horror in his eyes.

"Don't be angry at me, love." The words tumbled out of her. "I just wanted to be sure; strange, I've known for so long that this war was wrong and that Germany would lose it, but only now did I realize what that's going to mean for me—that charlatan Hitler seemed so strong that even I was fooled; I thought after his defeat the curtain would fall and we'd simply start a new number without him. . . . It never occurred to me that a time would come when Europe's hatred would turn against me, personally, that it would be I, Grete Baumann, who would foot the bill for the Germans who murdered; I should think it's only just, but I feel it isn't, my love . . . and now, when I have you, I'd finally like us to have a couple of happy years together, until . . . Look what's happened to me!"

He watched, distressed by her fear, as she quickly unbuttoned her long linen dress and pulled down her stocking. Baring a long, slender leg up to the hip, she pointed blindly with a finger, never letting her pitiful glance leave him.

"Here . . . !"

"I don't know what you mean. . . ."

"Can't you see," she practically moaned at him.

He brought his eye down to the place and finally spotted something:

dark blue lacework delicately embroidered on a small square of lighter skin.

"And what is it . . . ?"

"My veins have burst!"

He was so relieved he dismissed it with a wave.

"If you hadn't shown it to me . . ."

"Buback! If the world weren't falling apart around us and you had time to observe my legs the way you used to, you'd have caught it yourself. That's how it all starts. Take it from a former dancer who's seen the crippled legs of colleagues cut from the troupe before forty, except I wasn't even twenty at the time and thought I was immortal."

Now he understood: In her precarious solitude the theme of age had become a bulwark against the fear of death. Gratefully, he too switched gears.

"Did you find anything else?"

"Yes." She slid out of her dress, stripped off her white shorts, and turned her back to him. "Here!"

He scoured her beautiful figure but could find no flaw in it, and told her so.

"Come closer." She pulled him by the hand to the angled window. "Do you see those shadows?"

Logically there had to be some.

"Yes, so?"

"You see, you do see them!" she tormented herself triumphantly. "They weren't there not long ago. My flesh is sagging."

"What else?"

"My chin. It was totally firm. And now . . ." She pinched the skin under her chin between her fingertips. "Watch me pull on it!"

"You can stretch even the firmest skin that way."

He demonstrated on his wrist.

"We'll have to make love more often again," he said, "and you'll be even prettier all over, with your veins and wrinkles and everything else."

"Where do you see wrinkles?" she snapped, wounded. "I don't have any wrinkles!"

This spontaneous manifestation of female vanity made them both laugh.

"Except there's a catch, love," she quickly turned serious. "I can't now, not much. Suddenly I can barely feel you. I can't relax. First we have to survive the war. That means getting out of here. And if we're separated, finding each other again."

Now she was speaking from her heart.

"Do you have an idea?"

"Yes, I have a plan." She was animated again; the image of their meeting had banished thoughts of farewell. "The train station. The railways will be the first thing they repair. It's the easiest place to reach and the safest place to wait; there are always lots of people there."

"But where?"

"You choose."

"Do you have any relatives?"

"You'll be the only one, if you ever marry me."

"Likewise."

"All the easier to choose. Hamburg's too far, Berlin and Dresden blown to smithereens and nothing but sad memories. What's closer and not completely in ruins? Munich! Yes, love, we'll meet in Munich, what do you say? I'll be there a week after the war ends at latest, and won't move from the station until you appear."

Naked from displaying her supposedly aging body to him, she shuddered from the cold. And once again sorrow broke through his love and tenderness, sorrow that even together they were so alone against the war, and that despite his efforts and her hopes this might be the last time they would see each other.

"I'll do everything I can," he began carefully, "but I might be delayed longer than you think . . ."

"A month? Two . . . ?"

He would have to tell her.

"Defeated soldiers will face imprisonment."

"But you're not a soldier!"

"All the worse for me that I am what I am. It could take a while before the Allies are satisfied that not everyone in the Gestapo building worked in the Gestapo."

"How long, then?"

He did not have the heart to say what he really thought.

"Half a year, a year . . ."

Even that was enough to horrify her.

"No!"

"You know what?" He tried to reassure her by focusing again on their reunion. "If I don't return in four weeks, and you find work and an apartment somewhere else, look for me in Munich at the station the first Sunday each month at twelve, agreed?"

"The first and third Sundays!" she announced.

He nodded, but couldn't imagine in his wildest dreams that Grete, with her physical nature, could hold out alone for long, much as she might want to. He and Hilde had not needed to be close by. Even across the boundaries of distance and time their memories held them together. Grete's love demanded animal warmth; without it she would cease to exist. Her confession was foremost a warning not to leave her alone. But he loved her for this weakness as well.

Once again he longed for her. So instead he stood up.

"Agreed."

"What is it, love?" She panicked. "Are you going already?"

"I don't want to, but I have to. . . ."

She did not make it harder for him.

"I know," she said, and he could hear the fear through her courage. "Just tell me you'll come again tonight. You will, won't you?"

He did not believe he could manage it again today.

"I'll try, but—"

"Try, no buts! Keep the key."

"Yes. . . ."

"Maybe you'll even take me with you."

"Maybe . . . oh! I have something for you."

He pulled out the small pistol and was amazed to see how eagerly she reached for it, and how skillfully she checked that it was loaded.

"It's perfect! Thanks."

"I had no idea you were so attracted to guns."

She stopped.

"So why did you. . . . ?"

He repeated Meckerle's words to her.

She gave a husky laugh.

"You see, I want to have my life in my own hands, love. I'm glad your male vanity didn't stop you from giving it to me. But you don't have to worry. I won't be afraid anymore; if anyone tries to hurt me, I can just as quickly and easily turn him into dust."

The needle hunt in a haystack—there was no better term for it— went more sucessfully than Morava expected. The Czech police vehicle crossed the barricades without incident; at each point they tarried just long enough to find the person in command, usually a former officer, sometimes a colleague, and more and more often ordinary citizens determined to protect Prague even at the cost of their own lives. They would pass out two or three pictures with a caption, warn the recipients to be extremely cautious, and move on one block further.

On a city map, Morava marked barriers and their apparent permeability. He and Litera worked outward from the radio building, combing nearby areas in the hope that the murder squad had found the city center congenial; later it occurred to Morava that they would probably have headed for the Czech-German flashpoints, where they could continue their hunt. The first batch of photographs was running out and the second would be ready that afternoon. As Litera drove, he groped along the shelf under the wheel in the hopes of finding a cigarette butt. A key skittered off the shelf and onto the floor; Morava picked it up.

It belonged to Jitka; the last time she had used it was to open the door for her murderer, and it fell out of her skirt pocket on the way to the hospital. Litera had found it, put it away, and forgotten about it. Now Morava had this cold piece of metal in his palm, and the memory of their time together flooded back into his heart, when all he had to do was unlock the door to step out of the world of murderers (uniformed and otherwise) and into the small but boundless world of their love.

How can it be, he despaired again, that she's gone and her killer is still alive?

Then Morava caught Litera's sympathetic glance and turned to steel again. He would force himself through the door he had avoided ever since that day, and rid himself of that final weakness. His driver understood and agreed when Morava suggested they take Buback's thin German woman something fresh to eat; if the detective happened to be with her, they'd bring him back down with them. In the police canteen they gave Morava an enamel milk can filled with potato soup along with a quarter-loaf of bread. As usual they drove along the bank of the Vltava to the last tram stop, where they snaked up the hill on a narrow, wooded road. At the second bend some SS men unexpectedly stopped them.

"Hände hoch!" an angular sergeant bellowed at them. "Hands up! Out of the car!"

Their police uniforms had no effect this time; they were dragged rudely out of the vehicle, disarmed, and shoved onto the sidewalk: Morava tried to negotiate with them.

"We work for the criminal police, which is cooperating with the Prague Gestapo on—"

"Halt Maul! Shut up!"

The petty officer ignored them; he was completely absorbed in directing his men. Small groups of SS were bashing their rifle butts against the doors of the low houses.

The whole time he had lived in this corner of Prague with Jitka, Morava had rarely seen other people, only the occasional old ladies shuffling arduously out for a walk or to the store. Now for the first time all the inhabitants appeared on the street; it was a sorry sight, as if they were emptying out the old-age home and the poorhouse. An exception were the two youths they led out of the nearest house and put with the policemen. No one was paying attention to the foursome with raised hands at that moment; the SS troops were surveying their catch, driving the especially unsteady ones back into their houses.

"Who are you?" Morava whispered.

"Students. We ran from the Totaleinsatz, the work deployment. What do they want with us?"

"I don't know."

"We could run again," suggested the other, a vigorous blue-eyed blond with a handsome face. "They're not watching!"

He set off, bounding with long strides down toward the curve in the road. The sergeant turned almost casually and pressed the trigger of his automatic rifle. They could see the shots slam into the student's body, which kept running for several more seconds before starting to fall; even on the ground its legs jerked in a left, right rhythm. The horrible movement stopped only when the SS man walked slowly over to the dying boy and mercifully gave him one more shot . . . mercifully! Morava trembled. What a mockery of the word. . . .

"Amen. . . ." a pale Litera breathed.

The remaining student was about to faint. His arms began to fall.

"Keep them up!" Morava hissed at him.

The ease of that killing was a warning: These Germans were past caring. Then the shooter approached, looked at their hands and asked with what almost seemed like concern, "Does it hurt?"

Morava expected further savagery, but instead heard a piece of almost friendly advice.

"Put them behind your head, then!"

He remembered his dream. Even this death machine looked like a person and could probably act like one as well. How could he recognize him—or any of them—if they managed to escape, put aside their uniforms and become what they had been before? He had spent three months tracking a single murderer, trying to bring him to justice. But what about the thousands upon thousands like him? They murdered people as anonymously as this man here had, and at a moment's notice they could turn into upstanding teachers, shopkeepers and workers. How could anyone possibly prosecute the senseless death of the handsome, blond, blue-eyed boy? Was it moral to let them withdraw in peace? Were the Communists right this time, and not Beran?

He was still thinking about it when the SS assigned six older men and women to their group and led them away, leaving the dead boy and the police car behind.

Before they reached the top of the rise, they grew by a few more handfuls of Czechs and a heavily armed escort.

There were several dozen of them in the web by the time they reached the rows of modern houses ringing the Pankrác plateau. Across the valley, a stupendous view of the castle opened before them, but their attention was riveted on the drama they had been sucked into. Another SS company was driving younger men and women, some with children, from their houses.

The young Totaleinsatz refugee, still in shock from his friend's death, kept stumbling. Morava and Litera were practically carrying him.

"We're hostages, aren't we?" The boy's voice trembled.

The arrival of a staff car seemed promising; the lower officers saluted at attention and the remaining men stopped to look. But the pair who got out stripped Morava instantly of all hope. The tall SS officer with a pock-scarred face and the civilian with a skull-like shaven head were remarkably good personifications of a regime which, in its death throes, was baring its true nature again.

"Report," the pock-marked man requested in a half-whisper.

Despite this all the subcommanders heard him and rushed over to announce crisply that they were already finished. Except for one.

"I'm not done yet, major. They managed to lock themselves in the air-raid shelter. The building used to be a bank; it has steel doors."

"Are all of them down there?"

"One didn't make it."

"Bring him here."

They instantly hauled a middle-aged man forward; although it was afternoon, he was dressed in a bathrobe and slippers. Asked how many people were down below, he counted nervously in passable German until he arrived at six men, ten women, and eight children.

"Is your family there too?"

"Yes, a boy and a girl . . . my wife and mother-in-law . . ."

"Draw me the shelter!"

Shakily he drew a simple rectangle and a staircase with several turns on the back of some sort of receipt the officer found in his breast pocket.

"Where does the air come from?"

"There's a vent from the ground floor . . ." He drew it. "The garbage cans cover it."

"Will they hear you if you call down to them?"

"Probably."

"So do it!"

"What should I . . ."

"That I'll give them precisely three minutes to open up, otherwise I'll have you shot."

A hot flush appeared on the Czech's face, reminding Morava of the Klášterec priest, but the man gathered enough courage to ask a further question.

"And what will you do with them . . . with all of us then?"

With a gesture of his head he took in the whole street, full of exiles.

"Your people down in Nusle have blocked our way through the city. You'll walk in front of my soldiers as a human shield."

"But I can't tell . . . I can't just ask them . . ."

The scarface pulled a large pistol out of its holster.

"Go!"

My God, how can You let . . . Morava cut himself short: after all, that's exactly why he'd given up on Him last week. His heart ached for the unfortunate man, who had no choice. And it always works, every time; despite the faith, love, morality, and honor we acquire so painfully in our lifelong struggle for self-betterment, in moments of crisis what triumphs is a blind instinct for self-preservation. In that respect we humans are worse than animals, who defend their pack until torn to bits.

The man's gaze wandered to the Czech police uniforms. At that moment, Morava's stiff arms behind his neck stopped hurting him; he was glad that even in this garb he was treated no differently from the other hostages. However, the man suddenly smiled sadly right at him.

"If you survive, tell them that I loved them."

"In German!" boomed the major.

"You have no right!" the man retorted in that language. "We're civilians. You'll be punish . . ."

A shot ended the sentence.

The scarface stuffed his gun back and handed the sketch to his unsuccessful subordinate.

"Somewhere here is the opening. Throw a couple of sticks of dynamite in, and if they don't open up, a few grenades. Everyone else, on the double!"

With shouts and shoves, small groups of men, women, pensioners, and children were put together and the cordon of soldiers tried to goad them onward, but soon it was clear that many could not keep up the pace. At the nearest square the Germans weeded out the old and the very young. Morava helplessly watched parents' heartrending attempts to protect their children; some took them in their arms or on their shoulders, while others shooed them beyond the line of guards, calling out the addresses of relatives or friends.

The new groups trotted a few hundred yards further to the court building. At the crown of the street, which sank down into the Nusle valley in a long curve, tractors were shoving the last incinerated tram wagon from the German-captured barricade over to the edge of the carriageway; it was a rear car, and the pock-marked SS officer climbed up on its middle platform with the bareheaded civilian.

"An interpreter!"

The Czechs' experiences so far quashed any impulse they may have had to step out of the crowd that had become their last refuge.

On the second call, Morava volunteered. The officer indicated he was to join them on the tram, and nodded to his guide.

"Your fellow citizens have lost all reason," the skull roared at the throng. "They have blocked the path of hundreds of thousands of German soldiers who are defending Europe against Bolshevism. Since they did not let us pass, you will have to convince them; it is our right and your responsibility! Translate!"

Morava deliberately translated in the third person, making it clear he was not one of them.

"Anyone who insists you are civilians is lying. A handful of bandits have made all of you rebels, meaning you are not subject to protection. If we bleed needlessly, then so will the Czechs. Once your people cease their resistance, we will once again treat you as ordinary citizens under international law. That is all. Translate!"

When he had finished, he asked the commander, "May I add something?"

"No!"

"It would be in your interest for these people not to panic. I wanted to tell them an assault might not be necessary, because Colonel Meckerle is negotiating with the Czech National Council."

Both Germans were visibly shocked, each in his own way.

"How do you know that?" the SS man asked.

"How do you know him?" the civilian inquired.

"I told your men when we were detained that we are both"—he pointed to Litera—"members of the local criminal police working in close cooperation with your officers. This morning I was present at a meeting between my superior and a Gestapo representative; they're looking for a way to prevent further fighting. It's not in your interest to cause more pointless losses of life!"

They conducted the conversation on the tramcar platform, tensely followed by hundreds of Czech and German eyes. The major was evidently wavering.

"I'm also a confidante of Lieutenant General Meckerle," the civilian said, emphasizing the title. "Who was this envoy?"

"Chief Inspector Buback," Morava said and immediately realized he had made an error.

"Didn't I tell you?" The shaven head crowed triumphantly. "The Lieutenant General would never have entrusted a traitor—a deserter!—with such a task. Buback's authority has automatically devolved to me, and therefore my orders are still valid: clear a route!"

If Morava had briefly thought he could convince the SS man, the German's eyes soon disabused him of the notion. They clearly had only one goal: to get as far as possible from the scene of their crimes. The man turned to his officers.

"Get moving."

In a few moments the attacking tanks' motors roared to life. The hundred-strong Czech crowd was shoved into the wide, sloping street. One last gesture of false nobility awaited the policemen.

"I'll treat you as negotiators," the major announced. "You'll be returned to where you were detained."

Morava saw in his mind that ordinary man who had sacrificed himself for his family. Futile or not, his deed was a challenge. He glanced at Litera and saw agreement in his eyes.

"We'll go with them," he said. "Maybe a solution will be found . . . so long as you don't order them to fire prematurely."

"It all depends on your side," the officer retorted, and motioned genteelly to them to climb down first from the tram platform, as if he were waving them through a café door.

The tanks rode close behind them. Morava and Litera had to run again to catch up to the Czechs, who were now spread across the width of the street. Behind them were SS men with guns at their sides. The soldiers and Czechs were surprised to see two police uniforms pushing their way through them to get up front. The two of them did not speak the whole way down; talking was beside the point.

Why am I doing this, Morava mused: Jitka, my beloved, am I looking for the quickest route to you? Or do I want to give life without you some other meaning? But why am I dragging poor Litera with me? He shuddered; Litera dotes on his family as much as they do on him! Too late now. . . .

The scene was all the more unbelievable for taking place in broad daylight in a metropolis virtually unscarred by war. Two rows of lifeless, locked-up apartment buildings formed a channel, and a multitude of people who, a short while earlier, had been living quite ordinary lives in similar houses now filed along it toward an inescapable fate. Tanks rumbled behind their backs, their treads scraping along the cobblestones and tram tracks.

The front row reached the place where the sloping avenue turned right. A barricade about three hundred yards distant appeared around the bend. Tramcars placed end-to-end formed a sizable barrier just as they had uphill; here, however, they were reinforced by a high, impassable mound of cobblestones. Above them flew the Czechoslovak flag.

The Czechs stopped. Surprisingly, the soldiers made no immediate attempt to drive them forward. Gradually even the din of the tank treads subsided. In this place full of men and machines silence reigned, broken only by a strange sound Morava had never heard before. Then he realized he was breathing loudly to calm the wild beating of his heart. The unfamiliar sound was the agitated crowd's collective breath.

It had started to rain, but no one noticed.

The barricade too was silent. But they have to shoot; they have to risk it! Strange, Morava thought, now I have time to face the fact that in a few moments my life will be over, but I'm still not afraid. Did my sense of self-preservation—all my feelings, for that matter—irretrievably disappear when you did, Jitka? Or is it merely resignation, a consequence of realizing that once God is lost life itself has no meaning, since it can end so capriciously and stupidly time after time? A voice broke into his thoughts.

"Shouldn't we scatter? It'll open up the Germans and our side could shoot."

It was a very young girl to his right asking.

Why didn't I think of that, he wondered; she's right!

Before he could answer, fighting broke out from a completely different direction than they had expected; a wild cannonade and machine-gun bursts rang out behind their backs, somewhere up on the hill they had just left. Everyone, captives and captors, turned that way. They saw a tangle of sparks striking the treads of the rapidly turning tanks, and then confusion in the German ranks. The SS men left the hostages to their own devices and scurried behind the metal colossi.

"The Americans!" someone cheered.

Vlasov's men, Morava thought; thanks, Mr. Beran!

Many apparently had the same idea as the girl; suddenly they scattered toward the barricade, dragging the rest with them.

Immediately the barricade began to shoot past the fleeing hostages, but the Germans aimed their retaliatory fire right at their own prisoners.

Panic broke out. Some of the hostages flung themselves on the ground, others kept fleeing toward safety. Screams nearly drowned out the fire. The girl tripped on a body, lost her balance, and fell. Morava went back for her and picked her up. Suddenly he saw red. He blinked in vain. Then his forehead began to burn sharply. He reached up to it and felt a sticky liquid. Instantly strong hands pulled him forward and from somewhere he heard Litera.

"Come on, Jan, just a little bit further!"

He came to on wet sand originally covered by paving stones. The girl was binding his head.

"You sure got lucky, Mr. Policeman. Skin of your teeth!"

The distant battle still raged; here men and women were waging a noisy argument in its place.

His forehead burned agonizingly and his head would not stop humming, but at least he could see. He tried to look over his shoulder.

A familiar face leaped out from a small group of armed men arguing with an indignant crowd. He could not believe his eyes.

"Mr. Litera . . ." He looked around for him. "Josef . . . !"

"Lie down," the girl insisted. "You've lost a lot of blood. Your colleague is hunting up a car."

He strained his eyes.

It was him.

Rypl!

Then the image dissolved again like a phantasm.

The pretty boy behind the wheel of the Mercedes looked glassily toward the bridge; his chalk-white cheeks made the violet bruise under his right eye all the more noticeable.

"I hear he doesn't like us anymore," Lojza explained. "Should we give him to Pepík too?"

The driver's mustache trembled noiselessly like a guinea pig.

"Or what should we do with him, boss?"

The title warmed him.

DID YOU HEAR THAT, MOTHER?

"Any of you know how to drive?" he asked his men.

They shook their heads in unison. He repeated Lojza's phrase.

"His bad luck, then. He'll have to put up with us until we get a replacement. Pepík!" He handed the boy the pistol he had confiscated on the hill from that stupid cop in civvies. "The next one's yours as well. Forward!"

Then he looked at the bridge and was unpleasantly surprised.

"Where's . . . ?"

"I sent him over the edge," his boy crowed proudly. "He's gone for a swim!"

Over by the towpath's stone wall, the caretaker's body bobbed and floated close under the black tower, just above the weir. With this slow movement the past closed behind him.

NOW NO ONE CAN PROVE ME GUILTY!

Meanwhile the rain and the distant gunfire intensified. He decided to follow the battle's voice. However, false echoes plagued Prague's hills and valleys, and they were no closer to the uprising when they reached the last barricade in the Nusle valley. Here they were leery of turning up toward Pankrác, which was supposedly swarming with Germans, and he was just about to turn around when the messengers brought two pieces of news.

The first brought murmurs of horror: the SS were driving whole blocks of residents uphill as human shields. They were trying to break through to the city center, and that meant going through Nusle. The second seemed too wonderful to be true, but because enough telephones were fortunately working, several randomly dialed extensions in the suburbs immediately confirmed it.

Yes, they insisted one after the other enthusiastically, they were already celebrating; an hour ago the Russians had liberated them, or more precisely some Russian units disguised as Germans—no one really understood it, but the soldiers were definitely moving onward to clear Pankrác.

He ordered that the Mercedes be left in the next side street, so that in an emergency they would have it at hand, unscathed. The boy took the keys; the driver had obeyed him like clockwork since the incident with the caretaker.

MY APPRENTICE!

Not that he didn't trust the other two, but he felt absolutely sure he could always trust the boy with his back.

As the four well-armed fighters approached, a man in the uniform of a prewar staff reserve captain hurried over and welcomed them to his unit. He was trying, he explained eagerly, to bring some order to yesterday's chaos by securing an effective defense at the price of minimal losses in at least this one place.

Were any of them officers? He was the only one to come forward. Yes? And what rank? He remembered Brno and conferred on himself the rank Králík had been preparing him for.

"Sergeant."

"No!" The captain was overjoyed. "Heaven must have sent you!"

Taking his new sergeant aside, he confided that even after repeated requests for reinforcement, he still had no experienced men here, despite their strategic location. The sergeant's arrival had increased the barricade's firepower almost twofold; otherwise all they had was a light machine gun and a couple of ordinary rifles. The captain was nevertheless determined to defend the barricade and expected the sergeant to insure the precise execution of all his orders.

Once he had gotten rid of the old fool, he told his men, "My grandma knows more about war than that office boy. I've seen battle. Keep an eye on me. When I leave, we'll meet right away at the car."

"Watch it!" the boy warned the drooping mustache. "Run off early and I'll mow you down!"

To their surprise, a nearby pub brought them out some quite decent pork, dumplings, and cabbage, but afterward there was just more waiting and boredom. Meanwhile, they heard that reinforcements had gotten through to the Germans in the city center, the other central train station had fallen into their hands, and a new attack on the radio station was expected. He had already begun to consider heading in that direction when the captain hurried over. The Germans on the hill had moved, he announced breathlessly, and were driving Czech civilians in front of them as hostages, but in a short while—on good authority!—they would themselves be attacked from behind by General Vlasov's Russian corps. Their task on the barricade was to hold their fire and let the hostages approach, so they would have a chance to escape behind the barricade. He would remain at the telephone, while Sergeant Roubínek would see to it that there was no premature firing or a premature retreat.

The now-sergeant nodded at his men to indicate the final decision still rested with him.

A rumble reached them that could only be tank treads. The roadblock here was more than solid, a core of tramcars strengthened with various construction materials rising to the second floor of the corner buildings. Tanks could not roll past without partially clearing it first. He could imagine, however, what one tank grenade could do: Paving stones from the barricade would fly in all directions like huge fragments of shrapnel. Where would he aim, he mused, if he were their gunner? Over there, where the outlines of an openable passage were visible. He therefore selected a post on the opposite side.

The captain, he had to admit, had had his cement-bag gunners' nests atop the barricade built straight by the book; now he lay down behind them between Lojza and Ladislav. The boy kept watch on the mustache down below and—just in case—covered their backs.

In that strange suspended time that vibrated with an ever-louder rumbling, he could finally think over everything that had happened since morning. He had long known that nothing in his life was an accident. For years SHE had given him inspiration; from that other world it was even stronger than when SHE had been alive. Sometimes, when his strength unexpectedly deserted him, he had doubted himself. Now he knew SHE was with him again, showing him a path he had almost given up on.

FROM SHADOW INTO THE SUNLIGHT!

Antonín Rypl was dead, killed in the battle for the radio, and would never be reborn; he could not let a few whores threaten the new avenger of Czech shame. Not even Ludvík Roubínek, who had lent him his name and face, was a final solution. The man's unknown life concealed unknown people who might come looking for him. Mere exchanges would not help in the long run.

I NEED A BRAND-NEW ME!

His experiences yesterday and today showed, unfortunately, that even if a brand-new Czech state arose from the ashes of the Protectorate, its pillars would be the very same policemen. The fact that he was not alone gave him hope; for just under twenty-four hours he had led a small but determined company, which had now become the fighting core of this barricade. His inner voice told him something significant would occur here, placing him one step closer to his final goal:

TO TAKE POWER INTO MY OWN HANDS!

No, he didn't want to play the hero and perish senselessly on this godforsaken watch, but he definitely had to risk something to seize control and widen his power base. Then his NEW SELF would be born: a refugee from the Totaleinsatz, a freed prisoner, a partisan (or whatever, there was time to figure that out). The timid office mice of the new regime wouldn't dare question his past; they would give him any papers he asked for.

The din of steel treads grew stronger and the victims appeared around the bend of the road, a long line of men and women, and a second, third, and further one behind it. From several hundred yards away he could not make out the expressions on their faces, but their gait was the very picture of powerlessness and fear: some were holding hands, others had arms around their neighbors' waists, and their slow, loping motions betrayed the weakness in their legs.

The barricade defenders let out a loud, simultaneous gasp.

"Jesus Christ . . . ," he heard from one close by.

Now the first row of SS had appeared; they marched almost in step, guns held two-handed at their sides like hunters on the chase.

"What do we do?" the same voice asked, horrified.

The captain appeared again and tried to shout over the din.

"Retreat! Retreat to the next barricade! Vlasov is on the move, he'll be on them before we know it."

Lojza and Ladislav glanced at their leader. He was still down behind the embrasure and called to the officer, "So why drop back?"

"For the hostages' sake! Come down, Sergeant!"

"Stay!" he told his companions.

The boy was waving his weapon from below.

"Should I get my ass up there with the Panzerfaust?"

"No!" he roared. "Keep an eye on the car!"

The others were already clearing out.

"Sergeant! Didn't you hear me?"

"I want to cover them with my fire!" he shouted to him and his own men.

"Men, that's an order!"

The hostages and soldiers had just come within range and the first tank had crawled around the bend when the sky ripped open on the hill above them. Something there had evidently taken a direct hit and flown up in the air. A frenzied crossfire of light and heavy weapons followed.

The Germans stopped first, turning around hesitantly; their formation collapsed. The Czechs turned as well, but some inertia drove them onward; from the top of the barriade it was clear that in doing so they had opened up the Germans.

This was a target to die for!

A few paces away the machine gunner was also wavering. He clearly did not want to leave either and had taken aim at the Germans. It was time to decide.

"Fire at the Krauts!"

Three tommy guns and a machine gun carved deep swaths in the ranks of the SS. Through the deafening roar he could hear wild screeches. They came from the Czech crowd, which had run forward and scattered. The remaining German soldiers were lying on the ground, partially covered by the fallen, and firing like mad. Not seeing the gunners, the Germans had set their sights on the fleeing hostages.

"Stop firing! Stop firing!"

In the corner of his eye he could see the captain trying to pull the gunner away from the machine gun. Just then the other barricaders reached him, along with the first prisoners lucky enough to make the barricade.

"For God's sake, don't shoot!"

He stopped grudgingly because the Germans were in a blind retreat; the tank went first—he could have taken them all down! But with both superficial and more serious casualties among the Czechs—probably including a few deaths—the fuss was even worse than the one at the radio building.

The sergeant and his men had acted against explicit orders, the captain said, asking others to confirm it, like a little sneak. No, they acted like soldiers being led by a chickenshit, Lojza thundered at him, and the machine gunner agreed: It was their sacred obligation to attack Germans. The war wasn't over and every dead one counted; who knew how many other lives they'd saved? A few hostages shared this point of view, but the majority were insistent. There was no point staying here any longer.

"Pack up!" he told his men. "We'll get our payback somewhere else. Anyone want to come with us?"

Out of sudden instinct he turned to the machine gunner.

"Sure!" the man responded eagerly; a remarkably pale fellow, he looked too skinny and weak to handle the long weapon on its tripod.

"You must be crazy!" the officer snapped at him. "Without you we can't hold the barricade."

"Then drop back," the man scowled. "This gun nearly cost me my head yesterday and I don't lug it around to shoot rabbits for fun. You don't need weapons to retreat, anyway!"

"Cowboys!" the captain shouted at them, tears of rage in his eyes. "Just shoot up the town and move on, is that it? Our dead are on your conscience; there was no reason they had to die!"

A clearly audible "Hurraaaaaaah!" carried down from the hill.

As he led the way across the wet soil beneath the barricade, he nearly stepped on a Czech policeman whom a muddy young girl was trying to resuscitate. Drop dead, he wished malevolently.

The rain grew stronger as the battle slackened. And why not go uphill, it occurred to him. There'd be plenty of Germans to smoke out of their hiding places. In addition, the Czechs up there had just lived through an SS massacre and wouldn't be as squeamish.

Then he remembered another place they could dry out in peace and quiet and maybe even repay another debt. . . .

L ike a fire that suddenly flares up from charred rubble, the war reappeared to surprise Buback again. He was taking a shortcut, a trail that led down beneath the old fortress to a railway bridge, when the previously isolated gunshots melded into the cohesive hum of battle from several directions.

Standing in the rain, he wondered whether he should go back; everything in him wanted to be with her. Logically, though, it would not solve anything. On the contrary, it meant forfeiting control over their lives and entrusting them to luck. Logic won out, but his inner turmoil remained; part of him could not stop feeling her fear.

This time he needed his letter of transit at nearly every barricade, and twice the bedraggled revolutionaries shook their heads over it before giving in. He would not be lucky enough to get there and back tomorrow as well. If he was to save Grete, he had to arrange it today.

On the way he listened closely for rumors. The most credible one was that a couple of German units billeted in Prague, whose commanders had formally capitulated in return for a promise of free unarmed passage out of the city, had feared revenge from a now armed populace, and tried to force their way through to a safe retreat.

In front of the police commissioner's office he came across a familiar face. A broad-shouldered man looked inconspicuously around and informed him sotto voce that he was Matlák from Morava's group and was waiting here, at Beran's orders; Buback should follow him at a distance. Soon they were alone under the shelter of a crooked Old Town passageway, and Matlák poured out his story.

Beran and Brunát, he revealed to Buback, had been removed from their post and placed under some sort of house arrest. Why? Buback was flabbergasted. Because! The Communists had taken over the Czech National Council; they claimed Beran's acceptance of Vlasov's help was a gamble deliberately meant to insult their Soviet allies, as were Beran and Brunát's local agreements with the German commanders, which the Germans had broken without a moment's hesitation. Beran's message to Buback was that he could no longer do anything for him, his lady friend, or any other Germans. However, he still approved of any attempt to defend those decent and innocent German civilians, and hoped the majority of them would live to see peace without harm.

Could he speak with Beran's replacement, Buback asked despairingly. The broken truces were no doubt provocations by dyed-in-the-wool Nazis, who thought nothing of saving their own skins at the expense of their defenseless fellow citizens and exposing them to the enraged Czechs' vengeance. Matlák warned that it wasn't advisable. The garage manager had been named revolutionary police commissioner; since yesterday Tetera had taken the hardest possible line against the Germans and their Czech helpers.

The garage manager, realized Buback; my God, our informant is now in charge! But who can I tell?

Matlák informed him that on both sides, the radicals had simply swept out the moderates. All they could do now was try to prevent the worst from happening. He was among the few who had learned to appreciate Buback; therefore he was risking this conversation and would be glad personally to keep helping him as long as he was able. I need to get hold of Detective Morava urgently, Buback requested. He went somewhere with some soup; yes, Matlák repeated to the amazed

German, he had been there in the canteen when Morava and Litera had picked up a canister of soup and bread to take to someone.

Buback, of course, knew whom it was for. They must have just missed each other, so they would be long since gone from Grete's, but he was grateful all the same. He would risk one more trip to Bredovská for fresh news of the German side's intentions and then head back to Kavčí Hory; he couldn't leave her alone any longer.

"Please," he finished, "if you believe we're among those 'other Germans' who want to atone for the havoc Germany has caused, tell Mr. Morava as soon as possible that I'll be waiting for him at a familiar place."

"The house on the hill?" Matlák asked, and, seeing Buback startled, tried to calm him down. "I'm sorry, it just occurred to me; I'll forget it right away. . . ."

What occurred to Matlák could occur to others, said a fearful voice inside his head as he marched onward, showing the letter of safe conduct with its already invalid signature. At any cost he had to get Grete out of that place; it could become a deathtrap at any moment, and his only hope was Morava. Only? What about Meckerle?

Immediately he felt ashamed. Had he already sunk so low that he'd switch sides again? What set him apart, then, from Vlasov's traitors, whom he'd found so contemptible? But was this really a defection? Didn't he have the right, even the responsibility, to use any means available to save his love? If Meckerle could extricate himself and his men from this siege, the giant couldn't refuse to take her along. But then if Buback wanted to appease his own conscience, there was only one way: He had to stay to the bitter end, whatever it might be.

Mired in thought, he reached Wenceslas Square. The last Czech crossing point not only accepted his pass, but even tried strongly to dissuade him from continuing. The Germans had gone on the rampage, picking up every Czech who appeared on the street. And a hidden sniper was firing on anyone who tried to cross over. Buback bet on speed and luck to avoid him, and won. Around the corner, however, he was arrested.

What should have been a trifling problem for Buback, of all people, turned into a surreal scene with an ever wilder script. Before he could even speak, two SS men tackled him like butchers grabbing a meat calf and shoved him over toward a handful of men they had evidently picked up before him. He could not find the courage to dig his Gestapo identification papers out from his socks and shoes in full view and decided to remain anonymous until a less awkward opportunity presented itself. Besides, personal testimony of how Germans treated Czechs in these critical hours could prove exceptionally valuable in his coming conversation with Meckerle.

Shortly thereafter a covered truck pulled up and the prisoners were herded under its tarpaulin. None of the Czechs made a noise, and their escort was menacingly silent, although the Germans' gun butts proved more demonstrative. Buback sustained a sharp blow to the shoulder, but this only strengthened his determination to stay and observe what his kinsmen were doing.

Grabbing hold of each other to avoid falling over on the curves, the prisoners careened along the slippery pavement toward an unknown goal that could not possibly be Bredovská. Buback realized despondently that this was precisely how all Europe had come to know his people in the last five and a half years: as armed robots choosing victims at random, imposing their divine will on nations they judged less worthy. Anywhere else in the world, Buback's job would have been a perfectly respectable one, but here he belonged to these robots, was one of them, and bore full responsibility with them for each and every one of their deeds.

He had spent the whole war tracking cheats, criminals, and other wrongdoers in the Germans' own ranks. The front he knew only from rumors; as soon as they burned their evidence, they moved him one country further. Was that why he had been so sure his hands were clean? Blaming the German catastrophe on these blank-eyed savages, who had seen too little good or too much evil in their lives, was like blaming the hands of a clock for the time it shows. He, however, had been part of the mechanism—at first enthusiastically, later less so, but nonetheless an obedient cog in the workings of the Führer and Reich clockmaker.

Oh, Hilde, why didn't you argue with me years sooner?

Oh, Buback, maybe in your blindness you'd have left her. . . .

Oh Grete, if only late repentance could restore us to grace!

But who now would bestow it on the Germans? Even at this late hour, when all their lies were revealed and the Reich had reached the end of the line, they were loading inhabitants of a foreign city onto a truck like cattle destined for slaughter. What would come next? The only thing that made sense was to exchange them for Germans fallen into Czech hands. If that happened, he would offer to mediate under the condition that the SS finally start to behave in a civilized manner.

The truck stopped and the escort began to shove them out of the back. Anyone who misjudged the height or lacked agility landed on all fours. One older man could not stand and keened in pain; he had taken a bad blow to the knee. Buback looked around for the commander—now would be the time to step out of anonymity—but saw no officers in the circle around them. Two of the Czechs were already picking up the moaning man, their hands locked to form a seat beneath him, and carried him off after the others to a hall Buback knew well.

It belonged to the terminus railway station. International runs had never stopped here, only trains bound for the smaller Czech towns. In earlier days, it was the departure point for Prague children during the summer holidays. Despite the circumstances a memory of his mother caressed him: She pressed his teary face against her fragrant blouse and promised him that in seven days she and Daddy would come to visit. And he could even taste the mandarin oranges they always gave him for train trips to ward off thirst; oh, where are the snows of yesteryear?

The vast turn-of-the-century hall bore traces of recent fighting and swarmed with uniforms, overwhelmingly black in color. They pulled the prisoners at a swift pace to the front of the first platform. Strangely enough, there were no trains around, not even outside the hall where the tracks fanned out. And then, from out on the rails, a noise rang out like the cracking of an enormous whip. He realized what it was when they pushed the Czechs into long rows and began to count them off: one, two, three, four, five. Every fifth one was forced to jump down from the platform onto the rails; the four before him were herded between rows of guards into the parcel post storerooms.

As he waited among the last for them to get to him, a new salvo crackled from up front and he made a firm decision. It was barbarous of his countrymen to execute people this way when peace was just around the corner. As a German, he could only compensate for it by putting his own life on the line. If he were fifth, he would not speak up! To escape by condemning another man to death was beyond the bounds of humanity; he would cease to be himself.

If the worst happened, he would be sending his love to her fate as well, and would die with her in his thoughts.

All the Czechs knew what was happening—he could read it in their faces—but no one gave the slightest sign of despair. They all seemed to understand that their personal honor was the only thing they had left, and all their efforts were focused on preserving it. The foursomes not selected suppressed their relief, the fifth ones concealed their deathly fear. Buback had always found Czechs to be too cunning, too evasive, too openly selfish for his taste, but in this fateful test that arbitrarily consigned them to life or death, they seemed to him almost noble.

The Nazis were shifting the man with a wounded leg down to the tracks; a bullet would now end his pain. When the Germans reached Buback, he straightened up like the rest and stared them in the face. He saw nothing there but the effort to keep correct count. O German justice, point at me! He was fourth.

As they tried to drive him down to the storerooms, he finally reached down to his right sock and addressed his SS guard so imperiously that the man did not even check his documents, but hurried with him, as directed, out to the track branching. The guard obediently broke into a trot when Buback pressed him to overtake the condemned men from his own group.

From the end of the platform he could see the carnage. They were shooting the Czechs in front of the engine-shed wall, placing each new row a body's length in front of the one before. The dead formed an extensive, multicolored field in which red predominated. As another platoon of executioners stepped forward, the gunners just relieved all lit their cigarettes at once. Behind them, another dozen victims were arriving, among them men from Buback's truck.

The closest officer was a sergeant who seemed to be directing the executions. Buback pressed his document into the man's hand and quite exceptionally made use of his borrowed military rank.

"Sturmbannführer Buback, Prague Gestapo! What is going on here?"

The man turned his equine face toward him. Despite its expressiveness, two empty eyes once again stared out from beneath the helmet. After a brief pause he simply greeted Buback.

"The executions are to warn bandits."

"These are random pedestrians! I know because I was detained along with them. Stop this immediately; I will bring this case to the attention of Lieutenant General Meckerle!"

"You won't have far to go," the man said, pointing at a group of officers in conversation, protected from the rain by the switch tower's awning. "He's over there."

The giant had already spotted him and was striding over.

W e're almost there, beloved, his mother said; she was sitting in the driver's seat because when he had begun to choke, his father was at the castle (they'd fired up the furnace there to shoe the lord's horses, so they would not have to brave the snowdrifts), but his mother knew how to hitch the sleigh and the horse ran just as well for her as for Papa—breathe through your nose, beloved, she called out, worried, over her shoulder to where she'd balled him into a thick blanket . . . that word, Jitka was the only person to call me beloved, he thought, bewildered despite the burning pain in his forehead; why should my head hurt when it's my tonsils. . . . now she turned to him from the driver's seat, and it was Jitka, but he was already deep in his fever.

Then the sleigh stopped and he knew in a moment the kindly face of Doctor Baburek would appear over him. So he opened his eyes and saw Litera.

"Lie down, Jan," the driver insisted solicitously. "We ran over some glass shards; we're changing the wheel."

By the time they finished, he had come around and remembered everything. And when he realized they were in another police car, taking him to have his dressings changed properly, he stopped them immediately.

"We have to arrest him!"

"Jan," Litera cautioned, "it might have been your imagination after that bang you took. I didn't notice him."

Morava halted; yes, after all, he'd just seen his mother and Jitka . . . but his detective's memory rebelled.

"It was him! Rypl and his gang. And they're probably still there; turn around, we have to go back right away."

"You could get blood poisoning."

"If he gets away from me again, I'll have soul poisoning!"

Seeing that he was resolved to return on foot if necessary, they obeyed him.

They were too late; the gang was gone, but from the barricaders' stories and the descriptions of the foursome they realized Morava had been right. Strengthened by the addition of the machine gunner, the suspected Ryplites had headed up toward Pankrác in a Mercedes with Berlin plates as soon as it was confirmed the SS were on the defensive.

Morava instantly set out after them.

The square by the Pankrác court building, where two tanks were burning, proffered an unbelievable image of Czech and German brotherhood. The soldiers in Wehrmacht uniforms were, of course, the infamous Russians of General Vlasov. Their thick Slavic accents were ample proof for the Praguers, who had just lived through a day of horrors and celebrated them as liberators in their hour of need. Thanks to Beran and Buback, Morava knew these ovations would only deepen the soldiers' despair, since nothing now could save them. One of them was playing a wild melody on the accordion while the others danced a bravura display. They wore the faces of guests at their own funeral.

Morava caught these images in passing. All his senses were focused on his prey. He soon realized that they could go no farther without Rypl's picture, and sent the new driver off for another batch of portraits from Bartolomějská.

"If anyone's at the department, bring him along as well," Litera suggested. "Matlák's sure to be there; he's a crack shot. We can't go

after them barehanded. And if there are any decent German submachine guns lying around . . ."

Morava acceded, and because there was a first-aid ambulance a few
paces along, Litera coaxed him into letting them have a look. He was
glad in the end; the unsightly bullet wound, which had removed the
skin, had dried. Soon, a large bandage had replaced the turban so
similar to Brunát's. Then he began combing the streets again, stubbornly convinced that Rypl would come into his own in exactly this
sort of anarchy.

Confusion reigned on the square and the surrounding streets: Explosions of joy at surviving the day and perhaps even the whole war
mingled with laments for lost loved ones. There were rows of cellars
the SS had emptied with hand grenades. Volunteers carried the disfigured corpses out into the unrelenting rain and laid them temporarily
on canvasses in front of the buildings. The victims were predominantly
women and children.

Then a murmur rippled through the populace. A group of rebels
wearing RG armbands, all with trophy weapons, marched down the
middle of the thoroughfare. In their midst was a small crowd of
German civilians, mainly women and children. In one hand the Germans carried suitcases and bundles, as much as each could hold; the
other hand was raised above their heads. As their exhaustion grew they
shifted hands more and more often. The Czech onlookers left their
dead in front of the houses and realigned themselves along the pro-
cession route. Two columns of frosty silence greeted the parade of pale
faces.

What do I feel toward these Germans, Morava wondered, and was
suddenly surprised to find: nothing. The innocent rain-drenched victims on tarpaulins ruled out regret. But neither could he feel hate;
these were defenseless and horrified people paying for what were by
and large the sins of others. Most of all, he felt like packing every one
of them—even those who were born here—off to the ruins of their
ancestral homeland. Germany had unleashed this hell with their blessing, and he never wanted to see or hear them again.

Suddenly one of the Czechs, to judge by her expression half crazed
with grief, slipped through the escort and fell upon a tall German

woman with a blond braid, who even in her humbled state reminded Morava of the Nazi ideal of Germanic beauty as extolled in films and posters. As if lashing out at all Germans through this one, she scratched the woman's face with her nails and lacerated her skin. The victim cried out in pain, dropped her overflowing bag, and covered her face with both hands; two little girls beside her burst into tears.

Instantly two escorts were there; they pulled the attacker off and tried to return her as carefully as possible to the sidewalk, but just then pure hatred erupted. There was a forest of menacing fists, insults, and threats, gobs of spit flying over the guard's heads and onto them as well. Morava could see lunacy in many of the onlookers' eyes and realized he might have behaved just like this after Jitka's death, if his task had not imposed an iron self-discipline on him.

When stones started to fly, the escort commander drew his pistol and fired into the air. This drew a deafening whistle of contempt from the crowd; the threatening guardsmen began to fire as well, and a massacre seemed inevitable. Morava quickly formulated a plan.

"Litera," he shouted, "you take the back!"

Meanwhile, he pushed toward the front of the escort, where the commander was, and made himself heard over the restless crowd.

"Clear the way! In the name of the law! Offenders will be prosecuted! Clear the way for the law!"

Surprisingly, the presence of two uniformed policemen had the desired effect; the more levelheaded members of the throng helped calm the distraught ones. The German woman obediently hefted her baggage again. Seeing the bloody slashes on her face and the sobbing children helped the crowd's fever die down. The people returned to their dead, walking awkwardly past the attacker, who was now crying bitterly on another woman's shoulder. Morava sensed that for many of them—him included—the need for retribution clashed with the fear of becoming just like the men who so recently murdered their loved ones.

This brought him back to his original question: What would follow this war with the Germans? It was a wonderfully seductive picture: Czech would be the only language of Bohemia and Moravia, and the time bomb that had twice destroyed the Czech state would disappear.

However, it implied a new danger. Antonín Rypl was a Czech too—and now a national avenger. The killer's latest move unfortunately proved that despite his insane depravity, he was gifted with extraordinary intelligence and intuition. Morava longed for a quick meeting with Beran to try out his newest hypothesis:

Rypl had discarded his old identity upon finding the unknown corpse and was founding his own armed force. With their help, he would compel goodwill toward himself on the street and in the new revolutionary organs through exceptional brutality against Germans, thereby cementing his new persona.

Instead of just "Good work, Morava," he wanted to hear that Police Commissioners Beran and Brunát understood this terrible threat to the future of the free republic and would mobilize all the police reserves, even in the current situation. Once the country was cleansed of Germans, they could not allow a new bunch of scoundrels to occupy it just because they spoke the local language.

He learned from the grateful escort commander that for now they were rounding up the local Germans at a nearby primary school. This information triggered an instinct that was often more reliable than logic. The widow killer's choice of victims had never made the slightest sense, so why should the mass murder of Germans be any different? As the superintendent had once told him, intuition carries the same weight in police work as a lifetime's worth of experience, good organization, and dedication.

Why would Rypl, why would his hatchetmen leave this Eldorado, where the sort of mass psychosis he'd just seen would be congenial to butchers with primitive notions of revenge? Yes, he felt, they were here somewhere, but as he drew closer he realized it would be easier to find than to catch them. They must not frighten the gang away prematurely.

In front of the school where the column had disappeared, he instructed Litera to go wait for their reinforcements at the designated spot and bring them here as inconspicuously as possible.

Then Litera grabbed his sleeve and whispered excitedly, "There!"

"What . . . ?"

"A Mercedes . . . didn't they say it had Berlin plates?"

"Yes. . . ."

The car stood right opposite the entrance to the school, which was guarded by two youths; the policemen decided not to approach them.

"You go ahead," Morava urged. "Meanwhile I'll figure out what to do first."

"Don't you want to wait for us? So he doesn't kill you first?"

"He doesn't even know me. At most I'm a policeman he saw at the barricade."

"Do you have your pistol?"

"Yes."

Both simultaneously remembered the shot he had loosed by accident in the car. Morava laughed.

"No fear. In an emergency I'll try to bite him first."

Litera did not find it as amusing.

"He's got a small army with him."

"That's why I have to try to find out unobtrusively what their role is here. One advantage is that people will hardly join forces with a depraved murderer of Czech women."

"But how will you convince them?"

"I'll worry about that later. You'd better move along; our men might be there already."

Litera hurried off. Morava then slowly moved toward the Mercedes. Crossing the street next to it, he inconspicuously peered inside. Nothing caught his eye.

At the gates, he was shocked to find that the two guards, SS-gun-toting Czech youths in white armbands painted with the large letters RG, would not let him into the school.

"Who instructed you not to admit the police?" he asked incredulously.

"Our commander," the left-hand one said.

"Call him out here!"

"Get lost, you kolouš," the right-hand one advised him, "before we blow you away!"

What's a kolouš? he wondered, baffled.

M y love," Grete said, "know what I've decided?"
"No. . . ."
Buback could still see the horrible scene at the train station of his
childhood, and the trek behind him had pushed him to the limits of
his strength. He had seen unmistakable signs of the coming hunt for
German civilians and avoided the last barricade by clambering over
courtyard walls.

"Guess!"

He had found Grete lying prone on the bed, eyes fixed on the ceiling,
and let her be. He looked quickly around for an empty bottle before
remembering that there was not a drop of alcohol left.

"I give in . . ."

"I've decided how we're going to live until, as they say, death divides
us."

What must go through her head here, alone in this dilapidated hide-
out! He threw off his wet raincoat and then his soaking jacket, lay
down beside her, and tucked his arm beneath her head. For the moment he tried to put his recent experiences out of his head.

"Tell me. How?"

"We'll go to Sylt together."

"Aha . . . and why precisely . . . ?"

"Because that was the last place you were happy in peacetime. And
a little way from there, in Hamburg, mussels from Sylt kept me happy
for years. We'll go back there to recapture that happiness, and once
we find it together, you'll take a picture of me in the same place you
photographed them. The circle closes, and another begins. We'll be in
Germany, but almost not in Germany. Trying to be different Germans
than we were before."

It relieved him that she was not cowering in fear, but this strange
state of peace disturbed him as well. She laughed dreamily at the ceiling.

"We can start to give humanity back the greatest thing we took
away."

"Which is . . ."

"Goodness. At least you fought wickedness a little bit; I never
even tried. As a nation, we Germans gave the world great music, great

literature, great laws, and great evil. Evil became our music, our language, and our laws, until finally it came to embody Germanness. Humanity has a short memory; usually it fades in a few generations, but we're imprinted on it for all eternity. I've always regretted that I don't have children and never will, and now? You know what?"

"Now you're glad?"

"Now for the first time I'm truly unhappy as a result, can't you see? We'll never be able to make restitution for what was done in our name; our children's children might have a chance."

He closed his eyes and again saw that carefully arranged German harvest, a perfectly formed rectangle of freshly reaped bodies.

"You're right. . . ."

"We, and they after us, will have to replace that stolen goodness."

"But how?"

Now she smiled victoriously like someone who has solved an impossible puzzle.

"Each of us will have to find his own way. I'm going to dance again."

"Where?"

"Everywhere!"

"I don't understand."

"Didn't you like it when I danced for you? Didn't you like it so much there were tears in your eyes? Germans have had their fun, shouting and shooting, so now I'll dance for them. I'll go, stop somewhere, dance, and move on. Don't you think they might like it too? And maybe they'll be better for those tears than they were before."

Now he bent worriedly over her and saw that her usually clear eyes were cloudy and runny.

"Grete, what's wrong?"

"What do you mean, love?"

Finally he thought to touch her forehead. It was burning. What frightened him, though, was that her cheeks were their normal color.

"Are you ill?"

"No, no. . . ."

"It's as if you have a fever!"

"But I don't. So what do you say, love? Are you looking forward to Sylt?"

On a hunch he jumped up and gave the room a routine once-over. Nothing. There was a trash basket underneath the sink. He emptied it onto the floorboards and combed through the contents, picking up a cobalt blue bottle. It gleamed empty against the light. He uncorked it and sniffed. There was a faint smell of camphor. In a second he was at Grete's side.

"What is this?"

"What . . ."

"What was in this?"

Her eyelids closed heavily.

"Grete, speak to me!"

He slapped her cheeks, at first lightly, but when she didn't react, harder and harder until the pain brought her back to consciousness.

"Ow!"

His right hand did not stop.

"Ow, Buback, it hurts. . . ."

"Tell me!"

"Pills. . . ."

"What kind?"

"Sleeping pills. . . . Swiss ones . . . he gave me some from his . . ."

"Who?"

"You know . . . Meckerle. . . ."

"How many did you take?"

"What was left. . . ."

"How many?"

"Dunno . . . maybe five . . . or ten . . ."

"Or more?"

"Or more . . ."

He considered the matter quickly. However many she'd swallowed, her condition indicated that they had not yet dissolved completely. There was only one thing to do.

"Get up! Up!"

He grabbed her by the hands and pulled her up forcefully.

"Ow! Brute!"

He hauled her over to the sink so as not to have to drag her down the stairs to the toilet.

"Put your finger down your throat!"

"Leave me alone!"

"Do it!"

"I won't, you bastard!"

He stuck his own in. She bit him. Suppressing a scream, he managed to lock her in a vise grip with his left hand while forcing a toothbrush down her throat with his right.

At that moment she stopped resisting and drooped. It was all he could do to grab her with both hands around the waist before she collapsed, but she vomited obediently until he let her stop.

Then he laid her down on the bed again and sat next to her.

Her gray eyes slowly cleared and sharpened, but her mouth remained mute.

"Why?" he asked her. "For God's sake, why?"

"That dream . . . ," she whispered, "where I died, you know. It was so awful that yesterday I got drunk . . . and today at noon I had an even worse one. . . ."

"At noon?"

"I sleep constantly. What else can I do to keep from going mad?"

The unintended reproach stung him.

"And how was it worse?"

"They killed you. In front of me too. Then I woke up, and worst of all, I felt sure it had happened."

He attempted a smile.

"And did they kill me?"

Almost, he acknowledged, but did not say it, amazed that she had experienced his death at the same moment it had actually touched him.

"No. But they will!"

There was such despair in her shout that he trembled, as if only now feeling that elemental fear he had missed as they counted off.

"What do you mean?"

"Buback . . . ," she answered weakly in that gruff voice which had captivated him in the German House shelter, "my love, you and I have about the same chance of surviving as two goldfish in a pike pond. Don't you know that with each trip to and from I don't know where, you put your head on the chopping block? And once you lose it, as you undoubtedly will, I'm lost as well. I wanted to escape what they'd do to me then. . . ."

These were her most intimate fears, but he stubbornly rejected them. To accept them was to demolish the last barrier standing between man and death: hope.

"My love," he countered, addressing her with her own epithet, "it's no news that our lives hang by a thread, nor that you're worse off for it than I am. But our chances of getting out of here with our skins intact can't be less than one in two. How could you condemn me to go on living when you die? What kind of a life would that be, without you? Let's make an agreement: I won't leave you again to go you don't know where; I've learned that the best I can hope for is to save you alone, and that's what I intend to do. I believe Morava will come for us in time and find a solution; in fact, I'm counting on it. And if he doesn't. . . ."

Then Meckerle will arrange it, he hesitated to say. He recalled the bloodstained bank clerk explaining awkwardly that he had no influence over the executions because State Secretary Frank had ordered them as retaliation for the shooting of imprisoned German soldiers. He hoped at least to spare her that.

"If he doesn't come," he said instead, "and they get me first, you'll pull the trigger on your sweet pistol, agreed?"

"You're right, love," she said almost joyfully, yawning with exhaustion. "That way I can think of you right up till the end. But just now I'll have a little nap. I still owe you something . . . lots, actually, . . . more than . . ."

The primary school was the usual solid structure from the mid-twenties: Two wings, boys' and girls', were linked at the back by a building with a gymnasium and large auditorium. At the front was a courtyard with heavy bars and a barred gate guarded by sentries. While Morava stood ignominiously on the opposite sidewalk under the malevolent glare of both youths, they admitted another group of Germans and their escort, who were also adorned with RG bands.

What Morava had earlier dismissed as the invention of a few flag-waving patriots from Bartolomějská turned out to be a well-developed organization. Where had it come from in this part of the city, which until recently had been firmly under SS control?

A man in an old Czechoslovak Army lieutenant's uniform and an accompanying sergeant of the former Protectorate Government Forces were turned away from the entrance shortly after he was. Spotting Morava, they approached him.

"Sir." The officer saluted him. "We've been sent from city command to organize the concentration of German civilians as called for in the Hague Convention; once the battle ends, their deportation will be arranged. Could you direct the guards to let us in?"

"I'm sorry," Morava said, "but I'm not wanted here either."

"What's that supposed to mean? And what's the 'RG'?"

"I think it stands for Revolutionary Guards."

"I've never heard of them. Who are they under?"

"I have no idea."

A man came running across the schoolyard to the gate; from up close, Morava recognized the man who had brought him there, the leader of the RG escort. Seeing the uniforms, he hurried across the street to them. He was pale, and fear shone in his eyes.

"Please, do something!"

"What's happening?"

"In there . . . they're . . . beating and . . ."

For a moment he was unable to go on.

"Who?"

Mutely he pointed to his armband, slipping it off the sleeve of his leather jacket. Only then could he finish his sentence.

". . . and killing. . . ."

"What should we do?" the lieutenant asked helplessly.

"I'm expecting reinforcements," Morava said, "but now I don't know if there will be enough of them."

A car swerved sharply into the street and stopped directly in front of the guards. Three armed men in camouflage with RG armbands got out, as did a tall man in a black overcoat and hat; sunken black eyes ruled the man's thin face and black goatee. Why did he look familiar? Morava knew immediately: This was how he'd always imagined the medieval Czech martyr, Jan Hus. He stepped across the street.

"Hello," he called, drawing their attention.

The four of them stopped.

"What do you want?" the smallest snarled, bristling; what he lacked in height he made up for in energy, like a coiled spring.

"Do you have access to this building?" Morava asked.

"Why?"

It sounded like a bark. The other two soldiers and the shaken man with the armband in his hand came to join Morava.

"The lieutenant is supposed to prepare the Germans for deportation, but can't get into the building. They won't even let me in."

"They're following orders. Which say: no servants of former regimes."

For the first time in a long while Morava felt himself turn red with embarrassment; just like little Jan from the *Bartered Bride*, Beran had always laughed.

"I'm from the criminal police," he defended himself, "and the lieutenant served the republic, not the Protectorate. . . ."

"A republic of exploiters and capitulators," the coil announced. "But its time is up, and yours is too. We're the security forces of the future Czechoslovakia, where the workers will rule."

The lieutenant had meanwhile collected himself.

"Czechoslovakia will remain a democracy, represented by President Beneš and the government in Košice; I'm here at their orders. Are you planning a putsch, gentlemen?"

"Of course not," the man in black very quietly interjected, and it was immediately clear that he was in charge here. "We're also here from the legitimate government via the Czech National Council. Here."

He pulled out, unfolded, and displayed a sheet of paper.

"I have one too!" The lieutenant dug frantically through his pockets, finally finding it. "Are there two national councils, then?"

"Of course not," the tall man repeated, now reminding Morava of a patient teacher, "but there are different factions; democracy is being restored and we represent the political forces that have obtained a clear majority in the council. In accordance with its resolutions, we are creating a new revolutionary militia from people untainted by the past. Its task here is, among others, to prevent collaborators from the ranks of the domestic bourgeoisie and bureaucracy from eliminating German witnesses to their treachery."

"But that's exactly what's happening," the runaway guard member exclaimed.

"What?"

"They're torturing them!"

"Who? Whom?"

"Your people! Are torturing Germans. Civilians! Take it back. . . ." He stuffed his armband into the man's hand. "I don't want to be like the Nazis."

Another car pulled up behind Morava's back; its door slammed. Warily he turned and his soul leaped. Matlák and Jetel were there behind Litera; both of them had submachine guns. The forces were now balanced, and Morava quickly roused himself to action.

"Is torture one of your 'tasks,' then?" he asked sharply.

"Nonsense!"

For the first time, the black-suited man was upset and spoke loudly. Morava did not back down. He showed the man his badge.

"A charge of serious criminal activity has been made and we"—he pointed to his foursome, including the new police driver—"are detectives. If it's true, then the international convention on treatment of civilian prisoners—" Grete Baumann! A thought flashed through his head: How is she? Got to check as soon as possible! Then he continued, "is being violated as well. And if we're all part of one and the same government, then I appeal to you: Honor the reinstated law of this land and investigate the accusation together with us!"

The wiry one was about to object, but the man in the hat silenced him with a gesture.

"We have nothing to hide. But if it's a lie, then you'll prosecute him"—he pointed to the breathless man—"for slandering the revolutionary authorities."

Although the boys at the gate played soldiers for them again, no one paid them any further attention. The excited lieutenant hurried ahead toward the left and apparently main entrance, but once there timidly stood aside, despite the fact that it had started to rain again. The black-clothed man entered first, with Morava behind him. A stench from his childhood assailed his nostrils, the identical smell of primary schools everywhere: a pervasive mixture of dust, sweat, and disinfectant wafting from the toilets and the open cloakrooms lining the school classrooms. When they reached them they stood stock-still in amazement.

The lockable cubicles surrounded by metal grillwork were filled with people. Displayed before their eyes like animals in a zoo, but packed as densely as in an overfilled tram, the cage's silent inhabitants were primarily women, children, and the elderly. Occasionally one of the children would sob, and the newcomers would catch the fleeting movement of an adult hand covering the small mouth.

Only now did they notice the distant murmur of male voices. It suddenly intensified as the doors at the end of the hallway opened and three Revolutionary Guards entered. Seeing the police and army uniforms, the men rushed toward them, shouting hysterically, "Stop! Who let you in? What do you want?"

The man in black stepped forward in front of Morava, this time making no effort to back up his statement.

"My name is Svoboda; I'm a member of the Czech National Council and of the Central Committee of the Czechoslovak Communist Party. Who are you?"

The bristling trio drooped; their spokesman was almost embarrassingly unctuous in response.

"Excuse me, sir . . . I mean, comrade . . . I'm Lokajík, assistant to the local commander. . . ."

The black-clad man interested Morava more and more. He remembered his grandfather, father, and all their neighbors sitting in the taproom after Corpus Christi service, pointing at a diminutive man who stood at the bar, sipping plum brandy. Look over there, his father nudged little Jan, who had been teasing the house cat under the bench and was already a mass of scratches; that's a Communist! What's that, Jan had inquired, and he had learned: He doesn't go to church and wants to take everything we own away from us.

He had timidly watched the unshaven man with his luxuriant fore-lock, but the Communist's stubborn aloofness somehow attracted the boy at the same time. Whenever Morava heard or read about Communist crimes during the war he thought of this man, a black sheep in a pious and pitifully barren land.

The prisoners, crammed into children's cloakrooms, observed the scene mutely. It was as evidently unpleasant for the Communist as it was for Morava.

"Let's move along!"

They went around the corner into the entrance hall.

"Why haven't they been split among the classrooms?" he asked Lokajík quietly. "For God's sake, whose idea was it to lock them up like animals?"

"The team decided . . . ," the assistant commander said defensively.

"Well, they were acting like animals earlier!"

One of his escorts flared up.

"Do you know what they were doing? Throwing grenades into shelters with children in them! Chasing us with tanks!"

"These people?"

"A German's a German!" the man countered angrily. "An eye for an eye, a tooth for a tooth! And for the record: I'm a Communist too."

"Is that so?" Svoboda answered icily. "Then instead of the Bible, quote this: 'Hitlers come and go, but the German nation remains.' Do you know who said it?"

Once again Svoboda was a teacher, and the man stumbled like a pupil caught unprepared.

"No. . . ."

"Comrade Stalin. And if you're really a comrade, you should employ a class approach, not a nationalist one. Listen up!" Svoboda addressed the guardsmen, police, and soldiers, trying to rally the motley bunch around a common task. "Any Germans who have committed crimes will be punished severely and mercilessly, but we are depending on the German workers to help us bring about a worldwide socialist revolution. This human menagerie," he pointed to the hallway, "is a stain on our ideals. Comrades, transfer them into classrooms immediately, men apart, women with children!"

"Yes . . . ," his men chirped, including the rebel.

"And what's happening there?"

Svoboda pointed, and Morava could hear a clamor of men's voices in the distance. The trio were even more hesitant.

"There . . . ," Lokajík forced the words out, "that's where they're interrogating—"

"Who, whom, and why?"

"Our men are interviewing the Germans . . . about hidden valuables. . . ."

The high functionary headed toward it. The rest of them followed him wordlessly down that depressing hall past the cages, where only the sniffling of a child's nose could be heard. The din grew louder until only a door separated them from its source.

"You first," Svoboda ordered the three locals.

They proceeded behind him into the school gymnasium, so similar to the one where young Jan Morava had trained his muscles. It had never occurred to him that a gym could serve admirably as a torture chamber.

Like school classes practicing in teams on various contraptions, groups of guardsmen were gathered around the equipment. One of them always had a notebook, pad, or piece of paper in his hand, as if grading their efforts. The focus of their attention however, was not gymnasts, but half-naked men, each tied to an apparatus: one to the handles of the pommel horse, another to the crosspieces of the wall bars, a further one to the grips of the Swedish box. The fourth, on a diagonal ladder, was stretched out by his hands and feet, like in the dungeons of old. The final man was swinging, arms and legs bound, from low-hanging rings.

The outsiders' entrance attracted no attention; the guardsmen were apparently engrossed in the task at hand. On the rings nearby, the hanging man had just gotten a slap hard enough to start him swinging again.

"Make sure you remember all your stashes," the man with the paper encouraged him in German. "If we find any more in your apartment you can kiss good-bye to any hope of ever seeing your family again."

"We had all our valuables with us," the swinging man rasped brokenly. "You already took those. . . ."

Morava forced himself to suppress his emotions and scour the ghastly scene for his man.

It was clear that Svoboda was also on the brink of exploding.

"Put a stop to it," he ordered Lokajík. "Have them unbound and taken away. Then I want to have a talk with all the Czechs. And introduce me!"

The surprise order was not welcomed, but it was carried out. Morava, however, was already sure that Rypl was not in the gymnasium, and Litera, Matlák, and Jetel shrugged in unison as well. However, he saw an unfamiliar bald man hastily leave the room through the doors opposite. There had been someone similar in the radio station gang. . . .

"Where do those doors lead?" he asked Lokajík.

"To the stairs to the auditorium, to the cellar and the toilets. . . ."

"Have a look there," he requested Litera, "but be careful. . . ."

When only the Czechs were left and Svoboda had been introduced to them, he repeated roughly what he had earlier said in the entrance hall, but this time his voice rang sonorously through the large gymnasium; he must have been wonderful at political rallies. Morava noticed admiringly that even with these frustrated torturers the Communist did not mince words.

"Instead of revolutionary justice," he finished, "you've reintroduced the rule of torture, like in the Middle Ages!"

The guardsmen's initial respect for his position and appearance dissipated; they progressed from muttering to open disagreement. Even then the man in black managed skillfully to keep control.

"I am stopping all interrogations in this form. Procure some water and food for the interned. Then take personal details and question them, but in a civilized fashion. The guards we send to confiscate items from the apartments will find everything anyway. Or was anyone planning to make a private visit?"

Morava watched the gymnasium quickly divide into three camps: One group was visibly ashamed, another was hissing like wounded geese, and a third seemed deeply indignant.

"Look here." One of the note takers shoved his papers at Svoboda. "Every German mark, every ring, everything is recorded; I'm no criminal, I'm a patriot, and this is justified retribution!"

"Maybe not you, comrade," Svoboda responded, "but opportunities like this make criminals. We Communists will not permit people to muddy the waters and then go fishing in them for property that rightfully belongs to the whole nation."

To further his own goal, Morava quietly asked him, "Where's the commander?"

The black-garbed man rephrased the question. "Who's in charge here?"

"Captain Roubínek."

"They didn't tell you the RG doesn't take old officers?"

"He was a partisan. He brought a whole group here from the forests."

"And where is he?"

"They're in the cellar . . . interrogating Germans. . . ."

He! They! Now Morava was sure, but suddenly he felt nervous: Where was Litera? Why wasn't he back? He had Rypl's photos too!

"Should I go fetch him?" Lokajík asked ingratiatingly.

"We'll drop in ourselves," the envoy decided. "Meanwhile put things in order here, comrades!"

His speech had impressed Morava.

"Could I ask you for a couple of words in private," he requested of the Communist.

"Of course," Svoboda answered, still a bit defensively, "but quickly."

A few steps were enough to give them a noisy solitude. Morava looked him straight in the eyes.

"Call me a kolaborant, or a kološ, as they now say, but for the last three months my only 'collaboration' has been hunting a depraved murderer who sadistically tortured six women to death, killed three more people, and is now murdering Germans on a conveyer belt. That lieutenant of yours claimed that they're killing people here as well; I think we'll find the perpetrator in the cellar masquerading as one Captain Roubínek."

Svoboda listened intently to him without interrupting.

"I want to secure him and present him to our witness so he can be convicted. But he's already in charge of his own well-armed gang and has infiltrated your peacekeeping forces, apparently all the way to the top. Will you help us?"

The Communist tried to digest this.

"Are you absolutely sure?"

"Absolutely!"

"That's terrible. . . ."

These new Job-like tidings shook Svoboda, coming so soon on the heels of everything he had observed in his short time here, but he appeared to accept them.

"What do you suggest?" he asked, practical once again.

"He's the only one we know by name; we just have descriptions of the rest, and by now there may be more of them. The killer must have a diabolical charisma that attracts anyone who, deep in his soul, is a deviant; he knows how to unleash their blood lust. Mr. Svoboda . . . I don't know how to address you, I've never been interested in politics, but at the beginning of the Nazi era, all the psychopaths who had been waiting for their moment suddenly ran riot. I'm afraid now the stench of bloodletting is luring them here, even if many don't yet know they have it in them. What will it do to my homeland? And to your ideals?"

The dark-eyed man watched those leaving either nod respectfully or look angrily past him.

"I approve of any action that will remove this threat," he then said. "But what's the best way to carry it out?"

"Are your escorts reliable?"

"I'll vouch for them. Comrades from the Resistance."

"Then with us, my men, and those two soldiers"—he added them to the group as if it were self-evident and met with no objection— "that'll be enough. My colleague went off to find them; once he returns, we can decide how to take them."

The gymnasium had meanwhile emptied out; those who had not cleared off in a huff were busy shepherding the Germans from the cloakroom cages into classrooms. Only the group that had first met out on the street remained. Litera was still missing. Morava repeated his news for the rest of them in more detail, and Svoboda added a fiery conclusion.

"On the threshold of our revolution, which will secure peace and prosperity for our people without exploitation, we have met a great danger, one which has destroyed many progressive movements before us: Parasites and even ordinary murderers have slipped into our ranks amid the warriors. Despite the differences of opinion among us, I believe we are all of one mind on this matter. Where is your colleague?"

Litera was still absent.

"I don't know," said Morava uneasily. Suddenly a foreboding gripped him.

"I'll go have a look," Matlák offered, removing his safety catch.

"No."

"Why not?"

I've already risked too much, he feared. And someone else's hide, at that. . . .

"We'll all go; can I lead?" the sergeant asked. "I'm trained in house-to-house fighting."

Spring man was about to object, but Svoboda cut him off.

"Lead on."

Morava appreciated the Communist more and more. Unexpectedly he'd found a firm supporter in this man.

The sergeant described to them briefly how they should cover each other.

"If they fire first, let's hope we have better aim," he finished simply. "And if they don't fire?" He turned to Morava. "What then, Inspector?"

"I'm not an inspector," he corrected the sergeant, "but I still have to say that sentence."

"What sentence?"

"You know: 'I arrest you in the name of the law.'"

It sounded like something out of the good old penny dreadfuls. Everyone smiled, even Morava.

"Except . . . ," he admitted glumly, "I made a major mistake. . . . What if they're holding our colleague as a hostage?"

He met Matlák and Jetel's shaken eyes and had to answer his own question.

"Then we'll have to let him run. . . ."

No, there was no other possibility, and their only hope was that Litera, whom none of the murderers could know, had kept the gang in the dark until reinforcements could arrive.

"You'll arrest him later; we'll help you," the Communist said understandingly. "We'll hunt him down."

My new Beran, Morava thought gratefully. It was the second time in his life someone had won his trust completely. Once it's all over I have to introduce them, these two thoroughly different sides of the coin called a virtuous character.

The sergeant put himself at the front of the formation with Jetel's automatic weapon. Leaving the gymnasium, they found themselves at the foot of a ceremonial staircase. A sign in Czech announced that it led

K AULE

with an arrow pointing toward the auditorium. The part reading

ZU DER AULA

in German had for now simply been crossed out. The sergeant arranged the men with pistols—Morava and Svoboda—at the end. As they quietly ascended he demonstrated mutely how they could cover each other by firing if things turned ugly.

The double doors above the staircase's horizon were ajar; the great hall was empty.

They went back down, and the sergeant and Matlák checked the toilets, just to be sure. Nothing. Behind the staircase they found a door where wide, well-lit steps led to the cellar. The sergeant crossed the threshold and listened.

"Silence . . . ," he whispered encouragingly to the others.

Morava already knew it was the worst thing they could have heard. Meanwhile he checked the main door into the courtyard; it was not locked.

The bald one, he remembered. He warned them. Rypl has escaped again!

And Litera? He must be on their trail, of course, so the hunt could continue immediately. Beran's favorite driver was a policeman's policeman after all his years with the superintendent, a handy, wily Czech who could get himself out of any can of worms. Morava thought it unlikely that Litera would underestimate the danger and pounce on the bait.

His heart a bit lighter, he set out with the others to examine the cellar. The sergeant ordered them to maintain a decent interval between entrances. Morava was once again last, and halfway down the steps he could already read what awaited him in the posture of those who reached the cellar first. The arms with weapons ready slowly sank to their sides; the men stopped and looked wordlessly before them.

He held his breath and followed them in.

On the cellar paving stones lay a row of women bound with wire, all apparently sleeping; at first glance there were no visible wounds. Only the closest still had a long, thin knife sticking into her chest.

Despite this horrid sight he felt relief. Dear God, thank You for at least sparing . . .

Then he noticed that everyone else was now looking diagonally behind him, and turned around.

In a hidden corner next to the entrance Litera lay in a pool of blood next to a good-looking fellow with a mustache. Both throats had been cut.

S HE'S STILL WITH ME!
Lojza had popped into the gym just when the whole criminal squad came marching in, and he'd recognized the policeman who'd been pretending to be seriously injured down at the barricade. It could ONLY be HER doing!

They were in the middle of working over a rich lady; she had already confessed that she'd buried her jewels in the garden, and all that remained was to make her divulge the precise locations of her stashes. He immediately sent Pepík upstairs to sound things out. The boy ran right into the arms of the spy they'd sent, and handled things admirably: He'd poured out a story about some guy downstairs torturing a German woman while he ran for help. Then the fool drew his pistol and ran downstairs. The boy followed and managed to trip him halfway down the flight.

He could see it in the guy's eyes, just as he'd seen it in the caretaker's: The man knew he was Rypl. There was no choice; he had the man's hands bound. The cop even tried to frighten them.

"I'm in uniform! You'll get the rope for murdering a policeman!"

He taunted the cop with the new word he'd learned.

"But we'll get a medal for executing a kolouš!"

As a reward, he let the boy cut his throat. Pepík did it enthusiastically with a single stroke. Lojza did the driver, less expertly but with pretty much the same result. The chauffeur was clearly eager to turn them in, and as it turned out, the machine gunner, a chimney sweep in civilian life, knew how to drive. They finished on a sour note; Ladislav, who was already nervous, panicked and stabbed the last and most promising old hag before she could give them her address.

They left the school through the courtyard exit without any problems. The sentries greeted them, and a couple of fellows asked if they could come along; some big shot inside was getting on their nerves. Unfortunately, at the moment unfavorable conditions prevented him from recruiting a full-fledged detachment.

BUT I HAVE A PLAN!

Those three hours running the show here, where he had been welcomed by the leaderless horde, had given him new ideas. The Germans in Prague were just an appetizer for the meaty morsel that, by all accounts, awaited them in the Sudetenland. The sharper kids in the Revolutionary Guards predicted that the former border regions would return to the Czechoslovak motherland, and the Germans living there would be expelled (heim ins Reich with them!). In all probability the Krauts would only get to take what they could carry, just like in Prague, and then what would be left . . . ?

One man at the school had been expelled this way from the Sudetenland by the Germans in '38, after they shot his brother, a reserves member. He'd always thought he'd never hurt a fly, he told them, but now a need for vengeance had erupted in him. He'd take what they'd taken from his family, and something on top for damages. And if they so much as opened their mouths, he'd blow at least one of them away too!

The effect it had on the men was electrifying. A gold rush, Lojza gasped; didn't the boss think maybe they were needed there? He did. They were finished in Prague, he had to admit; even with an uprising going on, those damned Sherlocks had nothing better to do than chase him. They must have his description, probably even a photo, and he could not count on maintaining superior firepower.

THE SUDETENLAND IS MY CHANCE!

Once the Krauts in Prague were liquidated—and this was a question of days or hours—he and his men would take their Mercedes, move to a larger German nest, and seize power there. He was sure it would be as easy as it had been in this lousy school.

I'M A BORN LEADER!

By the time Prague could send out its official rats, he'd have his own bureaucrats, and policemen from outside would get sent right back to their mothers by his personal guard. It would consist of his most faithful men, who'd teach everyone to jump when he whistled, so long as he let them make the rest jump on their signal too.

For now he ordered them to drive just a couple of blocks further; the cops weren't organized enough to comb the whole city in this confusion. Here in Pankrác there were more Russians in German khakis than local inhabitants. They hung from tank turrets and hid behind the shields of cannons and machine guns, oblivious to the prolonged downpour that had driven even most of the insurgents to shelter, their tense alertness a sign that the fight went on.

No, the war was not over, and it would be crazy to leave Prague prematurely; being first in the border regions could mean being first to die, and that definitely wasn't what he had in mind. But where could they wait? Sleeping in the Germans' old apartments meant risking discovery; covetous neighbors or official confiscators might find them. He was about to ask the boy to take them home—at least he'd see how the kid handled his mother—but then a new idea hit him.

RIGHT UNDER THEIR NOSES!

The last places they'd look were where he'd punished those whores.

The embankment suited him best, except the dead caretaker was float-ing just beneath it, maybe even caught in the weir. The closest was the apartment where he'd spindled those two lesbians, but as they pulled up they saw a gaggle of people carrying the dead out of the house; well, there you go, in this case he'd just beaten the SS to the job! Of course, this morgue was now too lively for a hideaway.

Then his idea ripened as he remembered what flashed through his mind on the barricade.

THAT HOUSE!

That grubby house on a dead-end street where they set their trap for him! Whether it belonged to a policeman or someone who lent it to them for their dirty tricks, he'd see they got their deserts. First, though, the guilty party could be of use to him, like the half-pint on the train.

Of course, he didn't tell his foursome the whole story. HE didn't have to explain.

"Some kolousši live there," he informed them tersely. "If they're not home, we can catch a few winks till our clothes dry out, and if they are home it's their bad luck!"

He found the house by directing them to the cemetery and from there recalling step by step how he'd followed that whore a week ago. It was satisfying to approach it this time not as a foolish fox blindly chasing the bait into a trap, but as a victor and avenger. An idea for a new punishment was growing in his mind as well. He'd thought of it this morning for the first time, but it had already captivated him as completely as the picture in the rectory once had.

IT'S MINE! ALL MINE!

A work of his own imagination. And this morning, when he saw a gas canister attached to the Mercedes's mudguard, he knew it was foreordained.

Although hastily boarded up, he could see through the window that the house was lived in. All the better! He got out of the car first and rang the bell. When nothing happened, he rang twice, and, after an-other pause, thrice, pressing the bell somewhat longer each time.

He could feel their curiosity behind him, but also their deference.

They simply waited. And he did not hurry. He remembered, long ago, the way SHE had read him the fairy tale about the boy and the giant.

FEE FIE FOE FUM!

Four long rings. Suddenly the drumming of the rain ceased and footsteps resounded from within.

W hat could she owe me, he mused, once Grete had fallen swiftly into sleep. As he lay by her side and gradually recovered from the day's events, he fought a fatigue so strong that at times it robbed him of consciousness. Had time stopped? This day seemed as long to him as the whole war.

He forced himself to stand and noiselessly opened each drawer in the attic, until, to his surprise, he found what he needed: paper, even writing paper! And the fact that it was pink and decorated with a rather precious forget-me-not bothered him least of all.

He had never dared capture in words anything other than facts for work reports; thus he had never in his life written a love letter. When the war separated him from Hilde, his letters from the field contained only the superficial events of his life; the law of military confidentiality made this the easiest course. They both left their feelings for personal meetings.

Hilde's unexpected death taught him painfully that these might end with no warning. How terribly he had later missed those lines that might have given him back the sound of her words, breathed life into a dead photograph. And so he felt dogged by the need at least once to write Grete what he hadn't been able to tell her.

"My love," he began with Grete's favorite appellation, "my briefest and yet greatest love! Even though I can never understand why of all the men who admire you, you have chosen me, I am happy. If by some chance I pay that highest price for Germany's debt, I want you to know—"

"What are you writing?" he heard her say.

She looked sickly, but tranquil; only there was an unfamiliar gleam in her eyes, as if she were preparing herself for something exceedingly grave.

"A letter . . . ," he answered, confused.

"To whom?"

"To you," he confessed.

"Aha . . . and what are you writing to me?"

"You can read it. But not right now."

"I understand," she said, "yes, I understand. . . . But you should know first what I was really so afraid of that I tried to leave you and go I don't know where. . . ."

"What was it?"

"That we'd both survive."

He thought he had misheard.

"That we both wouldn't survive. . . ."

"No, the opposite! That we'd survive, and you'd finally learn . . ."

"Learn what?"

"Buback . . . love! You listened so patiently to my stories for so long, try just once more not to interrupt, no matter how much you want to. Promise me!"

It was less than fifty days since he first furtively scrutinized her in the sharp light of the German House air-raid shelter. An eternity seemed to have passed since that meeting. Fifty days ago, he admitted shamefully, he'd still believed in the possibility, however small it might be, that Germany could avoid a total and dishonorable defeat. And when he had despaired on realizing the truth, Grete had led him away from the pistol that would have ended his pain. Today it was she who had reached rock bottom.

"I promise!" he said.

"My love . . . as we were on our way here—it was only yesterday, but I've aged since then—I noticed that view, those breathtaking towers, and imagined the stony desert that awaits us at home; Germany lies in rack and ruin, defeated and humbled for generations, because revenge is sweet and the world is itching to enslave us as punishment: poverty, cold, and bondage will dog us till the end of this century and beyond, and I, unfortunately, am one of the many German women who let our men degenerate into barbarians that make your widow killer look like an amateur . . . now I can't remember which Greek poet said withholding pussy can become a weapon, forcing men to give up war so they can fuck again—what rubbish!—after all, millions of German women quivered with impatience to see whether their men would send French perfume or Russian furs from the occupied territories, and millions more, like me, convinced themselves they lived only for love, and hate had no place in their lives, so I too played my part in the destruction of our world, and now I'm going to fix it by dancing on Sylt? . . . oh, love—and pay attention now— that too was the fruit of my sick imagination, just like all the tales I fed my best lovers, so they would keep me as their femme fatale: the tale of the loving young husband, the tale of the mysterious Giancarlo or Gianfranco, whatever it was, and the tale of my tragic love for a theater star—because, you see, Hans finally chose his boyfriend over me, and if they haven't perished then they're still secretly in love; that mafioso Gianwhateverhisnamewas from Rome slept with me once in his elegant hotel and then disappeared, while I spent the remaining nights with the hotel chauffeur, who would bring me back after midnight to the pensione in a silver Lancia to the envy of my colleagues, but not, unfortunately, of Martin Siegel— to my sorrow he loved his beautiful wife from the very beginning to the bitter, dogged end, which his devastated spouse described to me so vividly that those adventures gradually became my own past, the kind I wished I had; I was so wild with grief that when this wound on my neck came up I completely blocked out my father the tinsmith, who when I was a child accidentally burned me with a blowtorch—yes, love, this truly is the truth, and in the end I served up all these lies to the first man I ever called my love, because he was the only one worth it, the only one who persuaded me to give up the sure for the unsure, and now, finally, has convinced me to entrust him with my true fate: that of an unsuccessful wife and a dime-a-dozen dancer— when I realized you were the only one who ever really loved me, and as your debtor I decided—and listen closely—to be worse in your eyes than I made myself out to be, so I could therefore be better than I am; do you understand me, love?"

She fell silent, but the question shone on in her gray eyes.

He had to answer, he wanted to, but he didn't have the right words, the ones that would express the feeling now filling him: that in her confession of false confessions he had found, after all his losses, the only worthwhile trace of his earthly wanderings.

"You don't respect me at all any more, do you . . ." she blurted, shattered, "but I simply had to . . ."

At that moment he knew precisely how to say it, but before he could speak, the bell below jangled.

"Who is it?" she asked fearfully.

"I don't know. . . ."

"Does Morava know our signal?"

"He might have forgotten. . . ." He wanted to calm her down, but did not believe it himself.

Someone gave the bell two long rings.

He could see fear taking hold of Grete and took action.

"Clothes! Quickly! And under the bed, with the pistol. Don't show yourself until I tell you to."

"But what if they—"

"I'll manage."

"But . . ."

A triple long ring.

"Do it!"

"Yes. . . ."

"And no panicking. You've got a weapon."

"Yes. . . ."

He waited for her to dress lightning-fast and disappear beneath the bed, which he managed meanwhile to make up. Anything of hers he saw he shoved over to her with his leg. Finally he was satisfied nothing would give away her presence.

The fourth ring caught him on the steps. Only now did it occur to him that they hadn't said farewell. But why should they have—why did he even think of it—he'd be back with her in a moment. It might be Morava's driver, probably with the food, but if not, both Buback's documents would, after a certain time, secure his safety with either side.

He opened the door wordlessly, waiting to see whether he should speak German or Czech.

When he saw the man at the bell, he knew it did not matter.

Morava cried as they brought Litera out. The tears he had held back since Jitka's death, so completely that some were scandalized, now streamed down his face; he could not see the steps and had to hold on to the cellar wall.

He felt his colleagues gradually take him by the shoulders and try to calm him, but the dam inside him, built with all his strength to fend off precisely this limitless despair, had finally broken.

The reason for his disintegration was simple shame. He had betrayed Litera because he had failed in his craft, acted like a rookie in sending an unsuspecting man to a pointless death.

Now he had found a powerful ally willing to set all the loyal Communists in Prague on Rypl's trail to stop his rabble from cropping up somewhere else. But instead of rejoicing, he was mourning the third death on his conscience. And three times, he repeated to himself in shock, three times the killer had been within his reach. Who else would pay for his incompetence?

Instantly he thought of Buback and Grete. Morava knew he was their only hope against the coming fury. And a new horror seized him.

To his own amazement, he had seen an old saying confirmed several times: A murderer does return to the scene of the crime. If so, Rypl too might be tempted to hide his band in the apparently deserted house. . . .

Eyebrows rose as what a moment ago had been a broken man now straightened up and called out to Svoboda.

"It's an emergency! Two cars and ten men!"

At first he took him for a copper still sniffing around for something, and he'd have had his knife ready if that idiot of a stoker
hadn't panicked and left it in the lady. Then they took a good look at
the guy and gaped: They'd caught a rare specimen, a real Gestapo
officer!

From the first the German was stonily silent, but he had no intention
of asking any questions. The less his men knew, the better; at any rate
they'd see living proof that the Krauts had been hunting for their
leader.

The loss of his knife was a symbol that the olden days were over.
He wanted to use this creature for his latest idea.

A NEW PURGATION.

He would reenact the words of Scripture that SHE used whenever
SHE remembered the Hungarians who had wounded him.

BURN THAT ROBBERS' DEN!

Why not extend it to Krauts as well? Why not frighten away the
darkness they had brought here—with their own torches?

He had the Gestapo killer bound with his straps, unwinding them
for the last time from his body; they too deserved a fitting farewell.
Then the men gasped as he strung the Kraut up by the feet from the
lamppost, which stood rusty and bulbless in a time of blackouts.

Darkness had just begun to fall on this long day, and he looked
forward to seeing all of them and the whole neighborhood nicely lit.

"The canister," he ordered.

The pain quickly passed from his bound ankles, which bore the
weight of his whole body, and the blood thrummed more and
more pleasantly through his head as it hung toward the ground;
strangely enough, he felt curious, as if this were not happening to him,
but to someone who would not be harmed by it.

As he turned slowly there and back, there and back, he glimpsed
unusual scenes from this birdlike, froglike perspective: there—above
his head, the pavement moved, shimmering after the rain; now back—
he made out a distorted lilac bush, whose flowers had just begun to

emerge; there again—he spotted guns leaning against the wall of the hallway; back—he saw one man working as the rest stood guard.

The pleasantly sharp smell of wet earth and greenery was supplanted by a pungent stench. He could guess its purpose, and because they had not gagged him, he was curious whether or not he would scream. The fumes made him feel dopey and light.

The only real surprise was that there was nothing especially noble about the end of his life. He should think about someone, that was it!

But he couldn't remember a name or even a face. . . .

H e slopped all the gasoline carefully on the rolled-up pants legs, the flannel shirt, and finally the hair.

Everything was ready, but he deliberately drew out the ritual so as to appreciate every detail.

That time in Brno, at the rocky beginning of the road that led him here, he had been so anxious and hasty that later he only remembered the disgusting parts.

He wanted to remember what made today festive and unique. He wasn't just a flunkey from the theater cellar anymore; now he stood on the stage, admired and feared, with a show far beyond what anyone here had ever seen.

I'VE REACHED THE GOAL, MOTHER!

"Matches!" he requested, and was even pleased that no one obeyed; they were all rooted to the spot.

He pulled out the box he had found in the kitchen.

H e swung around to face the man who had stood in the doorway. From up close he followed the fingers as they removed a single match from the box, closed the box again, and put the tip to the striking strip.

Then something moved in the doorway, someone—his eyes were

smarting, and he couldn't see who it was—left the house and came toward him.

Scrape. The match head leaped dazzlingly into flame at his side. Somewhere nearby the men shouted a warning.

The figure raised a hand with something gleaming to the man's head.

In that endless second before he burst into flames, Buback saw a brain splatter.

What Morava saw from the car looked like a giant gas cooker gone up in flames with a bang. Then he saw a burning spindle, a woman shooting, and four men in flight. In the clear flame a figure appeared, as if dipped headfirst into glass.

Now they were out of the car and could hear skin crackling in the deathly silence of the fire.

Grete Baumann, the gun still clutched in her outstretched hand, stared motionless into the flame.

The body in it began to shrink, moving twitchily about as if it were exercising. When the straps burned through, it jumped down and smothered Rypl's corpse in a glowing embrace.

AFTERWARD

Good evening, my beloved, he said and sat down across from her; so it's finally happened: Tetera (remember?—who liked you so much that I got jealous and had to let you know how I felt about you), our former garage manager and now the commander of Prague's National Security forces, had his candidate, but Svoboda, now a general and deputy interior minister, wouldn't have it otherwise—of course, it was Beran who decided it for me; believe me, Jan, he told me this morning at the hospital, you'd be my choice, he said, if I had one, just be careful, Jan, he went on, and that was all; I could only assume he was warning me not just about Tetera, but Svoboda too—you see, he's so used to staying outside politics and was so insulted by his short imprisonment that he sees filth wherever he turns, especially among the Communists; I tried to explain that these days there are riffraff everywhere and that there are Communists and Communists (I've seen Svoboda make order in a lion's den, and he accepted me in a uniform he personally loathes, despite what his lifelong comrades said); those five days of the uprising gave me more than all my years of schooling and service, Beran excepted, so I told him this, and I said that committed Communists like Svoboda will do this country more good than shortsighted democrats who refuse to admit that they caused the economic crisis and the Munich agreement—now they're calling on the West again, the same West that betrayed us before, and they're slandering the Soviet Union, which liberated us; oh, the lilacs are still blooming, beloved, the ones that blossomed overnight in Prague a week ago Wednesday, when the Red Army miraculously appeared in our hour of need and finally put an end to the war; people accuse the Soviets of hunting down their countrymen like rabbits and taking no prisoners, but after all, in helping Prague, Vlasov's men were just hiding their real reason for wanting to get to the West: to continue fighting against their motherland—that's what Svoboda says and I believe him: When Svoboda supported the exploited workers, our republic put him in prison, and still he spilled his blood in Spain for the cause; for six years he lived like an outlaw in basements and forests, fought while we just waited, his health is broken and he tires easily, but still he's like a pillar that holds up the bridge even during the worst floods; his attitude toward the imprisoned Germans has earned him respect and angered those who joined the victors in the thirteenth hour to reap what they didn't sow and avenge what they themselves didn't suffer—it was ghastly to find your murderer was one of them, my beloved: Fortunately he's dead, killed, as it happens, by the German woman who helped us and whom I've just helped, even if the others got away and we have no idea who they are, but at least Svoboda's been warned—in the turmoil of a revolution, people can barge into his quickly growing party from anywhere; it's unsettling and dangerous, but it helped me better understand the question he asked today: whether I'd like to join them and rise above the frontlines to where they're struggling for the future; why not stand by his side? . . . and I'm seriously thinking about it, beloved, I'm trying to decide what stops Jan Morava from letting people like Svoboda call him comrade; I've seen too much depravity and made enough mistakes myself—it's high time to join the side that has a vision for a better world, and to strive for it with them, for your sake too, that's what I wanted to say to you today, my beloved, so farewell until tomorrow and good night. . . .

The newly appointed superintendent of the Prague criminal police, Jan Morava, stood up from the bench where he sat silently every evening, as always touched the still-fresh tomb with both hands, and quickly walked off to the waiting car.

He had no idea he was rushing headlong into his worst mistake.

The idea for this novel arose on April 13, 1989, in San Nazaro, Tessin. The manuscript was begun on July 12, 1992, and continued to develop through March 9, 1995, in these locations:

Anacapri, Emmetten, Stuttgart, Düsseldorf, Hilesheim, Magdeburg, Vienna, Zürs, Zell am See, Prague, Sázava, Capri, Berlin, Dresden, Munich.